WHISPERS
OF A NEW
DAWN

MURRAY PURA

HARVEST HOUSE PUBLISHERS
EUGENE, OREGON

All Scripture quotations are from the King James Version of the Bible.

Cover by Garborg Design Works, Savage, Minnesota

Cover photos © Chris Garborg; Bigstock / diomedes66, idizimage, KMVS

This is a work of fiction. Names, characters, places, and incidents are products of the author's imagination or are used fictitiously. Any resemblance to actual persons, living or dead, or to events or locales, is entirely coincidental.

WHISPERS OF A NEW DAWN
Copyright © 2013 by Murray Pura
Published by Harvest House Publishers
Eugene, Oregon 97402
www.harvesthousepublishers.com

Library of Congress Cataloging-in-Publication Data
Pura, Murray, 1954-
Whispers of a new dawn / Murray Pura.
    pages cm. -- (Shapshots in History ; Book 3)
ISBN 978-0-7369-5170-8 (paperback)
ISBN 978-0-7369-5171-5 (eBook)
1. Amish—Fiction. 2. World War, 1939-1945—Participation, Amish—Fiction 3. World War, 1939-1945—Hawaii—Honolulu—Fiction. I. Title.
PR9199.4.P87W45 2013
813'.6—dc23

                                                    2012041417

Printed in the United States of America

13 14 15 16 17 18 19 20 21 / LB-JH / 10 9 8 7 6 5 4 3 2 1

The reviews are in! Murray Pura's books are a definite thumbs-up!

THE WINGS OF MORNING...

"Pura has created one of the finest stories of Amish fiction I have ever read...The reader will be applauding the exceptional writing, and the cast of characters demands an encore performance."

—Lindy J. Swanson, reviewer for *Romantic Times*

"Pura masterfully balances depictions of simple Amish living with the harm that can be caused when religious ideology overrides compassion and understanding."

—*Publishers Weekly*

"Pura's novel of an Amish community facing an unprecedented world war is accurate and winsome. But his portrayal of the two main characters, young people of integrity and maturity, is absolutely riveting. A book to be relished by any age, from young readers to their elders."

—Eugene H. Peterson, professor emeritus of Spiritual Theology, Regent College, Vancouver BC, and author of more than 30 books, including the Gold Medallion Book Award winner *The Message: The Bible in Contemporary Language*

"What a delight it was picking up an action-packed, historically informative and romantic novel as family-friendly as this one...I would recommend this book to all who enjoy well-penned prose; the story is a read-aloud feast...We enthusiastically give this book a five-star rating."

—Robin and Elaine Phillips, adjunct college instructors, Cochrane, Alberta, Canada

THE FACE OF HEAVEN...

"Pura's action-packed attention to military detail pulls the reader directly into the mechanics and the atrocities of a war that divided the nation. Still, the war is merely a backdrop to the personal conflicts of these young Christians who feel compelled to follow their convictions despite the impending consequences."

—*Publishers Weekly*

"A powerful literary masterpiece. A brilliant novel, destined to become a classic."

—Diana Flowers, OTT (Overcoming Through Time)

"If you love a good story, one set in a turbulent time in America's past, I recommend you get a copy of *The Face of Heaven*. This book has something to appeal to everyone!"

—Mary Ellis, author of *Living in Harmony*

"The message is life-changing, the writing superb, the characters believable. Don't miss this one!"

—Kathy Macias, author of *The Deliverer*

"*The Face of Heaven* is full of surprises and twists that fiction readers love. It keeps us turning pages and wishing the book did not have to end. But end it does. And all I can say is, write us another, Mr. Pura!"

—Connie Cavanaugh, author of *Following God One Yes at a Time*

WHISPERS OF A NEW DAWN

A Snapshots in History novel

The Snapshots in History novels are compelling romantic stories about faith-filled men and women caught up in the high drama of historical events of great significance.

World War I—*The Wings of Morning*
The Civil War—*The Face of Heaven*
Pearl Harbor—*Whispers of a New Dawn*

Acknowledgments

My thanks again to a super team at Harvest House Publishers—Nick, Laura, Shane, Katie, Paul, and the many others who help writers' dreams see the light of day with as much strength and integrity as possible. Thanks also to Jeane Wynn of Wynn-Wynn Media.

Thanks always to my beautiful family—my wife, Linda, my son, Micah, and my daughter, Micaela. And a big thank-you to my many new readers and friends who have gladly made my stories a part of their lives. God bless you all.

ONE

The de Havilland Leopard Moth, its single red wing on fire with the light of the afternoon sun, banked east and to the left, heading toward a massive purple thunderhead that filled the horizon. The young woman at the controls smiled as the two passengers seated behind her began to squirm in their seats and murmur to each other. She sensed the craning of their necks and the widening of their eyes as they peered through the glass of the canopy. Finally one of them reached forward and tapped her on the shoulder of her leather flight jacket.

"Miss Whetstone?"

She continued to smile her small smile and kept her eyes straight ahead. "How can I help you, Mr. Thornberry?"

"Is there some reason you are steering us straight into a lightning storm?"

"Well, it's hurricane season, Mr. Thornberry. It's difficult to avoid storm systems at this time of year."

"Surely we can go around it?"

"It would take us hundreds of miles off our flight path and we'd run out of fuel. You don't fancy a swim in the Caribbean Sea, do you?"

"Of course not."

"Though the water is very warm. Even far out from shore it will be in the mid-seventies. Perhaps warmer."

"Miss Whetstone." A woman's voice filled the cockpit. "I don't appreciate your cavalier tone. We have God's work to do on Turks and

Caicos. Mr. Thornberry and I would like to arrive there safely. The mission board assured us that your entire family was not only committed Christians but qualified pilots as well."

"We are, Mrs. Thornberry."

"May I ask when you received your license?"

"I soloed when I was fifteen, Mrs. Thornberry. In 1937 in British East Africa. I received my first license when I turned sixteen."

"Sixteen! And how much have you flown since then?"

"Quite a bit."

"Please give us a number."

"A thousand hours. Two thousand. Perhaps more."

The young female pilot heard a gasp of annoyance.

"Stop toying with us, Rebecca Whetstone!" snapped Mrs. Thornberry. "Two thousand!"

The pilot glanced back at her, turning a head with bright blond hair that had been pinned and tucked up under a leather flight helmet. "I don't mean to annoy you, ma'am. You can always pray if you feel your life and mission are in jeopardy."

"We shouldn't have to pray about your flying ability," growled Mr. Thornberry, his dark eyebrows coming together in a thick line of charcoal.

"I was raised to pray about everything," the pilot replied and turned to the front once again.

For a while there was only the sound of the four-cylinder air-cooled inline engine as it pulled them through the blue sky and over the turquoise sea. Then Mr. Thornberry leaned forward. His voice was light and pleasant. He had decided to try a different approach.

"Rebecca—"

"My friends call me Becky."

"I see. Well, I should like to be a friend. Ah, the mission board said you had been three years on the main island of Providenciales."

"That's right."

"And the church you planted with your parents has, what, just under two hundred people now?"

"One hundred and sixty-seven. That includes children. And newborns."

"I think that's remarkable. Remarkable." He paused, and Becky Whetstone imagined him staring at the clouds that loomed closer and closer, arrayed like black and purple pillars in the sky in front of them. "And all that time you flew back and forth from Miami frequently?"

"I did. So did my father and my mother. We often flew in and out of Cuba and Jamaica as well. Sometimes Haiti and the Dominican Republic. You can just spot the island Haiti and the Republic share over on our right. To the west."

"The board mentioned a brother."

"Nate is several years older than I am." Becky's voice suddenly lost its playfulness. "He chose to go to China as a missionary instead of joining us in the Caribbean."

"Is that where he is now?"

"We have not heard from him in three years. Not since 1938."

Mrs. Thornberry's voice had nothing of the frost of minutes before. "Where was his mission?"

"In Nanking."

"Nanking." Mrs. Thornberry's voice softened further. "Where the Japanese army was so brutal."

"Yes." Becky suddenly spoke in a tight and clipped manner. "Mother and Father continue to make inquiries. They refuse to give up hope. Every Sunday dinner a place is set for Nate. The praying in our family does not stop. It never stops."

"What was..." Mr. Thornberry hesitated. "What is your brother like?"

Becky saw the tall and slender body, the long sensitive fingers, the shy smile, blond hair always falling into his eyes and making him squint.

"He's beautiful," she said.

Moments after she said this, the stabs of lightning and the towering dark clouds cleared from in front of the aircraft. They were shifting to the right, heading west for Haiti and the Dominican Republic and Cuba. No longer in a teasing mood, Becky simply said, "The trade winds blow from east to west. I knew the storm system would be gone long before we reached Turks and Caicos."

With the thunderheads gone, the islands of the Bahamas were

obvious and Becky pointed them out to the Thornberrys. The water flashed jade and emerald and aquamarine and a dreamlike blue topaz. The Leopard Moth began to descend as Becky headed toward Turks and Caicos, just below the Bahaman Islands chain.

"How beautiful the water is!"

Becky twisted around and gave Mrs. Thornberry her full smile. It made her whole face come to life—her cat-sharp green eyes, her brown tan, the air and sun look of her hair. "It's like velvet to swim in, Mrs. Thornberry. So warm and clear. It's as if someone you loved put their arms around you. Someone like God."

The smile made Becky's beauty so obvious and so startling that Mr. Thornberry had to glance away, back down to the green sea and the islands with their white strips of sand. "The mission board is sorry you're moving on."

Becky faced front and continued to nose the Leopard Moth downward, completely unaware of the effect she had had on the older man. "It's a British territory. It's only right that British missionaries like yourselves carry on with God's work here."

"We're all his children. Nationalities don't matter. I wish you and your parents would reconsider."

"I love it here, Mr. Thornberry, believe me. The light brightens everything in a kind of supernatural way, as if we're not in this world but on the shores of heaven. It makes the island throb. Gives palm trees and waves and seagulls and people—everything—a fire. A divine color. I can't get enough of what God has done in the tropics."

Surprised by Becky's sudden chattiness, Mrs. Thornberry spoke up. "I agree with my husband. You really should consider staying on. It's clear that the Lord has ministered to your heart and spirit here."

"We've prayed this through, Mrs. Thornberry. Each of us agrees that it's time to return to America for awhile. My grandfather—dad's father, Grandpa Whetstone—died last month and we haven't been back to Pennsylvania since we arrived at Turks and Caicos. That was in '38 and now it's July of 1941—more than three years have gone by and we haven't set foot on the old homestead."

"I read that some of your family were farmers. Part of a religious sect." Mrs. Thornberry coughed. "I'm sorry. For want of a better word."

"Oh, they're Christians just like you and me." Becky's voice had tightened again. "They go about it a bit differently, that's all. But Jesus is everything to them." She straightened in her seat. "You can spot people on the beaches now and under the coconut trees. Are you both strapped in? Here we go!"

The plane roared over the glittering waters and palm trees and people waved as it swooped past. There was a crunch and a bounce and then another bounce, and the Thornberrys gripped the sides of their seats and watched coconut groves and pine trees with long needles stream by. The aircraft came to a stop by a hangar that gleamed silver. A cluster of people stood at the edge of the runway and once the propeller finished turning over they began to walk over toward the scarlet monoplane.

Becky opened up the canopy, waved to the people approaching, and helped the Thornberrys down. Then she dug out the luggage and tossed the cases to a tall man in white pants and shirt with brown hair and skin that had tanned a much darker hue than hers. He caught them and set them on the ground.

"Is that all?" he asked.

"Yes, Dad." She jumped down and kissed him on the cheek. "Miss me?"

"Three days is an eternity. How's Miami?"

"Crowded." She turned and hugged a woman with blond hair and green eyes like hers who wore a white blouse and skirt. "Hi, Mom. How was your second honeymoon?"

Her mother laughed. "A lot shorter than my first. Introduce me to your passengers."

"Mom. Dad. Everyone." Becky extended her hand toward the Thornberrys. "This is Mr. and Mrs. Thornberry of Essex. They're here to serve the wonderful people of Turks and Caicos."

"Welcome." Becky's father shook their hands. "God bless you."

Becky's mother took their hands as well. "We've looked forward to your arrival. The mission board made it sound like you were going to be here last week."

"Oh, delays of all sorts." Mr. Thornberry had already begun to perspire as he stood under the sun in his white shirt and tie and dark navy suit. "Everything's sorted out." He looked around him. "Are these some of the members of the church, Mr. Whetstone?"

"Jude. Yes, these are our elders. And Mrs. Hamilton here plays the piano and directs the choir."

"Splendid." He shook hands and bowed slightly as he met each person. "I'm so pleased to be among you. My wife and I have been praying about this for years."

Mrs. Thornberry, also looking warm in a maroon dress and a purple hat with white cotton flowers, smiled and took the hands of the men and women. "Mr. Thornberry is not exaggerating. We're so grateful to God to be here at last."

"And we also are pleased you are here." A tall man grinned. "I am John. Yes, we are glad to have you among us but sorry to see the Whetstone family go."

Mr. Thornberry wiped his face and forehead with a handkerchief from a pocket in his suit. "I understand. Indeed, Mrs. Thornberry and I asked young Rebecca if her family might not consider staying on."

"Did you?"

Mrs. Thornberry turned her brightest smile on Becky's mother. "Mrs. Whetstone. It would be wonderful if you could remain on the island. Even for another six months."

"Lyyndaya, please. Or just Lyyndy. Mrs. Thornberry, we'd be so happy to stay and never move an inch from this place. But we've talked it over, prayed it over, and read through parts of the Bible again and again. We believe we're supposed to return to Pennsylvania. Perhaps not forever. But for a season. Once we're there and have been part of whatever it is the Lord wants us to be part of, we expect we'll get a strong sense of where we're to go next. We have no idea where that might be."

"Why, it could be to return here." Mr. Thornberry fished a wide-brimmed white hat out of one of his bags and planted it on his bare head as sweat rolled down his pink cheeks. "Think of how welcome this climate will be when winter bears down with frost and snow and wind on Philadelphia."

Jude smiled. "No doubt about that. Five years in British East Africa—Kenya—and three here have softened us up quite a bit. If God opens the door, we'll run back to Turks and Caicos in a heartbeat."

Lyyndaya shrugged. "Or maybe we'll stay in Pennsylvania and give up flying. We could wind up threshing grain for the Lord and cutting hay and milking cows instead of climbing through the skies."

Everyone saw the quick flash of green fire that swept through Becky's eyes. "Not me," she said.

There was a long moment when no one spoke and Becky stood with what looked like flames flickering about her blond head as she removed her leather helmet. Then Mr. Thornberry smiled and laughed and said the new pilot would be with them in what he called a fortnight.

"Two weeks?" Jude frowned, creases cutting into his handsome face. "Why doesn't he let us pick him up in our plane?"

"Ah, well." Mr. Thornberry seemed embarrassed by the conversation he had started in hope of easing the awkwardness of the moment. "He's one of those types who isn't comfortable unless he's at the controls."

Becky's eyes ignited again. "You mean he doesn't trust women pilots?"

Mr. Thornberry swiped at his forehead with his handkerchief. "Ah… Denton…doesn't trust anyone—he might fly with your father—or he might not. In any case, he'll wait until you three return with it to Miami and then fly it back here himself." He squinted up at the sun. "I'm fairly cooking. Can we get under some shade, perhaps? Is there a glass of water or a large cup of tea to be had?"

"Of course, yes, forgive us." John picked up two of the Thornberrys' suitcases. "Your house is only a short walk. It's under the palms and very cool and the trade winds blow right through your windows. Come. Come."

Other men picked up the rest of the luggage and Lyyndaya accompanied Mrs. Thornberry off the runway and down a sandy path that ran through the trees. Jude remained behind with his daughter who, despite the heat, continued to stand by the Leopard Moth in a heavy leather flight jacket that was several sizes too big for her.

"You know," he began quietly, "you didn't need to make a scene over it."

The green cat eyes blazed. "Over what?"

"Going back to Pennsylvania. This guy Denton refusing to fly with a woman at the controls."

"I love Pennsylvania and I love our family there. I don't mind that they use candles and oil lamps or don't have cars or phones and it doesn't matter to me if they want to spend the rest of their lives riding horses and baking bread in woodstoves. But their God says don't fly, and my God says soar."

"We have the same God, Becky, you know that. They just feel called to a different life in order to honor him."

"Well, so do I."

"All right. All right. No one is trying to clip your wings."

Becky folded her arms over her chest. "Mother sounds like she's going to give it a try."

"Oh, she just misses living close to her family, her sisters and brothers. You know that."

"I love them all. Especially Auntie Ruth and Bishop Zook. I take them as they are and accept the life they wish to live. I need them to treat me the same way."

"They do. You know they do."

"If Mom wants to park her plane and put on a prayer *kapp* in her old age—"

"Old age?" Jude protested. "She's barely forty!"

"—that's up to her. But I'm nineteen and if you try to ground me—"

"No one is going to try to ground you, Beck."

"—I'll just make my own way through this world without anyone's help. I know God wants me up there. It's like that poem you read to me when I got my pilot's license. *A lonely impulse of delight drove to this tumult in the clouds.* It delights God that I fly. I know it does."

Jude gathered her into his arms and kissed the top of her head. "All right. All right. Shh."

"And I don't need a man either. Especially a man who doesn't think a woman can fly a plane straight and level. Or who doesn't believe any woman—or any man—should fly a plane at all. So don't try to be a matchmaker when we get to Lancaster County."

"What are you thinking? That your mother and I are hatching a scheme to get you married off this summer?"

"Who knows? I hear you whispering and my name sounds the same in whispers or out loud."

"Oh, Beck. Hooking you up to an Amish farm boy would be like putting a modern engine in an old Fokker triplane. Why, the stress on the wing struts would tear the plane apart."

"Yes." Becky's arms were still folded and the tip of her nose a burning red. "Exactly."

"Enough. Peace. We'll help the Thornberrys learn the ropes this week, okay?"

"I know that."

"Then we'll visit with Aunt Ruth and Bishop Zook and Pastor Miller and all the rest. For a month or two. Also okay?"

"A month or two? Oh, I guess."

"All the time we'll be praying, thinking, wondering."

"Yeah, yeah, okay. But I already know where God wants me to be and what he wants me to do."

Jude smiled. "Which is?"

"He wants me to be a pilot and he wants me up with the angels and the wild birds. I fly for God. I fly for the people he asks us to help. And I fly for me. That's it."

"A nice neat package."

"It is."

"Air delivery."

"Yes."

"Hey. Remember we love you." Jude tilted up his daughter's face with its fiery emerald eyes. "When Nate felt he ought to go to China we had big misgivings. But we let him go because he was a man and capable of making his own decisions. I want so badly to see him again and hug him. The same goes for you, Beck. If you believe God wants you in the air then stay in the air. Mom and I won't stand in your way. We may talk things over with you, argue a bit, make sure you know what's on our minds. But in the end it's up to you. You're nineteen now. An adult."

Becky's eyes glistened. "Thanks, Dad." She put her arms around him and hugged his body as tightly as she could. "You'll see Nate again."

"I know I will."

"I mean here. Not just there. Here. On this earth. You'll see him. I believe that."

Jude hugged his daughter back and closed his eyes, holding her. "I'd do anything to make that happen, Beck. Anything God asked."

Two

"Paradise!"

Becky opened her eyes. She had been half asleep, daydreaming about Turks and Caicos, the jade waters, her mother piloting the Leopard Moth to Miami, the president and vice-president of the mission board meeting the three of them there and taking charge of the plane, the long train trip up the eastern seaboard, miles of cities and towns, miles of cars, miles of flat fields. The monotony had made her doze. Now she saw tall green hayfields drenched in heat, men with straw hats and women with white prayer *kapps* driving teams of horses, a blacksmith shop with all its doors and windows wide open as the forge glared orange, a horse and buggy rolling along a dirt road by the track, a man with a long beard and hat and dark suspenders crossed over the back of his white shirt leaning on a shovel in a field and gazing at the locomotive as it steamed past.

Her mother put a hand on Becky's arm. "It has its own beauty, the Pennsylvania land."

Becky smiled. "I know."

"There will be many people at the station. Do you think you have all their names straight?"

"I know all your sisters and brothers—my aunts and uncles. Don't ask me to remember all their kids. You Amish grow families like you grow cornfields—they stretch to the horizon."

"*You Amish.* You're Amish too, Becky."

"No, I'm not. I've never been baptized like you and Dad. Never taken any oaths." She looked into her mother's clear green eyes. "Why don't they shun you?"

"Shh. There was enough of that when your father and I were young. The bishop and the people have made a kind of exception for us—an *Ausnahme*—so that we can come and go and still visit with them even if right now we are not truly one with them."

"*Right now?* How can we ever be one with them, Mother? We could never fly again."

"Yes, we could fly. The *Ordnung* of our community allows its members to travel short distances by air for business or family matters or medical care."

"No. *I* want to fly. I don't want someone to fly for me."

"Shh. There's no need to argue. No one is asking you to take the baptismal vows." Her mother looked out the window and smiled. "There they are. Bishop Zook is in his seventies and still straight and tall as the center beam in a barn."

Becky had no intention of smiling but couldn't stop herself as she saw the bishop in his black clothing and white beard towering over the others. "The gentle giant. I remember his piggyback rides."

Jude leaned over both of them as he peered out the window. "I think he could still do it. Though you and he did not call them piggyback rides, did you?"

Becky's smile grew, bringing all the color out in her eyes. "No. They were plane rides. I don't think Pastor Miller approved."

"Oh, well, that's Miller's way. But he's mellowed some since 1918."

Becky glanced up at her father. "He must have been a horror twenty years ago."

Jude shrugged. "A tough cud to chew. Eventually it goes down."

But Pastor Miller was as cheerful as Bishop Zook, both of them laughing and shaking hands and hugging with the vigor of twenty-year-olds. Beside Pastor Miller stood his son Joshua, taller than his father, covered in freckles, a big grin opening up his face. Becky knew who he was—the infant whose life her father and mother had saved by flying him to Harrisburg when he was dying of the Spanish flu. Pastor Miller had refused to allow the flight up until the last minute.

Now he had one hand on his son's shoulder, and his pride and joy were obvious.

"We must all get along to the picnic. *Ja,* we celebrate your homecoming with a picnic. The children are like balloons full of air they are so excited." Pastor Miller patted his son's back. "A blacksmith. Our new blacksmith."

Faces flowed past Becky's eyes. Grandfather and Grandmother Kurtz—her mother's parents. And there, too, her mother's sisters and brothers all grown up, with families of their own—Aunt Sarah, Uncle Daniel, Uncle Harley, and Uncle Luke. Pastor King and Pastor Stoltzfus, both old and stiff, but with plenty of light in their eyes and lots of goodwill in their greetings. Then there was her favorite, Auntie Ruth, her mother's older sister. Her raven hair was streaked with white and silver and her blue eyes were pale, but her arms around Becky were as strong as they had ever been.

Becky kissed her aunt's cheek. "Auntie Ruth. It's so good to see you again."

"And you. So tall. As beautiful as your mother."

Ruth had been widowed after only one year. No child had been conceived before her husband was killed by a kick from a Percheron he was struggling to harness. Ruth had never remarried and had returned to the Kurtz household to help her mother raise her brothers and Sarah. Now she did most of the housework though Grandmother Kurtz still had her hand in with the baking and sewing.

"Am I staying in the same room as you?" Becky asked.

"Is that what you want?"

"If I'm not an intrusion. We could talk so much more easily." Becky suddenly began to speak rapidly. "But perhaps you're not comfortable with that—you must guard your privacy—we don't have—"

"Hush." Ruth hugged her again. "Of course we will room together, my dear. There are always two beds and I've made up the extra one with fresh linen and feather pillows and placed a new candle on your table. You see, I'm all ready for you. If you hadn't asked, I would have insisted."

Becky laughed. "Great. Being with you makes all the difference in the world."

"The world is a large place and I have seen so little of it. But you've been to Africa and the Caribbean and know much more about it than I, so I will take your word for it. If God has arranged that I make all the difference in the world to you—*Lobe den Herrn.*"

"Yes, praise the Lord." Becky kissed her aunt's cheek again. "You are His gift to me."

Everyone climbed into the buggies that had been parked at the train station and they soon arrived at the Stoltzfus field, where the Lapp Amish had already gathered. Blue and yellow and white balloons were in the air, blowing across the freshly cut grass, and children were running after them and squealing. Becky and Jude and Lyyndaya went through dozens of introductions and Becky's head spun hearing the same names used over and over again—Yoder, Miller, Stoltzfus, King, Yoder, Yoder, Stoltzfus, Harshberger, Harshberger, Miller, Zook, Zook, Beiler, Beiler. She finally disentangled herself from the well-wishers and almost staggered toward the long tables that were laden with pies and pitchers of lemonade. A young man in a white shirt and dark pants with suspenders stood sipping from a glass as she came up.

"May I have a drink?" Becky asked an older woman behind the tables.

"*Ja. Natürlich.*"

The young man smiled at her. "A lot of hands to shake and faces to remember, *ja?*"

Becky laughed. "I've forgotten them all already."

"Oh, if you stick around long enough your brain will do the work for you. You won't have to think about it." He held out his hand. "So here is someone else to remember. I'm Moses Yoder. As if you needed another Yoder."

Becky took his hand. "Hello, Moses. I'm Becky Whetstone."

He nodded and continued to sip from his glass. "I know. We've been expecting you."

"Yes, this is quite a welcome. Which Yoders do you belong to?"

"My mother is an old friend of your mother's. She's the bishop's daughter Emma. Do you know who I mean?"

Becky took a glass of pink lemonade the woman offered her, said thank you, and glanced at the far end of the line of tables. "Isn't that your mother there? Handing out slices of pie?"

"Sure. That's her. How could you remember? It's been years."

"Oh, she's very tall and very attractive. She has those dark green eyes. And the dark skin. I wouldn't forget her." Smiling at Moses she realized he had the same height, the same color of eyes and skin, and the same kind of beauty, only it was more rugged and masculine. Suddenly embarrassed, she dropped her eyes. "Well, nice meeting you, Moses."

"Where are you going? Not back to your parents?"

"I…no, not my parents…" She fumbled with her words. "I'm… I'm heading over—"

"Listen. I'm in charge of organizing some races for the children. I'm starting with sacks, potato sacks. Would you help me, Rebecca?" When she hesitated he said, "They've left me all alone with this."

She smiled and finished her lemonade and set the empty glass down on the table. "Of course I'll help. Let's go."

After the sack race was the three-legged race, and after that was the wheelbarrow race. Then the children insisted some of the adults race and Becky won the sack race, was linked with her Aunt Ruth in the three-legged race, and teamed up with her mother to lose the wheelbarrow race four times. Before she could make her way back to the tables to get another glass of lemonade Moses asked her to help with the big scavenger hunt, which ranged from one farm to another and included children, teenagers, and parents. Becky, tanned face warm with the heat of the afternoon, strands of her blond hair loose and damp and dangling down her cheeks, became the heroine of many Yoders and Millers and Zooks and Harshbergers when she became the only one to find a four-leaf clover as well as the empty casing of an old shotgun cartridge. When the hunt was over she collapsed under an oak tree with Moses and the children and said she could hardly breathe.

"No more running, no more." Two girls were in her lap. "Ice cream for everyone."

"Not yet." Moses looked over at the tables where his mother was busy. "Food first. Fried chicken. Potato salad. Sausage. Fruit."

"Fine. Good. Everyone go get a plate of food."

A little boy stared at her and said something in Pennsylvania Dutch.

Becky raised an eyebrow. "What is that?"

Moses took off his straw hat and wiped his forehead with his arm. "He says how do they know you'll be here when they come back with their food?"

"Why didn't he ask me in English?"

"He's more comfortable with the Amish tongue."

Becky reached over and mussed the boy's blond hair. "Go get your food. I'm too tired to move. I'll still be under this tree at midnight. What is your name?"

His smile was a sudden flash of white. "Eli."

"Well, Eli, go and get a plateful of food. All of you can do that. Surely you must all be famished."

The fifteen or so children ran in a mob toward the food lines, where their parents were waiting for them. Becky leaned her head back against the tree trunk. She closed her eyes.

"What an afternoon." Her eyes remained shut. "Do they always have this much energy?"

"They're excited because you're here. And because you're kind to them." He paused. "You would make a good mother."

Becky opened one eye. "Mother? Are you kidding me? I'm only nineteen."

"Many of our women are married well before nineteen."

"Are they? Bully for them. I'm not against marriage but I think I'd like to fall in love first."

"Oh. You never have?"

"No."

"Not even a little bit? A crush?"

"A crush? No. Nothing." She opened both eyes and sat up. "I'm hungry."

"Of course." Moses jumped to his feet. "Forgive me. Let me bring you a plate. Here come the children."

Becky shielded her eyes with her hand as the sun dropped lower and found its way underneath the leaves of the oak tree. "Oh, my goodness. There are twice as many as there were when they left."

"They've told their friends. Is there anything special I should bring you?"

"Meat." She laughed, squinting up at him. "I'm starving."

"*Gut.* I'll be back in a few minutes."

"What will I do with them while you're gone?"

"Tell them to eat. Not to talk with their mouths full. To finish everything on their plates. If they do all that, you will tell them a story." He grinned and walked away, calling back, "Like a *gut* mother."

"Oh." The children swarmed around her, balancing their plates and glasses of lemonade and calling out to each other and to her in their language. "A mother, am I?" She put her arms around three smiling girls who were eating corn on the cob. "I feel more like Mother Goose." She kissed each of the girls and they giggled. "Do you know Mother Goose? *Mutter,* I think you say—yes, that's it. *Mutter Gans,* do they teach you about *Mutter Gans* here in Paradise? No, eat up, eat up, I'm the only one who can talk right now, the rest of you have food in your mouths. I will talk and you listen, all right? I have a story, a very good story, but you must all eat while I tell it to you, okay? *Ja? Gut?*"

They ate, their eyes on Becky. Once Moses arrived with a plateful of food for her, the roles were reversed, and she ate while the children talked. They told her about their schoolteacher, their ponies, their new buggies and wagons, their Percheron workhorses, their crops, and their pet dogs. Long streamers of cloud in the west turned purple and burgundy, and the fathers and mothers, a number of whom had been standing and listening at the edge of the circle, began to take their sons and daughters home, thanking Becky and Moses as they did so.

"Well, that's that." Becky stood up with her empty plate. "I should be heading home too."

"It's a ways to the Kurtz farm. I believe your parents have already left." Moses nodded with his head toward a buggy parked at one side of the field. "Permit me to give you a ride."

"That's all right. I don't mind walking."

"Please. It's not so often I get to speak with girls my own age."

"Moses, there are plenty of young women all around us."

He shrugged. "You're not the same as them."

They walked back to the tables with their dishes and gave them to the women who were washing up. Then they approached his buggy. The horse nickered. Becky rubbed its forehead and the spot between its ears.

"Milly." Moses patted the mare's neck. "I've had her since I was twelve."

"Really? That's quite a while. The pair of you must have a special relationship then."

"*Ja*. Very special. If I fell asleep holding the traces she would take me home and then whinny until someone came out."

"Are you going to fall asleep, Moses?"

He smiled. "No." He helped her into the buggy. "Please sit up front with me."

"All right."

They chatted while Milly trotted east along the road into the twilight and the first stars, falling into a long line of buggies and wagons. In minutes they were followed by another long line of buggies all going home from the picnic at the Stoltzfus' field. The air was warm and mosquitoes began to bite. When Moses saw her scratching her legs and arms he tugged a blanket out from under his seat and gave it to her.

"It's only cotton. It won't be too hot, but it'll keep off the hungry Lancaster bugs."

Becky pulled the white blanket over her. "*Danke*, Moses."

"*Bitte*, Rebecca."

He turned up the Kurtz's drive to the house. Aunt Ruth and her father and mother were sitting on a swing on the porch. Her father stood up as they approached.

"So there you are. We were wondering where you had gotten to." He smiled at Moses. "You are Emma and Adam Yoder's oldest son, aren't you?"

"Yes, sir." Moses helped Becky to the ground. "I didn't want her to walk home alone in the dark."

"Thank you very much. We're grateful."

Becky folded the blanket and gave it back to Moses. "Thank you for the ride. And all the games. I'm sure I'll sleep well tonight."

"It would have been very difficult keeping the children entertained without you. *Danke*."

"Oh, my goodness, I didn't do that much, Moses."

"You made all the difference." He touched the brim of his straw hat. "I hope I may see you again soon, Rebecca."

He drove away as Becky walked up the steps to the porch. Her father had his hands in his pockets and was smiling. Aunt Ruth and her mother were gazing at her from the swing.

"What?" She glared back at the three of them. "What is it? So a young Amish man drives me home."

Her father's smile grew. "I've never known Becky Whetstone to need assistance getting in and out of airplanes or boats or motorcars before. Or horse-drawn buggies."

Becky looked away quickly. "I'm exhausted. I'll see you all in the morning. Good night."

Jude watched her walk into the house and head up the staircase. Then he turned and looked at Lyyndaya.

"Emma's son," he said.

She nodded. "How strange life can be." Leaning back on the swing she began to rock more quickly. "It's past time that she took the notice of a young man. There was never any her age in Africa or in the Caribbean she felt she could talk to."

"But the Amish do not have boyfriends and girlfriends, remember." Ruth helped her younger sister keep the swing moving. "*Ja*, there is always friendship. But if young people feel anything more than that, it becomes a matter of courting and marriage. And he is the bishop's grandson. They will not be allowed to date as the English do."

Lyyndaya flicked her hand at a mosquito. "No one is talking about romance, Ruthie. Just a boy to be friends with. If she makes a girl her friend as well so much the better."

"Young Moses is considered quite the catch. So tall and handsome and sweet. All the girls will be jealous."

"Oh, Ruthie. Nothing will come of it. Becky will never give up her airplanes or the sky. No matter how charming Moses is."

THREE

The sunlight finally woke Becky when it fell across her face. After lingering a moment, she sat up, climbed out of bed, slipped on her dress, splashed some water on her face from the basin on the washstand, and rushed downstairs, pinning up her hair as she went. Grandmother Kurtz was alone in the kitchen, fussing with a tray of freshly baked loaves of bread. Her smile upon seeing her granddaughter was quick and bright.

"Ah, child. You must be hungry."

Becky hugged her. "Grandma, I'm so sorry I slept in. Where is everyone?"

"Up and about. Here and there. Your father is helping Luke with his hay cutting. Lyyndy just finished the milking. Grandpa is with the horses." She put on mitts and brought a plate of pancakes out of the warming oven. "Sit down. Give thanks. Eat." She placed a large mason jar of maple syrup on the table with a thump and added a rectangle of pale butter. "I just made the butter this morning."

Becky sat down and prayed and ate.

"When you're done just put your things in the sink." Grandmother Kurtz was placing loaves on the sills of open windows to cool. "Tomorrow we have the worship service in our barn. So Ruth is there with your mother getting it ready, laying down fresh straw. They would welcome your help."

"Of course." Becky drank her tall glass of cold milk in one gulp and pushed herself back from the table. "It was delicious, Grandma."

"*Vas?* You only ate three pancakes."

"I'm stuffed."

"It has to last you until lunch. Put this piece of bread in the pocket of your dress in case you feel faint."

"Grandma—"

Grandmother Kurtz stuffed it into Becky's pocket herself. "There. *Gut.* Now you go to the barn. They need you."

The barn was empty of horses or cattle or farming equipment. At first, walking from the brilliant sunshine into the gloom of the barn's interior, Becky couldn't see anyone. But then her mother called to her and as her eyes adjusted she saw Aunt Ruth was only a few feet away sweeping. Her mother was pitching clean straw over the floor.

"Becky, grab another pitchfork. There's one right behind you. There is so much else to do. We need to finish up in here."

Becky had no trouble spotting the pitchfork or the pile of hay her mother was using. She carried heaps of it to other parts of the barn and scattered it. Once Ruth was happy with her sweeping, she found a third pitchfork and joined Lyyndaya and Becky.

Ruth smiled at Becky as they tossed hay onto the floor side by side. "How did you sleep?"

Becky made a face. "It was perfect. But you should have awakened me."

"Did you get some breakfast?"

"No one can get past Grandma Kurtz without breakfast."

Lyyndaya leaned on her pitchfork a moment. "Or lunch. Or supper. Or bedtime snacks. That's the way she's always been."

Becky looked around the barn. "Are we going to sit on the floor?"

She had scarcely asked the question before there was a jingle of harness and a shout: "*Guten Morgen! Wir haben die Bänke!*"

Ruth propped her pitchfork against the barn wall and walked out to the farmyard. "There's your answer. The men have brought the benches over in a wagon."

Becky looked to see who was driving the wagon but her mother said, "Come. Let's finish this quickly now. There are some bare patches behind you."

Becky was still pitching hay when two men carried the first of the benches in. It was plain and sturdy and had no back. Behind them came two other men. She didn't know either of them and merely nodded, keeping her head down.

"Rebecca. *Guten Morgen.* How are you?"

She looked up to see Moses smiling and helping Joshua Miller carry a bench inside.

"Why, good morning, Moses. Hello, Joshua. I didn't know you were with the wagon."

"Oh, I drove it," Moses said quickly.

"And I helped," Joshua added just as quickly.

They set the bench down and positioned it in a row with another one. Then both straightened and looked at her, removed their straw hats, and put them on again. The older men were already getting more of the benches but Moses and Joshua hesitated, smiling at Becky.

"You're a good worker," Moses finally said.

"I think so too." Joshua was grinning. "I'll bet you've been at it since the crack of dawn."

"Joshua. Moses." Lyyndaya approached them. "Thank you. We do need those benches."

"Of course." The two of them almost ran out of the barn.

"You're proving to be a distraction." Lyyndaya gazed at Becky in her dress and pinned-up hair. "Perhaps I should send you to the kitchen."

Her daughter immediately lifted another forkful of hay. "Why? I'm working hard."

"*You* are working hard. I'm not sure Moses and Joshua will with you around."

"They brought in a bench."

"The other men have brought in two or three." She smiled. "Stay and pitch your hay. But perhaps you should keep your head down for now."

"Is that what you did?"

"What do you mean?"

"With Dad? Kept your head down all the time?"

Lyyndaya laughed. "Are you courting? Never mind. Do what you like. Your father always knew the color of my eyes."

The boys didn't speak to her again, not with her mother hovering nearby, but Becky could feel them gazing at her. Once she looked up and her eyes met those of Moses. Neither of them looked away. Sun slanting through a window made his eyes green and gold.

～

The next day Becky got up when Ruth did and went down to help her mother milk the dairy herd. The sky was still dark, for it was well before daybreak. At dawn there was a breakfast of oatmeal, sausage, eggs, and bacon and then everyone got cleaned up for church. There would be a communal meal after the service and Grandmother Kurtz had baked two large hams that she placed carefully in the warming oven.

"The women sit over here," her mother told Becky when they entered the barn for the morning of worship.

Becky made a face. "All right."

"It is the custom among the Amish. You remember that."

"I said all right."

Becky didn't know any of the slow hymns or understand the sermons given in Pennsylvania Dutch but she sat in respectful silence, head down, deliberately avoiding looking toward Moses and Joshua. She could feel their eyes on her, though, and decided the sensation was not unpleasant.

After the service, the meal tables were brought from a few wagons and placed between the benches. Becky found herself seated with Moses on one side of her and Joshua on the other.

"I remember the last time you were here," said Moses as they ate.

"So do I." Joshua swallowed a mouthful of ham and spoke again. "I think you were sixteen then, *ja*?"

Becky poked at her peas with a fork, liking all the male attention but not sure what to do with it. "Fifteen or sixteen, I'm not sure."

"And where were you coming from?" asked Moses, who wanted to be sure he stayed in the conversation.

"And where did you go to?" added Joshua as he carved up a baked potato, refusing to give his friend any advantage.

Becky suddenly laughed even though inside she felt tense and unsure of herself. "So many questions! I'll die of starvation if I try to answer them all."

Moses smiled. "Well, eat a bit and talk a bit and then eat some more."

Becky finished a piece of her grandmother's ham and wiped the corners of her mouth with a white napkin. "Okay. Before we visited here the last time we were in Africa."

"Africa." Moses thought about that. "I know about the amazing animals. Did you see any of them?"

"The animals? Yes. Lions, zebras, elephants, rhinoceroses. You must be careful, but they are beautiful."

"But what were you doing there?" Joshua drank from a glass of water. "What was the purpose of your visit?"

"It was more than a visit, Joshua. We were there five years. In Kenya. We helped start a church—Mother, Father, my brother, and I."

"Who is your brother?" asked Joshua.

"Nate. You didn't see him last time because he joined a missionary organization and went to China."

"China!" Joshua bit into a thick heel of bread. "Was he also helping with a church there?"

"Yes."

"What kind?"

"A Christian kind."

"Not Amish."

"Not Amish. But he taught them to follow the life and teachings of Jesus Christ."

Joshua shook his head. "We Amish don't do that. The bishop has told us many times—and my father has also said it—that it's not for us to go around the world chasing people and asking them to believe in God. There is the Bible. They can pick it up and read it. That's all that's needed. We must be about our life here. That's how we serve God."

Becky put down her fork and knife and looked at him. "You read a German Bible."

"*Ja,* sure, though I don't read it for myself, I listen to the pastors reading it on the Sundays."

"But the Bible was not written in German. Someone had to translate it into German from Hebrew and Greek. What would you do if they hadn't done that? How could you understand it?"

Joshua shrugged. "My English is okay."

"The Bible had to be translated into English too. Men and women were killed for doing that. Joshua, people are needed who will travel to a country, learn the language, and translate the Bible into that language. Otherwise people can't know the story of God's love. That's what we were doing in Africa and the Caribbean. Finding their words for the story and then using those words to tell them how much God cared for their families and friends. Talking to them about the Cross. Plopping a German Bible down in front of most people won't help them at all."

Joshua stared at her.

Aware that a touch of fire had come into her voice, Becky dropped her head and went at her cabbage salad. Moses and Joshua watched her for a moment, realized that something had fallen between them and her, and said nothing. Finally Moses tapped her lightly on the sleeve of her dress.

"Hey. We take nothing away from what you're doing. You have served the Lord in the manner you felt was most fitting. We're taught differently, that's all."

Becky didn't lift her head. "If you respect the Bible so much, what do you do about Paul's missionary journeys? All over the Roman world. Shipwrecks. Beatings. Mobs. All because he wanted to tell people God was love, not hate—that he was light, not darkness."

Moses nodded. "Of course we know those stories of his sailing trips."

"What if he had stayed home and said, 'Well, the world can read the Bible and that is all they need?' Especially if the world didn't have a Bible?"

Moses held up a hand. "All right. Tell us what happened before Africa."

"Why?"

"I'd like to know. We both would."

"Why?"

"Please. We're interested."

Becky kept on eating. "There was a lot of flying. We are a flying family. All of us are pilots. I was born in '22 and went up for the first time when I was five, strapped into my mother's lap. I was eight when I first handled the controls by myself, still in my mom's lap. The family became an act at shows all across America. The Whetstone Family Fliers. We did barnstorming, air shows, stunts of all kinds. It's how we made a living for years."

Joshua hadn't returned to his plate of food. "That sounds reckless."

"We took every precaution."

"But what good did it all do?"

"The crowds loved it. They cheered so loudly everywhere we went. It gave them joy for a few hours." Becky lifted her head despite herself and the two young men were treated to a dazzling smile that struck right through both of them. "You should have seen the kids. How excited they were when we took them up for a couple of dollars and they saw the world the way an eagle sees it every day." She looked at Moses. "My dad told me your grandfather went up with him and shouted praises to God."

Moses was startled. "My grandfather? I never heard of such a thing."

"He loved it. Dad reckons he would have been a flier too if the Amish hadn't decided to ban planes at the same time they said no to cars and electricity."

Moses took this in.

"So then you also learned to fly?" Joshua still hadn't returned to his food. "You are a pilot? A woman?"

Becky surprised herself by laughing instead of growling. "Yes. A woman. God's woman. Up there with the angels and the eagles and the swans—I did see a flight of white swans once." She drank her lemonade, her eyes gleaming over the rim of the glass. "I flew alone for the first time when I was fifteen. It was while we were in Kenya."

"And the Caribbean?" asked Moses. "What happened there?"

"More flying. Talking to people about the love of God. Medical supplies. Food. Clean water. Such beauty in the Caribbean. Flying over it all like a cloud. Or like the trade winds. That mission was one of the greatest blessings of my life."

Joshua ran a hand through his straw-colored hair. "Now I know why you are *Ausnahme*."

Moses grinned. "An exception. *And* exceptional."

Becky smiled at him. "Thank you, Moses."

"With all of that you must be ready to settle down now, *ja*? Is that the good news? Becky Whetstone has returned to Paradise for good?"

"Oh, I don't know anything about that. I'm pretty sure we're just here for the summer. After that, I have no idea."

Moses' eyes settled into a dark green like Becky had often seen in deep water off the coast of Turks and Caicos. "Surely you're going to stay? Don't you consider this your real home?"

"My father and mother might, Moses. It's really more their home than mine. Africa has that part of my heart. And the Caribbean. But mostly Africa."

"But we are your people. You come from Amish. You belong with Amish."

"I've never taken the vows, Moses. Never been baptized."

"But you will, won't you?"

"I—" Before she could finish, her mother approached the table.

It looked as if Moses and Joshua were going to bolt but she smiled at them. "Joshua Miller. Moses Yoder. Good day. How was the meal?"

"Very *gut*, Mrs. Whetstone."

"Everything was perfect, Mrs. Whetstone."

"I'm so glad to hear it. You will have to excuse Becky and me. We must help the women clean up. And the men will soon be wanting your help with the benches and tables." She glanced down at Joshua's plate. "What's this? Were your eyes bigger than your stomach?"

"Oh. I forgot." Joshua quickly attacked the food that he had left. "We were all talking so much."

"I see that. Well, perhaps you can visit again after the singing tonight. Good afternoon."

Joshua dipped his head. "*Guten Tag*."

Becky stood to leave with her mother and Moses got to his feet. "Good afternoon, Rebecca, Mrs. Whetstone."

A few minutes later as the two women walked toward the house carrying dirty dishes, Lyyndaya asked, "So how are you?"

"Oh, I'm all right. But things got awkward when they asked about our family being missionaries and flying planes. They don't seem to understand why we would do either of those things."

"No, of course not. They've been taught that missions aren't necessary and that airplanes are to be shunned. You'll just have to be patient and find other things to chat about."

"Mom, how much school do they take?"

"Usually up to grade eight."

"Grade eight? That's it?"

"They don't feel that any more than that is required. You know much more about the world than they do. Keep that in mind and don't push them too far."

"How…how can I talk with them? That's like being with kids who are fourteen."

"But they aren't fourteen, are they? They are strapping young men in their early twenties with all sorts of farming know-how and a great deal of common sense and Christian faith. And both are very good-looking. There are plenty of things to talk about that you don't need a grade-twelve education for."

Becky pouted, her lower lip fattening. "You made me finish grade twelve. And that was a hard year."

"So you are *Ausnahme*. That's why."

"Ha. I wonder if they will let us be *Ausnahme* forever?"

Lyyndaya shook her head. "They won't. I'm sure they'll speak with us about the matter before the summer is over. And they will certainly want to talk to you."

"To try to make me Amish?"

They climbed the steps into the house where women bustled about washing and drying and stacking dishes. "They won't make you do anything. It will be your decision. But Bishop Zook and the pastors will want to know what you're thinking. Hush now. We can talk later."

Long before the singing was to begin at seven o'clock, Becky wandered around the farmyard and eventually sat down alone in the barn. It held within it now not only the scent of the fresh hay she had pitched the day before, but the aroma of the food eaten. As she sat there thinking and praying she was certain she could smell the soap Moses used, which reminded her of long green fields and clover.

"Ah. Rebecca. May I?"

Becky half rose at the sight of Moses. "Oh. I didn't hear you come in." She sat back down and he took a seat next to her on the bench. "They won't let us sit together when the singing starts."

"I'll move when I must. How are you?"

"Much the same as I was a few hours ago."

"Listen. I've been turning over everything that was said during the meal. Joshua, myself, you, all our words. I'm certain we troubled you."

"No, Moses, it's just—"

"*Nein, nein.* We don't understand the world as you understand it. That's not your problem. It's Joshua's and it's mine. As you say, you haven't taken your vows. It's only right you should explore, travel, wonder about other ways. I'm twenty-one now and I didn't have my baptism until last year. So why should I be pushing you?"

"I didn't think you were pushing me."

"But I was. Because I…I find you intriguing. So different. So… beautiful…"

Becky felt the blood come swiftly to her face. "Moses—"

"And because of this I want you to stay. I want to see more of you. Want to listen to you talk. I want to hear what it's like to fly. How a person like Rebecca Whetstone feels when she sees lions in the great African fields. How alive a man may become if he swims in water the color of your—"

Moses stopped and looked away. He got to his feet. "I'm sorry. I rush ahead. So often this is my greatest fault. Words come tumbling out. I mean them, but they're not always appropriate. I'm saying to you things that are too soon."

"Moses. Please sit back down. You didn't do anything wrong. A woman doesn't mind being told she's beautiful. Please sit back down."

She patted the part of the bench where he had been a moment before. Slowly he took his seat again and removed his straw hat. He didn't say anything but when he finally looked at her she was smiling a small smile.

"Moses, I have no idea what I'm going to do. Mother tells me Bishop Zook is going to ask me how I feel about taking my vows and being baptized, and I don't know what to tell him. I'm flattered that you want me around and that you like me. I like you too. It's pleasant to be in your company. I like to listen to your voice and thoughts as much as you do mine. I don't know what is going to happen when it comes to the Lapp Amish and Becky Whetstone. But for now it's very good to be here. And very good to hear a beautiful man tell me I'm beautiful too."

Moses' face reddened under his tan. "Now I have no words at all. The Amish girls don't speak this way."

"Well, I do. I believe in being forthright." She touched his cheek with her hand. It seemed as if he would pull away but a different kind of light came into his face and he did not. "So I'm also going to ask you this, even though you say you have no words. Water the color of—yes? Can you finish your sentence for me?"

"What?"

"A moment ago you said a man could come alive swimming in water that had a special color."

He didn't look away. "The water would have the color of your eyes."

"Ah." Everything in her body and her face smiled.

He leaned toward her and Becky caught herself leaning his way as well, then straightened. "Maybe you should move to another bench now. They'll all be coming soon..."

Four

"So you've been here three weeks. What do you think?" Ruth was changing out of her dress into a nightgown.

Becky was lying on her stomach on her bed. Her head was pillowed on her arms. "I don't know what to think."

"Did you see Moses again today?"

"Yes."

"How did you two manage it this time?"

"He had a gift of fresh-ground flour for Grandma. One hundred pounds."

Ruth began to laugh. "He never runs out of ideas. The other day a big container of grease for our wagon wheels. Before that it was twenty pounds of cheese he said his mother didn't need. He likes you for sure. Is the feeling mutual?"

Becky's mouth was pressed up against the skin of her arm and her words came out muffled. "Of course it's mutual."

Ruth sat down on the edge of her bed, let out her hair, and began to brush it slowly. "If you'll get ready for bed I'll brush out your long golden locks for you, princess."

Becky didn't budge. "A month ago I just wanted to visit and leave. Now I don't know what to do."

"Are you thinking of staying?"

"If I stay I can't fly. All my life, God and flying have been the biggest things. There were no boys or men to complicate matters. Now I meet an Amish farmer who looks like a dream and suddenly everything is in a mess."

"A mess?" Ruth stopped brushing her hair. "Has he asked you to stay?"

"Oh, from the first day he wanted me to stay and I thought, *You're cute but I'm not becoming Amish just to stick around you.* But now…"

"Have you told your mother and father about this?"

"No. Mom watches me with the guys like a hawk anyway. If she thought I was getting serious about Moses she'd lock me up."

"Lyyndy won't be that bad."

"Would you like to place a wager, Auntie Ruth? On whether or not she'll impose further restrictions on my movements and who I spend time with?"

"I don't place wagers."

"I could do what I want, you know. I'm a woman of nineteen, not some skinny fourteen-year-old."

Ruth began brushing her hair again. "What became of the other knight?"

"What?" Becky turned her head to look at her aunt. "You mean Joshua?"

"Mm-hm."

Becky stared back at the ceiling. "He lost interest right from the day I argued with him about the importance of having missionaries. And he's uncomfortable with my flying. He doesn't know what to do with me. Any more than his father, Pastor Miller, does. So now he hangs around Rachel King a lot."

"You're okay with that?"

"Do you think I need three or four young men on a string to make me feel good about myself? I'm more than happy getting to know Moses. If I only knew how to stop feeling like a washing machine."

"And what does that feel like?"

"Well, like being the butter in a butter churn. But I'll be lucky if I come out looking like anything as good as butter."

"Eventually you'll settle down inside."

"When?"

"A year or two."

Ruth grinned. "Come. I said I'd brush your hair out for you and it's getting late. I want to go to bed. So get into your nightgown and sit beside me here."

Becky reluctantly got up, washed her face and hands at the washstand and toweled them dry, changed into her nightgown, and sat down by Ruth. "I don't know if I'll be able to sleep."

"I noticed you didn't eat much supper either. I'm surprised my sister didn't pick up on it." Ruth began to run her brush through Becky's blond hair.

Becky rolled her eyes. "The only reason Mom never saw how little I had on my plate was because she was too busy darting back and forth from the oven to the table. Her and her angel-food cakes."

"It's not as if no one sees what's going on. It's quite obvious the bishop's grandson is attracted to you. But the community knows nothing can come of it unless you're baptized into the faith."

"I think, *This is so foolish. I can't give up flying.* Then Moses looks at me with his green eyes, those deep-water eyes, and says something like, 'You are this special person. It's like watching the sun come up over the fields and I'm all alone and the air is so good.' What am I supposed to do with that? God throws this curveball at me—this handsome Amish farmer who is some kind of love poet too."

"What is a 'curveball'?"

"In baseball. A difficult pitch to hit with the bat."

"Hm. But you don't love him, do you?" Ruth stroked Becky's hair with her hand. "You've let it grow almost to your shoulders. I'm surprised. Usually you keep it short."

Becky mumbled. "Well. He says my hair is like—" She stopped. "Never mind what he says."

"The Bible says a woman's crowning glory is her hair."

"Moses says that too."

"The only man who may see it among the Amish is the husband."

"Yes. So he told me."

"And does he want to be the husband?"

"Just so he can see my hair?" Becky began to squirm. "Are you done yet?"

"With the longest hair I've ever seen on Rebecca Whetstone? Oh, no."

"Ouch!"

"You see? A snarl." Ruth slowed her brushing down. "You haven't answered my question."

"What question?"

"Do you love him?"

"How should I know? I told you. Everything is mixed up in my head." She groaned. "It's easier to fly upside down and do the kind of stunts where one mistake turns you into strawberry jam."

"Ugh. Please don't talk like that, Becky."

"Saying it doesn't make it happen, Auntie Ruth."

"Still. I don't want the image in my mind." She set down the brush. "There. That will do. It'll gleam like gold in the morning when Moses sees it."

"What makes you think he's going to see it tomorrow morning?"

"I thought you knew. He will be here at five to help your father repair the fences. The dairy herd escaped yesterday. And some of the horses got into the hayfield and almost ate themselves to death before a neighbor spotted them. Luke and Daniel and Harley are helping too."

"Why didn't anyone tell me?"

"It was just decided after supper. When you came up here to lie down."

"You thought I knew? How would I know?"

"Shh. Now I suppose you're going to have an even harder time falling asleep." She hugged Becky with one arm. "I'm going to pray for you. None of Grandma's homemade medicines will work on what ails you, my dear."

Ruth prayed in German for several minutes. Becky didn't understand any of it but by the time her aunt said *amen* she was calmer inside even if she still didn't feel like going to bed. Once she was sure by Ruth's breathing that she was asleep she peeled back the sheets and got to her feet. Moving quietly and quickly she left the room and went down the staircase and out the front door of the dark and silent farmhouse. The moon was half full, and she stood by one of the fields looking at the silver lighting up the heads of the tall hay.

So I will pray in English—if you don't mind. I've always felt you wanted me to fly and be a missionary pilot. Are you having second thoughts? Do you have a new plan? Is Moses part of it? I really can't think straight—half of me doesn't object to becoming Amish if he is the man I lie with every night and get up and face the day with every morning. It would be nice to have a sign from you, Lord. I would be grateful if you showed me something, anything, just so long as I understand what you're showing me when I see it. Thank you. I love you. Amen…and good night.

She made her way back to her bed and for the next several hours slept off and on, until four when she joined her mother for the milking. She heard her uncles—Luke, Daniel, and Harley—arrive in their wagons and saw Moses pull up in a buggy as she glanced through the open barn door. He looked around after greeting her father and her uncles and she felt like he expected to see her. Her mother noticed that Becky had her head up and was staring out at the farmyard.

"Finish your work. You'll see him at breakfast."

Becky leaned her head into the cow's side. "At breakfast? With all the noise and talk there will be at the table today I'll be lucky if he even hears me say hello."

Lyyndaya smiled as she worked the teats of her cow. "No matter. Your father thinks they will be at it tomorrow too. Just him and Moses. Would that sort of breakfast table suit you better?"

Becky stopped milking. "Just Dad and Moses tomorrow? Why?"

"He only needs one other pair of hands Thursday."

"And he chose Moses?"

"Yes."

"Out of the goodness of his heart?"

Lyyndaya picked up her bucket and milking stool and lantern and moved to another cow. "No doubt he was thinking of you."

"Me?" Becky started working on her cow again. "Ha. That probably means he wants to grill him. Am I right?"

"This isn't some sort of gangster movie."

"He will though. I know Dad. 'What makes Moses Yoder tick?' That's what's on his mind. Not me."

"Both of you are on his mind. Believe me." Lyyndaya glanced at her daughter. "Moses' mother, Emma, once vied with me for your father's affection."

Becky stopped milking again. "What?"

"Keep working. Ruth and Grandmother will have breakfast ready at six-thirty, after the men have put in an hour's work on the fences."

Lyyndaya watched to be sure Becky returned to milking her cow. "I tell you this because it would be just like Lydia Yoder to speak with you about it, thinking she's doing us all a good turn. So I was young and Emma was young, a great beauty, and we both fell in love with Jude. You know the story about him going overseas. Even then he wasn't sure which of us he should marry...if he returned alive. He was shunned because he went to war and we couldn't write him and he couldn't write us. Emma and I were good friends, despite being rivals for Jude, and we prayed for him and wrote him letters anyway, letters he never saw."

Lyyndaya got up and emptied her bucket into a milk can. Then she took her stool to another stall. Becky poured her milk into the container and moved to a different stall as well, carrying her lantern with her. She waited for her mother to finish the story, listening to the sounds of the dairy herd and the small creaks and groans of the barn. Finally Lyyndaya picked up where she had left off.

"You've heard the story about how your father enlisted to spare the other young men here persecution during the war and also to ensure the safety of the Amish community in Paradise. At the time, however, we didn't know why Jude had done what he had done, why he had joined the army and gone to France as a fighter pilot. Many felt it was because flying was such an obsession to him he couldn't resist the temptation. As time went by, Emma simply stopped believing in him and didn't want him as a husband even if he did return and repent. So she took up with another man in the community who she felt was more righteous and more Amish. She was, after all, Bishop Zook's daughter. Who can blame her? No one understood what Jude was doing or why."

"But you didn't stop believing in him, did you?"

Becky had stopped milking. Lyyndaya was going to tell her to keep going but then she stopped milking too and looked at nothing, her eyes light and dark in the glimmer of the lantern.

"I loved your father. And he told me when we met again that he realized long before he returned that it was me he loved, not Emma. He had one last letter I had written before the shunning and he read it over and over again before he took to the air every morning. The skies were dangerous in 1918 and my words in the letter and God's words in the Bible gave him hope and strength. Yes, I believed in him. I knew he must be doing something holy and good that none of us could comprehend but that one day God would bring it to light. And so he did. Your father was a hero and he saved lives here in Paradise as well as in France. He even saved his enemies' lives." She looked over at Becky and half smiled. "Who knows? Perhaps you will do something like that too. Save lives. Oh, what am I saying? You've already done that by having airlifted patients, brought in medical supplies—"

"It's not like what Father did. He had to be brave in a time of war when others were trying to shoot him down. That's different. That takes another kind of courage. I don't know if I have it."

Lyyndaya stood up. "I don't want to find out. If you truly have feelings for young Moses then I would be far happier if you married him and settled down here and grew wheat and corn and raised a crop of grandchildren for me. Even if you had to give up flying I would like that far better than you ending up in the skies over France like your father, with German bullets whistling by your head."

"Mom, they'll never let women fly combat aircraft. Not in this war anyways."

"Who knows how quickly that might change!"

Lyyndaya had tears shining in her eyes and on her face. Becky quickly got up and went to her, helping her mother to her feet and taking her in her arms. She stood a half-foot taller so that Lyyndaya's head rested on her daughter's chest.

"Mom. It's okay. They say America will never get into the war in Europe."

"They said that in 1914 too. But three years later there we were. All because the Germans sank American ships."

"The Germans won't do that again, Mother. We'll stay out of this conflict. Everyone says so." Becky kissed her mother on the top of her head. "And I won't go over. I have no desire to do that. I won't fly Red Cross planes. I won't nurse on the battlefield or anything—I'm no Clara Barton or Florence Nightingale. I don't know what's going to happen between Moses and me. Maybe I'll go Amish or maybe I won't. But I don't feel I have to take off into the air and prove I have as much courage as Dad did during the Great War. That's not in me. I may be a daredevil stunt flyer but I'm not going to play a game like that."

"Oh, this is so foolish, standing here in the barn crying." Lyyndaya swiped at her eyes with her fingers but didn't pull away from her daughter. "The milking needs to be finished, soon Ruth will be calling us into breakfast, there is baking and ironing—"

"All that can wait."

"You will want to see your young Moses."

"Yes. But that can wait too. He'll be there an hour from now, even two hours from now."

"You sound too proud when you say that, Becky, too sure of yourself."

"It's not that, Mom. It's that I'm sure of him. I know he cares for me. I know he'll be there." She smiled. "I guess I know he loves me. I only wonder if I love him too."

FIVE

A low boom rumbled over the fields from dark clouds away to the east. Moses Yoder glanced back. The storm wasn't any closer than it had been an hour before and the glow of the rising sun was lining the top of the thunderhead. He was certain the clouds would head out to sea or up the coast. Turning back to his buggy, he flicked the reins of his horse, Milly, and clicked his tongue.

"Come, girl, we must hurry."

They rushed past farms where his Amish neighbors had long been up and about seeing to their livestock in the dark. One or two waved to him, holding their lanterns, and he waved back. Soon the buggy was in Paradise, rolling through quiet streets where only a few cars were on the road that early. He snapped the reins again, biting his lower lip.

"*Bitte,* Milly, *bitte.*"

He emerged on the far side of town and immediately spotted the airplane in a field several hundred yards away. It was the field of Henry Parker, an English farmer. He had just taken his second cut of hay off it the week before. Moses could see Parker, recognizable by his tall, lean frame in the dim light of early dawn, and a smaller figure as well. He could feel his heart thudding in his chest as he drew closer and closer.

The sun cleared the cloud bank just before he stopped. Gold flashed over the plane and grass, over Henry Parker—and it flashed over Becky Whetstone, who stood by the craft in a leather flight jacket and helmet, goggles pushed high up on her head. Moses felt dizzy when he looked at her in that light. He almost fell out of the buggy, climbing out so hastily. Becky's eyes glittered with a smile.

"Moses Yoder. Good to see you, son." Henry Parker extended his hand. "Have you ever been up in a crop duster before?"

Moses shook Parker's hand. "No, sir. I've never flown in anything before."

"Well, you're in for a treat. My Curtiss Jenny is an old girl but she's solid. Sorry to say I won't be taking you up myself. I hope this young lady will do."

Becky looked like a different woman in her flying gear. Moses kept staring at her even though her hand had been extended for several moments. Finally she withdrew it and handed him a jacket and helmet and goggles.

"*Guten Morgen,* Mr. Yoder. Please put these on and climb into the front seat. Mr. Parker will see to it you are strapped in properly."

Moses tugged on the jacket. "Whose is this?"

"My dad's. He arranged for us to borrow Mr. Parker's Jenny and he was quite happy to lend you his gear." She came closer and whispered to him while Parker checked over the aircraft a final time. "Are you sure you want to go through with this? I haven't taken my vows. It doesn't matter what I do. But you've been baptized into the Amish faith."

Moses had an almost blank expression on his face as he looked at her. "I have never seen anything so beautiful as the way you look right now."

"Oh, my." Becky reddened. "You are the most romantic Amish farmer that has ever been born in Lancaster County. Are you sure you won't get into trouble for doing this?"

"No one will know."

"Of course they'll know. Everyone will find out."

"So if they shun me, they shun me. It will be worth it."

Becky helped him put on his helmet. "No Amish boy is as crazy as you. No wonder I like you."

"Like?"

She paused and put a hand to his cheek. "You know how I feel, my Amish man. *Ich liebe dich.*"

A smile moved over his lips. "So now I am ready to do anything. I could fly without the plane."

"Let's not try that this time." She kissed him quickly on the cheek. "Jump in. And make sure your straps are tight."

Henry Parker took care that Moses was safely secured in the forward cockpit. His brown eyes were warm. "Sometimes we risk all for the lady's hand."

Moses shrugged. "My grandfather flew before the planes were banned. I want to see what he saw. And I want her to be the one taking me up."

The older man patted Moses on the shoulder. "I'd do the same. She's a honey." He leaned in close to Moses. "Now you look out to the far end of my fields once you're aloft, young man. Just past all the corn. You look to the dirt road there. All right?"

"Yes, sir."

Moses watched in amazement as Mr. Parker spun the propeller and the engine howled and the plane started to move forward. Becky turned it into the breeze that was coming in from the west, and Moses felt his hair blow backward. They went faster and faster, faster than any horse he had galloped or any team he had driven, until the field on either side of them was a green streak. There was a lurch and they were in the air, the motor roaring, the Jenny rising higher and higher, roads becoming pencil lines, farmhouses little boxes, Henry Parker turning into a stick man. Moses felt a rush of fear and a rush of excitement colliding inside him.

Becky flew straight and level a few minutes, dove, then rolled the plane so Moses was hanging upside down. He could not help himself and began to laugh. He was still laughing when she came right side up and he twisted back to look at her. Becky saw his laughter and grinned, shaking her head. She shouted over the noise of the wind and the engine: "I—tried—to scare you—and all you do—is laugh?"

"I—can't—help it!" he shouted back.

"You are—one crazy Amish boy!"

She banked and Moses noticed the cornfield. He remembered what Henry Parker had told him and he stared down through his goggles at the earth far below. At first the road beyond the rows of cornstalks seemed empty. Then he saw a black buggy. Beside it was a tall figure, taller than Henry Parker, taller than anyone he knew except for his grandfather, Bishop Zook. A hand waved up at him and Moses leaned out of the cockpit in excitement.

"Grandpa!" he yelled, waving both arms wildly. "Grandpa! It's beautiful! *Es ist Gottes Schönheit!*"

"What?" shouted Becky from behind him.

"It's my grandfather!" Moses pointed downward.

Becky looked down. "What are you calling to him?"

"*Es ist Gottes Schönheit!* It's God's beauty!"

"Moses—he can't hear you! I can barely hear you!"

"I don't care! I am going to shout it anyway! God will hear if no one else does!"

Again Becky grinned and shook her head.

Moses twisted around in his seat as far as he could to look at her. "No one in the world could look as good as you do in such goggles! Everything you wear looks attractive once you put it on!"

"Oh, stop it! You are too much!" She threw the plane into a steep dive. "There! That will shut you up!" But even above the scream of the air and the shriek of the motor she could hear his laughter.

They stayed up for half an hour, circling over Bishop Zook again and again, sometimes heading east into the sun, other times heading north and south and west over lush hay fields and stands of trees as well as long rows of ripening oats and barley and tobacco. At one point a flock of white pelicans flew beside them. Moses kept slapping the flat of his hand against the outside of his cockpit and Becky was sure she heard him whistling. Sudden dives and barrel rolls and death spins only made him laugh with so much abandon she thought he wouldn't be able to stop to get his breath. When it came time to land she deliberately dove through a cluster of clouds white and cool as pearl and touched down on the far side of the field from Henry Parker, knowing it would take him at least five minutes to get over to them. The propeller hadn't even stopped spinning before she jumped clear of her cockpit and began tugging at the straps holding Moses safe in his seat.

"What is it?" he asked. "What's wrong?"

"Hurry. I want to show you something."

He followed her around to the side of the aircraft that was out of Henry Parker's sight. Then she pulled off her helmet and goggles so her blond hair flew loose around her face and shoulders. Moses didn't move. She ripped off his helmet, goggles with it, and kissed him full on the lips as hard as she could. His arms found her back and he brought her against his chest and jacket, kissing back with more and more strength until suddenly his lips were over her eyes and her hair and her throat. Now she was the one who began to laugh.

"Look at you," she teased. "A wild Amish man."

"Shh. This is not the time for words. *Es ist eine Zeit zum Berühren.*"

"What?"

"*It is a time to touch.*" He kissed her again and when he pulled away she gasped for breath. He smiled.

"How…how do you kiss like that when you have never had a girl?" she managed to say.

"It comes naturally…with you. Like the laughter coming out of my stomach. And then I can't end it." His fingers played with strands of her hair. "This is just like the sun. There is no difference. A woman's crowning glory is her hair. Now I must marry you, you know."

"Is that how it works?"

"That's exactly how it works among the Plain people." He put his hands on both sides of her face and kissed her slowly and softly. "You see? That is how we do it. No rush. No hurry. No English."

She closed her eyes and tilted up her face. "Please. I want some more Amish."

"My pleasure."

He kissed her again, slowly and deeply. Neither of them pulled away even when they heard the sound of hoofbeats and the jangle of harness and the creak of wheels. Only when Bishop Zook boomed, "*Wie geht es Ihnen?*" did they stop the kiss, but even then they didn't step apart or take their arms from around each other's waists.

"Hello, Grandfather," Moses greeted him. "We are good, thank you."

"Bishop Zook," said Becky. "I've never been better."

The bishop climbed down from the buggy and so did Henry Parker, whom the bishop had picked up and driven to where Becky had landed the Jenny. The bishop pushed his straw hat back on his head.

"So, so. Up in the air. Flying around. Barnstorming." He smiled at them through his white beard. "What shall we do with you, hmm?"

"Grandfather, Rebecca is *rumspringa*. She has not taken her vows."

"I know she is *rumspringa*. But what are you?"

"I? I'm in love with her."

"I see that. A hundred wagons coming up that road couldn't have made you two end that kiss."

"Not a thousand, sir."

"Hmm." He stroked his beard and turned his gaze on Becky. "So. Rebecca. What do you say?"

"He wanted to fly. Just like you flew twenty years ago. And me? Now that I have been in the air with him I want to marry him. Even if it means I must keep both feet on the ground."

Moses looked at her. "What? You want to marry me and you aren't teasing? Just like that?"

"It's not *just like that*. We were in the sky for thirty minutes." She hugged him. "And I have been praying about it all summer. I don't want you shunned or repenting of being up in a plane with me. Let the Jenny stay on Mr. Parker's runway from now on. You and I can plant our crops and have a farm, and our marriage can be what takes us into the clouds. Okay?"

"But you love flying planes—"

"Shh." Her fingers moved to his lips. "But I love you more." She glanced at Bishop Zook. "I want to take my vows and be baptized."

His thick eyebrows moved upward. "*Ja?* There will be a period of instruction."

"I'm fine with that."

"All things must be done in accordance with the *Ordnung*."

"Of course."

"Usually we have our baptisms in the spring. Marriages in the late fall or early winter. Well after harvest."

"Perhaps if I'm an exceptional student the timetable might be altered slightly?"

"Oh–ho—you think so?" He laughed. "I will talk to the ministers. Then I will decide. We should come to your place tomorrow morning after chores. Is that all right with you, Rebecca?"

"Yes."

"I will need to talk to your mother and father about it right away. Can I offer you two a lift back to your buggy? You should go home first, Rebecca. You should be talking to them about what is going on before I do my bishop speech. And Moses, you must talk with your mother."

"What about the plane?" asked Moses.

Henry Parker cleared his throat and stepped forward. "If someone will give the prop a twirl I'll get her back to the hangar and loaded up for a run over my apple orchards. You don't need to worry about Jenny."

Becky gave the old man a strong hug that startled him. "Thank you so much, Mr. Parker. It was a dream to be up in the air again. And to have Moses along. A dream. I'm so grateful."

Moses shook his hand. "I can't thank you enough. Your loan of the aircraft has changed my life completely."

Henry Parker smiled. "You're welcome. She's never been put to better use than she was this morning."

"Let me give the propeller the spin, Henry." Bishop Zook handed his hat to Moses. "Whenever you're ready."

"I keep my gear under the pilot's seat." He pulled out his jacket and helmet and began to tug them on. Then he climbed on board and adjusted his goggles. "Any time now, Bishop Zook."

The bishop smiled, spat on his hands, and gripped a propeller blade firmly. He threw down on it with all his might, and the engine sputtered, made a choking sound while he stood back with a worried look on his face, then rumbled and roared. Henry Parker tossed him a salute and steered the Jenny into the wind. He lifted into the air, circled once, and headed north to his farmhouse and the landing strip. Hands on his hips, Bishop Zook watched him go.

"If I could make horses fly," he murmured. He looked at Moses and Becky. "Well, shall we head over to your horse and carriage?"

The three of them climbed into the buggy and headed off to where Moses had parked. Moses and Becky sat holding hands in the back. She leaned forward.

"Bishop Zook."

"Mm?"

"I hope there will not be a great deal of trouble for Moses over this."

"The flying? There will be some mutters and scowls. But it will all pass like a sun shower the moment I announce you are going to take instruction for baptism and are leaving planes behind for good. Once it's made clear Moses intends to marry you when the baptism is over, and that you have every intention of being a good Amish bride, it will be as if the flight this morning never happened." He smiled back at them. "Except in your own hearts."

When they reached Moses' buggy, where Milly patiently cropped grass in the ditch, the bishop handed Becky a packet of letters once she had climbed down. "These came for your family just yesterday."

Becky turned them over in her hand. "Who are they from?"

"I don't know. Two of them have come a long way. First to Africa, then the Caribbean, finally to Paradise."

Becky examined the postmarks. "Why, those two are from the Hawaiian Islands. We don't know anyone there."

He shrugged. "Someone knows you. One has an army seal on the envelope." He squinted up at the sun. "You get started. I will show up fifteen minutes after you arrive at the Kurtz home. Is that enough time?"

"Yes," responded Becky. "I think so."

Once they were seated side by side Moses flicked the reins and Milly started along the road into Paradise. Becky leaned her head on his shoulder and squeezed his hand.

"Don't worry. I'll sit up straight once we come into town."

"Why should I be worried? I like your head where it is. It can stay on my shoulder right through the Amish farms."

"My brave man."

"Maybe not so brave. I get tight in my chest and throat when I think of talking to your parents."

"No, no, they're not that bad."

Moses moaned. "*They're* not bad. I am. What am I going to tell them?"

"That you love me and want me as your wife....or is it *frau?*"

"That's it? That will be enough?"

"Tell them we had a plane ride."

"Oh, sure."

"They had one, you know. Before they were engaged."

"How did that turn out?"

"Oh, Mom's parents wouldn't let her see Dad ever again."

"What?" Moses stared at her. "You tell me that now?"

"Relax. They're married, aren't they?" She kissed him on the cheek. "It will all work out." She sat up and dug around in the pockets of her flight jacket. "Excuse me while I pin my hair back up. And we should take these jackets off."

Moses shrugged the leather jacket off his shoulders and arms and turned around to throw it into the backseat. He saw the letters his grandfather had given her and the US Army insignia on one of the envelopes.

"So why is the army writing your father? I thought that was over with a long time ago."

"It is over with. I have no idea. Maybe they owe him money."

"You think so?"

"No." She put a final pin in her hair and posed. "There. What do you think?"

He glanced at her. "I think a woman's crowning glory is her hair blowing in the wind. But I'll take it short too."

"Don't worry. I'll have it halfway down my back for our wedding night."

Blood rushed into Moses' face. "*Ja*? And when will that be?"

"Christmas. I'll be your Christmas present. How's that?"

"But your baptism—" he began.

She tightened her lips. "I'm not waiting until 1942 just because they think they can only baptize people in the spring and marry them in the fall. I'll be baptized and Amish from the tips of my toes to the top of my head before we celebrate Thanksgiving. Just watch me."

Six

W ho is Ram Peterson?"

"A fellow I flew with during the war. We were in the same squadron in France."

Becky scanned the letter in her hand. "Why on earth does he call himself Flapjack?"

Jude sipped at his mug of coffee. "That was the nickname we gave him."

"Did he like pancakes or something?"

"I don't know."

"What was your nickname?"

Jude glanced across the breakfast table at Lyyndaya. Grandfather and Grandmother Kurtz and Aunt Ruth looked at her too. She smiled and dropped her eyes. Becky glanced up and saw the silent communication between her parents.

"What?" she asked. She looked at her father again. "Is it some big family secret?"

"My nickname was Lover Boy."

Becky stared at him and then burst into laughter. "Are you serious? Why?"

"Because of your mother. It was the letters back and forth that started it. Even after I couldn't get her letters anymore I kept re-reading the old ones."

Becky looked over at Lyyndaya. "Mom."

Lyyndaya shook her head. "Never mind. We were young and foolish."

"You were young maybe, but it doesn't sound foolish. It's sweet."

"Thank you."

Becky looked back at the letter. "So he wants you to come and help his company in Hawaii give flight instruction to army pilots?"

Jude nodded. "Apparently the military doesn't have enough instructors to make their pilots as combat-ready as they'd like them to be. Of course Flapjack trains civilians as well."

"Why do they suddenly need pilots in Hawaii to be combat-ready? We're not in the war. And Germany is so far away."

"It's not the Germans they're worried about in Hawaii, Beck. It's the Japanese."

"I heard America was working out some sort of peace settlement with them."

"Maybe." Jude rubbed his hands over his eyes. "We started cutting oil and steel and iron exports to Japan last summer. Our way of protesting what they have done in China." He paused. "And because of the way they are trying to expand throughout the entire Pacific region. But just the other week we upped the ante and imposed a full embargo on Japan—no oil, not so much as a drop. And we froze all their assets in the United States."

"What does all that mean?"

"Japan is a small island country. They don't have much in the way of oil to run their factories or their ships or their military. They don't have resources like iron ore to mine. So they have to get it somewhere else. If they can't import it from us, where are they going to go? And what are they prepared to do to ensure they can get the oil and iron and steel they want?" Jude looked down at the second letter from Hawaii, the one that bore the army insignia. "So things are getting tense. Japan wants to grow and we're saying no. Japan wants to do whatever it wants to do in places like Manchuria and China and we're saying no to that too."

"But still. There are the peace negotiations."

"Right now, yes." Jude tapped the letter in front of him. "This note is from another old buddy from the war—Billy Skipp. He was quite the daredevil pilot. Stayed in the military, and now he's a big-time officer in the US Army Air Forces, the USAAF. They just formed it in June."

"I haven't read it. What is he writing you about?"

"Same thing. He says he asked Flapjack to track us down and get us to come to Hawaii and help pilots hone their flying skills. Especially the kind needed for air combat—dives, spins, barrel rolls—"

Becky interrupted. "Barnstorming!"

"Yes. Stunt flying. So he's basically backing up Flapjack and asking your mother and me to come to the island of Oahu. That's where Flapjack's flight school is and that's where the military is based. The Pacific fleet has its anchorage on Oahu at Pearl Harbor."

"Flapjack doesn't mention me."

"But Billy does. And he mentions Nate. Up until we went to Africa we used to see the guys from the squadron every year at our reunions. And lots of them came to our air shows. Don't you remember?"

Becky shrugged. "No. Not really."

"We had big picnics. You met their kids."

"Sort of."

"Anyway, Billy asks about bringing you and Nate along. They do have female flight instructors."

"But I want to stay here. I want to get married to Moses."

"I know that."

"You're not going, are you?" Becky looked from her father to her mother. "Aren't you going to stay here with me and the rest of the family?"

Jude stared into his empty coffee mug. "They need us over there, honey."

"I need you over here. What about me?"

"Beck. You have your Aunt Ruth, your grandparents, Moses' mother and father, and more Yoders than you could ever run out of in a lifetime."

Becky stared. "Are you serious? None of that's the same as having your father and mother close by. We've always been together. Right through all the barnstorming years and the missions in Kenya and on Turks and Caicos. You can't be thinking of running off and leaving me behind!"

Lyyndaya was near enough to reach over the table and hold her daughter's hand. "We only got the letters yesterday. Your father and I are praying about everything. No one is talking about running off and abandoning you. But you are a woman now and making your own decisions about your life. Sometimes our paths will run parallel to each other. Sometimes they will diverge."

"This is all happening too fast." Becky wiped at the corner of her eye with a finger. "*Everything* is happening too fast."

Ruth was beside her and leaned over to give Becky a hug. "You will always have family here. I'm not going anywhere."

"Neither are we." Grandmother Kurtz smiled. "Certainly not to Hawaii. Pennsylvania is beautiful enough for us. You'll never be a lonely bride, my dear Rebecca."

"No one is talking about rushing off anywhere." Lyyndaya squeezed Becky's hand. "These people in Hawaii are good friends, that's all. We went through life and death with them. They deserve our prayers if nothing else."

"Okay. I know." Becky swiped at both eyes. "It's just that so much is going on. So many big changes."

"Yes. It's true. So we should pray a bit more." Grandfather Kurtz had his large black German Bible open by his teacup. "We are told that if we fix our minds on the Lord Jesus Christ—I think of nailing a board securely in place or having the bit firmly and safely in the horse's mouth—he will keep us in perfect peace, *nicht wahr*? So let us do that now."

He began to pray in High German. Becky bowed her head and was annoyed with herself when tears fell into her lap and onto her folded hands.

It's a time for happiness. Stop it, Becky Whetstone. You wanted to fall in love and now you have. You wanted to marry the man you fell in love with and now you are.

She understood certain phrases Grandpa Kurtz used. She recognized when Moses came into the prayer and also Nate. And her. Just as at other times when she had sat quietly and listened to prayers in languages she did not know, Becky felt calmness and strength work its way through her. When *amen* was pronounced she lifted her head—*I love you,* she mouthed at Lyyndaya. Lyyndaya responded with the lip movements for *I love you too.*

Aunt Ruth got to her feet, went to the stove, and returned with the large coffeepot. "Who will have another?"

Jude held out his mug. "Might as well. The bishop and pastors are late."

Ruth poured. "It's just as well. God's timing is better than ours. We had much to talk about."

"And we're still not finished." Grandmother chuckled. "But when are we ever finished in this family? And when is God ever finished with us?"

"Amen." Ruth went back to get the teapot for Grandfather Kurtz and placed it by his elbow. "There, Papa. You can drink all you like."

"If I drink all I like I will be in the washroom the whole time the bishop is here."

Each of them heard the whinnying as their horses in the paddock by the stables called out to horses arriving in the farmyard. Ruth glanced out the window and then returned to putting oatmeal and chocolate chip cookies on a plate. "They have all come in one buggy."

Grandfather Kurtz sipped his tea. "They have been meeting at Bishop Zook's before coming here." He winced. "A man could start a fire with this tea."

Ruth wiped her hands on a towel. "I thought you liked it hot."

"Hot, sure, but I don't drink tea with the devil." He got up. "I will get the door."

The bishop and pastors came in, put their straw hats on hooks, and were welcomed to the table, where they each took a seat. Coffee was poured, the teapot passed around, and the plate of cookies placed in the center of the table. Greetings were warm, but Becky felt the men brought a weight into the room as well as good cheer. Bishop Zook spied a newspaper her father had left by the sink.

"I have not looked at the news in days," he said. "But I like to pray about the world."

"The Germans are surrounding Kiev. I think the Russian resistance in the Ukraine is about finished. In the north they are moving on Leningrad and Moscow."

The bishop shook his head. "How soon will they be at Leningrad?"

"What is it now? Almost the end of August? A week. Ten days. Moscow in another month."

"*Ach. Es ist schwer*—it is grievous." The bishop was going to lift his cup of coffee then placed it down again. "Twenty years ago there was another war with Germany."

"But America is not in this one."

"I pray it may remain that way." He stared at Jude.

"I am not going in again, Bishop Zook. Even if something happens and the United States gets involved."

"No. Of course not."

"Like you, I pray. And I pray also there may be no persecution if America does take up arms."

"Amen." The bishop drank his coffee and looked at pastors Stoltzfus, Miller, and King. Then he nodded at Jude. "That is how this strange arrangement began. You went to war. You were shunned. Once the reason you went to war was understood, that you were trying to protect the Amish in Paradise from further persecution, the ban was lifted— and a great deal of tolerance was extended toward you and Lyyndaya. For years you were permitted to return and visit your father, Adam, and Lyyndaya was allowed to join you and spend time with her father and mother. You worshipped with us, broke bread with us. Even though all the time you were flying your Curtiss Jenny and performing airshows. Even when you went to Africa and the Caribbean the door was always open here, although you no longer embraced the Amish way or the *Ordnung*."

"We know this." Jude folded his hands on the table. "We have always expressed our gratitude."

"But have never returned to us to stay. Or live as Plain people once again."

"No."

The bishop drummed his fingers. "As bishop I have the final say in these matters. All the ministers discuss it with me and pray, but it is for me to say what will or will not be under the Lord and under the *Ord-nung*. For years, decades, we have the four of us agreed to let things remain as they were, to permit you to come and go freely. Eyebrows have been raised among the other Amish in Lancaster County. Bishops from other communities have expressed concern. Three years ago when you came to visit us after leaving Africa and were on your way to the Caribbean, I thought to say something, to tell you that you must decide if you would take up your baptismal vows again and live as God has called the Amish to live. *Ja*, that you must decide, and if you could not decide, to understand that you could not return. It was the pastors here who asked me to wait. *Ja, ein wenig länger warten*—wait a little bit longer. Pastor Miller was most persuasive and most passionate. So we have waited. I have waited."

He looked at Becky. "But now your daughter wants to take instruction. She wants to be baptized. She wants to marry my grandson, a fine boy. So I put this now to you, Jude, and to you, Lyyndaya. Rebecca Whetstone wishes to become Amish—what will you do? *Werden Sie jetzt als Amisch mit ihr zurückkehren?* Will you return to being Amish with her?"

Jude did not reply but looked down at his hands. Finally Lyyndaya spoke up. "We are praying about this very thing—should we be elsewhere or should we be here with Rebecca and my family and our people?"

Pastor Stoltzfus cleared his throat. "And you have no clear sign from God on this?"

"Not yet. We continue in prayer."

Pastor Miller rubbed his thick gray beard. "We would like to have you return and live among us. Very much."

"*Danke.*"

"It has been so very long."

Lyyndaya nodded and put a hand on her mother's hand. "Yes."

"You see, it has come to this." Pastor King's face tightened. "If you leave us again, you leave for good. If you stay, you stay for good." He looked around at all the faces at the table. "It has come to this."

"Of course." Jude offered a thin smile. "I knew it must. I regret putting you men in this awkward position. You have been more gracious than any other Amish community would have been. I thank God for you all." He turned his empty coffee mug over in his hands. "It's true, as Lyyndy says, that we're still praying this through. Last evening I went to my father's grave and thought about Rebecca and Nate and about the Lapp Amish."

Bishop Zook nodded. "Your family has much opportunity to pray. There are so many things in your hands."

"Rebecca is a woman, not a child. She is making her own decisions before God. Lyyndaya and I are happy she wants to marry Moses—happy she wishes to become Amish and stay here with all of you. That is a blessing—*das ist ein Segen*. And while our minds are not completely made up, I know Lyyndaya and I would like nothing better than to stay here with her, with all of you, and take up the Amish way once again. There is a very good chance that is what we will do."

Bishop Zook smiled, fingers in his white beard. "You would give up the flying? The planes?"

Jude glanced at Lyyndaya and she nodded. "Yes. She would. I would."

"Never to fly again? Never?"

"Never."

Becky found herself wanting to smile and wanting to cry, excited that her parents might live with her in Paradise for the rest of their lives, upset that they would give up soaring in the sky to do it. She rubbed her fingers under her eyes and brought a tissue from her dress pocket but did not use it.

"We must know." Pastor King again. "When will this decision be made? Next week? Next month? When?"

Jude shrugged. "Tomorrow morning we might say yes. Or a week from now. But we are here until Becky is baptized for sure. By then we will tell you."

Pastor King grimaced. "That's next spring. Almost a year away. That is too long."

"No, I will not be baptized next spring, Pastor." Becky stared at the four men. "I ask permission to take my vows at Thanksgiving. Or sooner. I will be an attentive student. You will see."

"We do not baptize in November," replied Pastor King.

"But you marry in November and December. I cannot wait a year to follow the Amish faith. And I cannot wait a year-and-a-half to be married to Moses Yoder. I ask to complete my instruction this fall. I can do it. I will apply myself."

The pastors were silent. Bishop Zook plucked a cookie from the half-empty plate. "And the flying is over, Rebecca?"

After a moment's hesitation, she said, "Yes...*Ja*."

"It is over for good? No more crop-dusting?"

Becky nodded.

"I don't need a vow from you. Not yet." The bishop bit into the cookie. "Well, well, we shall see. If your progress is good, if the Lord's hand in all this is unmistakable, who knows? Maybe a November baptism followed by a December wedding. Your teachers will decide."

"And who will they be?" asked Becky.

"The ministers. And their wives. Oh, yes. Six teachers." He winked at Becky. "And myself. No, we cannot leave out the bishop. How does this number seven suit you, hm? Seven Amish teachers."

Becky's eyes were sharp and green and stayed on his. "So much the better."

SEVEN

I have never milked a cow. I'm a grain farmer."

"Look. You just do this. Okay?"

"It seems crazy."

"My Aunt Ruth will be here in a few minutes. Come on."

Moses held the lantern away from the cow and toward Becky's face. "If she will be here in a few minutes then I'd rather do something I can't do when she's around—like maybe a milking kiss?"

Becky stared up at him from her stool. "A milking kiss? What are you talking about?"

He knelt beside her. "It's the least you could do for bringing me out here at four in the morning."

"I thought you wanted to come."

"Sure. But not for the cows." He set the lantern down carefully and put a hand on each side of her face. "I love you."

He began to kiss her slowly but deeply. At first she remained turned toward the cow she had started to milk. After a few moments she moved to face him and put both arms around his neck. Moments later she pulled away.

"You never know when to stop. How can I marry a man who wants to kiss me from morning to night and do nothing else? I won't last a year."

He put his lips against her cheek. "How were your classes last night?"

"The usual hard time from Pastor King and his wife. Pastor Miller always runs to my support."

"But you knew your Bible verses."

"Yes, I knew my Bible verses. And my German words. After three weeks of this I'm getting pretty good at my German."

"*Ja? Ich kann ohne dich nicht leben.*"

Becky slapped him on the chest. "Too many words. You're telling me there's something you cannot do but I'm not sure what it is."

"Well, I'll say it again in a week and maybe you will understand it then."

"What? I can't wait a week. Tell me."

"*Nein.*"

"Tell me!"

"*Guten Morgen,* you two. This is not a fight, is it?"

Becky and Moses jumped to their feet as Ruth entered the barn. "Oh, good morning, Auntie. No, it is just that Moses will not tell me what he said and I don't know enough German to understand it."

Ruth lifted a dark eyebrow at Moses. "And what did young Moses Yoder say?"

Moses shrugged and repeated the words. Ruth smiled and bent over to pick up a stool.

Becky glared at her. "Well? Are you going to be part of this whole game of his too?"

"I suppose I am." Ruth settled herself by a cow several stalls over. "It's not for me to tell you what his words mean. But they are very nice."

"I can't believe this!"

"Moses." Ruth glanced up. "You have not worked dairy before, have you? So sit beside me here and I will teach you."

Becky put her hands on her hips. "I was showing him."

"*Ja?* And how far did you get?"

Becky glared at her aunt a moment longer. "Fine!" She sat back down and went at her cow as if the milk would only come out if there were a fistfight. She worked in silence, her movements short and sharp, while Ruth and Moses talked and laughed as he got the hang of milking. Then all three of them worked alone in different stalls as sunlight began to make its way into the barn.

"Rebecca."

She didn't look up when Moses spoke. "What?"

"Your aunt has gone in to help with the breakfast."

"Good."

"So we're alone again."

"Alone again with seven more cows to milk."

Moses touched her shoulder. "Are you angry?"

"What could I possibly have to be angry about?"

"Do you want to know what I said?"

"I don't care anymore."

"Shall I tell you rather than make you wait?"

Becky picked up her stool and bucket and began to make her way to another cow. "It doesn't matter to me one way or the other."

Moses gently took her by the arms. "Hey."

"Let go of me." She tried to squirm out of his grasp.

"Hey. Do you remember who I am? The Amish man who can't stop kissing you?"

"Moses. I don't have time for—"

"*Ich kann ohne dich nicht leben*—I can't live without you."

"What?"

"You heard me." Moses kissed each of her eyes. "I'd sooner give up my air or my arms."

"Don't talk crazy."

"I mean it. *Ich schatze dich*—I cherish you."

She sank against him. "How am I supposed to stay in a sulk when you say such things?"

"Does this mean I can have another milking kiss?"

"You can have a dozen."

The first kiss seemed to last forever. Becky felt light-headed and considered sitting back down on her stool. But she wanted the other kisses, and she knew they would both be called in for breakfast very soon. So she let him take her whole weight as they started the second kiss.

"This is like flying for me," he murmured after the second one.

"Me too."

They both heard the car in the middle of the third kiss and broke apart to ask the same question. *Who is driving a motorcar to the door at six in the morning?*

They came out of the barn together as car doors slammed. Two men in suits and hats left the black car with whitewalls in the farmyard and walked up the steps to the porch. Jude was standing in the doorway.

"Good morning, gentlemen," he greeted them. "How can I help you?"

The taller man in a gray suit and hat and with an equally gray face showed him a badge. "Good morning. We're looking for Mr. and Mrs. Jude and Lyyndaya Whetstone."

"I am Jude Whetstone."

"Agent Hal Nordstrom, FBI. This is Agent Bill Jenkins. May we come in?"

"Why…of course…but what is this about?"

"We have some important information about a member of your family."

Becky felt a coldness sweep through her. As her father and the two agents went into the house she started up the steps. Moses did not join her. She looked back.

"Aren't you coming?"

"No. This is something serious. And it is something for your family. Not something for me. Whatever it is, you can tell me about it later."

"Moses. You worked. You deserve to eat."

"I'm fine. I have more than enough in me. I had the milking kiss, after all. Many of them." He waved his hand and climbed into his buggy. "God bless you in this. Whatever it may be."

She blew him a kiss as he drove out of the yard. Then she entered the house and saw the men sitting at the kitchen table, their hats off. Everyone else was at the table with them—her mother and father, Aunt Ruth, her grandparents. The two men turned to look at her as she walked in.

"This is Rebecca." Lyyndaya pulled back a chair for her. "Our daughter."

The men nodded.

Becky looked at her mother as she sat next to her. *What is it?* her eyes asked.

Lyyndaya didn't smile. "They have found your brother. He is alive."

"Alive?" Becky felt like clapping her hands despite the heavy mood in the kitchen. "Where is he? When can we see him? Thank God!"

Her mother put a hand on her arm. "Yes. We do thank God. But Nate is not well. The men are explaining matters to us."

Becky looked at the FBI agents. "He's ill? How ill?"

"Very." The agent named Nordstrom folded his hands in front of him near a cup of coffee. "The American public knows very little about what the Japanese army did in China and Nanking. There were reports in the *New York Times* and a few other papers but nothing extensive. And right now, because we have entered into serious and delicate peace negotiations with Tokyo, I am directed to advise you that under no circumstances can the details I am about to reveal to you leave this house."

Grandfather Kurtz nodded. "Very well."

"The Japanese do not make war as we do. Or even as the Germans do. It has something to do with their warrior's code of *bushido*. They treat prisoners with contempt and consider them cowards. They will work them to death or just kill them. Nor do they have any respect for the civilian population. In Nanking, to the best of our estimates, they killed at least 200,000, probably more. Infants, mothers who were with child, elderly men and women, it made no difference. Foreigners were generally left alone. There was a safety zone where citizens of other countries took shelter. A number of Chinese were in there with them. Most of the time the Japanese did not touch anyone in the zone. But other times they entered it at will and carried off hundreds of Chinese, raping some, torturing others, executing them all. Our intelligence services intercepted secret telegrams. Information came to us from contacts on the ground in China. The list of atrocities is endless. Your son tried to stop the murders."

Nordstrom looked into his coffee cup. It was full, steam still rose from it, but he didn't bring it to his mouth. "He wasn't the only one. Many did what they could. From what we can gather the Japanese had no regard for anyone of Chinese extraction. Chinese citizens were shot, bayoneted, burned to death after being drenched in gasoline, buried alive in holes in the ground where they suffocated, tied to landmines and blown apart. Your son rescued many from this fate—perhaps hundreds—hiding them in basements and attics in the safety zone. But one day he stopped a Japanese soldier from bayoneting a newborn still attached to his murdered mother by the umbilical cord. The soldier was injured, and your son was beaten and dragged off to where they kept the Chinese prisoners of war—though the Japanese did not want to call them that. They planned to do as they wished with them and didn't want to be bound by any code of conduct regarding prisoners of war.

"From that point it became difficult for anyone in the safety zone to find out what had become of Nate Whetstone. Many Chinese POWs were machine-gunned and bayoneted and thrown into the Yangtze River. It was only a few months ago that we found out Nate was alive—he had escaped the Japanese in 1938 and was with Chinese guerrillas in the countryside."

Into the quiet, Lyyndaya spoke. "When—may we see him?"

"At any moment." Nordstrom checked his wristwatch. "I asked our fellow agents to bring him here from the hotel in Lancaster at seven o'clock."

Lyyndaya put her hand to her mouth. "I can't believe it."

Nordstrom fixed his eyes on her. "To us he is a hero, Mrs. Whetstone, an American hero. But we can't say anything about it. Not now. Not yet. Nevertheless, the day will come when the world will know. For now, it is enough that you know. And we know." He looked out a window at the sun pouring over the sky and the fields. Then back at Jude and Lyyndaya and Becky. "This was all a preamble to help you understand his condition. He was starved and tortured along with the other POWs in Nanking. He was wounded several times in the years he fought alongside the guerrillas. Food was scarce, water was rarely clean, medical care was nonexistent. He's skin and bones, Mrs. Whetstone.

"We got him out of China after he was almost killed in an ambush. He's been in a naval hospital for several weeks. All that can be done for him by our doctors and nurses has been done. Now he needs good food and rest and—" The agent looked at his coffee cup again, his voice tightening. "He needs home. He needs all the love a home can give him. All the love Bill or I here or any of us would give to our own kids. I'd take Nate in myself and get Nancy to fatten him up. We'd treat him like the hero he is, I swear it. But he needs his own family. He needs you."

"How did you manage to find him and get him out?" asked Jude.

"I'm not at liberty to say. We brought out a number of American nationals along with your son."

Gravel and stones popped under car tires in the farmyard. Everyone got to their feet and began to move toward the door.

"What shall we tell our neighbors, Agent Nordstrom?" asked Lyyndaya.

"What they already know. He was a missionary in China. He was caught up in the Japanese attack on Nanking three years ago."

"But they will see him, how he looks—"

"He was a prisoner in a Japanese camp. He escaped and American officials overseas were able to get him back to the States. That is the story. They do not need more than that."

Three men in blue suits and hats were standing in front of the house. One of them opened their car door and another bent down to help a man climb out. The man stood up shakily as he pushed down on two canes. His arms and legs looked like sticks and the white shirt and pants in which he was dressed hung from his frame. One of the suited men went to take his arm as he moved forward but the thin man shook his head.

"Nate…" The word came out of Lyyndaya's mouth in a sudden rush of air.

His hair was gone. Everything about him was impossibly thin, including a face that was sharp as an axe blade. But Becky knew the eyes, and those eyes gleamed when they spotted her and her mother and father. She ran down the porch steps and threw her arms around him. He dropped one of his canes so he could hold her.

"Nate." She could feel the water and heat on her face. "We never stopped praying or believing. Never. Oh, God, thank you."

"Baby girl." His voice was rough. "I didn't think you would."

Lyyndaya had her arms about her son's back and was crying into his shoulder. Jude ran a hand over Nate's head and kissed him on the cheek.

"We missed you so much," Jude said. "Everything that was difficult an hour ago is nothing now that you're back."

Nate dropped his other cane and let his father and mother and sister take his weight as he sagged against them. "God knows I feel the same way."

Eight

"I was finally able to introduce myself to your brother at the worship service."

"Yes. I saw that. He hasn't wanted to venture out much yet. It's taken these three weeks to get him to go out of the house. It was the lure of the worship service that did it."

"He was very friendly. He seemed to know everything about me."

"Well. He is my older brother, remember. Once he knew I had a man in my life he peppered me with questions."

Moses brought Becky's hand to his lips. "I don't mind. I have nothing to hide."

"No? Be grateful I didn't tell him about the five-minute kisses. Brothers don't like things like that."

"*Danke* for sparing me. Whatever your mother is feeding him has made him fill out a lot. He looks utterly different from the first time I saw him."

"It's Grandmother. She's on him twenty-four hours a day with something else she's baked or fried or stirred in a pot on the stove. Poor Nate will never be skinny again."

They sat in Moses' buggy and watched the evening sun set in greens and purples. He had one arm around her waist and between them was a large paper bag of popcorn. Now and then he placed popcorn in her mouth or she placed it in his. Their fingers and lips shone with melted butter.

"Are we going to kiss?" Moses asked.

"When it gets darker. The term they use now in New York and Philadelphia is *necking*, by the way."

"What? Why necking?"

"Because we twist our necks around when we do it, I guess." Becky pushed three pieces of popcorn into his mouth. "We're going to taste like butter and salt."

"I like that."

"Yes?"

"What other flavors do you come in?"

Becky leaned her head against his shoulder and closed her eyes. "Oh. Lots. If I've had a cup of coffee, if I've had a glass of milk, if I've eaten an orange or a bowl of ice cream, if someone's given me a chocolate bar—"

"I'd like to try all of those kisses. Especially chocolate."

"No chocolate kisses unless I get my favorite candy bar."

"And which one is that?"

"Baby Ruth."

"Ah." Moses kissed her forehead. "Sure. I know that one. Named after the famous baseball player. The big hitter."

"Yes. Though the Curtiss Candy Company says it isn't. They just didn't want to pay Ruth any money." Eyes still closed, she smiled. "Is it raining?"

"No. How can it? The sky is absolutely clear."

"I felt something."

"This?" He kissed her on the forehead again.

"That. It's not rain?"

"Okay. Maybe it's rain. And I'm the rain cloud."

"No kissing until it's dark."

Moses played with a strand of her hair. "Does your brother talk about what happened?"

Becky opened one eye. "Not much. He tells us about living in the mountains with Chinese soldiers. He never talks about Nanking. Most of what he says, we're not supposed to tell."

"But you said the government men told you he saved tens of thousands of lives."

"Him and other Americans and Europeans in the safety zone. He refuses to discuss it. I've tried to get it out of him but he's simply not going to open up. The FBI said it was very bad in Nanking. I haven't told you the half of it."

"*Danke.* You can keep the rest to yourself. I hate war. It is one of the things I most appreciate about my Amish heritage—our mothers and fathers do not raise us to be killers."

Becky opened both her eyes. "I understand, Moses. But suppose the Chinese army had been strong enough to stop the Japanese troops? Suppose Nanking had never been captured? Then all those hundreds of thousands of men and women and children would still be alive."

"*Ja.*" Moses rested his hands on his knees and stared out over the darkening fields. "Soon it will be harvest."

Becky sat up and put an arm through his. "If the whole world were Amish, that would be one thing. But it's not. How do people protect themselves from armies that murder and burn and rape?"

"Not by killing."

"How then?"

"Prayer. The Bible."

"But in the Bible it tells us David fought."

"Sure. In those days. But Jesus has come, the Prince of Peace. It's different now. We follow him. Not David. Not Saul."

"Should my brother have done nothing?"

"Of course not. He was right to help the people hide from the Japanese soldiers. He didn't use a gun to do that, did he?"

"Thousands were murdered despite his best efforts. Suppose he and the others had been able to drive the Japanese away? Suppose the American army had been there to help them?"

"The American army?" Moses looked at her. "Why would they be there? America has no quarrel with Japan."

"Yes, we do. We have a quarrel with how they've shed blood in China and Manchuria. We have a quarrel with the fact they seem to want to go into other countries too and take the oil and steel they need."

Moses shook his head. "It's not for the Amish to quarrel or pick fights. We're not God, who is the righteous judge of the nations. Let him decide what should be done. We must continue on in the way he has called us to walk, a way without violence or hatred. That's how we bless America."

"Would you protect me?" Becky put a hand on his face. "Would you?"

"An Amish man will always care for his wife and family. I would never let any harm come to you."

"Even if an intruder forced you to fight?"

"No one will do that."

"How do you know? The Chinese men in Nanking tried to protect their women and were bayoneted or shot."

Moses' face hardened. "So if they should kill me I would die shielding you."

"And when you were dead they would rape me just the same."

Moses didn't respond. Silence and night draped over the buggy. Becky took one of his hands and laced her fingers through his.

"I've counted seventeen stars," she said quietly.

At first he remained silent. Then he brought her fingers to his lips. "Seventeen? That's good. But it's not what I wish to know."

"What do you wish to know? How many stars there are in the sky?"

"When will it be dark enough? That's the greater question."

"Well, I'm not sure."

He put a hand into his pocket. "Perhaps this will help."

"What is it?"

Moses offered it to her.

"Oh." She giggled. "A Baby Ruth. You crazy Amish guy. How could you have one in your pocket? I only told you I liked them a few minutes ago."

"It happens I like them. And so does my grandfather."

"You do not."

"I do. We both do. You should see how many he keeps in his study. Stashes them right beside his Bible."

"Can I eat it?" she asked, tearing the wrapper off. "I'm starved."

"Go ahead."

"You won't be offended?"

He laughed. "By your eating a candy bar?"

"I'm not good at sharing Baby Ruths."

"Don't worry. It's not the Baby Ruth I want."

"Mmm?" Becky was chewing.

"It's the woman eating the Baby Ruth that interests me."

"Just a minute." Becky swallowed and licked her fingertips. Then she leaned her head against his chest, closed her eyes, and parted her lips. "Okay, Candy Man. Come and get it."

Moses touched her lips gently with his. "Ah. Very nice. *Ich mag Schokolade.*"

"I know what that means. That you like chocolate."

"*Ich mag dich noch mehr.*"

"Too many words again. You like what?"

"You." Moses kissed her softly. "You're better than a thousand Baby Ruths."

"Oh, I don't think so—"

He reached over her, surrounding her with his arms and pulled her closer in a chocolate kiss. Finally she grabbed handfuls of his shirt in her fingers.

"I can't…I need to…breathe…"

Moses smiled down at her. "That's why God gave you a nose. So you could handle long kisses. Learn to use it."

"I—"

But he was kissing her again, cradling her body in his arms.

"You're not Amish," she said between kisses. "You kiss like some sort of movie star, like Clark Gable in *Gone with the Wind.*"

"I have never seen one of the motion pictures."

"Please don't. It will just give you more ideas. You're hard enough to handle as it is."

"I wanted to ask you how your classes are going. I forgot."

"I'm not surprised." She brushed her lips over his. "They're going fine, thank you very much. Pastor King is always going on about whether I'm becoming Amish for you or for God."

"And what's the right answer?"

"The right answer for them is God. The true answer is, I'm doing it for both of you."

"And God is not jealous?" asked Moses.

"Why should he be? He brought us together."

"Ah."

The kisses continued until Becky patted Moses on the back and tugged a shawl about her shoulders—the September nights were cooler than the nights of July and August had been. Milly took them slowly along the road to the Kurtz house where, at ten o'clock, a lamp was still burning in the kitchen. Once she had said good night to Moses, with a light kiss on the cheek that made them both laugh, she went up the steps and opened the door. Her father was still up, sitting at the table with an open Bible and a pad of paper.

Jude looked up and smiled. "Hi, honey. How was the sunset?"

"Full of stars."

"I'll bet."

She sat down and took an apple from a basket. "Are these the ones I picked yesterday?"

"Mm-hm."

"Are they washed?"

"Sure. The rain washed them a week ago."

She bit into it. "Why are you still up?"

"Nate and I were talking for an hour. He waited until everyone else had gone to bed."

"Was he telling you about Nanking?"

"Yes."

"And it was bad? As bad as the FBI said?"

"Worse. I guess he felt he needed to get some of it off his chest."

Becky sat still and put down her partly eaten apple. "Are you reading the Bible because of what he said?"

"I suppose. That and the request from Flapjack and Billy Skipp. I'm reading passages on war and peace."

"The bishop would not like to see that."

"No?"

"He would say the matter is settled with the Amish. And with the Whetstones. No war. Ever. No violence. The Amish are called by God to be a peaceful presence in America and the world. No enlistment. No guns. No uniforms."

Jude sat back in his chair, yellow pencil in his fingers. "Well, your barrel is full. Been thinking it through?"

"Moses and I talked about it. We almost got into an argument."

"How?"

"I said that Nanking could have been spared all the murder and rape if the Chinese army had been large enough or strong enough to defeat the Japanese. Then I asked him if he would protect me. He said he would even if they killed him. And I said if they killed him they would just go ahead and rape me anyway."

Jude twirled the pencil about in his hand. "It seems to me that the final thing for the Amish is, whatever else may be true, God has called them to be Amish. And to be Amish means you resolve conflicts— *all* conflicts, whether at home, in our cities, or between the nations— without violence. It is for others to bear arms. For the Amish to bear arms would mean they were rebelling against God's will for their lives. It would be a sin."

Becky rested her chin on her hand. "So at least I will never have to worry about Moses marching off to war and getting shot if America does end up in this fight against Hitler."

"No. Unless he has some sort of change of heart when he reads newspaper reports about the German army slaughtering people."

"He doesn't read the papers."

"Sometimes his grandfather does."

Becky shook her head. "Moses won't. He's not a reader. He's not a free thinker. He'll stick with whatever approach the Amish take."

"You mean he's not a free thinker like you."

Becky shrugged. "Nobody is everything. He has other qualities I like very much. I think we'll be very happy."

Jude nodded and smiled. "So do I, honey. He's a fine young man. Do you really think you'll finish your classes in time to convince them you should be baptized in November?"

"Yes. For sure. Even Pastor King and his wife can't stop me."

"Are they the biggest roadblock?"

"They think I want to be Amish just so I can marry Moses."

"And?"

"I do want to marry him. And I don't want to take him away from all this. It works for our relationship here. It may not work somewhere else. I think turning his back on the Amish way would totally destroy him. I don't think he'd know what to do or who to be. I can't risk losing Moses Yoder, Dad. He's too beautiful." She picked up her apple and put her teeth into it again. "So we're staying here. For good. I'll be fine."

"Even when planes fly overhead and you're not piloting one of them?"

Becky hesitated, taking the apple away from her mouth. "Even then." She stared at her father a moment. "Yes. Even then."

NINE

Becky glanced out the window as she washed her hands in the kitchen sink. Sheets and pillowcases were flapping wildly on the clothesline as the wind chased leaves back and forth across the yard. A chair scraped behind her and she turned to see her brother settling down at the table.

"Good morning, Nate. It sure is blowing today."

"Kept me up half the night. The window in my room rattles like a skeleton." He smiled through the sand-colored beard he had decided to grow. "I was chopping some wood."

"You shouldn't do too much. You've only been here a few weeks."

"I've been here more than a month, Sugar Plum."

Becky laughed. "Sugar Plum. There's an old nickname."

"I was wondering if I could get a coffee."

"Of course." She pushed aside a large wicker basket full of food so she could reach the coffeepot on the stove. "This was only made an hour ago so it should be okay."

"You mean it won't be like that stuff last week?"

"That *stuff* was half a day old."

Becky placed a mug by his hand and kissed him on the cheek. "Here." She put a large coaster on the table and set the coffeepot on it. "You can have the whole thing."

Nate poured as he watched her put a red-and-white checked cloth over the basket. "What's the occasion?"

"Oh, Moses and his father and some of their friends are shingling the Yoders' barn today. It got damaged during a hailstorm in August. I'm taking over a lunch in an hour or so. Moses' mother is taking care of the drinks."

"Heading off by yourself?"

"Well, Dad is over there with Uncle Luke and Uncle Harley. He's supposed to come back and pick me up about quarter to twelve."

"Sounds like a picnic. Am I invited?"

"Sure. If you help me with this crazy big watermelon." She was trying to keep it from rolling off the counter. "I can never cut the slices evenly."

Nate got up and came over, holding his coffee mug. "Aren't you going to wait until you serve it?"

"It's always so hectic. I like to have a couple of dozen slices ready. I'll pack the whole thing in ice."

"All right. Anything to get to one of your picnics. Where's the knife?"

She put a long knife in his hand. "Hey. Some of your hair is coming back."

"I'm surprised too. The doctors said it wouldn't. But they didn't know I had a grandmother who loves to make up poultices."

"Did she put something on your head?"

Nate began to cut into the melon. "It was our secret. We never told anyone. I slept with all these strange mixtures on my scalp the first two weeks. She kept them in place with cloths and string."

"Oh, my. I would have paid to see that."

"You could never have paid me enough to let you look."

"Just think what I could have done with a camera."

"Uh-uh, sis. No cameras among the Amish."

Hoofbeats sounded in the yard. Becky saw Ruth and Lyyndaya appear in the window with another load of washing to hang up and watched them turn in surprise and call out to the rider. She couldn't hear the response. Feet thudded up the porch steps and the door flew open.

"Excuse me. I'm sorry." It was Joshua Miller, his face flushed. "Please come, Rebecca. There's been an accident."

"What's happened?" Becky felt her body go rigid. "Is it my father? Uncle Luke?"

"It's Moses. A gust of wind took him off the roof. We've sent for the ambulance. No one wants to move him. He's badly hurt." He looked at Nate. "I've come by horseback to get her more quickly. Can she follow me by buggy?"

"Yes." Nate squeezed her shoulder. "I'll get Katie harnessed."

Both her brother and Joshua seemed strange to her. "I...I'm not sure what to do."

"Come with me and get in the buggy," Nate said. "I'll drive."

"You can't."

"I can." Nate looked at Joshua. "Thank you. I'll just harness the mare."

"Your mother and your sister are doing that," Joshua responded.

Nate put his arm around Becky and took her out onto the porch. Lyyndaya and Aunt Ruth were talking rapidly to each other in Pennsylvania Dutch as they got the mare harnessed to the buggy. Nate walked Becky down the steps. The two women threw their arms around her and held her tight.

"*Es wird in Ordnung sein,*" said her mother, rubbing her back. "It will be all right."

"*Gott ist gut.*" Ruth kissed her. "We will pray together on the way."

Nate slowly climbed into the driver's seat. His mother was about to say something but he shook his head and held up a hand. He grasped the reins. "Get in. Quick."

Ruth helped Becky up but Lyyndaya held back. "Grandmother and Grandfather are in the orchard. They won't know where everyone has gone."

Joshua was mounted on his large black gelding. "I'll tell them. You must go ahead. Please."

Nate snapped the reins and called out, and Katie set off at a brisk pace down the lane to the main road. They turned right to the Yoder homestead, wheels and hooves kicking up dust. Nate kept calling, *Hey, hey,* and flicking the reins. Becky hardly heard him or felt the motion of the buggy. Her mother and her aunt were squeezing her hands and praying at the same time in German. She understood most of the words but they didn't stay with her. In her mind Moses was sitting up against the barn with his arm in a sling, taking some water from her father, smiling, waiting for her, not as badly off as Joshua had made it sound. But when they arrived she saw a ring of men and women around a body on the ground, and the body had a sheet over it up to the neck. She ran across the farmyard. His tanned face was as white as limestone.

"Moses!"

His eyes opened as she smoothed back his hair. Blood swiftly covered her fingers.

"Hey." She could hardly hear him. "I'm…sorry…Rebecca…I think I did not…did not tie off the rope…properly…it did not hold me when I fell…"

"Shh. Shh." She ran her hands over his cheeks. "They've called for an ambulance. It will be here soon."

"But not soon enough…I was only waiting for you, that's all—"

"Hush. Don't say that. You'll be fine. You have to be fine. For me. I need you. Moses. Listen to me."

"I'm so sorry—"

"Moses!" In a flash, as if someone had snuffed out a candle flame with a quick pinch of their fingers, the light left his eyes. "Moses!" She threw her body over his, lifting his head and kissing his lips and face. "Moses! I love you! Don't…"

Blood was on her hands and mouth and cheeks. It trickled down her face as her father gently pulled her away. She buried herself in his arms.

"Oh, Daddy! What has God done? What's happened?"

"I am here for you. Always. I am here."

"I loved him! I loved him!"

Hands touched her back. She made out a few of the faces. One was Bishop Zook, tears sliding into his white beard. Another was Pastor Miller, his dark eyes darker than she had ever seen them. Another was Moses' mother, Emma. She felt Emma's kiss on her head. Then watched as her own mother took Emma in her arms.

The grief was the sharpest pain Becky had ever known. It cut into her chest and stomach and throat and raked her arms. Deep cries came from far inside, cries she had never heard come from her body before. She thought she sounded like a creature caught in a trap or sinking into a slough, its hope gone, desperate. She didn't want to eat, she didn't want to drink, didn't care if she took another breath. Sleep didn't come and she didn't care that it wouldn't come.

She had never seen a dead room but the Yoder house had one. Moses' body was washed and dressed in clean black pants and a clean white shirt and laid in a simple wooden coffin Bishop Zook had built for his grandson the very afternoon of the accident. The next day people filed past him in silence. Becky wanted to go to him, but part of her couldn't move. Her mother and Aunt Ruth and Emma helped her, walked over with her. No makeup was used as the English would have done. It was his face, his eyebrows, his perfect features. "How sweet you are," she whispered over and over again, "how sweet you are, my darling."

Bishop Zook wept as he spoke a message in the house about his grandson and the love of God. "No matter how we may hurt today, no matter how we may grieve, God is in this, he is not far away, he has his hands on this, he has Moses in his arms. *Die Liebe Gottes ist nicht aufzuhalten.*"

The love of God is unstoppable.

A long dark line of buggies wound its way to the graveside. The sun was hot and clear. *It is not right,* she thought, *that he should be dead on a day as beautiful as this, that we should be putting him in the ground on a day like this, that we should be covering him in earth when he loved the air and the sky so much.* Nate kept his arm around her the entire time. She couldn't stand on her own. He seemed to know that and she was grateful for his strength.

"Thank you, Nate," she murmured. "Thank you."

"Shh," he said in his quiet voice. "God knew I needed to be here and that's why I'm no longer in China. It's a small thing for me to do for you."

"It's not a small thing…"

"Shh. All right. I love you. We'll get through this."

"I don't see how. I feel like going down into the grave with him."

"We'll make it."

"Even if we do make it, I'll never be the same again."

"Shh."

"I won't."

One week later she tried to return to the classes. Everyone was gentle, everyone spoke quietly as they read verses from the Bible to her about the Amish way. Pastor King began to lecture about how becoming Amish was more important than anyone or anything, that everything else that happened in life was as dross compared to worshipping God as an Amish man or woman should, that nothing—not even grief or sorrow or loss—must blind her for a moment to the path he had laid out for her among the Amish people.

"No one must take the place of God. No one must be higher than him in our thoughts. No matter who on earth we love, it must be God whom we love more." He nodded at Becky as she sat silently in her chair. "Sometimes those we care for are taken away because we put them in the place where only God is supposed to be. In order to bless us more richly, he removes those we love too much so that he can love us more. No one can be where he should be in our heart."

Becky squeezed her hands tightly together. "What?"

Bishop Zook stood up and motioned for Pastor King to take his seat. "It is perhaps too strongly put. Remember this is a difficult time for the child."

"The Lord gives, the Lord takes away," rumbled Pastor King. "Often enough we are the reason he must take away. Blessed be the name of the Lord."

Becky got to her feet. "I must go. I'm sorry. I'm not well."

Pastor King folded his arms over his chest.

"I understand," Bishop Zook said. "These are rough waters for us all. Let me drive you home."

"Thank you. My brother is outside. He has been waiting."

"Let me bless you." He bowed his head and prayed briefly in German. Then he looked up. "We will see you here Thursday night?"

Becky didn't respond. She left the Zook house and climbed into the buggy beside Nate. The sun had set and a cool wind moved over the fields.

"How was it?" he asked as he urged Katie forward.

She didn't answer.

"You look as if you're carved out of stone."

"Maybe I am."

"Hungry?"

She shook her head. "I don't care if I ever eat again."

He clicked his tongue at Katie. "Is your next class Thursday?"

Becky stared straight ahead.

Nate tried again. "Are you going to the Thursday class?"

"I'm not going to another Amish class for the rest of my life."

He was silent a few moments as the horse's hooves clacked against the roadway. "Why?"

"King."

"What happened?"

"He said Moses had been taken because I made him more important than God." She put a hand to her eyes and bent her head. Nate saw the tears drop onto her dress. "I am not Amish. I can never be Amish. Not without Moses. This has been a great mistake." She jerked her head up. "Oh, my God, you know how much I loved him. But not more than you. Not more than you."

Bishop Zook came over to the Kurtz house that Sunday evening after the singing, parking his buggy in the yard. His visit was expected. Coffee and cookies were set before him but he didn't lift the cup or take anything from the plate. He folded his hands on the table.

"I received your note Thursday morning," he said to Becky. "*Danke.*"

"*Bitte.*"

"It is his way. The more so as he grows older. There is truth in what Pastor King says, but the way in which he delivers it is not always in the best spirit."

Becky didn't reply.

Her father leaned forward. "Do you agree with Pastor King?"

"I am not God. Who knows why he permits what he permits? It's a mystery we can never solve on this side. We must trust him. Regardless of the circumstances we find ourselves in."

Lyyndaya ran her fingers up and down the sides of her glass of water. "Do you truly believe God took Moses away from us because my daughter loved him too much?"

"Me personally? Not so much. But others do. As I said, who knows why he permits what he permits? Even if Pastor King is harsh, one must look past the wrapping on the parcel and concentrate on what is inside."

No one responded to this.

Bishop Zook looked about the table and nodded his head. "So what have you been thinking? In Becky's note she said she would not proceed with the baptismal instruction this fall. Are you all in agreement with this?"

"I cannot stay here!" blurted Becky. "It's not just the death of Moses. It's what you people think of me."

"No one thinks the worst of you, Rebecca—"

"Of course you do. The whole community does. Rebecca Whetstone loved Moses Yoder more than she loved God. It was the only reason she wanted to become Amish. To punish her, God took Moses away so that Rebecca Whetstone would set her heart in the right place." Tears began to make their way down her face as she pleaded with the bishop. "Yes, I loved your grandson. Yes, I wanted to be Amish with him by my side. But marriage to Moses was not the only reason I wished to take my vows. I love the simple ways here. I love the green roll of the land, the horses, the children. I love the people and their faith. I love the gentleness and grace." She wiped at her eyes with her hand. "Now I see a hardness. A judgment. I hear words being spoken behind my back. I hear you tell me Pastor King might be right—that

I am such a wicked person God had to remove Moses Yoder to set me straight."

"No one said you were wicked—"

"Don't you see I was committing myself to God and to all of you, not just Moses? Don't you see I was willing to give up the sky and the heavens, something I thought I'd never do? How can I stay here when I know what people are whispering once my back is turned?" She stopped trying to wipe the tears off her cheeks. "I'm leaving, Bishop Zook. I'm going back to my planes and cockpits and my tall white clouds. I should never have left. I should have asked Moses to come into my world rather than trying to fit into his." She smiled sadly. "But he loved all of you more than he loved me. He would never have left Paradise."

The bishop sat back and let out a long breath of air. He murmured something no one could hear. Putting his hands in his pockets he looked at Jude and Lyyndaya. "What are you going to do? Weeks ago you considered staying here with Rebecca. Are you thinking of leaving with her when she leaves?"

Jude's face was dark. "Perhaps."

"You remember what I said? That there is no turning back this time? If you go, you go?"

"I remember you said that, yes."

"Sure, I could try to smooth things over again, but what is the point? You're no longer one of us, are you? None of you are. Except Lyyndaya's mother and father. And Ruth. I don't know how you feel, Nate."

Nate didn't avert his eyes from the bishop's gaze. "I feel the same way my sister does. If she leaves I will leave with her."

"And I also, Bishop Zook." It was Ruth. "The Lord knows I love you. We all do. We are not ungrateful for all you have done for our family. But they will need me if they go from this place, and I feel that God would have me accompany them."

Lyyndaya looked at her sister in shock. "What are you talking about? You never brought this up before."

"Nevertheless, I've been praying about it. Especially since Becky returned with a broken heart from the time of instruction this week.

How many broken hearts does a young woman need, Bishop Zook? Is one not enough that the church must inflict another?"

"Ruth." Bishop Zook sat up in his chair. "Who will care for your parents?"

"I have talked with them about this. And my youngest sister, Sarah. No, I did not speak with Lyyndaya or Jude, but I spoke with the others in our family. They are all in agreement. I should remain with those who are being spurned and help them heal."

"No one is being spurned."

"Of course they are. Becky for loving your grandson with all her heart. Jude and Lyyndaya for not being able to make up their minds—and believe me, I understand why the church would be frustrated with them. Being Amish is not a merry-go-round a person jumps on and off of. It may be that my sister and her husband must follow God along a different path. I will help them find out."

The bishop tugged at his beard. "You will not be able to return without repentance."

"I know that. But it may be I will not return. Splinter groups from Amish communities have started new communities in other places. Perhaps that is what I will do."

Lyyndaya shook her head. "You can't do this, Ruth. It's too much of a sacrifice. And mother and father need you."

"Sarah and her family will come to this house to live. Harley and Luke and Daniel will pitch in. That has been decided. Mother and Father will be fine."

Grandmother Kurtz patted Ruth's hand. "We will miss you. But we shall be in good hands. And I can always pray that one day you shall return to us."

Lyyndaya stared at her parents and sister. "All this scheming going on?"

Grandmother Kurtz chuckled. "My tea is cool enough to drink now." She sipped at her cup. "Trying to follow God's will is not scheming, my dear. At the right time we have brought you into what we believe is right. You had already made up your minds about the Hawaiian Islands without us, hadn't you?"

Lyyndaya sat still. "I suppose that's so."

"The Hawaiian Islands?" Bishop Zook fixed his gaze on Jude. "What is there for you?"

"Friends who need help at a flying school."

"What? All the way there to help people learn to fly an airplane?"

"Some of it will be instructing army pilots."

"The army doesn't have enough teachers of their own?"

"Not who are skilled in stunt flying."

The bishop sat a moment. Then he reached for a cookie but didn't eat it, tapping it against the top of the table. "I said I didn't follow the war news very much and I don't. But I read enough of it to know how to pray. I understand what it means when Washington freezes the assets of Japan and stops the export of oil. The Japanese will either huddle together in their islands and give up any thought of making their nation mighty. Or they will fight." The cookie broke in half. "I think they will fight. America would. What is Roosevelt thinking?"

Jude nodded. "I realize he has backed them into a corner."

Bishop Zook bit into one of the broken halves of the cookie. "Roosevelt wants a war. He wants America in this conflict. That's what is going on. Where do you think the Japanese will strike us?"

Jude shrugged. "If they choose to fight? I think the South Pacific. Probably the Philippines."

"So if you go to this flight school you will be training pilots to make war."

"I know that's how you see it. For me, it's an opportunity to teach young men the skills that will keep them alive and give them a better chance of returning to their families."

"Of course. It is the young Jude all over again." The bishop looked into his cup. "May I have more coffee?"

Ruth got to her feet. "Of course." She returned from the stove with the pot. The dark liquid steamed as she poured. "This is so strong now it will make your beard black."

Bishop Zook laughed. "Some miracle that would be." He drank slowly. "I condemn no one here. You are a complicated family. But I cannot save you this time. If you go to the Hawaiian Islands and teach men how to fly warplanes and kill, you will be excommunicated. My other bishops will insist upon it. With the exception perhaps of Pastor Miller, our own leadership will demand it."

"Not Miller?" Jude asked.

"He will vote for it in the end. But he will not push for it. For Pastor Miller mercy is always the better path. That is who he has become in the past twenty years." He took a longer swallow from his coffee. "I feel as he does. But he is not in my place. I am required to uphold the *Ordnung* in a way he is not. The way people see it, you have broken faith. Broken the covenant with us. They believe much time has been granted you in order to allow you to change your minds and your ways and you have not done it. Now they will hear you are leaving again to help the army prepare for war. We are the people of peace. For hundreds of years that has been our way. You know that."

"It's not difficult to see you will have no choice." Lyyndaya drew a pattern on the tabletop with her finger. "Some feel Rebecca has been judged by God and our family with her. They will not be surprised if we leave. They want us to leave."

The bishop didn't answer her.

Grandfather Kurtz always had his large black German Bible at the kitchen table. "We read in Isaiah: *For my thoughts are not your thoughts, neither are your ways my ways, saith the Lord. For as the heavens are higher than the earth, so are my ways higher than your ways, and my thoughts than your thoughts.*" He looked up. "Who knows? Let us put the Amish of Paradise and the Whetstones and Kurtzes utterly in the hands of God. May I pray, Bishop Zook?"

"Please do so. And I will pray after you have finished."

Both men prayed for mercy and understanding and the triumph of grace over judgment. Then the bishop hugged and kissed everyone on the cheek before going to the door.

"When are you leaving?" he asked as he put on his hat.

"We will go by rail to San Francisco," Jude replied. "From there we will take a ship to Honolulu. Our friend who operates the flight school is paying for our passage." Jude offered his hand. "If we feel the Lord is still in this we will be gone in a week. Perhaps less."

The bishop shook Jude's hand with a strong grip. "Go with him then." He looked at Becky. "What a fine granddaughter you would have been for us. How we love you. Bless you, Rebecca."

Becky felt she was going to break down. "Thank you. I looked so forward to being closer to you. I wish you well in the Lord."

In his buggy the bishop paused and looked up at the family standing together on the porch in the lamplight. "*For as the rain cometh down, and the snow from heaven, and returneth not thither, but watereth the earth, and maketh it bring forth and bud, that it may give seed to the sower, and bread to the eater: So shall my word be that goeth forth out of my mouth: it shall not return unto me void, but it shall accomplish that which I please, and it shall prosper in the thing whereto I sent it.*" He picked up the traces in his hands, clicked his tongue, and the horse moved forward into the dark.

Ruth was holding Becky in her arms. "I will be with you. Your brother and mother and father will be by your side."

"It's my fault all this is happening to us."

Her father put a hand on her back. "No. It's many things coming together all at once—Nate's return, Moses' death, Billy Skipp's letter and Ram Peterson's plea, Pastor King's words, our violation of the *Ordnung*, the feelings that are running high among many of the people here, the anger of the other bishops. So now we're going where we're most needed. And we're going as a family. Our season here is ended."

"But we loved this place."

"We shall find love somewhere else." Her mother kissed Becky on the cheek. "All kinds of love. God is everywhere. His grace is without limits."

"Not love for a man." Becky's eyes were sharp. "No."

"You don't know that."

"I do know it. I will never love another man. Not on this earth."

TEN

R aven!"

"Yes, sir."

"Get in here."

The young man entered the room and snapped a salute. "Colonel Skipp. Lieutenant Raven reporting as ordered."

Skipp tossed him a salute. "At ease."

The colonel was standing behind his desk in a leather flight jacket. Raven had just watched him land a new P-40 Warhawk he had been putting through its paces. There was a touch of gray to his red hair but not much. Raven knew he was in his early forties but thought he still looked like a young man in his late twenties. Thinking about this, he remained at attention. Skipp didn't notice because he was looking down at a file folder that was open on his desk.

"Okay. Christian Scott Raven. Born in Oklahoma. Flying proficiency is rated high. Eyes like a carbine sight. Shooting is flawless—of course shooting at targets on the ground or streamers being towed by another plane is nothing like going after an enemy fighter, Raven."

"No, sir."

Skipp looked up. "What kind of name is Raven?"

"It's Cherokee, Colonel."

Skipp glanced back down. "Never been in the brig. Doesn't swear, doesn't drink, doesn't chew. Helps the padre with church parade." Skipp's eyes returned to Raven's face. "Blond hair. Blue eyes."

"My father was white."

"Still alive?"

"No, sir."

"Raven his family name?"

"My mother's. She's full-blooded Cherokee."

"You took your mother's family name?"

"After my father's death, yes, sir."

Skipp was back with the file folder, his left hand tapping out a rhythm, the gold band on his ring finger glinting from the sunlight that streamed through a window. "Rated high. Highest possible rating." He flipped the folder shut and looked Raven in the eye. "So what's the problem, Lieutenant?"

"I wasn't aware there was a problem, sir."

"No?" Skipp folded his arms over his chest. "You lack aggression. When it's an attack sequence you fly fast but not fast enough. Your barrel rolls are fat and sloppy. Your dives are shallow. You can't shake fighters off your tail quickly. Can't zig and can't zag well. What's the deal?"

"I—"

"Level with me."

"I suppose I don't see the point, sir."

"Don't see the point?"

"Of barrel rolls. And flitting all over the sky like a bat. And trying to shake pests off my tail. We're not in the war, sir. I know people think we will be, but I kind of doubt it. The Japanese will rattle their sabers a while and go home. The Nazis will take Europe and Asia and eventually we'll be doing trade with a German empire. Meanwhile Americans will just be flying around. And that suits me."

Skipp raised his dark red eyebrows and made a circle in the air with his finger. "Just flying around the good old USA."

"Yes, sir."

"And that's all you want out of your army career?"

"Pretty much. I couldn't afford a plane of my own. Uncle Sam had plenty. So I signed up and hitched a ride to the clouds." He grinned. "Sir."

"Mm-hm." Skipp glanced over at a calendar on the wall. "Another week and it'll be Halloween."

"Yes, sir."

"Two months until Christmas Eve. Not that it ever feels much like Christmas Eve in Hawaii. Not my kind of Christmas Eve anyway." He leaned over and began writing on a sheet of paper with a fountain pen. "But you can help me with that, Raven."

"How's that, Colonel?"

"By giving me a big fat Christmas present. By showing me you've got what it takes to become a real American fighter pilot. You've got two months before I kick you out of the air force and into infantry as a private first class."

"Sir—"

"Don't keep sirring me, Raven. Just do it. Or you can hang up your flight jacket for good." Skipp continued to scribble on the paper. "You'll recall I had something of a party at my house a week ago."

"I knew that, Colonel, but—"

"Do you know what the party was about?"

"Scuttlebutt had it that a friend you flew with in the war had arrived and was going to help you train pilots."

"Anything else?"

"Well. That he had a daughter."

Skipp laughed. "For sure he has, Lieutenant. A daughter who flew solo at fifteen years old. And would turn you inside out in the air, son. She knows barrel rolls and corkscrews and dives and death spins. Knows 'em so well I don't believe a German Messerschmitt could stay on her tail no matter how much glue they used. And while they were trying she'd whip around onto their own backsides and shoot them off."

Raven rolled his eyes while Skipp signed his signature. "She sounds like a real treat, Colonel."

"I saw that, Raven."

"Sorry, sir."

"Pity you can't do it in the air." He smiled a big smile and handed the letter to Raven folded up and tucked in an envelope. "But perhaps she can change all that. It's worth a try."

"What?"

"Take this to Ram Peterson at Peterson Air Services. It's a request

that Rebecca Whetstone take you on as a client with the express purpose of teaching you combat maneuvers."

"Sir—"

"Dogfighting, Lieutenant. I need to see those skills developed in you
before Santa slides down the chimney or you start 1942 in a helmet and
chin strap with a bayonet on your rifle. I'm not kidding, Raven." Raven
took the envelope reluctantly. "Go and see Peterson immediately. Ever
play Monopoly? Do not pass 'Go'? Do not collect two hundred dollars?
That's you. Go directly to Peterson Air Services. Get Skinny to drive
you over there in my personal jeep. Get it dealt with today. Heck, go
up this afternoon if she's free. You have eight weeks."

"Sir, honestly, I don't need a girl to teach me how to—"

Skipp's smile became even bigger. "You're gonna love her."

Skinny, Skipp's personal adjutant, had been listening at the door
and was ready with the jeep. "It's not that far from here, sir. I'll get you
there in five minutes."

"I'm not in any great hurry to arrive, Skinny."

"Dismissed, Lieutenant Raven," Skipp said, and then turned to his
file cabinet.

"Yes, sir," Raven replied and let out a breath as he turned to Skinny
and said, "Let's get this over with then."

Minutes later the two men sped across the airfield as Skinny tried
to reassure Raven. "Shooter and Lockjaw both went to her to sharpen
up their flying skills because they heard she was a whiz kid—and easy
on the eyes too. Of course Lockjaw put the moves on her."

"That's Lockjaw. What happened?"

Skinny snorted. "She slugged him."

"Are you kidding me?"

"No, sir. Five minutes with her was like gargling barbed wire, Lockjaw said. The word is she lost someone in a plane crash stateside and
isn't over it yet. Cut her hair off with a knife. It barely covers her ears
now. Shooter figures she hates guys and did it to drive them away. Juggler thinks she was a nun in another life."

"A nun? Do you believe in reincarnation, Skinny?"

"Not really, sir. To tell you the truth, I'm not sure what the young lady is. Here we are. Good luck."

Raven climbed out of the jeep and walked up to a building that said Peterson Air Services. For a moment he watched bright yellow Piper J-3s with dark stripes on their fuselage take off and land. *PASI* with a ring around it was painted on each cowling. Peterson appeared to have about a dozen of them, though Raven couldn't be sure how many might be in the air. As he looked over the runway and hangars he spotted a young woman in flying gear squatting and checking the struts of one of the Pipers. Her head was uncovered and the short blond hair, bright as sunlight, was obvious. She stood up and glanced around. Noticing him, she held his gaze a moment and then turned away quickly. A shock went through Raven that reminded him of lightning strikes in Oklahoma during tornado season, when the charge in the air would make his skin tingle and his hair rise. He took off his cap and ran a hand over his hair to make sure it was lying flat.

What was that?

"Can I help you, Lieutenant?"

A tall man with an easy grin and a thatch of sandy brown hair had come out of the office. He wore an old worn flight jacket with the name *Flapjack* embroidered on the chest. Raven handed him the letter.

"What's this?" asked the man, opening it.

"From Colonel Skipp, sir."

"Just Flapjack. My army days are done." Flapjack read the letter and his smile broadened. "Well, well. And here I was sitting at my desk worrying about how idle our little princess is. She's scared so many off." He looked up from the letter. "Will she scare you off, Lieutenant Raven?"

"No, sir."

"Let's find out. Come on." They began to walk across the runway together. "She did a lot of barnstorming with her parents long before she flew on her own. Even walked on biplane wings. She was a missionary pilot in Africa when she was fifteen. Just came up from doing the same kind of thing in the Caribbean. And she's not even twenty yet. Impressed?"

"She sounds unique. That's all. The circus is full of unique people."

"Oh, she's unique all right. Now listen. I don't know how you are among the ladies. But don't make any passes at her. She'll kill you. I'm not kidding. After the last guy, she started carrying a Colt 1911. So keep this professional. Got it?"

"Believe me, sir, I'd rather not be here. The last thing I'd want is any sort of relationship that extended beyond these flying lessons Colonel Skipp insists I take. From what I've heard she eats rocks for breakfast and broken glass for lunch."

"And men for supper. Well, good. I'm glad you have your priorities straight. You're here just for the flying so the old man doesn't ship you off to the infantry."

"That's right."

Flapjack glanced at him. "And you're not going to run?"

Raven narrowed his eyes. "No way."

"Or fall for her?"

"For her? Not a chance."

Flapjack's eyes sparkled. "Not a chance? There's a reason every guy has put the moves on her, Raven. And it isn't her personality."

"She could look like the sun, moon, and stars and I wouldn't be interested."

"Good. I like men who know their priorities. Your priority, son, is staying out of the infantry."

Raven knew she was aware of their approach but she was deliberately keeping her back to them as long as she possibly could, kicking the Piper's tires, examining the canopy, running a hand over the wings and ailerons. Finally she had no choice. Flapjack called her name.

"Becky. I have a customer for you."

She turned around and squinted at Raven in the sunlight. He opened his mouth to say something but couldn't think of a thing. Her lips were full and perfect, teeth milk-white, emerald eyes glittered like a cat's, blond hair was a fine silk that the offshore breeze moved back and forth over her cheeks. Her figure was slender and flawless even in a flight jacket several sizes too large for her and baggy brown pants that were tucked sloppily into her boots. Raven could feel Flapjack smirking at him but still had nothing to say, so he just thrust out his hand. She ignored it and had no smile for him.

"After the last fiasco, I no longer train men, Mr. Peterson," she said. "Find someone else."

Flapjack shook his head. "No, this one's yours. Colonel Skipp at Wheeler Army Airfield wants you to make a stunt flier out of him."

Becky's eyes spat green fire. "Why me?"

Flapjack handed her the letter. "No one else is good enough."

She shook her head. "I won't do it. End of sentence."

Flapjack shrugged. "Then you're fired. Pack up."

Eleven

B ecky seemed to grow six inches. "You can't fire me."
  "No?"

She glared at Raven's sky-blue eyes, strong cheekbones, and boyish good looks. "I don't want anything to do with him. My father can handle it."

Flapjack put his hands on his hips. "Actually he can't. He has a full slate of civilian and military trainees."

"My mother—"

"Right from the start we agreed your mother would only work with female students. We never made such an arrangement with you."

"Let's make the arrangement."

"No can do. We need this to happen."

"Nate then."

Flapjack shook his head. "You're grasping at straws. Nate's nowhere near ready to fly again. Maybe in the spring. Not today."

"I won't do it."

"You're out. Your flight status is revoked and you can get off my airfield now. I hear your Aunt Ruth is making a quilt—you can help her with that."

"My father—"

"Jude and I talked this over a few days ago. He told me that if you won't take orders or do the job to give you a swift kick out the door."

Becky flared. "He did not."

"Yeah, he did."

Becky turned on Raven. "What's your name?"

"Christian Scott Raven. Sir."

"What's your call sign?"

"Thunderbird."

"Raven. Thunderbird. What's with all the Indian names?"

Raven's eyes went to blue ice. "I'm part Cherokee."

Becky bit her lip but decided to charge ahead. "Your father's name?"

"My mother's."

"You took your mother's Cherokee name?"

"I never cared for my father."

"How old is the name Raven?"

Raven's face darkened. "Why all the questions? The Cherokee never had last names. Your people made them start that."

"*My* people? My people never lifted a finger to any Indian tribe. We kept our promises."

"Sure. You promised to take our land and you took it."

Becky looked at Flapjack, shaking her head. "No way, Mr. Peterson. I can't work with a guy like this."

Flapjack lifted his eyebrows. "Really? I think this is the best start with any of the army pilots you've had."

"You call this the best start?"

"Sure. All the others flirted with you until you blew up. This guy's not interested in you at all. And he can trade you insult for insult."

"I don't like anything about him and I don't want a pretty boy in my plane. Just give me female trainees and I'll be ecstatic and insult-free."

Flapjack started to walk away. "Take him up. Now."

"I'm not going to do that."

"I'll send Peachtree out with the jeep. He'll get you back to your parents' place. I hear the quilt has a kind of star pattern. Enjoy." Flapjack gestured with his hand as he headed toward the office. "Let's go, Thunderbird. I'll hook you up with someone else."

Raven took a step and Becky barred his path with her arm. "Stay here." Her eyes were flames. "I swear I'll shoot you if you lay a hand on me. Is that clear?"

Raven stared at her, his eyes hardening into a colder blue. "I haven't the slightest interest in you as a woman. I don't even find you attractive. So if all you want to do is teach me how to barnstorm that's fine. Because that's all I want. Besides, you're just a kid. And ugly and scrawny to boot."

Becky felt the heat rush into her face along with the blood. "Is that right?"

"That's right."

"You coming?" Flapjack called to Raven.

"No, he's not!" shouted Becky. "We're going up!"

"Thanks for letting him know." Raven took his cap from his head and crammed it into a pocket in his pants. "We Indians have a hard time speaking to white men on our own."

"I don't have anything against Indians. Neither do my people."

"And who are your people?"

"The Amish."

"What's that?"

"Pretty much like Quakers. With a German accent."

Raven grunted. "You don't have a German accent."

"How would you know?"

"I've been to Germany."

Becky tilted her head to one side and her tongue was in her cheek. "Oh, really. How did you manage that with a war on?"

"I was with the American team at the Olympics in '36. They were held in Berlin."

"I was in Africa at the time and fourteen years old. All I remember about the Olympics was a runner named Jesse Owens."

"I knew Jesse. Sometimes we trained together over there."

"Was he faster than you?"

"A lot faster. But then I ran distance races, not sprints. You *do* know the difference?"

Becky threw up a hand. "Okay. I was just trying to be pleasant."

"Don't bother. It doesn't suit you." He looked at the airplane. "I'll bet you can't even do a decent barrel roll. Isn't that why you're afraid to take men up? Because you can't cut it?"

Becky's face settled down into a hard burn. "You really know how to push it past the point of no return, don't you, Thunderbird?"

"Just taking my cues from you."

"Get in. Backseat. Instructor up front." She slid open the canopy and waved at one of the ground crew. "I need you to turn the propeller!" She gave Raven a glance so dark green it was black. "Let's see if you have the stomach for combat flying. My hunch is you don't."

Raven climbed into the backseat. "Do your worst."

She gave him a grim smile and adjusted her goggles. "My worst is my best. There's a bag under your seat for when you toss your cookies, Thunderbird."

He strapped himself in and put on his own goggles, offering up just a grunt in reply.

The sky was clear, the ceiling unlimited, and Becky put the plane into a steep climb and then let it fall and spiral around and around before going into a sharp dive and pulling up only a few hundred feet from the ground. She twisted her head around to look at Raven.

"You ready to walk on the wing yet, hotshot?"

"Yeah, but you better come out and hold my hand, Rebecca of Sunnybrook Farm." He began to laugh a deep laugh. "You even look like her, you know? Shirley Temple. She was all of, what, ten in the movie?"

Becky immediately went into a series of barrel rolls, so angry she didn't bother to count them and had trouble reorienting herself when she leveled out. Raven was quiet. She thought he had passed out and glanced back hopefully. He winked at her.

"When does the stunt flying start?" he asked.

Becky had intended to only stay up for half an hour but she found Raven so infuriating that she did rolls and corkscrews and steep dives and sharp pull-outs for more than an hour-and-a-half, trying to get him to fall apart or beg for mercy or use the paper bag. But nothing seemed to break his calm. Finally she headed in to make a landing.

"Hey." He tapped her on the shoulder. "When do I get to play the game?"

"Tomorrow. If you can still see straight. And Thunderbird?"

"What?"

"Don't touch me."

Before the propeller had stopped spinning Becky was out of the Piper and across the runway. She didn't bother to watch him climb down. Grateful, he put a hand against the fuselage to steady himself, began to walk, almost dropped, clamped his hand to the plane again, counted to twenty-five, and headed slowly toward the office, walking as erectly as possible. She was not there when he stepped in. Flapjack looked up from his paperwork.

"How was that, Lieutenant?"

"She can fly, that's for sure. Ought to be a combat pilot. Not that I'd tell her that."

Flapjack put his hands behind his head. "She's going to let you have the stick tomorrow. Says she hopes you kill yourself."

"Well, that's sweet of her. That would put her in jeopardy too, wouldn't it?"

"Not if she bails out." Flapjack grinned. "Still think she's ugly?"

"As sin, sir."

"Be here at seven. My driver will get you back to Wheeler." Flapjack tapped his pen on the desktop. "It works with her."

"Sir?"

"If you wanted her to go home thinking about you, Raven, today has been a success. You got under her skin."

"If I got under her's it's because she got under mine first. I wasn't raised that way, Mr. Peterson. My mother would smack my face for the way I talked to her. She'd probably kick me out of the house until I apologized to her on both knees and with three dozen red roses in my hands."

"Wouldn't work. Lockjaw tried roses after she slugged him. Almost crammed them down his throat."

"It would be my mother's idea. Not mine." He opened the door and adjusted his aviator sunglasses. "You going to give her any other men pilots to work on?"

"Only civilian women for now. We'll see how things work out with you. If you both survive, then sure, we'll line 'em up. No one flies like her, Raven. Except maybe Amelia Earhart. And she's gone."

"They never did find her, did they?"

"Nope. She missed her fueling stop and went down in the Pacific."

Raven was about to step outside when he glanced back. "Do you believe in reincarnation, sir?"

Flapjack frowned, his face creasing up. "No."

"Neither do I. But if I did, I'd bet Becky was another version of Amelia. Sent by God to test all men."

"Well, since you're the only man in her life now outside of her father and brother, try not to fail the test. You're representing all the rest of us red-blooded males."

"I really have no interest in her, sir."

"No? Tell me who you dreamed about when you show up here tomorrow morning. Seven sharp."

"Yes, sir."

Becky was waiting by her Piper J-3 at six-thirty. Raven showed up fifteen minutes later.

"Thought you'd thrown in the towel," she said.

"I don't know how to do that. Maybe you could teach me."

"Why don't we start with barrel rolls? You'll probably want to do towels after that."

"I'm game."

They took off and Becky let him have the stick once they had plenty of air beneath them. "You can't be casual about this, Thunderbird. The letter said you don't believe there's going to be a war. I don't care what you believe. I'm not interested in getting a reputation for doing a bad job teaching army pilots how to get out of trouble."

"Okay."

"Not that I care if you do get into trouble. It'll probably be your own fault and you'll only be getting what you deserve."

"Thank you for your confidence."

"I don't want it to look like I didn't know what I was doing. I have my pride."

"Are you running for office? When are the speeches over with?"

Becky turned around in her seat. "Be a wise guy, and eight weeks from now you won't be any better at flying than you are today and Billy Skipp will give you a nice new infantryman's uniform complete with a single pretty stripe."

"Yeah?"

"Yeah, and I'll have myself a good laugh every time I fly over your silly little head with its silly little tin pot strapped in place. Which would be great. Life has been rough and I could use as many good laughs as you can give me."

"Life has been rough?"

Becky nodded. "*You* make my life rough, Thunderbird. So you might as well be considerate and provide me with the laughs as well."

"Is there a barrel roll in our future?"

"Sure."

She threw the plane sharply on its side and keep turning and turning, finally leveling out after she counted four. "You see that, tough guy? Now you do it."

Blinking his eyes behind his goggles, clutching the stick more tightly than he would have liked, Raven began to bank the Piper to the left.

"Don't bank!" shouted Becky. "There's a fighter on your tail! He'll just keep shooting you full of holes! Go left hard and fast! Like this!"

Becky put them into another quick roll. When she had leveled out she raised her right hand and opened and closed her fist. Raven knew it meant to relax. He loosened his grip.

She shook her stick and jabbed her thumb at him. She wanted him to take over the controls and try again.

"Go ahead. Go ahead."

Raven flew straight and smooth for a few minutes. Then he banked left and did a slow loop and banked right and did another slow loop. His barrel roll was soft and round and he took his time. His dive was precise and gentle. Finally Becky tapped the top of her leather helmet to tell him to relinquish the controls. She took them back to the airfield and landed the Piper quickly.

"Thunderbird!" She was hollering at him the moment she pulled open the canopy. "How did you get a call sign like that? You fly like an old man who's afraid of speed. Peterson has souped-up Pipers that have almost three times the horsepower of the regular ones. They can do anything. If you wanted a pleasure cruise, why didn't you buy yourself an old Curtiss Jenny instead of telling Uncle Sam you wanted to be a combat pilot?"

"I'd rather fly my P-36 than a Jenny."

"You could be in a shooting war by this time next year. You won't last a day against the enemy."

Raven brought his sunglasses from a shirt pocket and put them on. "There won't be a war and there won't be an enemy."

"There already is a war and there already is an enemy. Haven't you seen the newsreels of the Germans bombing Poland and France and England? Of their tanks crashing through Russia and the Ukraine? Just the other week they were battering at the gates of Moscow."

"Far away, Miss Whetstone. It doesn't affect me."

"It affects me!" she exploded. "My brother was in Nanking when the Japanese captured it. They raped and tortured and mutilated and murdered for months. If China had an air force as good as the Japanese it would never have happened. Has it ever occurred to you that innocent women and children might be counting on you some day to save their lives?"

Becky stalked off. Billy Skipp was standing by Flapjack's office as she approached. She was used to seeing him and his wife at the house and, even though rage was all through her body and ripping apart the smooth skin of her face, she stopped to say hello.

"How's it going with Thunderbird?" he asked.

"It's not. There's no point in my taking him up again. He has no fight in him. No passion. No heat."

"Light a fire under him."

"I've tried."

"Try again." Skipp took off his Ray-Ban aviators and cut into Becky with the eyes of a hawk. "There are three or four top pilots on Oahu right now. You're one of them. Probably the best. If I could I'd give you Thunderbird's rank and plane and send you up. But I can't. So I'm doing the next best thing. Pouring you into him like water into a glass."

"He's not listening."

"Make him listen. People will be counting on us to defend our borders soon enough."

Becky shook her head. "He doesn't believe that."

"What matters is what you believe. You're the teacher. Put it into him."

"I can't."

"You have to. He should be as good a flier as you but he's not. He has the whole package—eyesight, reflexes, self-control—but he doesn't have the will to go hard and push the limits. You've always had that. It's your gift. Share it."

"He doesn't want it."

Skipp bit out the words. "*Make* him want it."

"Thunderbird doesn't like me, Colonel."

"And you don't like him. So what? You're the trainer—train him. You're the instructor—instruct him."

He put his Ray-Bans back on and waited as Raven came slowly toward them. She opened the door to Flapjack's office. Skipp gently took her by the arm.

"Becky. You can do this. I know you can do this. Or I wouldn't have asked."

She gave him a crooked smile. "You didn't ask. I'm your employee. You're my boss and this was an order, not a request. You made that very clear."

"And are you going to follow orders?"

"I'm taking him up every day, aren't I? I just think it's a mission we ought to abort."

Skipp took away his hand and turned to face Raven. "Not yet. Come up with another angle."

"I don't have any other angles."

"I don't believe that, Becky."

Twelve

"Do you think I'm scrawny?"

"What?"

"And, well, ugly?" Becky stared into the mirror as her aunt looked up from the large quilt she was stitching. "My eyes aren't the nice green that mother has. And they're too far apart. And my mouth is too big. And I really am skinny."

"This is too much vanity, Becky. You look the way you should look. Thank God and get on with your life."

Becky sat down at the table where Ruth had spread her quilt. "I know he doesn't like me. Why should he? I've been insulting him since the first day we met. It isn't the Christian thing and certainly not the Amish thing, but I can't seem to stop myself."

"What do you think of him?"

"Well, I don't like him any more than he likes me, and his tongue is just as sharp as mine."

"How much prayer have you put into this?"

"Not much. I'd rather just walk away. But Flapjack and Billy Skipp won't let me."

"Talk to your father." Ruth had been threading another needle and now she handed it to Becky. "Why don't you work on that side of the quilt while we're sitting here?"

"All right." Becky began to thrust the needle through the fabric. "At least I'll accomplish something." She stitched for several minutes. "Dad is on Flapjack's and Billy's side."

"Why? What's his reason?"

"His reason is the same as their reason. Christian Raven is too slow in the air and they think I have something that he needs."

"Something special?"

"I guess."

"What is it?"

"I don't know. Stuff."

"Stuff?" Ruth took a sip from a glass of lemonade. "I think the word is *spirit*."

Becky shrugged.

"Aren't things going well with your other students?" Ruth asked.

"Swell. But Raven is a combat pilot and they aren't. He could make a difference one day. The kind of difference that saves the Nankings of our world, you know? And I can't reach him. I just can't." Becky stopped stitching and stared at the needle in her fingers. "He's holding back."

"Why?"

"I don't know why."

"I suppose a lot of men think the same way about you."

"What?"

"They're polite. They ask you to the movies. To the restaurant. To a dance. And it's always no. Usually with a fair bit of heat attached. They probably wonder what a pretty girl like you is doing sitting around at home every evening. *What's holding her back?* they must be asking themselves."

"Let them ask. There will never be another man for me. Never."

"They don't know that. They don't know your story, about what happened in Pennsylvania. They don't know why you are who you are and why you act the way you do. It's the same with Christian Raven, isn't it? Don't you think there's a good reason he's holding back?"

"Who knows?"

"You have a reason for why you won't date a man. He must have a reason he won't fly as hard and fast as you want him to. If you find out what it is, you still may not be able to help him but at least you'll understand him."

"Never in a million years will he let me in on something like that."

Ruth put fresh thread through the eye of her needle. "He might if you let him in on what happened with Moses Yoder."

"What? I'm never going to tell a person like that about Moses!"

"'A person like that'?" Ruth pulled the needle through a corner of the quilt. "It's not as if there aren't stories going the rounds. Why not tell him the truth and let God take it from there?"

"What stories?"

"That you cut your hair off with a knife. That you had a friend killed in a plane crash and you were the one piloting the plane."

"What?"

"In church last week a woman asked me if it was true that you had been married and that your husband had divorced you because you wouldn't give up flying."

Becky put down her needle. "Why are so many people talking behind my back?"

"There's always talk going on behind all our backs. Now and then you have to decide where and when you're going to refute it. And who you think really ought to know the truth. Do you think Christian Raven deserves to know the truth?"

"Christian Raven! He doesn't deserve anything."

"So you're content that he thinks you chopped off your hair with a butcher knife and killed the man you loved when you flew poorly and crashed your plane?"

"I don't care what he thinks."

"Well, then, you're back where you started. You don't know why he's the way he is, and he thinks he knows why you're the way you are but he's wrong."

Becky got up. "I need a break."

The house Flapjack had found for the Whetstones was on a slope. To the south she could make out the waters of Pearl Harbor, and far to the left, Diamond Head. She walked through a grove of palm trees and looked toward Wheeler Army Airfield miles to the north. Watching the tiny dots of planes in the late afternoon sky she thought about Christian Raven without meaning to or wanting to. He might be flying his P-36 now—smooth, fluid, controlled, and without even the slight-est hint of fire in his bones.

He'd never have made it as a barnstormer. We'd have given him the lit-tle kids and their grandparents to take up for nice gentle rides.

She sat down on a rock. Now all she could see were palm fronds and pineapple plants. Without planning to, she began to pray, talking to God out loud as drops of light fell on her arms and face through the palm branches.

He said he believed in God but I don't really have any idea what he believes in. Of course we're not on speaking terms, are we? More like snip-ing terms. But I suppose in the end it doesn't matter what he does or doesn't believe or how he acts toward me or why he is the way he is. It just matters how I respond or act toward him. I haven't done a very good job, Lord. I haven't acted like a Christian in any way that you would recognize. I've been pretty nasty.

And not just to him. To all the pilots I've met. It's not like any of them pinned my arms behind my back and forced me to kiss them. They just wanted to ask me out and I'm still so upset about Moses all I could do was snap at them—"How dare you?" I expect all these men to know what hap-pened in Pennsylvania and that I've given my heart away to another for all time, and they don't know anything about Moses or the Amish or what hap-pened before we came here. I haven't been fair, have I? Not sure what to do next. I can't stand the thought of apologizing to Christian Raven.

He was waiting by the Piper the next morning as she walked across the runway. His sunglasses glinted in the sunrise as he smiled and pat-ted the plane's cowling.

"You're late," he said.

"Am I?" she responded.

"Were you hoping I'd pop into the front seat and show you how it's done?"

"I honestly wish you would, Thunderbird." Becky stood facing him a moment, her eyes hidden behind her own pair of Ray-Bans. Then she clenched her fists and took the plunge. "What have you heard about me at Wheeler?"

"Excuse me? What are you asking?"

"When men talk about me, what do they say?"

"Are you kidding me?"

Becky took off her glasses and her eyes were a mix of green and gold in the dawn. "No." She pocketed the glasses in her khaki shirt. "Some say I hacked my hair off with a butcher knife."

"I heard it was a bread knife with serrations."

"It was neither. I used a pair of scissors. Do you want to know why?"

"No. Let's just go up."

"A friend got killed. Did you hear about that?"

Raven hesitated. "Yeah."

"How do the men at Schofield Barracks and at Wheeler think it happened?"

"Some say it was pilot error—his. Others say you were reckless and doing a stunt that went wrong and he died because of it."

"There was no plane. We were engaged to be married. A strong wind gust took him off the roof of a barn he was working on."

Raven didn't say anything.

"He always loved my hair long. It was part of his religion, really— *a woman's crowning glory is her hair.* So I cut it off a few weeks after his funeral. I made a mess of it. My aunt had to trim it and make it right."

Raven still didn't respond.

"I made a kind of vow when I cut it off. No men. He was my life mate forever—even in death. So that's why I've been keeping men at arm's length, even movie stars like Lockjaw and Whistler. Not because I hate men. Because I loved the man I lost so much."

Raven finally spoke. "Why are you telling me this?"

"We got off on the wrong foot. And I was the one who made sure we did. Now I want you to understand why. His death has made me the way I am. Or at least the way I've dealt with his death has made me the way I am." She pulled back the canopy. "That's all. I'm a church girl and should know better how to treat people. I'm sorry, Thunderbird. Maybe we can start over. Maybe not. But let's at least stop cutting each other up, and let's try and make you the aviator Billy Skipp wants. I'd hate to lose you to the trenches."

A jeep came racing over to them with Flapjack's right-hand man in it.

"Hey," said Peachtree. "There's a storm brewing west of the islands." Raven and Becky both glanced that way and could see the dark cumulus building on the horizon. "The meteorologists say it will hit in an hour or so with a lot of big wind. So all planes are grounded for the morning. Maybe all day. Depends how long the weather sticks around."

"Okay," said Becky.

"You guys want a lift back to the office?"

"Yeah, I'll shove off now." Becky climbed into the back of the jeep.

Peachtree looked at Raven. "Coming, Thunderbird?"

"Stay with me, Becky."

Becky stared at Raven. "What?"

Raven took off his sunglasses. The blue of his eyes was piercing. "Stay with me."

Part of her wanted to say, *Why should I?* The other part didn't say anything. It just made her get out of the jeep.

"I guess we'll walk, Peachtree," she said. "Thanks."

"Suit yourselves." Peachtree roared off.

Becky gazed up at Raven. "What's this about, Thunderbird?"

"Let's sit in the plane and not go anywhere."

They left the canopy open at first. Raven leaned his head back against his seat and closed his eyes. "Can you hear me?" he asked.

"Loud and clear," Becky replied from the front seat.

"You're never going to get me to develop a fighter's instinct. It's not going to happen. We should save the time and gas."

"You want a tin helmet that bad?"

He said nothing more for a long minute. "You want me to spread the word about what really happened to you when you were stateside?"

"I don't care."

"I'm going to say some things about myself and I don't want anyone knowing about them. Understood?"

"All right. But why are you telling me if you feel that way? We don't have to play tit for tat. I said what I said. You don't owe me anything."

"No. I don't. But you tried to make a difference, so I'm going to respect that and tell you why I can't be the wonder boy you want to turn me into."

"Thunderbird—"

"I barnstormed too. With my old man. Mostly in the Southwest—Texas, Oklahoma, Nevada, New Mexico. I was born in 1917 and I was already flying alone at twelve—just short runs. Used to drive Mom crazy but the old man never cared what she thought. By '33, when I was sixteen, I was really cooking with gas. I'd do anything—fly under low bridges, go through barns, thread the needle between two or three trees. The old man made a lot of money off my stunts, always had some kind of bet going on with the odds against me and hundreds of people involved."

The sky had darkened and rain was coming in fast fat drops. Becky pulled the canopy shut and they listened to it drum on the plane for a few moments. Finally Raven sat up and looked out at the storm and spoke again.

"So my brother is, what, nine? The old man wanted him wing-walking but Mom really threw a fit so he let it go. Then he came up with a better idea how to make a lot of cash—Timmy flies the Jenny while I sit in front as a passenger. Timmy does the loops, the barrel rolls, the death spins—oh yeah, Becky, I learned all that stuff—and I've got my hands stretched out over my head to show I'm not doing a thing while we're in the air. So 'Timmy Dynamite' is the youngest barn-stormer in America and he goes under bridges and over hedges and through barns just like me, sitting on a stack of mail-order catalogues. Why am I in the plane? For only one reason—in case Timmy screws up. I'm supposed to somehow get to the back cockpit and take over the controls if that happens. Of course it's never supposed to happen because if we'd taken that part seriously we'd have realized how hard it was going to be for me to get into Timmy's cockpit."

Wind was rocking the Piper and the rain sounded like bullets on the wings and canopy and fuselage.

"The stunt was easy. He was going to do a figure eight with smoke. And the kid was never afraid, Becky, never. Into the eight he goes, I'm popping open the smoke canister, no one's looking at the wild geese coming in from the south. Timmy's going to bend right into them as he does his eight. The old man says he was waving his arms and screaming up at us—maybe he was, maybe he wasn't, we would never have noticed anyway. Timmy turned into the geese and they went right into the prop and the wings, tearing big holes in the fabric, spraying blood and guts all over the plane, breaking the propeller blade in half. Timmy's crying for me to help him, the plane's going into a spin, everyone thinks it's part of the act except the old man and Mom. I tried to haul myself into Timmy's cockpit, I couldn't do it at first, finally made it in time to see Timmy's white face and his big dark little-kid eyes before he fell out of the plane—his harness had been shredded. He landed in front of the crowd and sank a foot into the ground. I crash-landed the Jenny in a cornfield and walked out of it."

He stopped.

Becky had turned around in her seat, her eyes large and black. "Thunderbird. Christian."

"The drinking and the beatings came after all that. The old man blamed me and Mom blamed him and I blamed myself and God. There was plenty of blame to go around. Watch yourself now."

Raven hauled back on the canopy and the rain poured in. He was quick, pulling the canopy shut as soon as he was on the runway. He looked at Becky through the water streaming over the glass. Then he walked off into the storm.

Thirteen

"He turned in his wings."

Flapjack leaned back in his chair and looked at Becky. "And resigned his commission."

"When?"

"This morning. That's why he never showed up for his training flight with you."

Standing alone by the Piper, waiting for Raven to show up, Becky had felt something like this might be happening. What surprised her was that she had feelings about it. Her spirits sank like a rock in deep water.

"So that's it?" The dark feeling continued. "He's gone?"

"Not quite. Skipp gave Thunderbird three days to think it over. If he still wants to end his career in the air forces by Monday morning then that's that. But until Monday he's on leave."

Becky's mood lightened slightly. "That's good."

"Is it?" Flapjack began twirling his yellow pencil with his fingers. "Mind telling me what you guys talked about yesterday?"

"Yesterday?"

"Yes. Yesterday. The day before today. You sat out in the rain in that Piper J-3 for half an hour."

Becky shook her head. "I need to find him."

"I thought you didn't care about him."

"I don't care about him. But I need to talk to him."

Flapjack tapped his pencil on the desktop, his eyes locked on Becky.

"Funny thing is, I thought you might. Skipp grabbed Whistler and Lockjaw and they said he'll either be with his Coast Guard buddy or he'll camp out at a little cove he likes by Nanakuli. You know Nanakuli?"

"No."

"I thought you wouldn't. Here's a map I sketched for you. It's on the west side of the island."

"Who's his Coast Guard buddy?"

"Harrison. On the Coast Guard cutter *Taney*. Try Nanakuli first."

"Okay."

"Do you need a ride? Peachtree can take you there."

Becky looked at the map. "I can't have anyone else with me."

"Hm. Can you drive?"

"Not too well."

"I guess we're stuck then."

Becky folded the map and put it in a shirt pocket. "Give me a jeep."

"What?"

"Give me a jeep, Flapjack. Or isn't Thunderbird worth a jeep in case I crack up?"

"If you can get Thunderbird to fly like you fly it's worth a hundred jeeps." He tossed a set of keys at her. "It's the one with my call sign painted on the side along with the silhouette of a SPAD. Use the key with the red fob."

Becky ran out the door. "Thanks, Flapjack."

"Anything for my country."

She ground the gears and popped the clutch, but by the time locals had helped her discover a road that would take her to Nanakuli she thought the jeep was moving along pretty well. She had no idea why she was doing what she was doing except she knew if she didn't do it Raven would never fly again. Why that should matter to her one way or the other made as much sense as her driving an army jeep to the west coast of Oahu to find him. She had nothing to say to him. There was no reason to expect he would listen even if she did find something to say.

A dirt track took her to a deserted beach, where October surf was high and crashing over the sand. She got out of the jeep and walked through the brush to the shore.

There was no one around. That didn't mean Raven wasn't somewhere nearby. He could be back in the palms or up the slope on the hilltop. She began to head north along the beach, finally taking off her boots and socks so she could wade barefoot at the edge of the waves like she used to do in the Caribbean. After ten minutes of this her pants were soaked to the waist. She didn't care. All thoughts of why she had come to this beach in the first place were swept away by the surf until she spotted his head in the water. He was swimming in with the help of some five-foot waves.

When he came out of the water Becky was surprised at the tan that was over his whole body and how muscular his chest and stomach were. In his uniform he was broad-shouldered and slim but there was no hint of how fit he was. She hadn't seen a man in swim trunks since Turks and Caicos and she dropped her eyes for a moment. But she was not an almost Amish woman in an Amish community anymore and looked up again. There was nothing to be afraid of, she told herself, and she had no feelings for Christian Scott Raven whatsoever.

He approached her over the sand, wiping the saltwater out of his eyes with his hand. "What do you want?" His face was dark, his lips tight. "How did you find me here?"

Becky put on her sunglasses. "They told me you turned in your wings."

"What's it to you?"

"Nothing." She adjusted her glasses. "I thought you might want to talk."

"I talked too much yesterday. I should never have told you the things I did. But I—" He stopped. "So what do you want?"

"I want you to fly."

"You want me to fly? No, you want me to do stunts. I'll never do stunts again, Becky—no barrel rolls, no stalls, no steep dives, no corkscrews. You know why." He sat down on the sand and faced the ocean, legs bent, his arms resting on his knees.

Becky remained standing behind him. "I'm not asking you to do that. Not anymore. Let's just fly."

"That won't cut it with Billy Skipp or the Army Air Forces."

"We have until Christmas."

"Nothing will change. I thought it might. But it doesn't matter if I'm in a P-36 or a Piper J-3. I freeze up."

"If we go for a training flight every day for a half hour. I do some rolls and spins. We keep at it into November and December. Who knows? You might unwind."

"I doubt it."

"You might."

Raven twisted his head around. "Why does it matter?"

"It doesn't. Except I've never lost a student. Do you have to be the first?"

Raven laughed and looked at the sea again. "You're nuts."

"Well?"

"I'll think about it."

She waited a minute but he kept his back to her and wasn't going to say anything more.

She got up and left quietly.

All the way to Peterson Air Services she kicked herself for going after him to begin with—if he didn't care, why should she? Why did she have to go looking for him? Why did she say she'd keep taking him up when he had no desire to do anything she or Billy Skipp asked of him?

What is the matter with me?

Despite her anger she thought about him walking up out of the waves. His slender build reminded her of Moses. And his smile—the few times she'd seen it. How muscular Moses had been she would never know—Amish men did not go around in swimming trunks or with their shirts off. Raven's shoulders were broader and so was his chest. But he was older than Moses by a few years too. And his tan. It was so golden and all over him. Moses would not have had anything but a farmer's tan—face, neck, and hands, maybe a bit on each arm. But Raven had been out swimming. A lot.

"Stop it!" she shouted as she drove, startling a man walking on the shoulder of the road. "Stop thinking like that!"

The last time she had been swimming was in the Caribbean. She remembered the warmth of the water, its color like a turquoise gem, no waves, flat calm—and she had gone as far out as she dared, at least a mile, before turning around. She'd worn a white two-piece bathing suit. It didn't show too much, it was modest for the most part, and very comfortable, but it showed more than a one-piece did and her mother asked her only to wear it when she was alone and far from the gaze of men. Rolling her eyes, she had nevertheless done her best to find secluded places to swim, but the men had always seemed to find her, pretending to beachcomb or just be walking past, their eyes lingering on her whether she was in the water or out. Sometimes she liked the men and liked the sensation. Other times she swam to another beach to get away from them.

"Stop it, Rebecca!" She was on the paved roadway with army trucks behind her and beside her. "Stop being such a fool!"

Raven's eyes have never lingered on me. And they never will—he finds me skinny and unattractive. It doesn't matter anyway. Why am I thinking like this? We have nothing in common but airplanes, and I'm committed to Moses for life. All this daydreaming is ridiculous.

She parked the jeep in a savage mood and almost threw the keys in Flapjack's face. "Thanks. It still has four wheels."

Flapjack put his hand over the mouthpiece of the phone he was talking on. "Did you find him?"

"I don't know what I found."

Raven was standing by the Piper Cub when she arrived at Peterson's on Monday. They both had their Ray-Bans on, but as she walked toward him over the runway she had the same feeling of being looked at she'd had on the beaches in the Caribbean. She glanced around quickly as she walked—was it ground crew, another pilot, a student? There was no one else. The sensation was strong, she liked it, but it unnerved her at the same time—what if Raven was the one staring? It was easier to bicker with him and trade shots than to imagine him liking her or for her to start liking him in a way that belonged only to Moses. Still and always to Moses.

I hate that I want him to take his sunglasses off so I can know for sure if it's his eyes that are tracking me.

Raven's aviators stayed where they were. And there wasn't even a hint of a smile for her though she tried to muster one up for him.

"Hi," she said. The smile was lopsided. "I'm glad you decided to keep your wings."

"Half an hour lesson?" he asked her.

"Half an hour."

"When you want me on the controls let me know."

"I'll do a few barrel rolls first. And a dive with a little corkscrew thrown in."

"Whatever makes you happy."

But Becky wasn't sure what made her happy anymore. The other students she was training didn't. Going home and spending the evening with her family didn't. Going up in the air by herself and flying out over the Pacific didn't. Even her vow to Moses didn't. She hated it, but the one thing she looked forward to was climbing into the Piper with Raven. Even though his barrel rolls remained sloppy and his dives slow and shallow. Even though he never smiled. Even though she felt no warmth from him.

"Let's go up, Thunderbird."

"Yes, sir."

"Do the best you can."

"Yes, sir."

Two nights later, the dam broke. She burst into tears in front of Ruth, flinging herself on her bed and burying her face in the summer quilt. "I'm not going to be unfaithful to Moses! I'm not!"

"Hush, hush." Ruth sat on her bed and ran a hand over her back. "Why do you think you're being unfaithful to Moses?"

"I...I think about Raven too much...I think about him all the time...I don't even *like* him—but I can't stop—"

"And this is being unfaithful to Moses? How?"

Becky rolled onto her back and almost snarled at her aunt. "How? I said I'd never fall for another man! Never! That I'd be faithful to Moses through all eternity!"

"And Moses is in heaven where there is no marrying, no husbands and wives, just love for everyone. If he can see you, he is no longer thinking of you as he did on this earth. He is like the angels. And he loves you now like a sister in the Lord. No more."

"How can you say that?"

"The Bible says it. Shall I read it to you?"

"I know what the Bible says." Becky rolled over onto her stomach again, snatching a tissue from a box on her bedside table. "So you think I mean nothing to Moses now?"

"I didn't say that. I just said he doesn't see you as a wife anymore. He doesn't have those feelings. They don't exist."

"But *he* exists. Except now he has wings."

"Perhaps."

Becky wiped at her eyes. "This vow has kept me going for months. If I let it go I don't know what I'll do with my grief. I'll probably fall to pieces."

"Maybe not."

"I will. I'm sure I will. It's already starting to happen. I pick fights with Mom and Dad. With Nate. With you. I can't sleep. I don't have any patience for my female students. I talk out loud when no one's around. I'm a mess."

Ruth smoothed back Becky's short hair. "What if he said something to you?"

"Who?"

"This Christian Raven fellow."

"Oh, he says things to me."

"I mean nice things. Sweet things."

Becky blew out air. "Pah! Are you kidding?"

Ruth narrowed her eyes. "I am not. Do you think no one has noticed your moods and your fits of ill temper? We've been praying for you. All of us. Why may we not expect to see some return on our prayers?"

"He tried to be nice when we first met. I shut him down, and that was that as far as him being sweet."

"Didn't you say he believed in God?"

"He says he does. I don't know what that looks like because I don't think he's been showing his faith any more than I have."

"If you realize that, then the day will come when he will begin to realize it too. We all have bad days and bad weeks. We all go off on our own roads for a time. Finally the Lord brings us back to our senses and we repent and return to being the person we should be in Christ."

"I don't even know if he believes in Jesus."

"Well." Ruth sat back on her own bed. "There's one way to get to the bottom of it. Outside of coming right out and asking him to his face, you can offer to pray with him."

Becky lifted her head. "What?"

"You told me you prayed with your other students before each flight."

"That's different. He's an army pilot. A tough guy. Not to mention praying with me, even if he wanted to pray, is the last thing he is going to do."

"You don't know."

"I do know."

"You have to take the plunge sometime." Ruth unpinned her black-and-gray hair and took up her hairbrush. "That's enough for today. The Bible drama of Esther and the King of Persia continues tomorrow morning at seven sharp."

"Ha ha."

"There's a letter I put under your pillow. Not from him. From Bishop Zook."

"Bishop Zook? How can he write me?"

"You have never been baptized or taken your vows. Neither has Nate. So the bishop can have fellowship with you both. It's the rest of us who are out of bounds."

"Why do you put such things under my pillow?"

"So they don't get lost."

Becky sat up and lifted the pillow. The envelope was thin and had the red, white, and blue diagonal border markings that meant airmail. She opened it and took out a small sheet of paper.

"It's a short note. And it's on really thin paper."

"So the Amish are frugal. What does he say?"

"Shall I read it out loud?"

Ruth ran the brush through her long hair. "Only if you want to."

Becky scanned the note. "It's personal. But I'm going to read it to you anyway."

"Becky—"

My dear Rebecca,

God be with you. Not much time has gone by since you left us. I was going to wait until Christmas and send some of Mrs. Zook's special cake with the almonds in it you like. But after my time of prayer and Bible study this morning I feel compelled by the Lord to take up my pen and send you a note. I will not waste words. Moses, whom you love, and whom I love, is in heaven. He is like the angels now but greater, for not only has he been made in the image of God, he has been redeemed by the Son of God. His work on earth is done. He does not love you or me less but his love is of a different kind, a kind we cannot match until we join him in the eternal presence of the Lord.

So I say this to you—Moses is no longer a groom; he is no longer the husband you dreamed of. You must seek another. The Lord would have you free to find the partner he has arranged for you before the creation of the world. This man is in the world somewhere— perhaps here in Lancaster County, perhaps *there on the Hawaiian Islands. It is his call to love and cherish you all his life. Pray about this man. Look for him with the eyes God gives you. Above all, set yourself free from any vows you may have made to Moses while he dwelt on this earth. And so may Christ shine upon you, my dear.*

Bishop Zook

"So and what do you think?" asked Ruth.

"I think everyone is ganging up on me. Including God." She groaned, put the letter down, and looked out the bedroom window at a sky framed by palm fronds. A sense of being overcome and overwhelmed worked its way across her young face. "All right. I'll try. I'll put my best foot forward. With all the men I meet. I think it's a mistake. But I'll try." She glanced at her aunt. "Just because I do that, it doesn't mean he's going to respond in the same way. He might just stay a tight-lipped bulldog."

"Does he look like a bulldog?"

A thin smile curved Becky's lips. "Maybe not."

"Let me pray for you. Right now." Ruth put down her brush.

"Are you going to pray in German?" asked Becky.

"*Ja.* Why?"

"It seems to work better for me in Amish German."

Ruth smiled and took Becky's hand. "In Amish German it shall be. *Gott liebt die deutsche Sprache.* God loves the German language."

"Especially when the ones praying in it pray for life and peace." Becky closed her eyes. "All right. I'm ready to take the plunge back into the world I've shunned. Go ahead."

Fourteen

Instead of running three miles Raven ran six. Then he did five hundred push-ups in sets of fifty, with a two-minute break between each set. After the push-ups he went to Billy Skipp and asked if his driver could drop him off at Nanakuli. Once Skinny left him at the beach, Raven dove into the six-foot November waves, swimming against them and with them, fighting with the undertow, spitting out seawater, diving as deep as he dared, clawing his way to the surface once his air was gone. Twenty minutes of this and the waves threw him onto the sand. He struggled clear of the surf and sprawled on his back, letting the sun and wind dry him. The chaplain's words echoed in his mind.

Okay, Lieutenant, as far as I can see it there are three things, maybe four. You feel a lot of guilt because your kid brother was killed in an airplane you were supposed to bring safely to the ground. That's one. The guilt has blocked you from being a good combat pilot—you can't bring yourself to do the stunt flying that killed Timmy, so now you're not sure you should stay in the military. That's two. Three, you've been taking out your frustration on a female flight trainer. Why? Because she's the one that's been ordered to hone your flying skills and she sees only too clearly how you freeze up in the cockpit. It's humiliating.

And what's the fourth?

My guess is you're in love with her.

What? I am not in love with her.

I've seen this sort of thing before. Believe me, being a military chaplain is a lot more than blessing the troops and holding church parade. Hundreds of guys come to me to talk about their wives and their girlfriends or someone they just met who has them turned inside out and upside down.

Sir, I am not in love with her!

Why are you getting so worked up?

Because I don't love Becky Whetstone and I'm not getting worked up!

Raven lifted himself on one elbow and watched the thundering waves. Farther down the beach he could see three men surfing. Sitting up he reached over to where he'd folded his uniform and found his Ray-Bans. Putting them on, he stared out over the white-capped Pacific.

So what do I do?

With the first one? That's the biggie, Lieutenant. Your father put you in an impossible situation. That's the thing you have to realize. Your kid brother should never have been up there to begin with. Nine years old? And you're supposed to climb back when the plane's in a spin, get into his cockpit, grab hold of the controls, and pull off a three-point landing? Just like that?

He said it was my fault. I was too slow getting into Timmy's cockpit. I should have seen the birds to begin with. I ought to have snagged Timmy while he was falling out.

Sure. And did he tell you to find a phone booth and put on a red cape and fly after Timmy like the comic-book guy, Superman? You should have caught him before he hit the ground, right?

I don't know.

You do know. Your old man couldn't blame himself. So he made sure you and your mom took the blame. What did you tell me? That he said your mother should never have let Timmy go up that day? Even though he thought the whole Timmy Dynamite Air Show up and was making tons of money off it?

Not that day. He lost a lot of money that day. That was another reason for the beatings.

Did you ever fight back?

He had two hundred pounds on me.

Did you?

When he beat Mom, yeah. But it didn't do any good. After he'd taken care of me he always went after her three times as hard.

You have to take this off your back. He was the monster, not you. And you have to take it off this flight trainer's back. You're freezing up on the stick because of a death your father caused. Not because of anything the flight trainer's done. In fact, she wants the curse to go away, doesn't she? She wants you free, right? She doesn't want you to keep freezing up.

Yeah. She's okay.

But you treat her the way your old man treated you.

I haven't laid a finger on her!

You beat her up with your mouth, Lieutenant Raven.

He dove back into the waves, let them rough him up again, got out and waited for the sun to dry him, went behind a bush and changed from his trunks into his uniform, then started up a dirt track to the main road.

"Of course there's the whole problem about being a Christian," he said out loud as he walked. "Mom wouldn't call it a problem. For her it was always a path. 'Get back on the path and everything will sort itself out. You'll end up where you're supposed to end up.'"

He didn't speak again for fifteen minutes. When he did he was no longer talking to himself. "I don't do well at apologies, God. Or kissing and making up. Not that she'd be interested in the kissing-and-making-up part. It's one thing to say, 'Get back on the path.' What if getting back on the path means doing a bunch of things that are pretty difficult to pull off? Like getting somebody to listen to you without them spitting in your face? She's as tough as a steel cable, God. I'd have no idea where to begin. 'The first time I saw you I thought I'd been struck by lightning.' Lockjaw and Whistler would laugh themselves sick: 'A great line, Thunderbird, a swell line.' 'How about dinner? A dance at the officer's club? Church? Would you like to go to a great little church I know and pray together?'" Raven barked out a hard laugh. "She slugged Lockjaw for less."

Forget the dinner and dance stuff. There's nothing going on between Becky and you. You know that. So drop it. Just do the right thing—apologize,

make amends. Try to give her a barrel roll or two. Stay in the Army Air
Forces if you can. Get back on the path.

Once he reached the main road he stuck out a thumb for a ride.
Almost immediately he was picked up by an army truck heading to
Wheeler and then the Schofield Barracks. He spent the afternoon with
Harrison, who had leave from his Coast Guard vessel *Taney* and was
waiting for him at the bachelor officers' quarters, and in the evening
they linked up with Raven's fellow pilots Wizard, Juggler, and Batman.
The five took a Willys jeep into Honolulu, where a church was having
a barbeque on the beach along with a short service.

"It's Paul Thor who's talking, right?" asked Batman. "The tall guy?"

"Yeah," replied Wizard, who was combing his hair in the rearview
mirror as Batman drove. "He's all right. Even Lockjaw would listen to
Thor."

Batman made a sour face. "Sure. If we could ever tie him up and
drag him to a service." He glanced at Wizard. "What's with the comb?"

"Maybe I'll meet my wife there."

"Your wife? What wife?"

"The pretty church girl I hope to meet and marry. That wife."

Batman rolled his eyes. "Wizard, the top's down and your hair's
blowing all over the place. What good is the comb gonna do?"

"Women gravitate toward the well-groomed male. She'll be able to
tell my hair's been combed no matter what the wind does."

"*Gravitate*? When did you become the egghead with million-dollar
words?"

Wizard continued to look into the mirror and use his small black
comb. "Women prefer education and sophistication over brawn, Batman. That's why you'll be drinking punch and talking with Paul Thor
about God and I'll be drinking punch and talking to Hawaii's version
of Rita Hayworth about God. That's the difference between you and
me—I have the brains, I have the class, and I have the hair."

Raven turned to Harrison. "My apologies for what's lacking in our
conversation aboard this air force vehicle. I'm sure there is a much
higher standard in the Coast Guard."

Harrison laughed. "Oh, sure. I'm just glad to get ashore and get to church. Thanks for asking me to tag along."

"You anchored at Pearl?" Juggler asked.

"No. We're moored right next to it in Honolulu Harbor at Pier 6."

"I've been here since June and still haven't taken a walk along Battleship Row."

"Hey, I'd be happy to be your tour guide. Pick a day. We'll want to make sure some of the aircraft carriers are in. They're always sending them off somewhere."

"What carriers are in port?"

Harrison thought about it as the jeep sped along. "The *Lexington*. The *Enterprise*. That's it right now."

Juggler's forehead creased in disappointment. "What about the big battleships?"

"Don't worry. They're not going anywhere. The Navy doesn't move them around as much as they do the carriers and cruisers. Choose a date, we'll get clearance, and I'll show you the sights."

"Hey." Batman turned his head. "I want to get in on that."

"Me too," said Wizard who had stopped combing his hair for the moment.

Harrison smiled. "The Coast Guard can handle it."

There was already a fire going and a pig roasting when they arrived. Three men and a woman were playing guitars and leading singing for about a hundred people seated on the sand at Waikiki Beach, just down from the Moana Hotel. The five servicemen joined them. After a half hour of singing Paul Thor, dressed in a bright-red Hawaiian shirt with pineapples, palm trees, and flowers along with khaki shorts, got up and began to talk about forgiveness, his Bible open in his hand. He only spoke for ten minutes but when he was finished Batman leaned over to Raven.

"Hey. Thunderbird. That sure cleans out the pipes."

"Yeah," Raven responded, Thor's words still tumbling about in his head.

"Letting go and moving on."

"Yeah."

After grace they lined up for food and Raven put ten dollars in a bucket to cover the five of them. A woman sitting beside the bucket protested.

"Oh, no donation is necessary from servicemen, sir. You do enough for us already."

"I haven't done anything, ma'am, except fly planes in circles."

"You're a pilot?"

"All of us are. Except our friend in Coast Guard whites. He's from the cutter *Taney.*"

She gave him the ten-dollar bill back. "Do you fly the new P-40 Warhawks, Lieutenant?"

"I don't. Batman here does. And Wizard."

"Batman? Like the comic book?"

"He's a lot like the comic book."

"The P-36 is about to be mothballed." Wizard grinned.

"We'll see about that," grunted Raven. "It's a tough plane."

"It's as much a museum piece as Eddie Rickenbacker's SPAD. It can't do anything except look pretty in the sky."

"We'll see." Raven returned the ten to the woman. "Pastor Thor needs a new shirt. This is our contribution."

"Oh, my." The woman was surprised. "You don't like his shirt, Lieutenant?"

"We prefer blue. With coconuts and surfboards."

Juggler looked at the others. "We do?"

Wizard rubbed his hands together. "Come on. Move along. Let's eat. Grab a plate and fork and let me at the pig."

"What's the rush?" asked Batman. "The pig ain't going anywhere."

"But I am. The Hawaiian Rita Hayworth awaits. I need to discuss the Bible with her." Wizard looked around. "And there she is. The future Mrs. Wizard." He stopped dead. "Oh, boy. I really am in love. I haven't seen anything that beautiful in my very long lifetime."

"You're only twenty-one." Batman tried to find out who Wizard was staring at while he heaped potato salad onto his plate. "Where are you looking?"

"Over there. Under that palm tree. She's talking to Pastor Thor, for pity's sake."

"Oh, yeah. Oh, yeah." Batman smiled. "I see her. Whooo. She's as hot as the sun."

"Hotter."

No one else was paying any attention. Harrison and Juggler and Raven were digging into the greens and pineapple spears and people were bunching up in the line behind the group. Finally Juggler nudged Wizard.

"Hey. Romeo. Grab some chow and keep moving. You gotta eat, love or no love."

"Man. She kills me. I'm dead. I don't need food. I don't need anything."

"Oh, yeah? Glad to hear it. So maybe you'll leave my mom's Christmas cake alone when she sends the next batch over from Wisconsin." He glanced up from the slices of roast pig. "Okay, where is the princess?" He spotted Pastor Thor. Then he gave a low whistle. "Oooo. I see what you mean. I think I've lost my appetite too."

Batman helped himself to a glass of punch. "You know who she is, right? That little slice of sunlight and volcano?" He took a drink and looked at Pastor Thor and his companion. "That's Thunderbird's flight trainer."

Wizard reacted. "What?"

Raven looked up from a platter of rice. "What?"

"Isn't it? Isn't that her?" asked Batman.

Her blond hair ignited as the sun dropped into the mountains behind them. Pastor Thor had said something that made her laugh and she tossed her head.

Like a wild mare, thought Raven in surprise.

She wore a Hawaiian skirt with red and pink flowers and a simple white T-shirt with a necklace of small seashells. Her arms and face and legs were gold in the sunset. Now and then she would draw her hand back through her hair and it would spark. Again the pastor made her laugh and she lifted her foot so that only one toe was touching the sand. Then she touched a finger to her lips and rubbed it back and forth slowly while she nodded her head. There was another necklace of sea-shells on her ankle that caught the last of the sun. It swung with every movement of her leg as she traced a pattern with her toe on the beach. Once she looked toward Raven and his friends. There was a final flare of light and her green eyes burst into flame.

You have tiger eyes.

She put a hand up to shield out the sun. Seeing the men in their uniforms she gave them a smile that made Wizard groan, it had so much strength and beauty.

It opens up your face like a breaking wave curls white and opens up the sea.

She kept looking at them and Wizard put down his plate in the sand and started toward her. "I'm not passing up this chance to meet the Lord's woman for me."

"Hey." Batman chewed and swallowed quickly. "Wait up."

Juggler gulped his punch and ran after them. "May the best man win." He glanced back. "You guys coming?"

Raven lifted his glass in a toast. "Enjoy her company. See you back at the jeep."

Harrison was sitting in the sand, busy with his plate of food. "I'm sticking with Thunderbird, guys. See you later."

Wizard and Batman and Juggler shook the pastor's hand and crowded around Becky like a football team going into a huddle. Raven heard her laugh a third time, a sound he realized he'd rarely heard. He turned away, trying to sip at his punch.

Harrison looked up at him. "They can think what they like, Thunderbird, but she was looking at you."

"Forget it, Harrison."

"I mean it. Where her eyes landed was pretty clear to me." He bent over his plate again. "The smile was for you too."

"I doubt it."

"Yeah?" Harrison popped a cherry tomato into his mouth. "When do you go up with her again?"

"Tomorrow morning at seven."

"Dollars to doughnuts you're in for a big surprise. When love happens, and God opens the heavens, I want you to remember who told you so. And I want an army breakfast of bacon and beans on the house."

Raven sat down on the beach next to him. "I'm good for that."

Harrison smiled. "Glad to hear it. I just hope you remember once she turns you inside out and has you doing hoops and loops over Diamond Head in your P-36."

"How about I just do a victory roll over your ship instead?"

Harrison shrugged and continued to eat. "Okay with me. So long as it comes with bacon and beans."

Fifteen

Raven was up at three. He ran four miles, did his push-ups, then lay on his back and looked at a sky that was half stars and half dawn.

The old man is a shadow to me, Lord—I can hardly make out his face. All I've ever wanted to do is get back at him. Now you're telling me to forgive him and move on. Not so easy. But I'll give it a shot if it will make me a free man. I need your help with that. And hers. I just don't know how to ask.

He was at the Piper J-3 at six. Weeks before he'd started showing up early to get under her skin. Now he admitted to himself a stronger reason had been in play from the first—the pleasure of watching her walk across the runway to him. She moved like a breeze, and her spirit couldn't be diminished by the cloud cover or his own fears or by the sunrise itself—her beauty and heart was stronger than all of it. Whether she felt his gaze on her each morning he didn't know. But he did know he had pushed all his feelings for her as far away as he could and denied every one of them. It was time to say something, to make it or break it.

"Hey!"

Her shout came across the airfield to him. She was walking across the tarmac and waving, holding her goggles and leather helmet with the other hand. The sight was as wonderful as ever—her oversized flight jacket, a white T-shirt, pants that were snugger than her usual pair, short hair loose in the dawn air, a smile he hardly ever saw being given to him, pure and strong, like white terns, *manu o ku,* in the Hawaiian sky.

"Hey." She was still smiling. "I saw you at the barbeque last night."

Her smile and friendliness startled him. "Yeah. I was there with some of the guys."

"Why didn't you come over and say hello?"

"It looked like you had your hands full."

She rolled her eyes and laughed. "Did I ever."

"They were all pretty excited this morning. Every one of them got hot dates with Becky Whetstone."

"Hot dates? Is that what they told you? Coffee with Batman, breakfast with Juggler, oh yeah, a movie with Wizard. Does it—" She hesitated and dropped her smile. "Does it bother you, Thunderbird?"

"I never noticed you had freckles before."

She looked up at him, her emerald eyes taking in the sun as it rose out of the ocean. "I don't."

"You do. Right over the bridge of your nose. Really small. You'd have to look real close to see them."

"I guess I haven't looked close enough."

"You know…I'm not sure how to talk to you…there's been so much of the other stuff…I'm not sure what words to use…to be sweet and tight…"

"I'm not sure either, Thunderbird."

He felt an urge to touch her. It seemed to him that something in her was almost compelling him to do that. He reached out his hand and stopped. She wasn't smiling. But there was no anger in her eyes either. The moment confused him. He reached out again, ready to pull away if she said something. She didn't. His fingers touched her skin and a shock went up his arm.

"This is nuts," he said.

"I guess."

"Is it okay?"

"Yeah, Thunderbird, it's okay."

He smoothed back her hair and ran his thumb along her chin and the line of her jaw. Her green cat eyes stayed on him and took on more and more of the fire of sunrise. It seemed like a daydream to him.

"I've been a fool, Becky. I haven't been honest to God or honest to myself. The Lord knows I haven't been honest to you."

"Thunderbird—"

"I had to step away from my old man so I could see he was standing in front of you. It's this crazy thing. One minute it's night and the next it's daybreak. Light changes the whole world. Have you noticed that? I can see Becky Whetstone." He stroked his thumb over her lips. "You're easily the most beautiful thing God ever made. You're more than the ocean and the volcanoes and the islands. You're more than everything."

A soft smile took over her face. "A really handsome aviator once told me I was ugly and scrawny."

"He was wrong."

"And he said I was nothing more than a kid."

"The guy didn't know what he was talking about. Forget him."

"I'm having a hard time doing that."

"Can I help?"

"I wish you would."

"Hey!" Two of the ground crew drove up in a jeep. "You guys need a hand getting airborne?"

Raven pulled away his hand and stepped back from Becky. "Sure. Yeah. Thanks."

"We'll get the wheel blocks and the prop. This is Piper Eleven, isn't it? We gassed it up last night."

"Great."

Raven tugged back the canopy and began to climb into the backseat. He looked down at Becky who hadn't moved.

"Hey." He smiled. "You coming?"

She held back. "Do you need me, Thunderbird?"

Raven took off his aviator glasses. "Yeah. I do."

"Really? Or are we just trying to make up and be nice to each other?"

"I need you."

She kept her eyes on his. "Okay."

"Becky."

She was putting on her helmet and goggles. "What's up?"

"You really think the guy was a hotshot aviator?"

She sprang up and had her hands on both sides of the cockpit. She looked back at him. "Are you serious?"

"Yeah. After all these weeks. I'm serious. Finally serious."

"I *know* he's a hotshot aviator."

"You know it?"

"Yeah, Thunderbird. I do." She jumped into the cockpit and had her back to him. "So now show me."

"Beck—"

She turned around. "If everything's changed this morning and it really is a different world, a world where you're freer than you were twenty-four hours ago and your old man's out of the picture—" She stopped. Then she reached across the space between them and gripped his hand. "The kind of world where you can have feelings for Becky Whetstone and she can have feelings for you—then show me that world. Show me you care for her, Thunderbird. Do a tight barrel for Becky Whetstone. Just a bit is enough." She let out her breath in a rush. "I'm scared."

"Scared of what?"

"Scared of liking you. Scared of getting close to you. Scared I'm making a mistake. Sure I can act bold. Even brazen. But all kinds of things are in my closet, Thunderbird. If you break free I'll believe in what's been dropped on us out of the clear blue. I'll believe it's happening. And I won't run." She paused. "*If* you break free."

They took off. Once they were a few thousand feet in the air she waggled the stick and jabbed her thumb at him. He took over the controls. There was a tightness in his chest and a coldness in his mind. His little brother's face came and went. He could feel sweat slipping out from under his helmet and moving across his forehead. It got under his goggles and into his eyes. With his free hand he pulled back the goggles and wiped it away. Then he closed his eyes, put the goggles back in place, prayed a fast and hard prayer—*God, this has to be one of your immediate responses—I don't have weeks and years—it has to happen now—or I'll stay locked up forever*—and threw the Piper into a dive as steep and sharp as the Hawaiian cliffs. He waited until they were almost in the ocean before pulling up sharply. Becky did not react. As they gained height he put the plane into tight spirals. When he had the air he wanted under him he leveled out a moment before suddenly throwing the Piper to the left as hard as he could. He kept it up, going left again and again, strong and smooth and tight, over and over. Finally he straightened out over Diamond Head, other trainers ahead of them and above them, blinked, and let the aircraft slide to the right. It soon went into a spin. They hurtled downward, everything blurring and colors flashing. He fought out of the spin and put the Piper on its back, flying upside down for several minutes, and flipped it upright as they roared low over Waikiki, people waving their arms as the yellow Piper buzzed the beach. Zooming over the rooftops of hotels, Raven headed inland for the airfield. The gas needle was trembling at zero. They landed in a rush and skidded to a stop.

The prop still churning, Becky threw back the canopy and jumped to the ground.

"Get down here, Christian Scott Raven!" she shouted above the prop noise.

He sprang down and she threw her arms around him. "You crazy fool! No wonder Uncle Sam wanted you! You fly like a hurricane!"

Raven felt drained and empty but not too drained to take in the warm sensation of Becky Whetstone's arms being around him or the scent of her hair or skin or the sweet leather of her flight jacket. His arms brought her in close. Her face with its small freckles and full lips was inches away.

"Becky—" he began.

Her eyes rippled with green and gold. "Go ahead, Thunderbird. I'm trying to live again too. And the only way I know how to do it is to plunge in with both feet and both arms and all of my body and soul."

"It's happening fast, Beck."

"After all the weeks we've wasted I don't think it's happening fast enough." She smiled and her lips parted. "Go ahead, Thunderbird. You're cleared for takeoff."

"Hey! What was that?" Flapjack leaped out of his jeep, Peachtree at the wheel. "What was all that?"

Raven pulled away from Becky. "Barnstorming."

Flapjack looked at Becky. "Were you at the controls?"

She shook her head. "From two minutes after takeoff it was all him."

"You're kidding me."

"No, sir."

"I'm getting phone calls from hotels up and down Waikiki Beach saying you buzzed them. The Royal Hawaiian claims you stripped a flag off its roof and the manager's howling mad."

Raven shrugged. "No one got hurt, did they?"

"Not so far as I know."

"It couldn't be helped, Flapjack. I was breaking out of jail and I had to keep running."

Flapjack stared at him. "What?"

"And there was this girl I was trying to impress."

"A girl? A *pretty* girl?"

"Pretty's not a strong enough word, sir."

"No?" Flapjack looked back and forth between Raven and Becky. "What word would you use?"

"I don't think there is one word. But *dazzling* comes to mind. Spectacular. Striking. Fabulous. Superb. Magnificent. Gorgeous. Stunning."

Becky's face reddened. "Will you stop it?"

"If I did it for anyone, I did it for her, sir."

"You hardly know her."

"I'd like to change that flight status, sir."

Flapjack snorted and put his hands on his hips. "You remind me of her old man. We called him Lover Boy." He shook Raven's hand. "Well, shoot. If she can pull that kind of flying out of you I'm all for the relationship. You can even fraternize on duty."

"Thank you, sir."

Flapjack got back into his jeep. "Some of the stunts I saw were still a little rough around the edges."

"I'm sure my flight trainer can rub those off."

"I'm sure she can." He threw them a salute. "I'll leave you alone. Your next student's here in twenty minutes, Whetstone."

"I'll be ready, Mr. Peterson."

"I have a phone call to make to Billy Skipp."

The jeep drove off.

They looked at each other. Becky reached out and played with the chain that held Raven's dog tags. "That was pretty impressive, hotshot."

"It was hard coming back from the hole I dug for myself."

"I'll bet. I know a little something about trying to get out of holes." His fingers stroked her blond hair gently.

She put her hand on his. "Airfields don't work for us."

"I guess not."

"Do you have any other ideas?"

"When are you off?"

"My last student's at three. I'll be ready at four."

Raven nodded. "I have a maintenance check on my Hawk. And some other chores. But I'll be waiting here with a jeep at four."

"Are you sure?" she asked.

"Yeah. I'm sure."

"You want to go ahead with this?"

"That's affirmative." Raven twined a strand of her hair around his finger. "You?"

"It's not easy. I loved the man who was killed in Pennsylvania."

"I know."

She shook her head. "No. No, you don't know. He was my world. My gift from God. I didn't want anyone else. After he died I still didn't want anyone else. I swore I'd never touch another man. I vowed it."

"What changed that?"

"You did. No matter how hard I fought it I started getting feelings for you. And people close to me reminded me Moses was in heaven and was no longer connected to me the way I wanted to stay connected to him. I wasn't his bride. I wasn't even a date. Or a woman. He was like an angel and had moved on to other things. So it was up to me to have a life down here. Or not." Her fingers returned to his dog-tag chain. "I closed both eyes and jumped." She looked into his eyes. "I wanted you to come to me last night on the beach."

"I…I wasn't ready…not with Batman and Wizard and Juggler as an audience—"

"Are you ready now?"

He untwined her strand of blond hair. "Yeah."

"Four o'clock?"

"Four o'clock."

She tugged on his dog tags and smiled. "Promise?"

"Cross my heart and hope to die."

"No. Not that, please. Just come in one piece."

Throughout the day she felt a mixture of euphoria and guilt.

At four o'clock when he showed up, she was leaning against the side of Flapjack's hut. Not sure if she was doing the right thing, she got into the jeep without a smile or a greeting. Clenching her hands in her lap she said nothing while Raven drove.

"It's okay," he finally said. "We don't have to do this. I can take you home."

She glanced at him. "Is that what you want?"

"No. It's not what I want. But what I want is for you to be here with me, not somewhere else. Things have moved too quickly for both of us. I'll take you home."

He took the turnoff toward her neighborhood.

Her lips were tight. "Turn around."

"Beck—"

"Turn around."

"You don't have to jump into the deep end your first time back in the water after a drowning."

"You did."

"I did?"

"What happened this morning, Christian? Spins, dives, barrel rolls, treetop flying. All the things you've been afraid of doing since your brother died. You didn't ease into it. You dove in head first."

"Because I knew I might not do it if I didn't throw everything into it."

"It's the same for me. I know it is. I'll die a slow death if I don't love again. Turn around."

"What about Juggler and Wizard and Batman? And Lockjaw and Whistler will want to get in on it once they find out."

She smiled her small smile. "They'll get their dates."

"And me?"

"You're in a different category. Stop and turn around, Thunderbird, or I'll take back the controls."

He did a U-turn and got back on the main road.

She leaned her head against the seat. "Where are you taking me?"

"Nanakuli."

She looked over at him. "Are you serious?"

"I like it there."

"So we're going to walk the beach, is that it?"

"Well, if it's not taking it faster than it already is, I'd kind of hoped I could get you swimming."

"Really? Wouldn't I need a swimsuit for that?"

"Sure, but—"

"I don't normally pack one along with my flight jacket."

"I didn't think you would."

She raised her golden eyebrows. "So? Are you planning to have a beach wedding and then take me into the water as is?"

"Not yet." He patted the seat. "The PX carries swimsuits for women. So guys can buy them for their sweethearts. Or the brass for their wives. Look under your seat."

She kept her eyes on him. "You bought me a swimsuit? How would you know my size?"

"I guessed."

"You guessed?" Her eyes flared. "Did Wizard and Lockjaw lend you a hand?"

"Take it easy, Becky—"

"I am taking it easy. Just answer the question."

"No one lent me a hand. Not even the nice lady at the counter. I really did guess."

"*I really did guess.* How could you do that when you've only seen me in a flight jacket four sizes too big?"

"I've—" He stopped while he turned off the main road. "I've watched you walk out to the Piper for weeks. Walk right at me."

Blood rushed into Becky's face. "I thought you didn't notice."

"All part of my tough-guy act. Didn't you feel it?"

She slapped his arm. "Shut up, Thunderbird." She put on her Ray-Bans and stared straight ahead. "I felt it all right."

When they reached Nanakuli she stood up in the jeep before Raven brought it to a stop. "I like what I see."

"Those are seven-foot waves."

"I've been an island girl since I was sixteen. I can handle it."

Once Raven parked she took the paper bag from under her seat and darted into the bushes. "Stay in the jeep until I call you."

When she did call it was not from the bushes. "Thunderbird! Come on in! The water's great!"

He came down to the beach. She was in the surf up to her neck, letting the waves break over her and cover her in foam.

"How do you like the swimsuit?" he asked.

"It's a little snug but I love it. You have good taste."

"I can't see it. Come out of the water."

"No."

"Why not?"

"Because I'm too shy, that's why not. You have to come in."

Raven had his trunks on under his uniform. He removed the uniform quickly, folded it, and put a stone on top. Then he ran up to the edge of the waves and dove in as a large one crashed onto the sand, hurling spray. When he came up he could not see her but suddenly a hand grabbed his and she surfaced beside him, grinning and blinking the saltwater out of her eyes.

"I want to see the swimsuit," he said.

"Is that all you have on your mind?"

"I've never bought one for a woman before."

"Go stand on the shore then. I'll come to you."

Raven waded out to the surf line and turned to face her. At first she remained in the white boil of the waves with the water as high as her throat. Then she began to walk out, water and foam sliding off her arms and chest and stomach. The swimsuit was a black two-piece with a white *pikake* flower embroidered on the bottom piece and another on the top. She walked like she walked on the airfield, with a soft roll to her shoulders and her hips. He watched fascinated as she emerged, her skin glistening as the sun struck her, her long legs breaking free of the surf. She tossed her head when she reached him so that the spray scattered over his face and eyes. Then she put her arms around his neck.

"Hey. Thunderbird."

"What?"

"Kiss me."

He leaned forward to her and kissed her gently. He pulled back... and then took her close to him and kissed her again, this time with more confidence. She whispered something in his ear but he couldn't hear it. He kissed her again, lifting her in his arms and carrying her into the waves. The sea broke over them and she ran her hands and fingers over his face and hair and back as the foam streamed off their shoulders and arms.

"Are you still scared?" he asked.

A wave smashed into them. Her fingers went to his mouth. "Yes. But I don't want to stop if that's what you're asking."

"It's not what I'm asking."

"What are you asking then?"

"If we can keep going until the sun drops behind the mountains and the stars come out."

"That's a long time."

"Can you handle it?"

"Am I scrawny?" she asked, smiling as the water roared all around them, her fingers still playing with his lips.

"No."

"Ugly?"

"No."

"A snot-nosed kid?"

"No."

"Then maybe I should be asking if you can handle me. Can you?"

"How am I doing so far?"

She stopped smiling, silver water drops beading on her face. "You're taking the heart out of me. And putting it somewhere else. Somewhere safe. And I like it." She pulled his head toward her with both of her hands locked together and covered his mouth with her own, putting all her strength and spirit into the kiss. In a few moments he didn't feel the ocean surge against his legs and chest anymore or hear the breaking of the waves against their bodies.

Sixteen

"Has it become serious?"

"Yes."

Ruth looked up from her quilting. "Have you told your mother and father?"

Becky traced a pattern on the tabletop with her finger. "I've told them a little."

"And how are you feeling about it?"

"Sometimes I'm up. Sometimes I'm down. But—"

"But?"

"I want to keep going. I really care for him."

"And how does he treat you?"

Becky smiled. "I feel cherished."

Ruth returned the smile. "And how long has it been serious?"

"Since he kissed me. Two weeks ago."

"Have you given Moses back to God then?"

"I think of him. I love him. But I've taken what you and Bishop Zook said to heart. Some days it's easier to let go of him than others, though." She looked out the window at the sunset. "Now and then Raven reminds me of him—the gentleness."

"What about what was damming this Raven up inside? Has he come to terms with that?"

"Yes."

"Did you help him? Did you pray for him?"

"Yes."

"I noticed him at church last Sunday. He is a handsome young man and appears to be polite. And he attended to what Pastor Thor had to say." She made a stitch. "Are those men with him pilots also?"

"Most of them. The one in whites is with the Coast Guard."

"They all seemed friendly enough with you."

"I like them. They're good guys."

"You must introduce me sometime. Your mother was talking about having some of them over for Thanksgiving."

"They'd love that. "

Ruth sniffed. "There's nothing like good solid Amish fare for a man." She held up the corner of the quilt she was working on. "Hm." She put it back down and smoothed it out. "You're still helping this Raven hone his flying skills?"

"Not anymore. He doesn't know it but tomorrow morning things take on a new twist."

"Oh? And what is that?"

"I'll tell you after tomorrow." Becky stood and stretched. "I'm turning in. Four o'clock always comes too fast for me. *Gute nacht.*"

"*Gute nacht,* my dear."

Raven was waiting for Becky by Flapjack's office when her father dropped her off.

"That old jeep of your dad's is still putting in a day's work, eh?"

"It is." She placed a kiss on his cheek. He gathered her up in his arms, lifted her off the ground, and kissed her on the lips, holding the kiss for a long minute.

"Hey." She laughed. "Since when do you kiss me like that at six in the morning?"

"I missed you."

Her green cat eyes gleamed as she smoothed back his blond hair. "And I missed you. But we weren't apart that long."

"Even a minute can be an agony."

She arched her eyebrows. "Agony? Have you been reading Shakespeare?"

"Just the Bible. Same kind of English, isn't it?"

"Pretty much." She hugged him. "I love how you feel in my arms. Especially when you have your flight jacket on."

"Exactly how do I feel, Becky?"

"Just right." She kissed him quickly on the lips. "Now tell me why you're standing here instead of waiting out by the plane?"

"Well…you walk out to me every morning—and I'm watching you—and I got to thinking—suppose the walk makes her uncomfortable—you know, my eyes on you the whole time and all that—"

"All that? You nut." She hugged him again, harder this time. "I loved the feeling it gave me before you ever took me in your arms. What kind of feeling do you think it gives me now?"

"I just didn't want you to feel embarrassed by anything I did."

"I'm not. I feel special when you look at me. I can see what's in your eyes."

"What's that?"

"Me." She mussed his hair. "Wizard would kill a person for doing this to his hair." She started to pat it down again. "Anyway. You'd better get out to the Piper."

"Aren't you coming?"

"Not today. You don't need me anymore, hotshot."

"What are you talking about?"

"You've got the stunts under your belt."

"Beck—"

She put her hands on both sides of his face. "Hey. It's been great. It brought us together. Now you have to do what a combat pilot does all on your own." She went on her tiptoes and kissed his forehead. "Except you won't be alone up there today, Thunderbird. Watch your back."

He gave her a puzzled look, his eyebrows coming together. "What are you talking about?"

"I'm not supposed to tell you. But, after all, I am your girl, right?"

"You are."

"So check with Flapjack before you go up."

Glancing back at her he opened the door to Flapjack's office. Lockjaw was in the chair.

"Yo, Thunderbird. Whassup?"

Raven stared at him. "What are you doing here?"

"They asked me to cover."

"Where's Flapjack?"

"Search me."

Raven closed the door and turned back to Becky. He shook his head and grinned.

"You're worth fighting for," he said.

"Yeah? Well, that's what you'll be doing in the air a few minutes from now."

"Okay, beautiful, what's going on?"

"Flapjack is coming up after you. He'll be on your tail."

"Flapjack. Is that it?"

"No. My dad's going to be on your case too."

"Your dad. Jude Whetstone. The ace. People talk about him the way they talk about Eddie Rickenbacker. He was that good."

"He's still that good. Watch yourself."

The early color in the sky lit his blue eyes. It made her smile.

"What's so funny?" he asked.

"Nothing's funny. You're gorgeous, that's all."

"Sure I am." He looked toward his Piper. As he did he noticed two other J-3s warming up on the runway. "Is that them?"

"It is."

"Baron von Richthofen and his Flying Circus?"

"Yup."

"Wish me well."

"Of course." She suddenly wrapped her arms around him and gave him a fast and hard kiss. "You've come a long way. Now keep going. God bless you, Christian Scott Raven."

"It's just a game. There's no war."

Her eyes were a dark jungle green, the kind of green he saw when he hiked back into the thick growth of Oahu's forests. "People are dying by the millions, Raven. In Europe. In Russia. In China. There's a war. You're supposed to save them. Remember? You're a fighter pilot. Promise me you'll save them."

"Aren't you going just a little bit overboard?"

"Ask my brother. He watched pregnant women get raped and their newborns bayoneted."

"Beck—"

"You're my man now. Aren't you?"

"Sure, Beck, but—"

"Save them."

He ran a thumb gently over her dark blond eyebrows. "You have so much beauty inside and out. How can a guy say no to you?" He began to head across the runway. "I miss your walk to the J-3 already."

"I'll do other walks for you, Thunderbird."

"Where and when?"

"I'll start when you come in for your landing."

"You're going to come to me?" he turned and walked backward a moment, grinning.

She hugged her leather jacket around her. "I'll run."

Lockjaw came out of the office once Raven took off. No sooner was Raven up than the two Pipers that had been waiting lifted and headed after him. Raven went for height and Jude and Flapjack split apart, one going to Raven's left, the other to his right.

Lockjaw grunted. "They take all this stuff with the Japanese seriously, don't they?"

Becky hugged herself more tightly. "So long as they remember it's a training exercise, not the real thing."

Lockjaw popped several Chiclets into his mouth. "Babe, every time you go up it's the real thing." He glanced at her. "Don't worry. He knows how to take care of himself."

"I just…I just don't want him to come in too low…hit buildings or trees by mistake—"

"He won't."

"Twisting and turning to get away from two war pilots? How do you know?"

"He has a better reason to land than he's ever had before." Lockjaw grinned and chewed. "Lucky stiff."

Despite her anxiety Becky couldn't hold back her smile. "You're crazy, Lockjaw."

"That's what Mom always says."

It began. Jude, in Piper number five, went at Raven head on. When Raven dove to avoid him Flapjack pounced on his back. Raven swung left and right and finally barrel rolled, flew upside down, then looped around on Flapjack's tail and would not be shaken off until Jude bore down on him from above. Raven dove sharply to treetop level, and Becky was sure she saw palm fronds spin into the air, snapped lose by the turbulence. He was closely followed by Jude while Flapjack maneuvered to get above him for an attack once he pulled up. But Raven fooled them both, actually touching his wheels down on an open field, the dust flying, while Jude ripped past overhead, then jumping up onto Jude's tail, gaining height rapidly, finally breaking away to dive on Flapjack, who suddenly found himself a thousand feet below Raven.

Lockjaw popped more Chiclets. "Your boyfriend seems to be holding his own. But now comes the tough part."

Becky slipped her eyes onto him. "What are you talking about?"

"They didn't tell you because they knew you'd tell him. Surprise." He jerked upward with his chin.

An aircraft flashed out of the sun at Raven's Piper. Becky's mouth opened. It was a P-40 painted army green. She knew Raven would have to be as startled as she was but he kept his cool and waited until the P-40 was on top of him before dropping quickly and making it tear past just as Jude had been forced to do minutes before. Then he was up and on the Warhawk's tail. This lasted only a second before the P-40 streaked away. But now both Jude and Flapjack were on Raven's back.

"That isn't right!" Becky was shouting. "These souped-up J-3s can only go one-forty tops. The P-40 can go twice as fast!"

Lockjaw chewed. "Actually the Warhawk can go more than twice as fast—three-sixty."

"It's not fair! How can he fight against that?"

"War's not fair, babe. Let's see how he does."

"See how he does? Three against one, and the P-40 goes almost four hundred miles an hour?"

Lockjaw chewed rapidly. "Don't worry. It's Billy Skipp. He was an ace too. He knows what he's doing."

The P-40 roared over Raven's Piper as it fled Jude and Flapjack and then banked to come back for another pass. Raven decided to go into a corkscrew, diving and spinning away from the Piper J-3s and the Warhawk. Billy Skipp went after him, diving sharply on the spiraling yellow plane.

"Are they crazy?" Becky yelled. "They could kill someone!"

"The whole area's been cleared. No one's on the ground. No other Pipers are up. In fact no other aircraft are allowed in this zone."

"What if Raven heads out to sea and over the beaches?"

"They'll go after him. But they'll stay high."

"These guys are all cowboys! Who knows what Skipp will do?"

"Who knows what the enemy will do? The Zeros are fast and can turn on a dime. Same with the Messerschmitts."

"How can Skipp be sure he won't ram him?"

"Well. He's pretty sure. Skipp's quite the aviator."

"What if Raven jigs instead of doing the jag that Skipp expects?"

Lockjaw only chewed and did not respond.

The tumbling and turning and twisting and diving went on for another fifteen minutes before Skipp waggled the P-40's wings and vanished. First Jude landed and then Flapjack. Raven waited until they were down, circled the airfield once, then suddenly streaked in low and buzzed the two men as they climbed out of their Pipers. They ducked and Flapjack went sprawling.

Lockjaw laughed. "Cheeky brat! They'll spank him for that!"

Becky's eyes flashed. "It's no more than they deserve."

"Don't be too hard on your dad. When the day comes this kind of training could save Lover Boy's life." Lockjaw glanced at her. "And the lives of others."

"I'm going to him, Lockjaw."

"That's the right thing to do."

Becky started to run. Raven brought his J-3 in while she ran past her father and Flapjack. He had hardly leaped onto the tarmac before she hurtled into his arms and pulled him close.

"Hey. Easy." He laughed. "You trying to finish the job for them?"

"I can't believe they did that to you. Are you okay?"

"It was quite a party. And the P-40 takes the cake."

"You took the cake. I'm so proud of you."

"All I did was hang on by my fingernails."

"Three on one. They're crazy."

"The infantry and the Marines crawl under barbed wire while guys fire machine guns over their heads. I guess I'm lucky the P-40 didn't make it a live-fire exercise."

She drew back to look at him. "You aren't upset?"

"Well, I—" He grinned. "I haven't had so much fun since I barnstormed on my own. Before Timmy Dynamite and the old man's wild ideas."

"Are you kidding me?"

"I felt like I was alive." He tilted up her chin with a curled finger. "Almost as alive as when you love me up."

"But not quite."

"Not quite."

She looked behind her. "They're being gentlemen. Dad and Flapjack are waiting by the office to talk to you."

"Come with me to the other side of the plane."

"Why? Do you have a bullet hole to show me?"

"Hey. I'll have to check."

They walked under the wing to the side facing away from Jude and Flapjack and Lockjaw and he suddenly pinned her up against the fuselage and put his arms under her jacket and around her white T-shirt.

"Listen. I want to tell you how good you look."

"Oh, yeah?"

"I don't care if it's a black bathing suit or Hawaiian skirt with a seashell necklace or your flying gear with a jacket big enough for two men to climb into. The first thing I thought after the dogfight was, *Great! I get to see Becky Whetstone.*"

"A woman likes to hear that. I spend a lot of time picking out my clothes every morning."

"Yeah?"

She smiled and put her head against his chest. "No."

"Of course you could wear a sack and look stunning."

"You and your superlatives. Why don't you just kiss me? Isn't that why you hauled me out of sight behind this Piper?"

"I like the word *superlative*. I should use it more."

"You use superlatives enough, believe me."

"*Of the highest order or quality or degree. Surpassing or superior to all others.* Isn't that it?"

"So are we in college or behind an airplane in Hawaii?" She reached up for his dog tags and yanked on them. "Hey? What does a girl have to do to get some attention around here?"

"A girl like you? Not much."

His kiss was slow and deep. When it ended he immediately began another. She tried to say something after that but a third kiss, longer and more penetrating than the other two, took away her words. He was going to start a fourth when she put her fingers on his lips.

"You've proved your point," she said.

"You want me to stop?"

"No, I don't want you to stop. But Dad and the other two are still waiting by the hut and if we don't go there soon I know for sure they'll cross the runway and show up here."

He began to kiss her neck and ear. "So can we get together after you finish with your students?"

She closed her eyes as he kissed her. "Christian Scott Raven, I am trying to convey the sense that we need to get somewhere else quickly before somewhere else comes to us. You're not helping."

"One more kiss then, and we're off."

Long and sweet. You remind me so much of Moses. He pulled me behind an airplane so he could kiss me too. And he kissed me until I had no more strength. You do the same thing. I don't care if my father and Flapjack show up. Let them come. I'd rather be here in your arms. I'm blessed here.

"Lieutenant Raven."

It was Billy Skipp.

Raven jumped back from Becky and saluted. "Sir."

"I was going to say as you were, but perhaps not." He smiled and put his hands on his hips. "I landed the P-40 at Wheeler and had Skinny drive me back here. I think it's important to talk to the aviator responsible when a Piper J-3 gives a P-40 Warhawk grief."

"I'd hardly say I gave you grief, Colonel. Sometimes a slower plane just makes it harder for a fighter aircraft to react appropriately."

"I see. Thanks for the tip."

"You had me dead to rights a number of times, sir."

"And you dodged me a number of times, Lieutenant." Skipp looked at Becky. "So here we have your trainer, Miss Whetstone."

She was standing at attention beside Raven. "Sir."

"Lord knows how I'd love to have you in uniform and in a cockpit." He waved his hand. "Both of you stand down." He put out a hand. "I was being rough, bouncing you with a P-40. But you were being tricky. Well done."

Raven shook Skipp's hand. "Thank you, sir."

"Becky. You put everything you had into this pilot. You helped him break through a lot of barriers. I had no doubt you could make the difference. Now he's on his own."

"Yes, sir."

"I may have a few other air force pilots to send your way. Think you can handle it?"

"I can handle it, sir."

"You don't need to fall in love with them. Just teach the boys to do barrel rolls quick and tight."

"I'll do my best, sir."

"I'm sure you will." He snapped them both a salute. "We shouldn't be saluting one another, Whetstone. But it only seems right. Carry on."

Skipp walked off, ducking under the engine and heading back across the runway.

"Hey," said Raven. "He kind of indicated that you fell in love with me during training. Is that true?"

She grinned and punched him on the shoulder. "Shut up, Thunderbird. If it ever happens, trust me, you'll be the last to know."

Seventeen

"Happy Thanksgiving, everyone. I'll ask Mr. Whetstone to say grace." Lyyndaya smiled at the pilots seated around the table. "He used to be Captain Whetstone."

Jude stood up. "Twenty years ago I was a lot of things. Now I'm a flight trainer and the happily married father of two. Let's give thanks."

After he had prayed the food began to make the rounds. Besides family there were Shooter, Lockjaw, Juggler, Wizard, Whistler, Batman, and two naval men, Harrison of the Coast Guard and his buddy, Dave Goff of the *USS Arizona*. Everyone was seated at a large table set up outdoors on the patio. Becky had invited two of her Hawaiian women students, Kalino and Hani, as well as one of the new Hawaiian pilots Flapjack had hired, Manuku. Flapjack and his wife, Shirley, sat next to him. Raven had been seated as far away from Becky as he could possibly be placed, with Nate on one side and Jude on the other.

"I love these dresses you ladies are wearing," said Wizard. "*Muumuus*—right?"

Lyyndaya nodded. "That's right."

"Bright and flowery. All of you look swell."

"Thank you, Lieutenant."

"Mrs. Whetstone," Juggler spoke up between mouthfuls, "this is just like a good old homegrown Wisconsin meal. Where did you get a bird this big in Hawaii? Nobody breeds turkeys on Oahu, do they?"

Lyyndaya smiled a small smile that made everyone think of Becky.

"You just have to know where to look, Juggler. I'm glad you like the meal. It's actually very Pennsylvanian. With a few Hawaiian touches."

"Thank goodness for that." Manuku grinned. "It's great to see the *kalua* pig dish and the blue marlin. Who grilled the marlin?"

"Why?" responded Lyyndaya.

"It's top-notch."

"The guy sitting beside you. Your boss."

Manuku stared at Flapjack in surprise. "You're kidding me."

Flapjack dug into his white turkey meat. "I've lived here long enough to know how to grill like a *kanaka maoli*."

"Most nonnatives would have overcooked the marlin, boss. They always do. It's traditional for them to burn it."

"I started a new tradition. This *kama'aina* does it like a local."

"Well, boss, I guess you're pretty local now." Manuku spooned up some soup. "You make the *saimin* noodle soup too? And the *poke* with the tuna and red cabbage?"

"Not me. Kalino did the *poke*—"

"No, my mother," Kalino interrupted.

"Excuse me. Kalino's mother did the *poke*. And Hani—or her mother—did the soup."

Hani smiled. "My grandmother."

Flapjack lifted his knife and fork high in the air. "There you have it. Authentic Pennsylvania Amish cuisine meets authentic Hawaiian delicacies."

Manuku pointed with his knife. "What kind of pie is that?"

"Too soon for pie, Manu."

"It's shoofly pie," answered Ruth. "A molasses pie."

"A molasses pie." Manuku looked doubtful. "Will I like it?"

"You'll love it. I'll cut you a Hawaiian-sized piece when you're ready."

Manuku smiled at her. "Thank you, ma'am. I'll burn through this plate and be ready in five."

"Ruth. Not ma'am."

Manuku inclined his head. "Ruth it is. A great name. What does it mean?"

"Lifelong friend."

Manuku stopped eating. "Lifelong friend? I love that."

"Thank you. And what about your own name? Manuku?"

"A bird. Moving in the air like a bird."

"Well. That's appropriate for an aviator."

"I used to be afraid of planes. The ones with two wings. Monoplanes looked better to me. Safer than cars. So Mom and Dad paid for my lessons instead of sending me to college."

Ruth looked down the table. "What about Kalino? And Hani? What do they mean?"

Kalino was buttering bread. "Bright one."

Hani was dipping into a mixture of cabbage and potato. "Hani means to move lightly." She smiled at Becky. "So I want to move lightly in the air and please my instructor."

Becky winked. "You're doing very well, Hani. And, the truth is, you do have a light touch. So do you, Kalino. It's a pleasure to go up with you both. Pretty soon Mr. Peterson will be offering some more contracts for instructors and the pair of you will be first in line."

Kalino glanced at the pilot next to her. "Some names are harder to understand than others."

Lockjaw still had his Ray-Bans on. He grinned. "Kalino. Trust me. If you knew me you'd know my name was easy to understand."

"And Wizard? Whistler? Batman?"

Batman looked up from his grilled marlin and *poke.* "Bite me."

She laughed, her dark eyes flashing. "What?"

Whistler downed the last of his punch. "Now you know. Bats bite. Some draw blood."

Flapjack wiped his mouth with a red napkin. "It's amazing you've been able to put all these mainland dishes together, Lyyndaya, considering the shortages in the shops."

"I couldn't find anything I needed for a dessert I wanted to make," Shirley, his wife, said. "So I picked up coconut and pineapple and bananas instead."

"The ships are bringing in defense material." Jude put his empty plate to one side. "Airplane parts. Aviation fuel. Ammo. Rifles. Trucks and jeeps. There's no room for much else. The shopkeepers are pretty sore."

Flapjack reached for a toothpick from a glass cup. "What do they expect? Every week things get worse with the Japanese. What was it the ambassador from Japan promised the secretary of state a few days ago?"

"Nomura told Cordell Hull they would pull some of their troops out of China in return for a normalization of relations between the US and Japan. Some of their troops, not all of them. The White House said that wasn't good enough so it was no deal."

Nate spoke up. "Will there be other offers, do you think?"

Jude glanced at his son. "From Tokyo? I hope so. Cooler heads sometimes prevail."

"What will it take?"

"From where America stands? Complete withdrawal from China. Nothing less."

"Will we get it?"

"I don't know."

Ruth stood up. "Let's try and keep things lighthearted, shall we? It *is* Thanksgiving Day." She began gathering up plates and Becky rose to help her. "Who wants dessert?"

Manuku raised a hand. "Shoofly pie, please, Miss Ruth."

"Hang on to your extra fork then."

Nate turned to Raven and whispered, "Do you think they will land an army here like they did in China?"

Raven shook his head. "I'm no expert, but if they land troops anywhere it will probably be in the Philippines. We have a big base there."

"You're positive they wouldn't come here?"

"Not positive. But Hawaii's pretty isolated and doesn't have the resources they need. There's really nothing they want. The Philippines have iron, copper, and nickel as well as good anchorage, and they're a lot closer to Japan."

Nate's face was pale. "Would they send you there? Or my sister? Or father?"

"No. Your dad isn't in the military anymore. And your sister never was. They're not going anywhere."

"What about you?"

"I don't know. They might move planes and pilots to the US base there if things get worse with Japan."

"They're not getting any better. Excuse me."

Nate got up from the table and left the patio. His father noticed. And Becky, who was serving pie. She set down a plate and came toward Raven.

"What's up with my brother?" she asked.

"I'm not sure. He seems pretty worried about the Japanese invading Hawaii."

"What did you tell him?"

"That there's nothing here. They'd be more likely to put an army in the Philippines. Then he got anxious about you or me or your dad being posted there. I reminded him that you and your father were not in the military and couldn't be sent anywhere. But it didn't seem to calm him down."

"Come with me a minute."

They left Ruth chatting with Manuku and the pilots hovering around Hani and Kalino while Flapjack and Jude sat with Harrison and Goff. Nate was sitting on a bench under a cluster of tall palms about a hundred yards from the house. Becky took Raven's hand.

"I'm worried about him. Instead of getting better he's been getting worse since we moved to Hawaii."

Raven watched Nate put his head in his hands. "I'm no Army shrink but I can see what's eating him. He's afraid of getting caught up in another Nanking. Or those he loves getting caught up in one. So whether the Japanese land troops here or in Manila Bay or anywhere in the world it doesn't matter—it puts fear in his gut. He's even treating me like family, worked up I'll get shipped to the Philippines or somewhere else in harm's way."

"I don't know what to do."

"Neither do I, Beck. But you and I have both bottled things up that took the heart out of us. He's doing the same thing. Nanking is chewing on his soul like a worm." He began to walk toward Nate. "Let's try."

He sat beside Nate. "Is it okay if I park myself here?"

Nate looked at him with large blank eyes. "It doesn't matter. They could show up at any time."

"Nate. I couldn't fly well for the longest time. Did you know about that?"

"Sure. I know something about it."

"There had been an air accident. My little brother was killed. I blamed myself. Swore I'd never do stunt flying again. Which meant I could never do combat flying."

Nate clasped his hands together so hard they turned white. "Yeah."

"So it was your sister, Nate. She helped me. Just by giving me a safe place to talk and get it off my chest. It wasn't an overnight cure, but it started the ball rolling. I'm shaking the fear of stunt flying, Nate. They're not going to kick me out of the Army Air Forces after all. I'm getting out from under it."

"That's good."

Becky knelt by her brother and put a hand on his arm. "You know about Moses. I don't have to tell you how his death devastated me."

"It devastated all of us."

"I know. But he was going to be my husband, Nate."

Nate said nothing.

"I swore I'd never love another man. Never. It made me a holy terror. And when I started having feelings for Christian I was frightened. Frightened of breaking my vow. Frightened I wouldn't be capable of having any sort of intimate relationship with him, that I wouldn't know how to talk or listen or show him that I cared."

"So? You're doing that now."

"Bit by bit. Only because I told him about the man I loved and lost. Only because I let go of Moses and let him be in heaven while I went about trying to live on earth. Only because Ruth talked to me about it and Bishop Zook. Only because I prayed to be free of what happened that day in Pennsylvania."

"What is it you want me to do?"

Raven leaned back. "We kept the stuff that hurt us and ate at us right inside." He put a fist over his stomach. "It made us sicker and sicker. Like holding in poison instead of spitting it out."

"You think I'm doing that?"

Becky rubbed Nate's arm. "He talked about his brother's death. I talked about Moses' death. Maybe you can talk about the death of the people you tried to save in Nanking."

Nate's face contorted and turned blood-red. "It was thousands. Hundreds of thousands. Every day the Japanese bayoneted and raped and buried people alive. Every day they shot. Every day they beheaded. One day two officers had a contest to see who could decapitate the most people without replacing their sword. One officer killed a hundred and eight, the other a hundred and five. They laughed about it and drank *sake*. The Japanese newspapers treated it like a baseball game: *The two officers went into extra innings.*" Nate gripped the front of Raven's uniform. "It wasn't just your brother." He looked wildly at Becky. "It wasn't just Moses. It was thousands of babies every week. Thousands of women. Thousands of men. Children. Grandmothers. Grandfathers." He grabbed Becky's hand and squeezed it until her bones cracked. She winced but did not pull away. "Every day I was covered in blood and gore from head to foot. Do you know what that's like? Head to foot."

"Tell us," she said.

"You can't handle it. Go back to your Thanksgiving dinner."

"Tell us."

"I can't…it puts the faces back in my head…"

"The faces are there anyway, aren't they, Nate?" asked Raven. "Eating? Sleeping? Don't they always come to you? My kid brother always came to me. Falling out of the plane. Looking at me with those dark eyes of his. And my father would show up—angry, yelling, hitting me with his fist, telling me I killed him."

Nate put his head into Raven's chest and began to weep, his hands grasping for Raven's shoulders. "I hid as many as I could. They found them. Pulled them out of the closets and basements. Shoved bayonets down their throats. Again and again. I prayed…but they killed again and again—"

"They didn't kill them all." Becky put her hands on his back. "You saved children. You saved families."

"We couldn't stop them. There weren't enough of us. The Chinese didn't have enough planes. They didn't have enough tanks. They couldn't fight. They had nothing left."

"We'll fight them, Nate," Raven said. "I promise. If they come to the islands. We'll use all our planes and all our ships. We'll do it here. We'll do it in the Philippines. Everywhere we have to."

"They'll overwhelm us."

"No."

"God knows they'll overwhelm us."

"Then God knows we won't give up. We'll keep on fighting back with rocks we dig out of the earth with our fingernails."

"It's no good. It's no good."

His weeping intensified. Raven and Becky put their arms around him. She glanced back at the house and saw her father standing at the doors of the *lanai*. He was alone.

"If I could lie down." They were barely able to make out what Nate was saying. His voice was suddenly weak.

Becky stood up. "There's a hammock right over here." She helped Raven get her brother to his feet and shuffle the few steps to where the hammock was slung between two trees. They laid him down in it, balancing him, careful to make sure he didn't suddenly roll out. He seemed to fall asleep within moments. Raven sat down with his back to one of the palm trees.

"It'll take more talk," he said. "A lot more talk."

Becky looked down at her brother. "I know that. But it's a start, isn't it?"

"Yeah." Raven gazed up through the palm fronds at the blue November sky. "The old man was smart. He wouldn't hit me anywhere others could see. Nothing on the face or hands or neck. But under my clothes, that's where the bruises were. All in different stages of healing. Fresh ones were purple and black. Not so fresh and they had more of a red tinge. Yellow and green? Healing pretty good."

"I'm sorry, Christian."

"Funny. He didn't care where he hit Mom. Didn't care if people saw her black eyes or broken nose or swollen cheeks. But for me it was all under my shirt and pants."

She knelt and put her arms around him. "You mean a great deal to me. Not many men would talk to another man the way you spoke with my brother."

"The wounded helping the wounded."

She snuggled up next to him. "Put your arm around me." He did. "Tighter." He did that as well. "Pray for me, please, will you? Not just for me. For Nate."

"I'm not a big one for praying out loud in front of an audience."

"It doesn't have to be long. And I'm not an audience. I'm your woman."

"Are you?"

"I am."

"I like the *muumuu* on you. The color of the dress goes with your eyes. And the white flowers on the dress go with your teeth."

"My teeth?" She closed her eyes and leaned her head on his shoulder. "You nut. How's Nate?"

"Breathing deep and slow."

"Thank you, God. Now pray a bit, please, Christian."

The sound of male voices raised in song suddenly came down to then from the house.

> *Eternal Father, strong to save.*
> *Whose arm hath bound the restless wave,*
> *Who bidd'st the mighty ocean deep*
> *Its own appointed limits keep;*
> *Oh, hear us when we cry to Thee,*
> *For those in peril on the sea!*

"That's Dad's favorite hymn," Becky said, her eyes still closed. "He always gets us to sing it at Thanksgiving and Christmas and Easter."

"That's about sailors, though."

"They added another verse or two to the hymnbook last year. Just wait."

O Spirit, whom the Father sent
To spread abroad the firmament,
O Wind of heaven, by thy might
Save all who dare the eagle's flight,
And keep them by thy watchful care
From every peril in the air.

Raven closed his own eyes. "I've never heard that before. I like it."

Becky hummed the tune. *"Save all who dare the eagle's flight, and keep them by thy watchful care from every peril in the air."*

"God." Raven began his prayer. "You know what Nate's been through. Clean and bandage his wounds. You know what Beck's been through—please do the same for her. I like to fly, Lord, but I'd rather not fly to kill. So please bring our world to a place of peace. That won't happen overnight in places like China or Europe or Russia. So until that time of peace defend the nations. And give the nations the means and the will to save the innocent. In the name of Jesus."

Becky was asleep, her fingers curling around his as her breathing deepened. He took in the scent of her hair, a wonderful mixture of heat and perfume and skin, kissed her on the top of her head, and let her rest. She murmured something over and over again but he could not make it out. The men's voices drifted down from the house a final time.

O Trinity of love and power,
Our brethren shield in danger's hour;
From rock and tempest, fire and foe,
Protect them whereso'er they go,
Thus evermore shall rise to thee
Glad praise from air and land and sea.

Eighteen

Becky rolled over on her back behind the sand dune and bushes. "I'm cold."

Raven was toweling himself off. "How can you be cold in Hawaii?"

"The sun went behind a cloud."

He looked up. "It's a small cloud."

"And there's a wind."

"What wind?"

"Breeze. Wind. Whatever you want to call it."

"Beck, come on."

"Hey. It's my invitation to you." She extended her arms. "Warm me up, Thunderbird."

He lay down beside her and she rolled into his arms.

A minute later she sighed. "It's working."

"What's working?"

"I'm warmer already."

"Warm enough?"

"Oh, no, not warm enough. You can't shake me that easily, hotshot." She hugged him closer.

A moment later he said, "It's like flying."

"What is?"

"You are. The way you make me feel."

She kissed his neck softly. "Flying?"

"Yeah. Flying fast and high through the cumulus, right through it to the perfect blue on the other side."

"Sounds good."

"Except this is better."

She brushed her damp hair back and forth over his face and eyes. "Yeah?"

"Oh, yeah."

"How fast and how high are you flying now, hotshot?"

"Ceiling—forty thousand feet. Air speed—five hundred and twenty-five miles per hour."

"That's pretty fast, Thunderbird. I don't think we have any plane that can go through the sky that fast, do we?"

"Not yet. Someday though."

They lay together on the beach quietly. Then Becky whispered, "Pick me up and carry me into the surf."

"But you're dry and warm."

"Exactly. And getting dry and warm was all the fun. I want to do it again."

Raven shot to his feet, scooping her up so suddenly she shrieked and laughed. He ran over the dune and out of the bushes to the beach. Five or six men were surfing a hundred yards away and two women lay on their towels but that was it. He plunged into the big waves, her arms around his neck, and waded out until the ocean was crashing over their heads and practically knocking him off his feet. Becky shrieked again and again as seven- and eight-foot breakers pounded them.

Interlacing her fingers behind his neck she pulled his face toward hers and kissed him slowly, just as a wave knocked them to their knees. He laughed and grabbed at her hand, walking with her, both of them staggering, out of the crashing sea and back to their hideout in the bush behind the dunes.

"Did anyone ever tell you how perfect you are?" he asked.

"I'll never tell."

"How much you're like Hawaii?"

"How can I be like an island?"

"Your beauty. Eyes like green palms. Hair the color of light. Skin as smooth as sand, freckles like—"

"Oh, shut up about the freckles."

"But I love them."

"You love my freckles? Do you love me?"

He bent forward and kissed her gently.

"Does that answer your question?"

"Yes, but don't stop. Keep telling me."

"I thought you might want to head back into the water again."

"No. Let's just stay like this." She put her hands on both sides of his face. "Your eyes are bluer than the sky is. Let me float around in them instead." One finger curled around his dog tags. "Christian Scott Raven. What about your other names?"

"I don't have any other names."

"You must have. I was thinking about it at Thanksgiving. My students are native Hawaiians. So is the new pilot. Their names mean something."

"So does Rebecca. It means captivating. Which is exactly right."

"I didn't know that. I heard it had other meanings."

"Trust me. I'm a Hebrew scholar. That's the right meaning. And my name means a follower of Christ."

"Okay. But you're native. Like our Hawaiian friends. Except you're Cherokee."

"On my mother's side."

"Do you have a Cherokee name?"

Raven grew quiet. "We don't share the names."

She ran a finger over his mouth. "Sometimes you do."

"How do you know?"

"I'll bet you do."

He pulled away and sat on the sand beside her. "It happens."

"Hey." She put a hand on his arm and got into a cross-legged position. "I'm sorry. I didn't mean to tease you about that. I know it's a serious thing. I should have throttled back. Forget it. It doesn't matter."

His blue eyes rested on her. "Sure it matters. Knowing the name will give you a certain measure of power over me. So the Old Ones believed."

"I don't want power over you."

"Well, you have some already, in case you haven't noticed."

She kissed his hand. "That's different."

"Love makes it different." Raven smiled. "It's okay, Becky. I was raised by my mother to believe in a higher power than all that. I've given my entire life over to Christ. He has the power. No one and nothing else. Still, I wouldn't tell just anybody my name. It's kind of a special thing."

"I understand that."

"As a matter of fact, I've never told anyone else. Only Mom knows. A chief back in Oklahoma knew but he's dead. You'll be the only other person in the world."

"Really. It doesn't matter. I'm sorry I brought it up. Just take me in your arms again and let's—"

"*Waya*. Wolf."

"*Waya?*"

"That's the name." His eyes seemed to take on a deeper blue.

"When can I use it?" she asked.

"When we're alone."

"How about the times I pray for you?"

"Sure. But I want it to be a you-and-me name. You're very special to me. I trust you. I want this secret to reflect that."

She put her arms around him from behind. "That has to be the greatest compliment you've ever paid me."

"It's bigger than a compliment. It's truth."

Becky hugged him. Then she turned her head so that her cheek rested against his back. "Tell me about your mother."

"My mother?"

"All I've heard about is how rough your father was. Say something about your mother."

"You sure? Talking about mothers isn't likely to promote romantic passion."

"I can wait for the passion."

"Really?"

She slapped his arm. "Hey. Just stifle it and tell me about your mom."

"She was where I put down roots. She was the one who prayed with me and read the Bible to me in Cherokee. Tucked me in. Wanted me to fly—but not for money. To worship God, to worship him with my wings, with my flight, like a falcon or red-tailed hawk."

"Or eagle."

"Yeah. The eagle. But then the wolf came into the picture."

"Hard to say something good about the wolf. Especially after going through the Bible. They're always a symbol of some kind of evil."

"A superficial reading takes you there. But the man who named me was one of the Old Ones and a Christ Walker." Raven interlaced his fingers. "So he brought two verses together and made something new."

"What?"

"Habakkuk 1:8—I'd be *more fierce than the evening wolves.* But he coupled it with Isaiah 65:25—*the wolf and the lamb shall feed together… they shall not hurt nor destroy in all my holy mountain.*"

"So what does that mean?"

"He wouldn't tell me. He said it was for me to figure out. I had to fast and pray. Worship the Creator. Honor the Christ, the Messiah who had come to our people by surprise—surprise because he came with people who were harsh to us. And cruel."

Becky gently turned his shoulders so he was facing her. "Not me."

He rested his hands on her shoulders and stroked her cheekbones with his thumbs. "No. Not you. My mother thought my name and the Bible verses had to do with protecting the weak and the innocent, those who were pretty much defenseless. The fierce wolf who uses his ferocity to safeguard life, not take it. Maybe I'm on that path again. I don't know. I've been off it a long time."

"Because of your father. Because of your brother's death."

"Well. You can't blame the world forever. Eventually you have to do what's right. I thank God you showed up with your white T-shirt and oversized flight jacket and cat's eyes."

"*Cat's eyes?*" Becky drew her knees up to her chest. "I didn't do much really."

"You did everything."

"No, I didn't. You had to do things. God had to do things. But I'm glad I helped a bit."

"More than a bit." He kissed her lightly on the lips.

"Yeah?" She smiled into the hand that cupped her face.

"Yeah."

Becky leaned her head into his. "I don't know how far I can go with this. Maybe as far as marriage. Maybe not. But that probably doesn't interest you."

"Why couldn't you go as far as marriage?"

"Because I was almost there once. And even with giving Moses back to God and trying to get on with my life I'm finding it difficult to picture being at the altar."

"With me?"

"With anyone."

"What about engagement?"

"I don't think I can do that either."

Raven gave her a big smile. "Well, don't worry, I haven't given either of those things a thought."

Her eyes flashed. "Oh, you haven't?"

"No. Just being with you keeps me busy enough. What to say. How to act. I don't have time for the stuff you mentioned. Just you, right now, that's enough."

The cat's eyes emerged. "But you're a wolf."

"I am."

"Are you a nice wolf?"

"A very nice wolf."

She lay back slowly on the sand. "So then be nice to me."

He ran his hand gently over her cheek and neck. "I'll do my best."

Nineteen

O kay. We stick together. Both jeeps. No one takes off on his own. The Shore Patrol is keeping an eye on us, so everybody be on their best behavior. Okay, Lockjaw? Batman?"

Batman squinted over the water at Ford Island. "What do they think we're going to do, Harrison? Run off with a battleship?"

Harrison leaned over the wheel of one of the jeeps. He was in his whites. "I think the SP is more concerned with some sort of Army-Navy rivalry turning into a Monday-afternoon brawl."

Harrison's buddy, Dave Goff, also in his whites, was at the wheel of the other jeep. "I thought the SP only dealt with stuff on shore—you know, sailors on leave, the ones hanging out at bars."

Harrison shrugged. "They're around. So let's all be good."

"Aye, aye, skipper," said Shooter.

Harrison put his jeep into gear. "We have clearance. We don't want them to revoke it. Let's head over the causeway. We're coming in at the north end of the island and starting down the eastern shore."

The two jeeps drove slowly to Ford Island. Harrison, Batman, Juggler, Shooter, Raven, and Becky were piled in the first jeep. Goff, Jude, Kalino, Hani, Wizard, Lockjaw, Whistler, and Manuku in the second. Wizard was wedged up against Hani and Lockjaw up against Kalino. Harrison began to speak loudly and point as the big ships loomed larger and larger on their left.

"Okay, so we're at the north end of the row. The first one is the *Nevada*. Fore River Shipbuilding laid her keel in their yard in Quincy,

Massachusetts. Launched in July 1914. Roosevelt was Secretary of the Navy then and he attended that. Her twin sister is the *Oklahoma*. Identical ships for the most part. We can't see the *Oklahoma* too well from here. It's way back and anchored next to the *Maryland*. Right behind the *Nevada* is Goff's ship."

The jeeps pulled onto the island and were waved ahead. Harrison took a road that led as close to the water's edge as he was allowed to go. He stopped in front of a ship that towered over the *Nevada* moored in front of it. He nodded at Goff.

Goff stood up in his jeep. "My lady. The *Arizona*. Roosevelt was there when they laid the keel in Brooklyn. Launched her in 1915. Pennsylvania class—you can see how much bigger it is than the Nevada class. Hull number BB-39. The Navy modernized her at Norfolk in 1929—new antiaircraft guns, among other things. We were based in California until last year. Now the whole crew has turned Hawaiian."

Manuku, Hani, and Kalino laughed.

"How many of you?" Manuku asked.

"Fourteen hundred."

Batman whistled. "That's a handful for your Shore Patrol, Goff, if they should come out and try and take on the Army Air Forces."

"It would be over before the Shore Patrol could show up, sir."

"Unless we went easy on them."

Goff grinned. "Unless."

"It's massive." Becky was staring up at the funnels. "It looks like an ordinary gray warship from shore and now I'm sitting under a giant."

"Yes, ma'am. It's pretty easy to feel like a dwarf on Battleship Row."

Harrison eased his jeep forward down the line. "This is the *Tennessee*. Anchored alongside is the *West Virginia*."

Becky looked back and forth between the *Arizona* and the *Tennessee*. "Is it possible that the *Tennessee* is larger than the *Arizona*?"

Goff snorted. "Not by much."

Harrison smiled. "The *Arizona*'s about 608 feet long but the *Tennessee*—I boned up on all this for y'all—is 624. *Tennessee* displaces almost 41,000 tons but *Arizona* only a bit over 37,000. So you have a sharp eye, Miss Whetstone. Glad you're an aviator." He pointed. "*West Virginia*,

'Wee-Vee,' is one of our three Colorado-class battlewagons. Those are our newest and best. Sorry, Goff."

Goff folded his arms over his chest. "Matter of opinion."

"Wee-Vee was launched in '21 at Newport News in Virginia. Fourteen hundred officers and men—like *Arizona*. Incredible armor protection. Different lines than the ships built in '14, '15, or '16, like the *Nevada* and *Arizona*. Her sister ship is the *Maryland,* astern of the *Tennessee*—see how similar she is to the *West Virginia*? Built in Newport News too, launched in '20, exact same length. And anchored alongside her—*Oklahoma*. 'Member I mentioned it was sister to the *Nevada* that's at the top of the row? Same class, same lines, launched in 1916, New York." He pointed. "Glance back at the *Nevada* and compare the two. Both of them are a lot smaller and shorter than ships like the *Tennessee, West Virginia, Maryland.*"

He glanced around. "Have I lost you? The guys call me the Professor. How's everyone doing?"

Raven gave him thumbs-up.

"Waiting to see a sailor's hornpipe," said Wizard.

"Or some swabbie swabbing the deck," added Whistler.

"It's like driving beside great tall buildings." Kalino craned her neck. "With men all over them."

"Forget the Navy men," grunted Lockjaw. "The Army's all you need."

"I like to fly, Lockjaw."

"The Army Air Forces, I mean."

"But aren't those Navy planes beautiful?" Kalino pointed. "Wouldn't you like to fly one of those?"

Six aircraft painted dark blue zoomed over them, motors snarling.

"They're from the Naval Air Station here on Ford," said Goff. "Grumman F4F Wildcats."

"Yeah, we know." Shooter put on his Ray-Bans. "We're on the same side."

"The paint's all wrong," grumbled Lockjaw. "You need green or silver."

Kalino smirked. "A plane is a plane."

Harrison inched ahead with his jeep. "Okay, take a look—we've got *California* here. And right across the water from it—there on the main shore, moored to the quay—that's *Pennsylvania*. The *California* was built in California—yeah, really—at Mare Island Naval Shipyard, launched in 1919, and was once flagship of the Pacific Fleet. *Pennsylvania* is another old girl, putting on the years but still sturdy, launched in 1915 at Newport News—hello?"

The occupants of both jeeps were staring at the huge ship that loomed up astern of *California*.

"Which carrier is that?" demanded Batman. "I don't see them that often."

"The *Enterprise*," Harrison said. "The Big E."

"What kind of planes operate off it?"

"Oh, I don't know. Dive bombers like the Douglas Dauntless. Douglas Devastator torpedo planes. Wildcat fighters."

"All those?"

"Yes, sir. The *Enterprise* can handle almost eight dozen aircraft—ninety on the nose."

Batman stood up in the jeep as it continued to move toward the huge carrier. "Ninety planes? Taking off and landing out at sea? With all the ammo and fuel and chow the aviators would need?"

"Yes, sir," responded Harrison. "All that and more."

Another formation of Wildcats swept by overhead. Wizard squinted at them. "We've been at Wheeler too long. No one ever talks about the Navy planes up there."

"Or the carriers." Lockjaw tapped Goff on the back. "Can't we get any closer?"

"No, sir. She's taking on supplies. What's today—Monday the twenty-fourth? Thanksgiving's over and they could weigh anchor anytime. Scuttlebutt has them heading out for a training exercise soon. A longer one."

"When?"

Goff shrugged. "Pick a number. The boys on the *Arizona* say by the end of the month. Some say December."

They watched supply trucks pulling up and sailors busy on shore and on deck with cargo. Officers marched about giving orders and sometimes lending a hand.

"You know, y'all are pretty lucky," said Harrison. "The ships are in port at the same time because we're here on a Monday. They haven't been at Pearl together on a weekend since July fourth. Either there are six battlewagons out at sea as Task Force One on a Saturday and Sunday or there are another three out with Vice Admiral Halsey's carrier task force. They trade weekends back and forth."

"Ha." Lockjaw rolled a pair of Chiclets around with his tongue. "So what's the skinny on the *Enterprise,* Harrison?"

"Another Newport News child. Commissioned in '38. Just over 824 feet. Top speed about thirty-two knots. Twenty-two hundred in the crew. That includes the aviators."

Lockjaw slipped three more Chiclets into his mouth. "I wouldn't mind trying that. I wouldn't mind at all."

"Not much of a runway," grunted Wizard.

"That's all the room I need." Lockjaw glanced at him. "You're just worried the wind on deck would mess up your hair."

"Where's the *Saratoga*?" asked Jude.

"Not in Pearl. Not today. And not for a while." Harrison pointed with his chin. "But the *Lexington's* on the east side."

Harrison steered the first jeep south of the landing strip as three Dauntless dive bombers came in over their heads and touched down one after the other. Goff followed. Lockjaw remained standing as the *Arizona* sailor drove, his eyes glued to aircraft that flashed through the sky. He spotted the *Lexington* and slapped Goff on the back.

"Willya look at that?" he almost shouted.

She was tall and long and gray. Unlike the *Enterprise* she was not taking on supplies and sat silent and grim in the water. Harrison and Goff pulled over and stopped. Everyone except the two drivers got out to stretch their legs and look the carrier over.

"*Lady Lex.* Almost 900 feet in length." Harrison draped his arms over the steering wheel. "Handles seventy-five aircraft. Started out as a battleship. They changed her over during construction. Just shy of

50,000 tons for a deep load. Launched in '25 and commissioned in '27. Quincy, Massachusetts. Over twenty-seven hundred in the crew."

"What kinds of airplanes?" asked Lockjaw. "Since you're a walking naval encyclopedia."

"Same as the *Enterprise*. She has the Devastator and the Dauntless—but no Wildcats. The *Lady* carries Brewster F2A-3 Buffalos for fighters. The battleship in front of her is the *Utah*. She's the Old Girl, launched in 1909. She's been refitted and rearmed. They do a lot of gunnery training with her."

Lockjaw looked from one ship to the other. "Maybe not a Navy man. But a Navy pilot."

"Aviator." Harrison held out his hand for some Chiclets and Lockjaw gave him two. "Naval aviator."

"Bite me," grunted Batman.

Jude stared at the *Lexington*. "No news of deployment?"

"Not that I know of," replied Harrison. "Maybe Dave's heard something."

Goff shook his head. "There are always rumors. Once the supply trucks roll up we'll hear more rumors."

"You thinking of jumping ship, Lockjaw?" asked Whistler.

"Dunno. What do you think I should do, Kalino?"

"Jump." She squeezed his hand.

They wound up back at the Whetstones, where Ruth and Lyyndaya had prepared a supper of hamburgers and potato salad. Manuku immediately went to Ruth's side.

"Can I help you with anything?" he asked.

"Yes. You can help eat all the food."

"No, really."

She smiled at him. "No, really. I don't need your help with anything right now. But you can give me a hand with the cleanup later."

"I'd like that." He jabbed over his shoulder with his thumb. "I'm going to pull up a couple of chairs outside by the banana plant. Join me?"

"Yes. I will as soon as everyone is served."

"Great."

Nate came over to Raven. "How was Pearl?"

"It was swell. We got close to the ships. You have no idea how huge they are until you're standing next to them like that. Especially the carriers."

"Did you hear?"

"What's that?"

"Nomura presented another proposal from Tokyo. He's told Washington it's the final one."

"When was this?"

"Back on Thanksgiving Day—the twentieth."

Raven handed him a plate with a burger and potato salad. "You eating?"

"Yeah, thanks. Where's Becky?"

"In the kitchen." Raven took his own plate and salad and a bottle of Coca-Cola and sat down on a couch. "Tell me about the Japanese terms."

"They said they'd cease operations in China. All military operations."

"And withdraw their troops?"

"I guess so."

"In exchange for what?"

"A million gallons of aviation fuel."

Raven whistled and bit into his burger. "That will put a lot of Zeros and Vals into the air."

"Do you think Roosevelt will give them what they want?"

"Maybe. If they think the Japanese are serious about pulling out of China. If they think it will avoid a nasty armed conflict." He looked across the room to where Ruth was just stepping outside with Manuku. "Hey, Ruth. This hamburger is terrific."

"I didn't make all of them, you know. Becky's mother did quite a few."

"I'll thank her as soon as I see her." Raven turned back to Nate. "The bigger question is whether the Japanese want to avoid war or if they think it'll help them get what they want—places they can capture that will furnish them with the oil and iron and rubber they need."

Nate had hardly touched his food. "Sometimes I think I've shaken the old bugbear. But things bring it back."

"It's not just you, Nate. I have memories of my kid brother that can come on so strong it makes me wince at the controls. I swear I'm going to break the stick in two, I squeeze it so hard. So go easy on yourself."

"Maybe I won't make it back."

"You'll make it back. Beck mentioned you'd asked about going up with her."

"Yeah. She said I'd be better off with Mom or Dad. I told her no, I needed to get back in the air with my wild flying sister."

Raven finished his Coca-Cola. "When?"

"Next week."

"I think it's a great idea. We'll get you into a P-40 in no time."

Nate shook his head and nibbled at his hamburger and bun. "I don't think so."

"Unless you want to go Navy and fly a Wildcat. Lockjaw's got his blood up about that all of a sudden."

"Navy?"

"Aw, he saw the Grummans and the Douglases tearing air when we were at Pearl. The idea of heading to sea and taking off and landing from the *Enterprise* or the *Lexington* got him going on all cylinders."

Nate looked out the patio doors to the palm trees and the sky. "I used to love flying. More than Mom or Dad. As much as Beck. Now I freeze up when I think about it."

"So did I. If Becky could point me in the right direction she can point you there too."

Nate half laughed. "I used to do a corkscrew and a barrel roll at the same time when we were barnstorming. Wouldn't that make her jump in the cockpit if I pulled one of those off again?"

"Do it." Raven got to his feet. "Can I get you a Coke? I'm going to get myself a spoon for this salad. And another burger."

"Sure. Thanks. That would be good."

The sun vanished and stars appeared in the warm velvet dark as Nate and Raven sat together. People continued to eat and talk. Finally Raven went looking for Becky. He couldn't locate her anywhere in the house so he wandered outside, hands in his pockets, and found a spot where he could get a good view of Pearl Harbor. Lights gleamed on the quays and on the battleships and carriers. He wondered what it would be like to try to land on the *Lexington* or *Enterprise* in the dark with a storm howling about your plane and oil leaking from the engine back over your canopy. He saw himself at the controls, lights on the flattop giving him something to shoot for, coaxing his Wildcat or Dauntless down and down, wings swinging from side to side, trying to match contact with the deck with the pitch and roll of the sea.

"Hey, stranger." A warm hand slipped into his pocket and wrapped itself around his fingers. "Sawbuck for your thoughts."

"Sawbuck?" Raven put his arm around Becky. "That's a lot of money."

"It's worth it."

"Yeah? Where have you been? I haven't seen you since you helped your mom and aunt serve the food."

"Oh, I had some letters Mom wanted to see. My grandparents wrote me and Nick from Pennsylvania."

"They didn't write your mom?"

"No."

"Are they your dad's parents?"

"No, they're Mom's."

Raven gave her a puzzled look, his forehead creasing. "What gives?"

Becky leaned her head on his shoulder. "I'll try to explain. Mom and Dad were baptized into this certain religious group—the Amish— when they were young. The group doesn't believe in war and doesn't permit its members to enlist in the military. And it doesn't allow anyone to assist the war effort in any way either—you know, like buying war bonds or attending a parade of soldiers or even joining the medical corps. So Mom and Dad are helping train Army pilots to fly better—or at least Dad is, since Mom is only teaching woman civilians. But they lump them both together for coming out here and helping Peterson, and no one is permitted to write them."

"No one is permitted to write them. Even though your mom and dad are serving their country?"

"They don't care if Mom and Dad are serving their country. They don't want them serving their country."

"But you're training Army pilots, Becky."

She squeezed his hand. "That's different. I've never joined the church. Never been baptized. Never taken any vows. So I can't be cut off or excommunicated. It's okay for Grandmother and Grandfather to write me. Nate too. Neither of us has joined the church yet."

"Whew. That's a relief. I don't know if I could handle you being like that."

"I guess it does make them sound harsh. But the Amish people are really very beautiful, Christian. You would like them."

"Beck—" Raven started to protest.

"No," she interrupted. "You would. They're kind and cheerful and they take care of one another. You would have no problem because you haven't broken any vows. They would welcome you and feed you and bless you. Of course, not showing up in a uniform would help first impressions."

"Hm. I could fly dressed in civilian clothes."

She laughed and looked up at him. "Poor Thunderbird. No, you can't do that either. The church people aren't allowed to pilot planes or drive cars or use phones or have electric lights. If you want to visit them you must make up your mind to accept that it's still 1880 in their world."

"What?"

"That's how it is with them."

"They sound like a cult."

"No, no, they are not a cult. They believe in Jesus and in the Bible just like you and me. They just go about things differently, that's all. But they are not a cruel people."

"They won't write letters to your father or mother or your Aunt Ruth. What do you call that?"

Becky sighed. "The shunning can be deceiving. It can make them look far worse than they really are."

"I think I'll skip the trip to Pennsylvania to find out."

"Okay, look." Becky tugged an airmail envelope out of her jeans. "I'm going to let you read this out loud to me. I haven't opened it yet so I haven't had a chance to censor it or change anything. And I won't try to take the letter away from you if I don't like what's in it."

"That's odd. Why? I'd rather walk on the beach with you."

"Oh, Christian, we can do that later. Right now, I want you to read this letter out loud."

"Really, why does it matter? I don't care."

"The Amish people are not simply about shunning and turning their backs on planes and cars. I want you to know that."

"Beck—"

"It matters to me."

Raven shrugged, took the envelope, and opened it, tearing along the side. There wasn't enough light so he moved closer to a window. He scanned the page.

"There's some German in it," he complained.

"Skip over the German."

"Who is this from? A secret admirer?" He grinned. "Sure you want me to read it?"

"You goof." She shoved him into a palm tree. "It's the bishop of the church."

"You gotta be kidding me."

"Just read it, okay?"

My dear Rebecca,

I want you to know I think of you often and pray for all of your family. And I'm not the only one. The whole church prays for your mother and father and for your Aunt Ruth. We love them and look forward to the day we can all be reconciled in Christ Jesus our Lord.

So I am going to say some things that are not very Amish. I say them because I believe they are true. Now and then I look at the war news in the newspapers even though what I read puts a great stone in my heart. So much death. So much destruction. Oh, God in heaven, that those made in your image would beat their swords into plowshares, their tanks and guns and bombs into pruning hooks. This is my deepest prayer.

But then I think—between my praying of this prayer and God's answer of it, his resounding YES, what happens? How many more people are slain? How many children orphaned? How much land is ravaged and how many cities burned to the ground? So I bear in mind that the Lord does not call everyone to be Amish, only a few. Those few he charges with being salt and light in the manner in which the Amish are to live and pray and conduct their business and raise their families. Not everyone is called to this. Yet those who are not can still serve the Lord.

So what of these others who believe in Jesus Christ? What does the Lord call them to do if he does not call them to be Amish? To pray and worship of course. To raise their families in his sight. To conduct their business in a manner pleasing to him. Even if it will not be exactly as the Amish do it, their way can still honor our Lord.

I look at the war that covers the earth and I ask, What can be done, oh, God, what can be done in the measure of time between our cries

for peace and your granting of that peace?
Who will strive with those who would rule the
earth and imprison whole nations? Who will
stand between the slayer and the mother with
her children? Who will blunt the blow of the
wicked?

This is what I think—it is not just the task of
unbelievers to stand between the evildoer and his
victims. God has appointed some Christians
to be Amish, it is true, but he has appointed
other Christians to maintain decency and order,
to bring to an end the ways of the wicked, to
safeguard the widow and the infant and bring
about peace in God's name. So some will be
pilots, my dear, and do this. Some will be
soldiers. Some will command great ships. But
they will do it for God and for the people God
made in his image.

I could not do this. I recoil from such a task.
It is not in me to lift a gun. But God may
put this in others who are his children—not
because they love to do it, God forbid, nor even
because they want to do it, but because they are
compelled to do it by the living God.

Yes, yes, I am aware that many who do not
believe in Jesus Christ bear arms and fight,
and some fight for what is good. I do not
judge them. It is not for me to weigh their

sins against their righteousness. All of this is in God's hands. I know he raises up to do his bidding those who know him not—he did this with Cyrus the King of Persia when he wanted Cyrus to set the Jews free. What the unbeliever is called to do, this I leave with God. But for the believer I say, if you will not be Amish, yet do God's will in God's way. So if the believer fights to set people at liberty, to stanch the flow of blood, to shield the innocent from those who thrive on evil, let him do it as one doing the very work of God. That is what I wish for; this is what I pray for. If you must stand in the gap with the sword, let it be the sword of a righteous God and may you stand as one who stands on his very words.

How strange this must seem to you, my dear Rebecca. Such talk to come from an Amish bishop. But I look and see darkness spreading over the earth and I know there is yet more darkness to come. Some are called to dam the flood of evil. I believe this with all my heart. Just as I believe it is not for the Amish to do, never, for they are called to make a different stand in Christ Jesus our Lord.

But something is coming. Something more is coming. And it may be it is for you to deal with. Already you have trained a few pilots.

Perhaps you will train more. Perhaps your
father and mother will train more. Perhaps it is
what you and they are called to do. And there
was mention in your last letter of a young man
whom you favor. Who knows—perhaps you are
in love with him? You say he is a Christ man,
a Jesus follower, a Christian. So maybe it is
also his destiny to guard, to protect, to deliver
the people of the earth. Only if he does it let
him do it in the Spirit of the Lord. We are
frail, we are weak, we sin, yet as far as it is
possible with this young man, let him fight in
the Spirit of the Lord, not in his own might or
the might of those who would usurp the beauty
of the world.

I will write again for Christmas. God bless
you, my dear. The Lord be with you forever.

Bishop Zook

Raven stood holding the pages of the letter in his hand. After a moment he folded them up and gave them back to Becky. Then he walked away from the house and looked down again on the lights of Pearl Harbor. She followed him but did not touch him or speak.

"You asked for my thoughts a half hour ago," he finally said. "I was thinking about what it would be like to be a naval aviator, of how hard it would be to land on a carrier in the dark in the middle of a storm. But I was just beginning to think of other things when you showed up. How I'm likely to be transferred to the Philippines with the Army Air Forces. That the war with Japan will be there. And you will have to remain in Hawaii, far away from me. I will never see your eyes, touch your lips, pick you up, and carry you into the waves. Can I bear that?"

Becky didn't speak.

"If I was a naval aviator, flying a dive bomber or torpedo plane or fighter, if I was assigned to a carrier that had Pearl Harbor as its home base—well, that would be a different matter. Sure, we'd go on deployment, we'd be away for weeks or months at a time, but not for years, and we'd always come back here." He turned and ran a hand down the side of her face. "Your hair is getting longer."

"The Bible and the Amish say a woman's crowning glory is her hair."

"So now I have the Amish to thank for that and for the letter."

"I had no idea Bishop Zook would say those things. He could actually be cut off from the community for writing them down."

"He said you might be in love with me."

"Yes, I adore you—I can't think of any better way of spending my time than being with you. But love? Love is a big deal. I loved once and lost. A lot of things may be healed inside me but not that. I'm afraid the moment I say love you is the moment you'll be snatched away from me. I'm afraid to go where love is again."

Her young face looked so troubled Raven cupped it in his hand and kissed the freckles that made their way across the bridge of her nose. "Hey. I'm okay. I've had rough landings before."

"I don't want you to have rough landings." Tears made their way to the corners of her eyes. "I want you to know you're cared for. Prayed for. Dreamed about. That when we're apart I ache for you. You mean so much to me. I can't stand the thought that I'm making it hard for you."

"You're not making it hard for me."

"Of course I am. Any other woman would have said the words by now. But not me. I can't say the words that would make you happy."

"The happiest man on earth." He kissed her cheek. "I can wait."

"What if it never happens?"

"Are you trying to frighten me off?"

"I'm just saying—"

"Because it's kind of hard to frighten off an army pilot. Especially one who wants to be a naval aviator. Who wants his home base to be Pearl Harbor so he can love you up forever." He gently kissed the side of her neck and she closed her eyes. "Not to mention that I'm *Waya*. The wolf doesn't run, Becky."

"I don't want you to run," she whispered. "I just don't want to break your heart."

"Shh. Christmas is right around the corner. Who knows? There's a little something extra in the air that time of year. Anything could happen to your heart. To my heart."

He kissed her. She clung to him as he held her tighter and tighter, never breaking the kiss. Finally he pulled away.

"Do you—do you love *me*?" She ran her hands over his face, looking into his eyes, her own face tight and anxious, her lips parted. "Do you, Thunderbird?"

He smoothed back her hair and stroked her cheek. "Remember the first time we met? I put out my hand and you wouldn't take it?"

She looked even more anxious, her eyes widening in the dark. "I'm sorry, I'm so sorry—it seems like all I ever do is hurt you."

"Before that I saw you when the jeep dropped me off at Peterson's office. You were checking over your J-3. At first you were bent over and almost out of sight. Then you stood up. I thought I'd been hit by lightning. A buzz went right through me. It was like I'd been standing out in a field during a thunderstorm and electricity had gone through me." He snapped his fingers. "It happened in a flash. For a moment I lost my breath. Do you remember spotting me at the other end of the runway?"

Becky nodded.

"No woman's ever affected me like that in my life. One look at you just about knocked me out. But then came our weeks of quarreling and fighting, so I had to distance myself from that lightning burn as fast and as far as I could. I never quite made it, though. And the afternoon you walked out of the sea at Nanakuli I was finished." He took her chin between his forefinger and thumb. "So help me, there has never been anything more beautiful on the face of the earth or in the face of heaven than you. You think I'm just spinning a line. But you're wrong. I'd die for you. You have no idea how strongly I feel about Becky Whetstone. From the moment you stood up on that runway I was yours forever."

He put both of his arms around her and pulled her in, kissing her gently. He took her breath, he took her strength, her thoughts and words, and she felt suspended in the air, held by him above the earth, nothing but sky beneath her feet and sun above her head.

"You wanted to know," he whispered. "So I told you."

"No. I need to hear you say it."

"I did."

She shook her head, tears cutting down her face, hands on his chest and shoulders and twining around his back. "No. I need your words. If you mean it. If it's true. I have to hear your words. Tell me, Thunderbird. Tell me what you feel for me."

"Beck—"

"Tell me."

"I love you. I love you with all my heart. Everything. God knows how much I love you."

His kiss came again. When he released her, the tears were slipping along her face, her arms still wrapped around his back with the last of her strength, he put his lips to her ear, kissed it, and whispered, "The sun's come up for you again, girl. And so long as I live and can take you into my arms it doesn't set."

TWENTY

"Hey!" Becky walked into an empty house in her flight jacket. "Where is everybody?"

"I'm out here!" Jude called.

Her father was standing at the edge of the hill the house was built on, looking south toward Pearl Harbor, a large pair of binoculars to his eyes. "Take a look at this."

Even without using the binoculars her father passed to her, Becky could see what he was excited about. "One of the carriers is leaving. With an escort."

"A big escort. I count three heavy cruisers and eight or nine destroyers heading out."

Becky refocused the binoculars. "I think it's the *Enterprise*."

"I think so too. Judging from where she started out."

"Did you hear anything about this, Dad?"

"They're on a weekend training op. Be back in Sunday night. Or Monday, December first."

"Why now?" She handed the binoculars back.

"Did you hear what happened to the Japanese offer?"

"The one about a million gallons of airplane fuel in return for stopping the war in China? Has Washington said yes?"

Jude had the binoculars back at his eyes and was tracking the task force as it left Pearl Harbor behind. "They're sticking to an easterly course. Washington said no, Beck. Rumor is Japan is still sending reinforcements to China and has no intention of pulling her troops out.

Who knows? But Tokyo said that was their final attempt to normalize relations with us. So anything could happen now."

"That's why the Big E's suddenly doing a training exercise?"

"Well, we saw them taking on supplies last week, remember? Everybody knew they were heading out sometime. Today it's a weekend exercise. Tomorrow, maybe something longer. Maybe all the way south. Or west. Or north."

"What does that mean?"

"We have a large base in the Philippines so that's a good bet—south and west. Midway Islands are north and west, we might reinforce them—we have an airstrip there. Wake Island and Guam are pretty much due west of here and a lot closer to Japan than Hawaii is—Guam's practically in Japan. So are Manila and the Philippines for that matter. I can see task forces being sent to all those places and probably a lot more I haven't thought about."

"But the *Enterprise* is going east."

"For now."

"I thought—" Becky stopped. "You sound like you're talking about war. I thought we might be past that."

"Not with the U.S. turning down the last offer from Tokyo."

Becky glanced back at the house. "So how come you're the only one home? Where's Mom? Where's Aunt Ruth?"

"Your mother's doing some extra flying lessons this evening. Nothing to do with the *Enterprise* heading out, just civilian students. Ruth—well, Ruth's going up pretty soon."

"Going up? What? In a plane?"

"I hope so."

"How can she go up in a plane? She's Amish."

"Amish and shunned for not being Amish enough because she dared to come to Hawaii and continued to talk and eat with us. So she thought she might as well enjoy herself. Bishop Zook went up after all."

"Twenty years ago." She stared at her father. "Are you pulling my leg?"

Jude put an arm around her shoulder. "Manuku asked her. He's the pilot."

"She's going up with him in a J-3?"

"Yes."

"Why, he…he's only—"

"Thirty-eight. Your aunt's forty-four. Six years between them. Not so bad."

Becky's mouth was partly open. "Are you serious?"

"Ruth is. As serious as she's been since her husband was killed. Haven't you noticed?"

"She's never talked about it."

"I don't think she wanted to talk about it or analyze it. Sometimes that spoils things, doesn't it? I don't recall wanting to talk to the guys in my squadron about your mother. I wanted to keep it inside and secret." He smiled and walked with her into the house. "Isn't that how you feel about Thunderbird?"

"I guess everybody knows I adore him. But I'm not sure I can ever really and truly love him, Dad."

"Why not?"

"It's not really about Moses. It's not that he has to be Moses. I like Thunderbird just as he is. But I have this—this thing inside…where I feel if I let myself love him…he'll be killed."

"You believe that?"

"I don't want to believe it. In my head I don't really believe it. But all my emotions believe it and I don't know how to stop that."

"I can pray with you if you like."

"I *would* like that. Maybe it will help me make my way out of this." She sat on a stool in the kitchen and peeled a banana. "He told me he loved me, you know. The night after we toured Pearl." She smiled with her eyes and her lips. "He made me pretty happy. And every time he says it again I'm even happier." Her eyes turned a dark green. The smile vanished. "I can't make him happy in return. I can't say it."

Jude poured Becky a glass of pineapple juice. "I'll bet he's a happy guy just to have you as his girl."

"That's what he says. But I wish I could say to him what he said to me. It's like I've got something caught in my throat."

"I think Thunderbird is a patient guy."

"He says he is. But he won't wait forever."

"How do you know?"

"No man will, Dad." She drank the juice in one long swallow.

Jude opened the fridge. "What do you want for supper?"

"I don't care. What does Nate want?" She looked over her shoulder into the rest of the house. "Where is he?"

"He's up too."

"What?"

"He went up with Thunderbird."

Becky stopped as she lifted the glass pitcher of pineapple juice. "He's up in a Piper J-3 with Thunderbird."

"No, sir. Not a J-3. They're up in a Curtiss P-36 Hawk. Billy Skipp gave the okay. I have no idea where they are right now. Maybe tracking the *Enterprise*?"

"Dad! Nate could barely handle the stick when I had him up this week. How can he handle a fighter? Even an old fighter like the P-36?"

"Don't let Thunderbird hear you say that. He's pretty fond of his bird. Figures it can handle anything."

"I know what he thinks. How did he get involved with Nate?"

Jude put a plate of fried chicken and coleslaw in front of her. "Nate called him up last night after you were in bed."

"So Nate was sneaking around."

"He knew you'd be upset. That you wouldn't think he was anywhere near ready to handle a fighter plane."

"And he's not. Who put that idea in his head?"

"You did."

"Me?" Becky pushed away the chicken.

"Didn't you tell him he'd feel more comfortable handling a bigger plane? That the Piper was too small and light for him?"

"Sure I did, Dad. But just to encourage him. He was so stiff and tight. His clumsiness at the controls was bringing him down. You know how good he was before China. I was just trying to buck him up."

"Well, you did. He was smiling just enough after the phone call to make your mother thank God at bedtime and all the way to the

Peterson airfield this morning. Thunderbird was supposed to pick him up at our house at one o'clock."

Becky pulled the plate of chicken back and began to nibble at a drumstick. "I'm surprised. But Christian's with him. And he's talked with Nate several times. He's very good. Very gentle, more gentle than any man I've known except for Moses." She didn't want to laugh but did. "I can just see them crammed together in the cockpit. I'm sure it'll be a short flight."

"Short or long, if it helps Nate it's worth it."

"Of course it will help him. Thunderbird's a great pilot. And a great guy." She shook her head and played with the other pieces of chicken. "I just can't tell him that in the way I ought to." Becky clenched a fist and jammed it against her chest. "I can't stand being trapped inside, Dad. I hate not being free."

Jude wiped his fingers on a napkin and reached across the table to take his daughter's hand. "Time to talk to Eternity about it."

She bowed her head. "Could you pray in German, Dad?"

"Will you understand the German?"

"Some of it I will. It doesn't matter. He'll understand it."

"All right, honey."

Jude began to pray quietly. "*Herr, setze meine Tochter Becky in Freiheit.*"

Becky understood that much. *Lord, set my daughter Becky at liberty.*

His prayer grew and the sentences became longer and more complicated and Becky got lost trying to follow the German. So she calmed her mind and let the words flow through her and through the air and find their way to God while peace worked its way into her mind and into every part of her body. The only thing she found herself doing was whispering, "*Gott sei gelobt, Gott sei gelobt, Gott sei gelobt.*" *Praise God, praise God, praise God.*

When Jude had pronounced *amen* she opened her eyes.

"Thank you, Dad. I always feel a lot better when I'm prayed over in German."

"Do you feel free enough to say what you want to say to Thunderbird?"

"I don't know." She folded her hands in her lap. "Do you ever miss being among our Amish family and friends?"

Jude leaned back in his chair, toothpick in his mouth. "Sure. There are many people I love. Your mother and Nate feel the same way. And of course Ruth. But then I remember how some of the Amish in Paradise felt God had taken Moses away because of your great sin of loving him too much. I remember that they will not let me fly. Or serve my country. I look at the faces of my students—" He tapped the side of his head. "I see them right here—and I know how satisfied I am that the skills they're learning can keep them alive when they fly, whether they're civilians or military."

He leaned forward and took the toothpick out of his mouth. "And today's civilian is tomorrow's fighter pilot if we go to war. So if we train them well the odds improve as far as some of them surviving combat and returning home to their parents and their wives and their children. It's hard to think of throwing that over to return to the Amish church. In fact, I won't. Neither will your mother." He looked at her steadily. "We're never going back, Becky."

The door opened before Becky could respond. Her mother rushed in, blond hair loose and blowing back, flight jacket open, green eyes flashing, a smile opening up her whole face. "My goodness, what a day. My students were as sharp as tacks. I haven't done so many loops and rolls since the '20s. And Ruth! Quiet Ruth! I have never seen her so animated in my life."

She kissed her husband and daughter and took a seat, immediately peeling a banana. "Manuku must have had her in the air over an hour and a half. He handed the stick to her seven times, he says. And there was Ruth on the runway, twenty minutes after landing, and she still had a leather jacket and helmet on—they fit her perfectly—and she didn't want to leave the plane. But Manuku had several students to train so she finally walked back to the hut with me. Her eyes were as bright as a sixteen-year-old's. And her hair came loose when she pulled her helmet off, pins flying everywhere, and she left it loose. I've never seen her look so becoming. The silver and white in her black hair made her so—so—" She ate the banana in small bites and hunted for the word she wanted. "Well, she was enchanting. Not a very good Amish word. But that's what she was."

Lyyndaya finished the banana and reached for the pitcher of pineapple juice. "Flapjack had all this music blaring, he always celebrates a bit when it's Friday, and I was sure Ruth would complain, but do you know what she did? My Ruth? She knew the words to that song Judy Garland sings, 'Somewhere Over the Rainbow,' and started to sing along. Not loud. But she's always had a pure, strong voice. Everyone could hear her. Then it was 'You Are My Sunshine' and Billie Holiday's 'God Bless the Child.' She knew more of the songs by heart than Flapjack did, than anyone did. How is that possible? What has happened to my Amish sister?" She poured the juice into her glass.

Becky didn't know what to say. "Where was I when all this was happening?"

"You were up. Or gone. A lot took place after you were gone." She sipped at the juice and smiled at Jude. "And you too, my dear. The best thing of all happened after you left."

"And what was that?" he asked.

"Nate showed up with Thunderbird. Flying the P-36."

"No kidding!"

"They circled the field twice. Threw the canopy back so we could see who was doing what. And Nate had the stick. He brought her in. A little wobbly. A little flat. But he made the landing. He was all smiles. It did my heart good. *Gott sei gelobt.*"

"No one—came back with you?" asked Becky. "Not Nate? Or Thunderbird? Why not?"

"Oh, Wizard and Lockjaw showed up to whisk Kalino and Hani away for hot dogs at the Black Cat and then off to the movies. Batman and Shooter and Whistler were supposed to meet them there. Some sort of double feature along with a Bugs Bunny cartoon. *Maltese Falcon* and a movie about General Custer, it has Errol Flynn in it—"

Jude put his hand over Lyyndaya's. "You've had quite an evening. So where's Nate?"

"Nate and Thunderbird borrowed some of Flapjack's fuel and took off again. Like a pair of brothers. Headed out to Pearl and the open sea. They'd heard the *Enterprise* had left port."

"It did. Along with an escort."

"So what does that mean? Is there trouble somewhere?"

"It's just a weekend training exercise."

"Yes?" Lyyndaya glanced at her daughter. "Why so glum?"

"I'm not glum."

"I come in here at attack speed and I haven't even asked you two how you are."

"I'm okay, Mom. Just a little bowled over at the idea of Aunt Ruth dancing and singing 'Somewhere Over the Rainbow.'"

"She wasn't dancing."

Jude cleared his throat. "Becky and I were discussing our Amish church in Paradise when you flew through the doorway. She was asking if I missed the people and the Amish way. So I said, yes, there are some things I miss, some people I miss very much. But honestly, I wouldn't trade them for training these young people and helping all the American people, not just the Amish ones. I told her you felt the same way I did."

Lyyndaya stared at her daughter. "Your father is right about that."

"I could tell when you barreled in here, Mom."

"Are you angry because I'm happy?" Lyyndaya asked. "Because Ruth and Nate are happy? I thought you were happy."

"I...am...I guess I am—"

"What's happened? Is it Thunderbird?"

"Yes. Of course it's Thunderbird. He's turned me inside out. Even when he doesn't mean to."

"What did he say that has hurt you so much?"

"He said he loves me."

Lyyndaya blinked. "Excuse me?"

"He loves me. He told me he loves me."

Lyyndaya looked at Jude and then back at Becky. "And this hurts you? How?"

"I...I can't say it back..."

"You don't have to say it back right away."

Becky's face filled with blood. "I'll never say it back. I can't."

"Shh, shh."

"I thought we might return to Pennsylvania. So I can get away from him. Stop breaking his heart. It hurts me to break his heart, Mom; he's such a great guy, but I need to leave." She ran her hands back through her hair and the tears started. "But now you all want to stay here. Ruth, Nate, you and Dad, no one wants to be Amish anymore. No one will come back to Paradise with me. I don't know what else to do."

Lyyndaya got up and pulled her chair over beside her daughter and took her in her arms. "All right. All right. Even if no one is going to jump on a boat with you and head to San Francisco, that doesn't mean we don't care or won't do all we can to help you."

"How can anyone help me when I can't even help myself?"

"That's usually when we do need help, my girl."

"I have no idea what would help. I want to love him but I can't. I want to look into his beautiful blue eyes and say, 'I love you,' but I can't."

"Why can't you?"

"There's just a block, that's all. Dad's prayed with me. I've prayed. But I just can't."

"But it is Moses, isn't it?" Her father's voice was quiet.

"No, it's not Moses—I told you, I'm over Moses, I don't know what it's about."

"You loved Moses and he died. If you love Christian he will die too."

"I don't—"

"But you can go back to Paradise. Go back to the Amish. Go back to Bishop Zook. Take your vows. Be baptized. Perhaps you'll find peace. Perhaps Christian will be spared. And if Christian is spared then your heart will be spared also."

Becky didn't reply. She sobbed into her mother's shoulder as if she were twelve. Lyyndaya began to rock her and whispered, "Do you really think this is what God does? Do you really think you must scheme like this trying to make sure the man you love won't be taken away a second time?"

"I don't know…In my head, I know, but in my heart…"

"Do you honestly think God wants less love in the world? In this violent and hate-filled world? Do you think the God of love who loves you and this whole earth does not want you to love a man he also loves and who he put in your life to touch your heart and your soul? Didn't God heal you of the loss of Moses, and wasn't this man part of your healing? This man you love? Do you truly think God wants to take him away from you? Or does he want the two of you to put more love on the earth?"

"Mom, I can't—"

Lyyndaya hugged her daughter more tightly and kissed her hair. "Raven is the man you love. And he is the man God loves."

TWENTY-ONE

"Hey. Batman."

Raven lifted the comic book off Batman's face. The sudden rush of sunlight failed to make him open his eyes.

"What happened?" Raven flipped through the comic book. "The adventures of Batman and Robin put you to sleep?"

"No."

"Come on. Get up. Skipp's briefing us in the hangar in five."

Batman opened one eye. "We at war?"

"We're at Christmas—almost. Less than a month to go. He wants to hold a big dinner and dance, and you get to swing down on a rope and snatch up the prettiest girl."

Batman opened both eyes and grinned. "That would be Becky then. Would you mind?"

"Me mind? No, I'd have the Christmas spirit. Jolly and fat and ho-ho-ho. You need to ask if Becky would mind. Remember what happened to Lockjaw."

Batman had been slumped in a deck chair near the runway. He climbed to his feet and stretched. "I met a sweet little nurse who works at the naval hospital. Think I'll stick with her instead."

They began to walk.

"What were you doing at the naval hospital?" asked Raven.

"Getting blood drawn."

"For what?"

"I was doing a medical."

"Your army medical not good enough?"

"Not for the navy. Did you see that Abbot and Costello film *In the Navy?*"

"Missed it."

"Well, if you'd seen it that would explain the whole thing."

Raven glanced at him. "Are you looking to transfer over to flattops?"

"Yes, sir."

"When are you going to get your carrier training?"

Batman put on his aviator sunglasses. "All in due time. Today I'm still on army time. Let's see what the old man has to say."

"I thought Lockjaw was going to make the transfer."

"I bumped into him at the hospital. He had Kalino in tow. Guess he can't give blood without her."

The others were seated on chairs with their backs to the open doors of the hangar. Billy Skipp was sketching out a pattern on a chalkboard, rapping the chalk down sharply to make dots when he wasn't drawing in a line or a circle.

"Good of you to join us." Skipp broke his piece of chalk and picked up a fresh one. "So the concern is saboteurs. That's why the P-40s are being placed in the middle of the airfield—we're kind of stacking them. That way an enemy agent can't sneak out to the edge of the strip one night and damage all our fighters. The sentries can see what's going on easily enough when all the Warhawks are out on the open and in the same place."

"Who's the enemy?" asked Shooter.

"Who do you think? Mussolini."

The pilots laughed. Raven raised his hand to shoulder height. "Sir. What about the P-36s?"

Skipp dusted his hands off by slapping them together. "I know you like your kite, Thunderbird. But saboteurs aren't going to go after them. They're almost museum pieces. The P-40s are our first concern."

"I told you," whispered Wizard. "You're just a target balloon for the Zeros."

Raven grunted. "Shut up, Haircomb."

Skipp broke into the fresh wave of laughter. "Speaking of Zeros, let's see how you guys are doing with aircraft identification." He turned to a flip chart set up on an easel and pointed. "Wizard?"

"That's the Zero, sir, that's the Zeke."

"More, please."

"Mitsubishi A6M. Currently, so far as we know, the A6M2, Type 0, Model 21. Maximum speed more than three hundred miles per hour. Two machine guns in the engine cowling, seven-point-seven millimeter. Two cannon in the wings, twenty millimeter. Fast and maneuverable."

"Very good." Skipp tapped the chart. "Juggler. What about this?"

"Um. I'd guess the Kate, sir."

Skipp's eyebrows lifted as high as anyone had seen them. "You'd guess?"

"Uh. It *is* the Kate, sir."

"And what does that mean, Lieutenant?"

"It means...B5N, sir. Nakajima B5N."

"What're its weapons, Juggler? *Hashi*—chopsticks?"

Juggler reddened while the others laughed. "Torpedoes, sir. It's a torpedo bomber."

"Thank you." Skipp's eyes darkened. "Okay, Lockjaw, our latest defector, if you think flying off carriers in an ocean swell is duck soup, why don't you tell us what this is?" Skipp's face was tight.

Lockjaw protested. "I'm army all the way, Colonel."

"Is that right? Well, I have to approve all transfer of personnel to other units, so maybe you and I had better have a chat after this briefing."

"Yes, sir."

Skipp scanned the group. "That goes for any of you who are thinking of going Navy. Anybody who wants to fly Grummans when they could be flying P-40s. See me first. Or you may be surprised by what's in your sock this Christmas. Understood?"

As one, the pilots responded, "YES, SIR!"

"That's given you enough time to think. What's the silhouette, Lockjaw?"

"The, uh, the..." Lockjaw seemed flustered by Skipp's aggressiveness. "The Val, Colonel. The Aichi D3A. Dive bomber."

"Tell me more, navy boy."

"It...uh...it...has a maximum speed of two hundred forty-two miles per hour. Ceiling of thirty thousand five hundred feet. Uh— two machine guns in the wings, seven-point-seven millimeter. One facing the rear, manned by a gunner, also seven-point-seven millimeter."

"Range?"

"Range? Range is—is something like nine hundred miles."

Skipp's eyes slitted. "Something like?"

"Nine hundred and change, sir."

"How many nautical miles?"

Lockjaw chewed furiously on a Chiclet. "I don't know that, sir."

"You want to be a naval aviator and you don't know nautical miles, Lockjaw?"

"No, sir."

"Exactly seven hundred and ninety-five. Even a dumb army officer knows that, Lieutenant."

"Yes, sir."

Skipp tapped the chart with his piece of chalk. "You haven't said a thing about the payload."

"Uh...I...I'm not sure—"

"Not sure?"

"No, sir, I—"

"A five-hundred-and-fifty-one pounder, sir." Raven's voice was clear. "Or a couple of hundred-and-thirty-two pound bombs."

"Thank you, Thunderbird. I don't recall asking for your help."

"You didn't need to, sir. I'm Lockjaw's wingman. It's my duty to cover him in all combat situations. I don't need to be told to do that."

Skipp stared at Raven. His eyes were made of rock. Then a slow smile made its way across his face. "That is correct. Thank you for reminding me of that, Lieutenant Raven." He turned back to the chart. "We'll cover the scouting aircraft in a moment. Let's go back to the Zeke, the Zero." He drew a white circle around its silhouette on the chart with his chalk. "The A5M wasn't that hard for the Chinese to bring down using their Russian-built aircraft. But in August 1940 the A6M2 saw action in Chungking and totally dominated the skies, bringing down Polikarpov I-16s and I-153s with ease. In one engagement thirteen A6M2 Zeros flamed twenty-seven I-15s and I-16s in less than three minutes without losing a plane. I kid you not. Of course they have yet to meet up with British or American fighters. Maybe Washington will make peace with Tokyo and the Japanese and American fighter pilots will never meet. But my hunch is we'll be seeing action in the new year."

Skipp faced them, putting his hands behind his back. "To tell you the truth, I don't really care if you go navy or army. Just remember this. We don't know much about the Zero except that it's deadly. The few times over the past year when the Chinese have scored some successes it's been because they hit the Zero with good strong bursts, not short and fast ones. That's what I've picked up from the intelligence reports. The Zero is light and quick and highly maneuverable. So if it's light it probably can't absorb a lot of punishment. Don't try to out-twist or out-turn it. Dive on it, get it in your sights, put as many shells into it as fast as you can, and get out of there. If the pilot is in your sights, kill him. He'll zip around and get on your tail and do it to you if you don't do it to him first. Questions?"

There were a few moments of silence before Shooter spoke up. "Is the *Enterprise* coming back, sir?"

"That's a navy matter."

"Is it?"

"The Big E is on a routine training exercise. Nothing more. She'll be back at her berth by Sunday or Monday."

"What if she isn't?"

Skipp folded his arms over his chest and shrugged. "You can place odds on it if you like. I'll spot you twenty bucks she'll be home-sweet-home when you fly over Pearl on Tuesday morning."

Shooter smiled. "You're on, sir. I'll give you three to one. I have a twenty says she'll be hundreds of miles away by Tuesday."

"All right." Skipp looked over the squadron. "Anyone else have something on their mind?"

Juggler half lifted his hand. "Are we going anywhere ourselves, Colonel?"

"Not before Christmas. So maybe this is a good time to talk about our Christmas dance. I want—"

"Are we going to the Philippines in the new year, sir?"

Skipp tilted his head. "I don't know, Juggler. I told you chances were good we'd be mixing it up with the Empire of Japan in '42. If I'm right we won't be leaving the Army Air Forces on this rock. I expect we'll be deployed to places like Wake or Guam. Or Manila Bay. I have a hunch if it boils over with Japan it'll boil over with Germany too. For all I know this squadron could be sent to England. With brand new P-40s for everyone. Including you, Thunderbird."

Raven shook his head. "My P-36 can knock anything out of the sky, Colonel. I'll stick with it until you cut my fuel line."

"Never mind Thunderbird's rocking chair," said Wizard. "I'm interested in this dance you mentioned, Colonel."

"I've set the date for the third Saturday in December, the twentieth, just three weeks from today. I want this well organized. Wizard, Lockjaw, Whistler, you're on balloons and streamers—and the tree—I want a beautiful pine tree with silver balls all over it."

"A pine tree?" Wizard looked at the others. "Sir, where do you expect us to find a pine tree on Oahu? This ain't Minnesota or Montana."

"I don't care, Wiz. Just find it and decorate it. That's an order. Batman. Work with Juggler and get us a band. A really good band. Jimmy Dorsey or Glenn Miller."

Batman smiled. "Not a problem, sir. If it's the 'Chattanooga Choo Choo' you want, you'll get it."

"Actually I was thinking more along the lines of 'By the Light of the Silvery Moon,' Lieutenant. Sweet and slow for Mrs. Skipp."

"Easy as pie."

Juggler looked at Batman. "What?"

"Have no fear. If we can't get an army band we'll get a navy band."

"What if that doesn't work either?"

"We'll take trumpet lessons."

"Food!" Skipp clapped his hands and rubbed them together. "Food and drink. Can't have a Christmas party without that. Thunderbird. Shooter. Grab whoever you need and get the grub—I'm sure Boxcars and Bandit have time on their hands. The dishes can be Hawaiian or American. I don't care. So long as it tastes good and there's plenty of it. Hit up your girlfriends for help, if you need to. You go to that Pastor Thor's church, don't you, Thunderbird?"

"Yes, sir."

"Maybe some of the ladies there can help."

"Well, they're having a beach party on December sixth, Colonel. Right on Waikiki by the Royal Hawaiian. Why don't you drop by and ask them yourself? A colonel in full dress uniform should motivate dozens of them to cook whatever we might want."

"Me? In a church?"

"It's on the beach, sir. Ocean, sand, palm trees."

"I'll think it over, Thunderbird. Okay, that's about it. We'll do the Japanese scouting planes next time. Have a good weekend. Some of you have instrument checks, so get gassed up. Dismissed. Lockjaw— let's have that fatherly chat."

"What about you, sir?" asked Shooter.

"What about me? You want me to increase my bet on the *Enterprise*?"

"Sure. You sound pretty confident about where it's gonna be next week."

"In harbor."

"Right. But I'm thinking more along the lines of this Christmas dance you're so hepped up about. You've got us running after pine trees and the Glenn Miller Band and prize turkeys and geese—it sounds like you want Christmas in New Hampshire."

Skipp grinned. "Not a bad idea, Shooter."

"So while we're making the impossible happen, what will you be doing?"

"I'm glad you asked. Sending out the invitations. Admiral Kimmel and General Short will be just two of my invitees. Would you like the job of going to them and asking them to attend?"

Shooter put on his aviators and stood up. "No, thanks, sir. You win this round. We'll see how you do with the *Enterprise*."

"I'll do just fine. Keep your greenbacks handy."

"Yes, sir." Shooter fell in step with Raven, who had picked up a parachute and was walking toward his airplane. "Do you think that church of yours will give us a hand?"

"I'm pretty sure they will. But the old man has to give us some idea of numbers—are we feeding a hundred, two hundred, five hundred?"

"My girlfriend can help out."

"Peggy?"

"No, Megs. Peggy took up with a marine corps pilot."

"Before or after you took up with Megs?"

Shooter lifted one shoulder in a shrug. "How about Becky? Can she cook?"

They reached Raven's P-36. A member of the ground crew gave him thumbs-up. The canopy was open and Raven tossed his parachute into the cockpit.

"I don't know, Shooter. Her mother and aunt can cook up a storm. What Beck can do I'm not sure."

"Ask her."

"Sure I'll ask her. Next time I see her."

"Wouldn't that be now?"

"What are you talking about?"

"Isn't that her? Looks like her."

Raven followed Shooter's gaze to the far end of the airfield where a jeep had stopped by the hangar they'd just left. It was now racing across the runway toward them. The driver's bright blond hair was flying and the sun glinted off her sunglasses. Her face was a mask of determination, set in stone.

"Yeah." Raven took off his glasses and squinted. "That's her."

"Maybe she's coming so quick just to settle my nerves and tell me, 'Hey, Shooter, it's your lucky day. Twenty prime geese, plucked, gutted, stuffed, and roasted. Delivery December twentieth.'"

"I'm sure that's what she's going to say."

Raven had no idea what she was going to say. He had no idea what she was doing at Wheeler Field. He knew she was booked solid right through December with students on both Saturdays and Sundays—and today, the last Saturday in November, was no different. Flapjack always let her book off church time on Sunday mornings so he had expected to see her at church tomorrow and hopefully tomorrow night. It had been a couple of days and he missed her. But he had no idea what the mad ride across the airstrip was about.

The jeep skidded to a stop and Becky jumped out. "Hey."

"Hey," Raven responded.

She was in her flight jacket, white tee, and Levi Strauss jeans. "How's it going, Shooter?"

"Great."

"Thunderbird?"

"Can't complain."

"You going up?" she asked.

"Yeah. Instrument check." He looked at her as she stood there in the Hawaiian heat, Ray-Bans on her small face, freckles scattered across her nose. "What's up? I thought you had students from dawn to dusk."

"I do. This won't take long."

"What won't take long?" Raven asked.

"Just this." Becky approached him. "You need to know you achieved what I thought was impossible. You made me fall for you. Long and hard. Now I can't live without you. No matter what the risk."

"What?" Raven glanced to Shooter who cleared his throat and said, "Maybe I should—"

"It's all right, Shooter," Becky said. "I don't care who knows."

She put her arms around Raven's neck and pulled him into a kiss.

He squirmed a second, then, not knowing what to do with his hands, finally placed them on the back of her leather jacket and hung on until Becky pulled back.

"I love you," she said. "You need to know that."

Twenty-Two

Sunset sent up a burst of bronze and copper clouds from the sea. The sky glowed white for ten or fifteen minutes before the night rushed in like dark water. It glimmered with stars like minnows that sparkled as they rested in the deep. Becky, lying on her back in the sand, reached over to take Raven's hand but he pulled it away sharply.

"Hey, hey. No touching until the moon is up."

She let out her breath in a gust. "You and your games. The other week it was no kissing."

"I like it. Heightens the anticipation."

"My anticipation is already sky-high, in case you hadn't noticed."

"I know. Your eyes are smoldering."

"*My eyes are smoldering?*" She rolled over on her stomach. "How can you tell in the dark?"

"The sparks."

She threw her head back and laughed.

"I think mine are smoldering too," he said.

"Really."

"They're unusually warm. Know what I mean?"

"No, I don't. Come on. Relax the rules. I want to play. We haven't seen each other since—well, since Saturday."

"Since you told me you loved me."

She dropped her eyes. "Yeah. That."

"A pretty sweet moment."

"Thank you. It took all my nerve."

Raven pushed himself up on his elbows. "Why?"

"Because…because I was afraid to say it. I was afraid where saying it might take me. Might take us."

"Well, I'm sure not. I didn't need a plane to fly for the rest of the day. I haven't needed a plane since, actually."

"Yeah?" She looked up and he could see the white of her teeth in the tropical night. "You left me that note at Peterson's explaining why you weren't at church Sunday. You didn't say anything about planes in it."

"I had other things on my mind."

"So I read."

"Share the note with your mom and aunt?"

"Are you kidding?" She propped her elbows in the sand and rested her face between her hands. "So tell me what happened after I left you standing on the airstrip on Saturday. You haven't said a thing about it."

"How do you talk about a tidal wave?"

"Please." She gave him the biggest smile she could. "How did your instrument check go?"

"Not that great. Considering I could hardly read the gauges or focus on the needles."

"Ah. Sorry about that."

"I do remember doing a victory roll over Pearl Harbor and Honolulu Harbor. I did it twice over the *Taney* until Harrison came out and waved his arms at me."

"What was that about?"

"He told me weeks ago you liked me. I said you didn't. It was kind of a bet, I guess. I said if you ever fell for me I'd do a victory roll over his ship."

She grinned. "Is that all?"

"I owed him a plateful of bacon and beans. Had to give one of the mess cooks a fiver to get a plate big enough for him."

"Bacon and beans? Is that how I'm going to be remembered? Not cake? Not wine? Not roses?"

She ran her hands back through her hair to get the bangs out of her eyes. Damp from a swim, it remained upright in a kind of wave.

"There." Raven smiled as he looked at the wave. "That's how you're going to be remembered. As gorgeous under all conditions."

She rolled her eyes up to try to see. "Oh, sure, gorgeous—with my hair sticking up in the air like a freak."

"You're stunning."

"You see? You're absolutely hopeless. You think I'm cute no matter what I look like."

"Well, you always look the same."

"I always look the same?"

"Yeah—beautiful. Like a Pacific sunrise. Or a sunset. A night with stars. The sea in a storm."

"You're a nut. I tell God you're a nut."

"And what does he say about that?"

"He says I should love you anyway."

"Yeah? So do it."

"Do it?"

"Love me anyway."

She raised her eyebrows. "So I can touch you now?"

"The moon. The full moon. That's what we're waiting for. All week it's going to look like a full moon. But the meteorologist told me Wednesday, December third, was the actual full moon. That's why I dragged you here."

"Dragged me here." She made a sour face. "You're the one who's been playing hard to get."

"Not my fault. Skipp had us do all this extra stuff with our planes on Sunday. Like he knew something was up. When the *Enterprise* didn't show on Monday he really went into high gear. Way too many drills. Too much chalkboard talk. Flight patterns till we were sitting in our cockpits with our eyes closed and fast asleep."

"I missed you."

"Believe me, I missed you more. A guy doesn't normally have a gal that looks like you come waltzing up, kiss him like a volcano, then disappear for a week."

"*A gal that looks like you.* You always make so much of me."

"It's not hard to do." He suddenly swung around. "Here it comes." A Bible was holding down his uniform. He reached for it. "Now don't do anything. I want to read you a verse."

"Who can do anything? You have more rules than the Amish *Ordnung*."

The moon rose silently over the palm trees of Oahu and the brightness slipped over the beach and the crashing surf, making the waves whiter and the pages of Raven's Bible gleam. He traced his finger over the lines of type. Becky moved closer.

"Can I help?" she asked, putting her face close to his.

"Uh-uh. This is something I have to do."

"You act as if I touched you you'd explode."

"I would." He sat up straighter. "Now listen to this. You can't interrupt me or tempt me while I'm reading the Bible. These words are from God."

Becky hugged her knees to her chest. "All right. What are they?"

"Really. These are words of God. But tonight I'm reworking them a little. They're from me to you."

"*A good woman who can find? For her worth is far above rubies. She rises early in the morning and gives meat to her household. She layeth her hands to the spindle. She is not afraid of the snow. She openeth her mouth with wisdom—*"

"Shh. No fooling around."

Raven faced her, holding the Bible open in one hand. For a moment she was reminded of an Amish minister preaching. But it was impossible for her to hold the image long—Raven was tanned, muscular, his hair tangled from seawater and sun, and he was sitting cross-legged on a tropical beach in his swimsuit. She put a hand to her mouth to stop the laughter gurgling up inside her.

"Are you listening?" he demanded.

"Yes, yes. I had a crazy thought, that's all."

"Well, hold that crazy thought for a few minutes. I've been thinking about this since Skipp had me up and flying in the moonlight Sunday night."

"That must have been something."

"It was something. Are you here?"

Becky smiled softly as she watched him start to read the Bible to her. "I'm here."

"Okay." He looked up. "*You are beautiful, my love, as Tirzah, comely as Jerusalem, awesome as an army with banners. Turn your eyes away from me for they have overcome me.*"

Becky's smile deepened. "Where did you get this from? The Song of Solomon?"

He took a piece of paper out of the Bible. "That part I read pretty much straight. But I, uh, I went to the chaplain to see if he could help me put something together that was…a little more modern. He's actually a bit of a scholar when it comes to Hebrew and Greek. So we came up with this. It's accurate. Just not as formal as the old language the Bible uses."

"I'm happy with that. What did you tell him you needed the translation for?"

"A Christmas present."

"Is that true?"

"It is true. Three weeks to go. This is a warm-up." He lifted the paper so he could see it better. "*Your teeth are lambs, pure and white and freshly washed and perfect. Your temple is like the halves of a pomegranate, cleanly sliced and smooth, lying gently under the covering of your hair. My dove has no flaws, no blemishes—everything in her is as it should be, and she is the only daughter of her mother. Who is she? Who is this young woman? She comes to me like the dawn, fair as the moon, radiant as the sun, majestic as a sky glittering with stars.*" He put the paper down and stared at her as the moon carved her face and figure with light. "*Before I was even aware of it she made the soul inside of me like the chariots of a prince.*"

Knees drawn up to her chest, Becky had leaned her cheek on the tops of them. "Aw. That makes me feel special. You have no idea."

Raven's hand followed the path of the moonlight to her face. "*U-wo-du-hi. U-wo-du-hi. U-wo-du-hi.*"

She let him stroke her cheek, not closing her eyes. "What are you saying to me?"

"*Beautiful. Beautiful. Beautiful.* It's Cherokee."

Her eyes glimmered. "Okay. You can't read all those verses to me from the Bible and tell me I'm beautiful in Cherokee and expect me not to cry."

"*Gv-ge-yu.*" He touched his lips to hers as lightly as he could.

She continued to look at him, tears moving slowly along the curve of her cheek. "If I had to guess I'd say you were telling me you love me."

Raven kissed her lightly again. "*Aloha au ia 'oe.*"

"I know that's Hawaiian."

"*Aloha nui loa.*"

"Tell me what you're saying to me, Christian. No more games."

"I could choose more languages, I suppose. I know it in French and Spanish and German too."

"Let me do the German." She traced a heart over his face with her finger. "*Ich liebe dich.*" Her lips brushed his. "Am I right?"

"Yeah. You're right." He kissed her. "You taste perfect."

"What does perfect taste like?"

"It tastes like someone who is strong, gentle, intelligent, compassionate, altogether lovely and holy and—"

"Stop." She pressed her fingers against his lips. "I asked you not to play any more games."

"I don't think you realize how much I think about you and how often I thank God for you. He must get tired of me. *It's Raven going on about Becky again.*" He stood up, stooped, and took her up into his arms. "Will you stay with me until the moon sets?"

"Yes."

"Will you wait for me if I am sent far away with my squadron?"

"I will."

"Can I keep using superlatives when I talk about you?"

She wrinkled her nose. "I guess. So long as we're alone. But no more speeches to others about me."

He carried her toward the surf. "You're dry as a bone."

"And warm. What are you going to do about it?"

"If I get you wet you'll want to hug me all night, won't you?"

"Probably."

She squealed as he ran into a big wave and let it smash to pieces on their backs and shoulders, filling their mouths with water and covering their eyes.

A roller knocked him off his feet and they were both buried in white foam. They came up spitting and shouting, and the surge churned them around and flung them onto the beach. She pounced and pinned him down.

A wave hit and threw her off him and they both spun and rolled in the swirl. The current pulled them back into the ocean and they treaded water next to each other in the swell.

"You look great!" he shouted.

"Sure I do. With my hair all plastered down."

"You know, the guys were talking about giving you a call sign. After all, you are a pilot."

"Not a combat pilot."

"You're better than most of them."

"I hate to think what your crew came up with."

"Lava. Rocket. Tiger. Volcano."

"I'm not like that!"

"I wanted to go for Green Eyes."

"What?"

He spat out seawater. "The Jimmy Dorsey hit. You've heard it on the radio."

She slapped water into his face. "Oh, cut it out!"

He began to sing it.

A breaker pushed Becky up against him and he put his arms around her, managing to hold on even though her skin was wet and slick. "*Green Eyes, I love you.*"

"So is that my call sign then? Green Eyes? I don't mind it."

"It was going to be your call sign. The guys liked it but they vetoed it."

"You make it sound like this was a vote in Congress."

"They have call signs for Kalino and Hani too."

"Great. Probably nice Hawaiian names. So what did I end up with? Spotted Leopard?"

"Another song. Lockjaw wanted to go with 'Choo Choo'—"

"No!" Becky swallowed water and gagged.

"And Wizard voted for 'Chica Chica Boom Chic.'"

Becky was still sputtering. "What—stop goofing around—what did—"

"Artie Shaw. Doing Hoagy Carmichael's song, 'Stardust.'"

"I don't—know that—"

"Gee, even the Amish must know, 'Stardust.'"

"Sing—it—"

"I'd need a trumpet or trombone. It's a solo."

"What's so great—about it?"

Raven lifted her up out of the water. "What's so great about it? Are you kidding me? Everyone loves the song—just like everyone loves you."

"Everyone does not—" A whitecap smacked into her mouth. She coughed and choked.

"Whistler told us the saying goes, *If you seek God you will find him in Artie Shaw's solo in 'Stardust.'*"

"That's—"

Because she had her face toward the sea the surf always found her. A wave silenced her, filling her mouth. Finally she twisted around in Raven's arms so that, like him, her back was to the breakers.

"Whew. That's better." She looked at his face as sea foam ran off his cheeks and forehead. "So, *Stardust?* That's it? That's me?"

"That's you. I can't believe you've never heard the song. It's got incredible swing. It's soft. It's got the right amount of energy and beat. It's you, baby. When you hear it you'll be impressed that the guys tagged you with it."

"*It's you, baby?* Since when do you call me baby?"

"The guys do, so why can't I?"

"Swell. *The guys do.*"

"Don't take it the wrong way. Lockjaw's interested in Kalino and Wizard's head over heels with Hani and Batman is googly eyes over some nurse at the naval hospital. They're not after Becky Whetstone anymore. They just plain like her." He gave her a quick kiss before the sea broke over them again. "When you hear the song you'll get it."

"And when will that be?"

"Let me look into it. Did you know Harrison plays the trumpet? No kidding, Batman and Robin have him lined up for the Christmas dance band at Wheeler." He began to wade out of the crash and roar of the ocean with her in his arms. "Cold yet?"

"A little."

"*By the light of the silvery moon, I want to spoon, to my honey I'll croon love's tune, honeymoon keep a-shining in June, your silvery beams will bring love dreams, we'll be cuddling soon, by the silvery moon.*" Raven ran up the beach. "You ready to spoon? And don't tell me you don't know what that means."

"I know what it means, hotshot. I just can't figure out what's gotten into you. All these songs and tunes, and now suddenly I'm Stardust and fair as the moon and majestic as the stars in the heavens."

Raven placed her down on the sand and laid himself beside her. "You can't figure it out?"

"No, I can't."

"This is the first time I've seen you since you told me you loved me and you can't figure it out?"

"Well, I..." She looked up at him, using her hand to shield her eyes from the bright moonlight. "You're like a bottle of Coke someone shook up and popped open."

He laughed. "Hey, that's good."

"I can't have had that much of an effect on you. There's something else. Or someone else."

"Are you kidding me? You think that?"

"I don't know."

Raven looked at the drops of water that slid off her face and arms and stomach. Becky's skin glowed under the full moon and the drops were like tiny silver mirrors. Her eyes were dark, half-closed, watching him. He picked up one of her hands and placed it against his lips.

"You are the most beautiful woman alive," he said.

"Christian, you don't have to say—"

"I've talked to Billy Skipp about taking carrier training next year and getting posted to a flattop based in Pearl. A number of the guys have approached him—Batman, Wizard, Lockjaw. At first he was pretty upset about it all. Then he calmed down. He has lots of pilots who want to stay in the army. And he realizes it has nothing to do with his leadership. He said to me, 'I'd be seeing stars too, Thunderbird. Her beauty and spirit are enough to turn any man inside out. I'll see what I can do about your transfer.'"

"He did not say that."

"He did say that."

"How embarrassing. He's known my parents forever."

"Why is it embarrassing?"

"He's exaggerating. You're all exaggerating. I'm just—"

He put a hand to the side of her face. "You're already dry. Are you warm enough?"

"I guess."

"You have no idea what your eyes do to me, do you? The feel of your hair in my fingers. What it's like to kiss you." He sat up and took both her hands in his. "God. Creator. Redeemer. Thank you for the gift of this woman. She doesn't see—so help her see. She doesn't know—help her know. She doesn't believe in what you've put inside her and what you've made out of her—help her believe in what you've created and what you have died for and how precious she is to you and to others. I've needed freedom—a lot of it. So has Nate. So has Becky. But I think she needs even more so she can be everything you put it in her to be. I ask you, our Father, on this night of a moon of white fire, that you will speak into being Becky's freedom. Turn back the darkness. Bring in more of your light. Set her loose—your daughter, your child, your angel. Open up the ancient gates and set her free. And may she tonight, this very night, here on the shores of this vast sea, know also this—how much a man can love her. How much a man can be faithful to her. How much a man can be blessed by her. In the name of the strong son of God, Jesus Christ, our Lord."

He released her hands.

"Lie beside me and hold me. My love."

He lay down and she curled into him, tucking her head against his chest.

"Becky—"

"Shh. No. You've said all that needs to be said. I feel your prayer at work in me. I feel God unbolting doors and cracking open windows. I believe you love me in a way not even Moses could love me. I believe God won't take you away from me. He's making something more out of me with the love you have for me. It's astonishing. Miraculous that you can cherish me like this and it can make such a difference to my heart. This is the most perfect night of my life. Hold me closer. Don't say anything more. Let's listen to the sea and gaze at the light of the moon and for now, just for now, let the breeze kiss us, the warm breeze, let it put its lips to our skin, let the Holy Spirit fill us up with all his silver and all his gold, and let the love of God be enough for us. Later I'll want you to tell me again how much I matter to you. Later I'll want you to light another fire in my heart. But for now just let God speak, and his ocean speak. That's all we need to hear."

In a few minutes, his arms wrapped around her and her head over his heart, her eyes closed and she slept. But it was not in Raven to sleep. He had never felt so alive or so grateful or so full of hope. It seemed as if the blood was singing through his bones and fingers and throat. He had all the air he needed, all the soul he needed, all the faith he needed.

He made an effort to wake her after an hour.

"Hey. Stardust. Hey."

But her breathing was deep and regular, her features like a child's, and he didn't try again.

TWENTY-THREE

Lyyndaya Whetstone was bringing baked chicken out of the oven, when Becky walked through the door in her flying gear and dropped into a chair.

She leaned her head back. "What a day."

"A lot of students?"

"A lot of students and I was bone-tired to begin with. Thank goodness I have tomorrow off. I'm going to sleep till noon."

Lyyndaya cut open one of the chicken pieces with a knife and examined it. "What time did you get in last night?"

"Four."

Lyyndaya licked her fingers. "You'll be twenty in March. The old gray mare ain't what she used to be."

"It's Thunderbird. He's the problem. He has the energy of a seventeen-year-old. I'm having trouble keeping up."

"Shall I phone him and ask him to come over and carry you up to your bedroom?"

"Don't. He'd probably fly over in his P-36 and do it." Becky pushed herself to her feet. "I'm hitting the hay."

"Don't you want some of my Caribbean chicken? We're eating once your father gets home."

"I don't think I'll make it."

"So I'll put some aside on a plate in the fridge." She opened a cupboard. "What do you find to do until four in the morning?"

"If you want to know the truth, Mom, not much more than

reading the Bible and praying. He does a lot of that. And I fell asleep for a couple of hours too."

"Hm." Lyyndaya looked up as she placed a breast on a plate along with a few spears of pineapple, and her eyes went to Becky's neck. "Is that your father's flying scarf from the Great War?"

Becky started up the staircase. "Yes."

"Why are you wearing it?"

"I found it lying around. The silk is comfortable. I like the feeling."

Lyyndaya licked her fingers again. "Lying around?"

Becky kept going up the stairs. "See you."

Ruth was spreading out a quilt on her bed as Becky entered the room. "There. It's done."

Becky stared. "It's beautiful. But the Amish wouldn't know what to do with it."

There were patches of pineapples, banana plants, waves, palm trees, and Diamond Head.

Ruth straightened the quilt. "The Amish don't matter. It's for Manuku."

"Manuku. Who needs a quilt in Hawaii?"

"It's not a heavy quilt. He likes to sleep with all his windows open. Now and then if the wind is rough the apartment gets cool. So this will help." She smiled at Becky. "A Christmas present."

Becky walked closer and stood over it. "The colors are amazing. So are you. My aunt is quite the artist."

Ruth waved a hand. "It's a simple thing. But I hope he'll like it."

"Of course he'll like it. He likes you, doesn't he?" Becky peeled off her leather jacket, tossed it over an armchair, and flopped on her back on her bed. "I wish I had a talent like that. There's nothing I've made I can give Christian for a present." She locked her hands under her head and looked at Ruth. "How serious are you about Manuku?"

Ruth raised her eyebrows and pursed her lips. "Sure, I like him. I do like him. How serious are you about Christian?"

"After last night? Very."

"What was so special about last night?"

"He read to me from the Bible. He prayed for me. It was just a very spiritual night."

"The full moon couldn't have hurt."

"Moonlight never hurts. But he was even gentler than the moon was. He was so kind to me and so patient. I fell asleep in his arms and I felt totally safe and protected. Nothing was going to hurt me." Suddenly she sat up. "Ruth, I love him with all my heart. I thank God for him."

"I'm glad."

Ruth sat on the quilt. "I'm not so far along as you. The Lord himself knows I wasn't even looking. I haven't been looking for years. But Manuku also has been kind and patient—and persistent. Now I feel so alive. So alive, Rebecca."

"I'm glad."

Ruth looked up at the ceiling and began to pull the pins from her hair. She grinned. "Oh, the plane ride, the first one—that was something else. All of them have been good but that first time in the sky—my goodness."

"Why, Auntie Ruth, how many plane rides have there been?"

"Four. I'm getting much better with the stick."

"Four!"

"The last few weeks have been like wave after wave coming in on Waikiki. The dancing was also good."

"Dancing…you danced?"

"At a nice place in Honolulu. Very clean. Everyone dressed modestly."

"What did you wear?"

"Well, he—Manuku—he bought me a gown. I tried to say no. But he can be very charming. It was not expensive. He showed me the sales slip."

"Where is it?"

"In my closet."

Becky got up and opened the closet doors. Hidden behind several plain Amish dresses was a black gown. Becky took the hangar off the rack and ran her fingers over the material.

"This has to be silk, Aunt Ruth. It's like the scarf I'm wearing. It's beautiful."

"Yes, of course it's silk, but not too expensive. And as plain as a gown can be, I suppose." She raised her palms in the air. "So I'm shunned, and what does it matter? Lyyndaya has been encouraging me."

"Silk is one of the most wonderful things a woman can wear in this climate. I plan to get something white and in silk for the Christmas dance. I'd never tell you not to buy silk. Or to turn down a gift of silk." Becky unwound the scarf from her neck. "Dad had this during the war. Mom kept it in a paper bag inside a drawer, with cedar chips. It looks brand-new."

Ruth nodded. "I remember that scarf. He gave it to your mother for a wedding present, I think."

"He did?"

"Or an engagement present. I can't recall which."

"I'm so happy about you and Manuku. I never expected you would…"

Ruth laughed. "That I might fall in love? I'm not saying I have, Rebecca. I'm at an age where we tend to take these things more slowly than you who are young. I take it one day at a time. One prayer at a time. It wasn't expected; but then many of God's blessings arrive unexpected. No one has been more surprised than me. But I made up my mind last week to enjoy this. For who knows what may happen another day or another month?" She looked down and began to pick pieces of lint off the quilt. "He is a beautiful man."

"Yes, he is."

"Knock, knock." Nate leaned against the door frame. "Am I interrupting?"

Ruth straightened up and put her hands on her knees. "Not at all. Come in."

Nate remained leaning. "Just a few things. Dad's home early so Mom wants to serve supper in ten minutes."

"I'm not eating." Becky walked back to the closet to hang up the gown. "I'm going to bed. I can hardly keep my eyes open."

"Really." One corner of Nate's mouth lifted in a smile. "There's also this." He extended a small white envelope to Ruth. "I was up with Manuku this afternoon."

Ruth got up and took the envelope. "Thank you. Excuse me a moment while I read it, please."

"Why were you up with Manuku?" asked Becky. "He and I had an hour together in the morning."

"Well, Flapjack took me aside while you were up and said he liked what he was seeing—and that if I continue to progress he'd think about offering me an instructor's position in the new year. If I was interested."

"No!" Becky laughed.

"So he wanted me to go up again and he asked Manuku to take me after lunch."

Becky got up and hugged him. "Oh, that's wonderful. You're coming back to life and everyone is starting to notice what a fine pilot you are."

Ruth, standing by the window, looked up from her letter. "That's a blessing, Nate. Did you enjoy your time with Manuku?"

"It was swell." He put his hands in his pockets. "I'm not out of the woods yet. I still hold back. You know it. Manuku knows it."

Becky kissed his cheek. "Give yourself more time. There's plenty of time."

"Yeah." He cast his eyes down for a moment and then gave the two of them a crooked smile. "Finish your note yet, Aunt Ruth?"

"Just. You act like you know what's in it."

"Manuku told me. As a matter of fact, one of the things I wanted to tell you two was that the phone call was actually from Manuku. He'll be here in an hour."

"What phone call?" asked Becky, pulling back from her brother. "I never heard the phone ring."

Ruth folded up the note and placed it in the Bible on her pillow. "We don't have a great deal of time, Rebecca. We'll need to eat and get dressed quickly."

"Get dressed quickly? Get dressed quickly for what? I'm going to bed. I'm exhausted."

"You don't look exhausted," said Nate.

"I'm just excited for you," Becky said. "And for Aunt Ruth. Really, I don't know what's up with the phone call and note, but this gal needs her beauty sleep." She plopped herself on her bed.

"You look great, sis. No sleep needed."

"Ha ha. My noble brother. It won't work. It won't work for anyone." She grabbed her pillow and tossed it at him. "Now go. Have a nice evening, both of you."

"Hey!" A face popped into the doorway. "You ready, Stardust?"

Beck shot back to her feet. "Christian!"

"Did you get my message?"

"What message? There was only a note for Ruth and a phone call from Manuku."

"There must have been a mix-up. But this is for you." Raven walked into the room with a huge bouquet of red roses. "You're the absolute most."

"Why—" Becky couldn't count the roses there were so many. She brought them to her nose and breathed in and they covered her face completely. "Christian—"

"I want you to dance with me, baby. Tonight. Double date with Ruth and Manuku. Skinny is the chauffeur. Billy Skipp's lent us his brand-new Packard One Eighty LeBaron. A metallic carmine-red Sport Brougham. Can you believe that?"

She smiled up at him with her eyes half-closed. "I have no idea what you're talking about."

"When you see this car you'll flip."

"I'll flip?"

"You'll flip, baby."

"I'll go anywhere to dance with you. But if this place is at all posh—"

"It is."

"—what is a gal like me to do? All I have are flying helmets and leather jackets and jeans. How can you take Amelia Earhart to the ball when she doesn't look like Cinderella after the magic?"

"I lucked out buying you the swimsuit so I tried again."

Her eyes came fully open instantly. "What?"

"I'm just glad your dad got here with it in time."

"My dad?"

Jude took his cue and entered the room with a white silk gown in his hands. Becky dropped the bouquet but Ruth reached out and caught it. Becky had a hand to her mouth, her eyes wide and bright green.

"Of course your mom helped this time." Raven watched Jude give the gown to Becky. "I didn't want to mess up taking my baby to the prom. So it was a family affair."

Becky put the gown to her cheek. "How did you know I wanted white?"

"I didn't know. But I wanted it. You're an angel."

Her eyes were shining. "You have a crazy love for me."

"I know."

"Don't stop, okay? No matter what else happens. Don't stop."

He put up his hands and shook his head. "I got no brakes, baby."

"*Baby.*" She smiled. "It's beautiful. But I don't have any shoes to go with it. Nothing. Are they going to let me dance in bare feet?"

"On the beach it doesn't matter. But in the club that could be a problem."

"So—"

"Enter Mom to save the day."

Lyyndaya walked in flashing her smile. "All this drama, Thunderbird. I thought you'd never get to me."

"Sorry, Mrs. Whetstone, I guess I do like my games."

Lyyndaya held out white high heels to her daughter. "Not from the Amish in Lancaster County. But they'll fit. I know my girl's ten toes."

"Mom! What's going on here?"

"Just trying to raise my child in the best way I know how."

Becky held the shoes and gown and struggled with tears. She looked at Raven. Stumbling for words, she managed, "I…I have to get changed…"

"I'll leave you to that. I can hardly wait."

"For what?"

"To see you come down that staircase looking like a dream."

When she did come down the stairs it was more than Raven expected. The high heels made her four inches taller. Her legs were shimmering in stockings of sheer white silk. The gown flowed to just below her knees and her arms were bare down to the white gloves on her hands that matched the dress. The gown was fastened in the middle with a gold clasp. Ruth had brushed her hair until it sparkled like diamonds and had helped her apply things neither of them knew how to do well—eyeliner, eye shadow, mascara. Raven had never seen her eyes look so much like the turquoise of the tropical waters or so large they seemed like the green sea itself. Becky had used lip gloss as well and her mouth had a soft gleam. A flesh-colored cream covered the blemishes on her neck. He took her hands in his and breathed in the scent of her perfume.

"Well?" She squeezed his hands. "Aren't you going to say anything?"

"I don't have words."

She brushed his cheek with the back of her gloved hand. "My baby doesn't have words? Since when?"

"Since you stepped out of the clouds and into my arms."

She smiled and laid her head on his uniformed chest. "Those are pretty good words. Where is everyone?"

"Outside looking at the Packard. Skinny just pulled up with Manuku."

"Is Ruth out there too?"

"Yes. The whole crew."

He kissed the top of her head, drawing into himself the richness of her gold hair. "Milk and honey. And lemons."

"What?"

"Sometimes you're like freshly baked bread too. But my favorite is when you've been out in the sun and you smell like cookie dough rising in a warm oven. Chocolate-chip cookie dough. That's the best."

"You really are a nut."

"You look like moonlight in that gown. Do you know that?"

"Well, now I know." Her gloved hand brought his head down. "I feel like a bride. This is for you. You make me feel like a woman."

A car horn honked twice outside. Jude came to a window and tapped.

"Cinderella, your carriage awaits," he announced with a grin.

The warm night was full of sailors in white uniforms and caps striding across the streets between cars and spilling over the sidewalks in small mobs. The crimson Packard pulled up in front of a club surrounded by coconut palms and beds of tropical blossoms. A doorman immediately opened the passenger door and Manuku stepped out in his white suit and offered Ruth his hand. She slipped along the seat and put her black high heels on the sidewalk. Standing erect, she was as tall as he, and her upswept hair, high cheekbones and perfect posture made sailors walking past slow down and linger. One or two whistled. Manuku smiled at this but Ruth grew rigid and tightened her lips.

"They're just saying they like you in the Navy man's way," Manuku said as she slipped her arm through his.

"It's so much not the way I was raised. I like dressing in silk and dancing with you. But I'm not comfortable having strange men gawk at me."

"Yet how could they not notice you?"

"Manuku—"

"Your look is dark and strong and perfect."

"Perfectly mismatched, you mean."

"No, that's not so. You are a wonder. Put you back in your Amish dresses and stick a thousand pins in your hair and you are still a wonder."

She gave him a smile as her eyes flashed. "Take me inside, charmer, and hold me in your arms, please."

Raven was helping Becky out of the backseat. Her white heels and long legs came first, and sailors and soldiers hung back and offered more whistles. She smoothed the white silk of her dress as she stood next to Raven and took his hand, reddening as several Army pilots stopped to clap.

"Are my aunt and I some sort of show?"

"Looks like it." Raven, his uniform immaculate, lifted his hand to the pilots. "I'd be clapping if I could get away with it."

"Don't you start, please."

"You're pretty gorgeous, Stardust. So is your aunt dolled up like that. Have some mercy on the guys."

"Whatever I look like on the outside I'm still a good thirty percent Amish under my skin."

"Thirty percent? Do you know that for a fact?"

She tightened her grip on his hand. "Take me into the club, please, Christian."

He started toward the door that was being held open. "I thought you didn't mind an audience."

"Where did you get that idea? I always mind an audience."

The club was huge, and dark but for a few table lamps. Colored lights rimmed the dance floor, at one end of which a tall man conducted a band of sixteen or so players. The floor was full of men and women who were dancing to a fast swing number. The headwaiter ushered them to a table and they sat and watched the quick, precise movements of the dancers.

"I can't do that." Becky leaned into Raven and spoke into his ear while the trombones blasted. "Can you hear me? I can't do that."

"Well, you can fly, can't you?"

"What does that have to do with it?"

"If you can fly you can dance."

"I have a plane when I fly."

"God gave you a plane for dancing. Your legs."

"What?" She stared at him.

"You have great legs. You can go anywhere on those legs."

"Christian, I can't do everything you say I can just because you think God dropped me out of heaven into your arms."

"Look."

Raven gestured with his head. Ruth was laughing as Manuku swung her about the dance floor with ease. Becky couldn't believe the freedom in her aunt's shoulders and legs as Manuku guided her smoothly between other couples, spun her in circles, and brought the kind of big smiles to her face Becky had never seen in a lifetime. Suddenly Raven was stripping the gloves off her hands and pulling her onto the floor, and she was whirling and gliding as he tugged and pulled and tossed her past blue and red lights and the glittering brass of polished trumpets. Fear became astonishment, and astonishment became laughter that burst out of her stomach and chest, laughter she couldn't stop. She was a kid on the swings, on the slide, on the seesaw. In the blur she saw pilots and sailors and soldiers circling the dance floor and swinging their right arms down again and again with the beat, cheering her on.

"What—what—" she gasped.

"They want us to go faster. Come on." He smiled as perspiration ran down his face.

The song changed to a more rapid beat and three women began

to sing into the microphone—something about a boogie-woogie boy from Company B.

"Just do what I do," Raven said, whirling her around the floor.

"Oh, sure," she panted.

The servicemen were clapping and shouting in rhythm with the dancing. Becky sensed herself loosening up, her arms and legs keeping time. She began taking charge of some of the moves and leaped halfway across the floor when Raven threw her out of his hands, spinning on her own so quickly she couldn't get her breath. The soldiers and sailors and pilots roared. To her it really was becoming like flight. She leaped again and landed in Raven's arms, twisted loose and danced on her own, swinging past Ruth, and coming back for Raven to toss her in the air and catch her.

"I love it—but I can't—keep it up, Thunderbird—"

"Sure you can. You're serving your country."

"What?"

"Give the guys something to cheer about. Come on. You look terrific."

They danced until the band seemed to explode and come to a sudden stop. The women stopped singing, the room broke into applause, and the bandleader spoke into the microphone.

"Ladies and gentlemen, how was that?"

Shouting and clapping and whistles.

"So who do we have here tonight? Any sailors from the *Arizona* or *Oklahoma* or *Tennessee*?"

An eruption of shouts and yells.

"How's about the *West Virginia* or the *Maryland* or *California*?"

Another burst of hollering.

"We got any flyboys here? Ford Island? Hickam? Wheeler? Ewa?"

Becky clapped with the others and Raven took a bow along with other pilots scattered through the crowd.

"And we can't forget our army men. Who's here from Schofield Barracks?"

A huge roar made Becky laugh and put her hands over her ears.

"You want to keep dancing?"

Another roar.

"You want the lady in black to keep dancing?"

It was like thunder. Becky looked over at her aunt whose face was red to the roots of her long black hair. She couldn't tell if it was from embarrassment or fast dancing—perspiration dotted her cheeks and forehead. As the applause continued Ruth put a hand over her eyes and dropped her head.

"What about the lady in white?"

The whole club seemed to blow apart. Men shouted and whistled. The clapping was like big surf breaking at Nanakuli during a storm.

"I thought you said this was a posh club," Becky said to Raven, feeling the heat in her face.

"It is posh. No drunks. No fights. Hardly anyone smokes."

"What am I supposed to do?"

"Keep dancing with me."

"Christian—Thunderbird—I don't run on aviation fuel—"

"You're young."

"I *was* young. I'm twenty and ancient in March."

"You've got a long way to go till ancient, baby."

The band struck up again and Raven began to swing her arm to help her get into the rhythm. "Now just stick with me, kid."

"Kid yourself, old man. Anything you do, I'll do. And if I decide to cut loose and go solo, catch me if you can."

Flying and whirling and sliding. Sometimes Raven was with her and sometimes she was alone. She saw the band and the trombone players on their feet, saw the sailors and soldiers and pilots waving at her and whistling with their fingers in their teeth, saw her aunt laughing in Manuku's arms, felt Raven's quick kiss on her cheek, thought she could just about reach the ceiling if she jumped a little higher and stretched a little farther. Finally the music ended for the second time and she collapsed into Raven's arms as the room erupted.

"That's it. I can't. No matter how loud they clap and yell."

"It is pretty loud."

"I don't care. I've served my country. I've made up for all the Amish who never served America during a time of war. I need you to take care of me now."

"All right. I'll do that."

Slowly the clapping and whistling died down. The band was silent. No one was singing. She leaned against him and closed her eyes.

Suddenly a blue spotlight came through her eyelids and she lifted her head. "What's this?"

"This? Why, this is you."

"This is me? What are you talking about?"

The dance floor was empty except for the two of them.

The bandleader came up to the mike. "Ladies and gentlemen, this little lady isn't just another pretty face. She's a flight trainer at Peterson's and has worked not only with civilians but some of our army pilots to make them the best in the world."

The army men cheered and someone shouted, "What about naval aviators?"

"So the Army Air Forces decided to give her a call sign. I expect we all could give a gal as sweet as her a lot of call signs. Without thinking too hard I could come up with a couple of dozen myself." Everyone laughed. "But the boys at Wheeler gave her something special. I don't think any man of you will be displeased with it now that you've seen how she sparkles and shines. Ladies and gentlemen, our lead trumpeter, Mr. Benny Hart, with Hoagy Carmichael's immortal 'Stardust.'"

Becky looked at Raven in surprise. The trumpet notes rang out pure and clean and he brought her in close and moved with her gently across the open space. As it sunk in with the servicemen what her call sign was, they began to clap enthusiastically but without any whistles or shouts, warmly expressing their approval of what the men at Wheeler had come up with. A tear came to one of Becky's eyes and remained at its corner, glittering like a drop of sapphire in the spotlight. The beauty of the music washed over her body and spirit. She felt it going on deep inside her. Raven's lips brushed her damp hair.

"What do you think?" he asked.

"I love it. It's such a perfect melody."

"Just like you. I told you that."

"Don't be crazy. But thank you for the vote of confidence."

"Every man in this room agrees with me." He tilted her chin and kissed her lips. "Shall I take that vote, Stardust?"

The band joined in with the trumpeter. The bandleader said, "Everyone dance, please, everyone dance." Becky was aware of other couples around them, aware of the slow and sweet movement of men holding women. Once she opened her eyes because she felt something, and she saw her aunt smiling at her, her head resting on Manuku's white-suited shoulder. She smiled in return and closed her eyes again. Raven continued to dance her softly in the dark, the spotlight gone.

"It's all so wonderful," she whispered.

"Yeah, Stardust. It is. Thank God."

Twenty-Four

"H ey. Wake up. It's Christmas morning."

Becky pulled the covers over her head. "It is not."

Nate placed a tray of food on her bedside table. "Bacon. Scrambled eggs. Toast with marmalade. Coffee with cream. A cinnamon roll. Looks like it."

Becky sat up, blinking and wiping at the corners of her eyes with her fingers. "Who made all this?"

"I did. I was up with Manuku and came home after that. Dad lent me the jeep."

"What time is it?"

"Two."

"No!"

"I thought you might be dead so I checked your pulse."

She took the tray and put it on her lap. "Christian has had me living at the pace of a sixteen-year-old." She bit into the toast and marmalade. "Thank goodness I had the wisdom to beg off for Friday." She smiled. "It's great to have Christmas breakfast three weeks early. Bless you."

Nate sat down on the edge of her bed. "Aunt Ruth flew for fifteen minutes on her own today. Manuku said she has rock-solid nerves and is cool as a tray of ice with the stick."

"That's amazing. But it doesn't surprise me. I don't even feel comfortable calling her Aunt Ruth anymore because she's changed so much. She's a completely different woman from the person I knew in Pennsylvania. You should have seen her dance last night."

"Boogie-woogie?"

She sipped her coffee. "Yeah. She's a natural. Just flows with the music. She looked about twenty-nine when she was dancing to 'In the Mood' with Manuku."

"I heard from him you weren't much of a slouch yourself."

"Ha. He exaggerates. Christian knew how to move his feet though."

"Well, Jesus danced at Cana."

"It doesn't say that."

"It was the culture. He would have danced. It was what you did as a good Jew."

"And good Jews kept their friends from being humiliated by brewing wine for them."

"That too."

Becky plunged her fork into the scrambled eggs. "Did you put ham and cheese into these eggs?"

"Yeah."

"They're very good. Well, I never was Amish anyway. Not really. For a few weeks I took instruction. That's all. It's Ruth—Aunt Ruth—who has thrown it all out the window. As if she were *rumspringa* like you and me."

Nate made a face. "I don't even consider myself *rumspringa*. Mom and Dad never raised us Amish. They raised us as stunt flyers and missionary pilots. Sure, a few German prayers popped up from time to time. But I have nothing Amish to toss out the window because I was never Amish to begin with."

She chewed and swallowed a mouthful of cinnamon roll. "Who baked this?"

"Ruth."

"I knew it. Mom uses more raisins." Becky popped a piece of bacon in her mouth, then wiped her mouth. "You never had an Amish girl you fell for. But I had Moses. That's how the Amish way got into my blood. There's a lot of good in it, Nate."

"I know. But would God be able to heal me like he has if I weren't able to sit in a cockpit?"

"I guess not. But if you had been raised Amish, real Amish, you wouldn't have been flying to begin with and you never would have been allowed to go to China as a missionary."

Nate's face darkened. "I might say *amen* to that. But if I hadn't been in China many of those people would never have heard about a God of love. And many wouldn't have been saved spiritually or physically. The Japanese weren't able to kill all the ones we hid." The look passed, and he patted his sister on the knee that was drawn up under the blankets. "Listen. A couple of things. First of all, the *Lexington* left today. It had the *Chicago, Portland,* and *Astoria*—they're cruisers—with it. And nine destroyers."

"What? Where is it going? To meet up with the *Enterprise*?"

"Who knows where the Big E is? Some say it's another weekend exercise."

"Oh, like *Enterprise's* weekend exercise that isn't over yet?" Becky finished the cinnamon roll.

"Right. So no one believes that. People have *Lady Lex* going to the Philippines, to Guam, to Wake, even to Australia. We're never going to find out. At least not right away."

"What else?"

"The Pan-Am clipper brought in a bunch of mail today. The good bishop wrote me again. I thought you might want to have a look at his note."

"So soon?" Becky put the tray back on her bedside table, plumped up her pillows, and leaned against them with her coffee in hand. "Read it to me."

"Okay. But I'm not going to read all of it line by line. He says right after he sent the letter to you, what he calls his un-Amish letter, he felt the Lord tell him to read Isaiah 55. He asks if I remember Grandfather Kurtz reading the verses from that chapter—you know, my thoughts are not your thoughts, your ways are not my ways, says the Lord."

"Sure. At the kitchen table. I remember that."

"Then he asks if I remember that his last words to us were from the same chapter—as the rain and snow come down from heaven and don't return without watering the earth so is God's word, which will not return to him empty but accomplish what he desires. We were all standing on the porch."

"And he drove away in his buggy. That was goodbye."

"So he writes out verses 12 and 13 and says he believes they are for me and also for our entire family."

For ye shall go out with joy, and be led forth in peace: the mountains and the hills shall break forth before you into singing, and all the trees of the field shall clap their hands. Instead of the thorn shall come up the fir tree, and instead of the brier shall come up the myrtle tree: and it shall be to the Lord for a name, for an everlasting sign that shall not be cut off.

"But what does it mean, Nate?"

"Well, it's about change for the good, isn't it? Something is bad but now instead of the bad a beautiful thing is going to replace it. There was a bush of sharp thorns and it's gone and a tall fir tree stands in its place. There was a tangle of briers and it doesn't exist any longer because a myrtle tree is where it used to be."

Becky set down her coffee cup, drew up her other knee under the covers, and wrapped both arms around them. "It sounds like us."

"What do you mean?"

"It was a thornbush as far as my heart and Moses went. Then God brought Christian into my life. After China your life and soul were a tangle of briers. But God gave you back the sky. It's changing you. A myrtle tree is growing up inside you instead."

He smiled. "Yeah." He patted her knee again. "Not just us. Ruth and Christian too, don't you think?"

She thought about it. "Yeah." She looked at Nate. "So did Bishop Zook send it for us? I mean, is it just about us?"

"He doesn't know himself. He ends by writing that he's not sure exactly who or what these verses apply to. Just that he felt he was meant to send them." Nate stood up. "You know there's a Christmas meeting at the house tonight. I promised Mom I'd do cleanup to make sure the house is ready."

Becky snorted. "Oh, sure. Clean it up so the army pilots can mess it up."

"Something like that. Want to help?"

"I'll be right down."

That night several of the pilots were lucky enough to drive up to the Whetstone house in the crimson Packard with Billy Skipp, Skinny happily at the wheel. The others came by jeep. Somehow Kalino, Hani, Manuku, and Ruth were drawn into the planning group, but Skipp didn't care. He said he'd grab as many as he could if it would help the squadron pull off a great party.

"If I do invite Admiral Kimmel to stop by I want the best food, the best band, and the best tree." He sipped at a glass of fresh pineapple juice. "And the best Santa Claus. Who's eager to put on the red?"

No one spoke up.

"I'm not asking you to do a suicide mission. You're sure to come back alive from this one. Juggler? Shooter? Whistler?"

Shooter shook his head, still wearing his aviator glasses in the house. "No can do, sir. Bird and I have the chow detail and that's taking a lot of work, let me tell you."

Skipp nodded at the attractive young woman sitting beside Shooter. "Peggy, is it?"

She smiled and shook her head. "No, sir."

"Ah, I'm sorry. It's Megs."

"No, sir. Sydney. My dad is chief of your ground crew."

"Archer. You're his daughter?"

"Sydney Archer, yes, sir."

"You don't look at all like him."

"Thank you, sir. He's put on a lot of weight in the last six months."

Skipp leaned toward her. "What do you think? Is the chow going to be good?"

"Oh, yes, sir. I have Mrs. Whetstone, Ruth Kurtz, Kalino, Hani, and Shirley Peterson on the team. And your wife."

"My wife?"

"Yes, sir. As of noon today. Mr. and Mrs. Peterson are supposed to be joining us this evening. Perhaps that's them now. Mrs. Peterson can tell you all about what your wife's going to do."

They could hear car doors slamming and Flapjack's loud voice.

Sydney carried on. "We also have Pastor Thor's church on the runway, sir. All sorts of lists are being circulated. But we do need to know how many to expect. Have you sent out your invitations, sir?"

"Well—" Skipp drank from his glass which was empty. "I don't want to be premature—"

"So here's where half my flight school is—goldbricking." Flapjack walked in wearing an orange-and-pink Hawaiian T-shirt. "Please don't wait. Just start without me."

He flopped down on a couch next to Manuku and Ruth. "I hear you were up when *Lady Lex* stretched her legs."

Manuku nodded. "Ruth was actually on the stick."

"How was that?"

"Impressive sight, sir, with the three heavy cruisers."

Ruth had her hands folded in her lap. "I loved watching all the wakes. So many of them. So white. Like knives slitting water open."

"I meant, how did Ruth do?"

Manuku grinned and put his arm around her shoulders. "Great. Just great."

Ruth drew close to him. "Thank you."

"I've been baking, baking, baking." Flapjack's wife, Shirley, came into the living room, her round face dotted with pink splotches and her curly red hair damp with perspiration. She was carrying several tins stacked on top of each other. "Shortbread. I don't care where a person lives in the world. You celebrate Christmas with shortbread." She looked around at all the faces. "Tell me, Lyyndaya, when was it that you and your husband decided to adopt a squadron?"

Lyyndaya took the tins from her. "I have no idea. It started with Becky and Christian. Nate got into it somehow. Then the church. Of course knowing Billy since 1918 probably helped."

Shirley took one of the tins back. "I want the boys to try them out.

The others are for your freezer. You said you wanted to fill it up, didn't you?"

"I do, Shirley. Thank you."

Shirley pried the lid off, folded back the wax paper, and gave the large tin to Batman. "You just take a few and pass them on, please, Lieutenant."

"You can count on me, ma'am."

Shirley sat down next to her husband. "What did I miss?"

"I have no idea." Flapjack raised his eyebrows as high as he could. "I think they were talking about food."

Billy Skipp raised his empty juice glass to Shirley and Flapjack. "Food and the number of guests. I'll say three hundred." He turned to Sydney. "How's that?"

"That's a lot."

"See what you can do. Invitations go out Monday." He caught Batman's eye. "How's Glenn Miller coming?"

"We're doing the best we can, sir, with what we have. Juggler has the list, sir."

Juggler tugged a ragged piece of paper out of his hip pocket. "Um, we have Harrison for lead trumpet."

"Who's that?"

"Radioman on the Coast Guard cutter *Taney*, sir. He's really good. We've listened to him."

"Good, huh? I'd like to hear him play for myself."

"Sir, he'll be at the service on the beach Saturday night." Juggler kept his eyes glued to the list. "He's going to play a hymn. You could drop in."

Skipp pointed at him. "We need at least ten players to give us a big sound. Never mind the state of my soul."

"Our friend David Goff—"

"Who's this Goff?"

"USN, sir. He's talking to guys on the *Arizona* and *Maryland* and *West Virginia*. I think we have a drummer and a bass player lined up."

"We need more brass."

Batman spoke up. "If the colonel could suggest some of his pals in the upper ranks, we'd be happy to teach them how to blow a horn."

"Ha ha, wise guy. It won't be much of a party without a band, will it?"

"Juggler is doing navy. I'm doing marines and army. Even if we only have six players we're setting up our first rehearsal for Sunday night."

"That's more like it." Skipp turned to Wizard. "What about my pine tree?"

Wizard had just been whispering in Hani's ear and she snorted and put her hand over her mouth to stop a laugh.

"Well, do share, Lieutenant." Skipp looked around Lyyndaya's shoulder as she poured him more pineapple juice from a pitcher. "We could all use a good laugh."

"Nothing, sir. Private joke."

"Let's make it a public joke, Lieutenant, shall we?"

Wizard made a face and shrugged at the same time. "Lockjaw's on snowflakes. And a cold front. We're hoping the meteorologists will bring subzero temperatures in from Russia for the party. I want Hani to do a hula dance during the blizzard we plan to come up with."

"Wizard—"

"Whistler's on ice skates and frozen ponds and hockey sticks."

Hani laughed out loud.

Wizard shrugged with both his hands and shoulders. "Look, sir, there aren't any of the right kind of firs growing in the Hawaiian Islands. We could get something shipped in from the States, say Washington or Oregon, but it would cost as much as your Packard and a tank full of gas."

"No excuses, Wizard. If Juggler and Batman can put together a band—"

"We have pine trees." Manuku released Ruth's hand so he could show its height. "This kind grows up to two hundred feet high. I am sure there are some on Lanai. Or Maui. We call it the Cook Pine. It's very slender but it has beautiful needles and cones."

"Two hundred feet!" Skipp's eyes gleamed as he downed his glass of juice in one go. "Perfect for the hangar. Imagine Kimmel's eyes when he sees that all gussied up for Christmas."

Lockjaw gave Manuku his death look. "Sir, a two-hundred-foot tree? We'd need an aircraft carrier to bring it in. Or one of the battlewagons."

"The *Lexington* will be back on Monday."

Shooter perked up. "Would you like to put some money on that, sir?"

Skipp jabbed his glass at Shooter. "You have enough of my greenbacks." He glanced around the room and his eyes stopped on Flapjack. "Everything's coming together. Grub, music, a Christmas tree strung with lights and tinsel—can you think of anything else?"

"Sure." Flapjack grinned. "Eggnog. Hot chestnuts. Figgy pudding— like in the song." He began to sing off-key, "*Bring us some figgy pudding, bring us some figgy pudding—*"

Shirley swatted his arm playfully. "Shh!"

"He's right." Skipp's juice glass had mysteriously filled again and he put it to his mouth. "Thunderbird. What about eggnog?" He looked around the room. Not seeing Raven he fixed his eyes on Shooter. "So where is he?"

"Search me."

Becky jumped up. "Uh, he just went to get a glass of water, Colonel. I'll tell him you want to know about eggnog."

She went to the kitchen but Raven wasn't there. Glancing out the windows she spotted him sitting on the grass with a tall glass in his hand.

"Hey." Becky sat down next to Raven. "Whassup, baby?"

He laughed. "Well, baby, I needed a break from Billy Skipp's latest obsession. If he doesn't have us in the air flying after imaginary Zeros and Messerschmitts, we're trying to create a New England Christmas for him in the tropics."

"The colonel's just having fun. So are the guys."

"Moon's only a shade off full now. Nice yellow color this low in the trees. What do you think?"

She slipped an arm through his and leaned her head on his shoulder. "Lovely. But nothing will ever match Wednesday night for me. The moon was completely full and God was everywhere. God and love."

"Yeah, it was pretty special. But so was the dancing last night."

"It was a lot of fun. But nothing like the night on the beach."

"I guess you're right." He put down his glass and wrapped his arm around her. "Tomorrow's the sixth."

"Right you are."

"I have this note in the margin of my Bible back at Wheeler, you know. All it says is *Becky Whetstone* and a verse is underlined. There's the date—November sixth. Oh, and a heart."

She lifted her head. "There is not."

"Nothing Michelangelo would own up to, but it's there."

"What happened on the sixth?"

"I'm not sure exactly. Was that when we agreed to stop insulting each other for breakfast each morning? Did I have a dream? Was I thinking about you a lot?"

"I hope all three."

"The verse is from Proverbs. It goes sort of like this—there are three things that are too wonderful for me, four which I do not understand. The way of an eagle in the sky, the way of a serpent on a rock, the way of a ship in the middle of the sea, and the way of a man with a maid."

"You underlined that and put my name next to it a month ago?"

"Yeah. And I remember daydreaming about how an eagle slips through the sky, how snakes glide when they want to move fast, what it looks like from a plane to see a carrier and its task force cutting their way across the ocean—and how a man loves a woman. Then I daydreamed about holding you in my arms and kissing you. It was really wild because we were nowhere near that stage yet, and I'd argue with anyone who thought I was falling for you. But I dreamed that dream. And now it's real."

Becky leaned into his arms. "No one is more surprised at that than I am. I never thought…"

"Meet me on the flight line tomorrow morning before your first student," Raven said. "It's our one-month anniversary. I'll have something special for you."

"I'll be there at six."

"I'll be waiting for you."

And he was. Becky showed up at quarter to six. No one was in Peterson's hut. She began her walk across the runway to Piper Eleven. For a moment it looked like the plane stood alone. Then a tall figure emerged from behind the aircraft.

I feel your eyes on me again and my skin tingles—it's good, so good. I'm back in October and I'm walking over the tarmac and wondering who it is that's gazing at me, which one of the ground crew or which one of the flying instructors or students. And all along it was you, the guy I swore I'd never love, never touch, never kiss. Thank you, God, that my life turned out differently from my vow.

"Morning, Stardust."

"Morning, Thunderbird."

"You look terrific."

"Thanks. You don't look so bad yourself. I love seeing your blue eyes early in the morning. It's like getting twice the sky."

"Charmer." He dug a small box out of his pocket. It was wrapped in blue paper with a blue bow. "Speaking of blue. This is a small token of thanks for the way you walk across runways."

"Shut up, Thunderbird." She punched his shoulder hard. "Can I open it now?"

"Definitely."

She ripped at the paper like a child. Inside the box that emerged was a smaller box. Inside that box was an even smaller box. She yelped and punched his shoulder again. "I can't take it. What are you trying to do to me?"

"One more box."

The smallest box opened to a wad of pure white cotton. Under the cotton was a gold chain. Its links were larger than the usual ones used in a woman's necklace. The chain gleamed.

"Just right," he said, reading her thoughts. "A whole lot of beauty. A whole lot of ruggedness. And pure gold."

"Aw." She carefully lifted the chain out of the box and was surprised to see a gem attached to it. "What's that?" The jewel was blue and green, and it turned the color of the Hawaiian sea as the sun, not yet over the horizon, continued to spill light into the air. "Oh, my goodness, Christian. It's beautiful. I've never seen anything like it. It's as if the ocean has been set in stone."

"You must have seen it before. It's your birthstone. For March."

Becky held it in her hand while the chain slid over her fingers and sparkled underneath her hand. "I don't know anything about birthstones. We never practiced such things. Too much Amishness in my family's bloodline."

"It's aquamarine. Your eyes have that color of green mixed with blue sometimes. Usually when you're swimming or flying."

"You don't see my eyes when I'm flying."

"I did when you were my instructor. Whenever you turned around to glare at me or fire off an insult."

"You shouldn't have been thinking romantically at those times."

"I didn't think I was." His fingers touched hers. "Do you mind if I do the honors of placing it around your perfect neck?"

"*My perfect neck.*" She smiled up at him. "As if I'd mind."

He took the chain from her hand and circled her throat with it, gently closing the clasp. "The way of a man with a maid." He glanced to the east. "When's sunrise?"

"About six twenty-five."

"I want to hang around long enough to see what happens when dawn and your eyes and the gemstone meet. When's your first student?"

"Seven. That's your old slot."

"Do you mind if I wait here till six twenty-five?"

"No. But you have to help me look over the plane if you're bent on seeing eyes and gems and dawns come together."

"My pleasure."

When he knelt to check the tires she encircled him from behind with her arms. "I'm your gold chain. And we're both out of sight."

"Hey, did you trap me or something?"

"Yeah, hotshot. Try to get this Zero off your tail." She drew his head back into her stomach and leaned over him. The gemstone dangled just above his eyes. "I'm going to take all your air. You know what that means?"

"I'll crash."

"Right into my arms. That's the plan."

"I usually don't like losing. But this is okay."

"Just okay?"

He reached his hands up and back until he had them behind her head. "It's the best." He drew her head down until their lips touched. When the sun found its way under the wing of the airplane the gemstone ignited as it lay over his heart.

Becky took her students over Diamond Head and over the ocean all day. She gave Nate the stick and let him take the two of them out to sea for miles. Often she closed her eyes, praying and dreaming.

In the evening the sun was still golden and above the palm trees when she walked from the parking lot of the Royal Hawaiian onto the beach. Harrison was standing by the water, and the pure notes of "Amazing Grace" rose from his trumpet. He was in white and the sun on him was the color of the chain at her neck.

Praise God for beauty.

Her family was already there. And Raven. She walked past Dave Goff, who was singing the hymn with such power and depth that it startled her. She lingered nearby for a minute. He smiled and lifted his hand in greeting, then closed his eyes and continued to offer up his voice and the words.

You walked on the beaches of Galilee and you walk on the beach here. We honor you.

Becky reached Raven on the fourth verse of the song. He took her hand, kissed it quickly, and continued to sing. She joined him. It was not the final stanza. Pastor Thor had added several extra ones she had hardly ever heard.

The Lord has promised good to me,
His Word my hope secures;
He will my Shield and Portion be,
As long as life endures.

Yea, when this flesh and heart shall fail,
And mortal life shall cease,
I shall possess, within the veil,
A life of joy and peace.

The world shall soon dissolve like snow,

The sun refuse to shine;
But God, who called me here below,
Shall be forever mine.

She bowed her head as the hymn came to an end. The beach was silent. Even the gulls did not cry out for a few moments. When she looked up the sun had set and the sky to the east in front of them was the color of a crimson rose.

"*Red sky at night, sailor's delight.*" Raven continued to hold her hand. "It's good to see you here. You and the stone look magnificent."

She smiled her thank-you. "Harrison plays so well."

"Yeah."

"Did you hear David singing?"

"If it was that rich and deep male voice—"

"That was him. He really surprised me. Billy Skipp should think of asking him to lead us in some of the carols at Christmas."

"Well, if we heard him I'm sure the colonel did too. He's over there with your dad and Flapjack." Raven gestured with his head. "And the wives are all together by the shore."

"What are Flapjack and Skipp both doing here?"

"I don't know. To hear Harrison?"

"They could hear him anytime. And this isn't 'In the Mood' or 'Boogie-Woogie Bugle Boy.'"

"Maybe Shooter bet they wouldn't show and they did to make sure he lost a lot of money."

"Ha. Knowing Shooter, he set them up. Dared them to come but acted like he knew they wouldn't. Probably bet against the odds. Laid his money on Flapjack and Skipp showing up to spite him."

"Could be. But they're here now. And they don't look like they're going anywhere."

"Where does Flapjack get his shirts? Now it's yellow and orange and purple."

"And Thor's is red and black. He obviously didn't use that ten we left for him last time."

"You wanted blue?"

"Prayed for it."

"Maybe God likes red as much as the pastor does."

Pastor Thor prayed and then spoke for about ten minutes. He tied his message into the hymn they had just finished and spoke about the love of God.

"A lot of things come our way in life. There are many ups and downs. Few things endure. A great deal collapses or fades or falls apart. Our buildings do, our machines do, our bodies do—even our lives come to a stop. But the love of God is unending. The love of God is ceaseless. In a world where so much does not last, his love is the one thing that does. It's why I steer people to Jesus. His face is the face of God—his warmth, his kindness, his strength, his courage, his power. You measure a man by his character and his actions and his words. Some of us can size a man up just by looking in his eyes. If you do that with Jesus you see God and you see greatness. You see a bright, clear, and steady dawn."

Raven started walking her away from the crowd of worshippers as Pastor Thor asked Jude to pray a final prayer. Becky kept her eyes closed, listening to her father's words, feeling Raven guide her over the sand and to the edge of the water so that the surf ran over her sandals and toes. Soon she could not hear Jude's voice but still kept her eyes shut.

"You can open them now if you want."

She saw Diamond Head in the last trace of rose and scarlet with the night sweeping in like a strong dark sea.

"It's rock steady." Raven stared at the volcanic cone. "Like God. But God is more than Diamond Head. So is my love for you. I want you to know that."

"I do know it."

"I'm not going anywhere, Becky. And there's no one else. You're my lady. This is our one-month anniversary and there's going to be a thousand more."

"I believe you."

He ran a thumb slowly back and forth over her lips. "I'm not going to ask you to stay up all night again. You're at the airfield early for your students like you were always at the airfield early for me. I just want you to stand here and hold my hand and wait until the moon rises out of the sea. Okay? That's how I'd like our anniversary to end."

"Can I say I love you?"

"I'd like that."

"And I'll see you at church tomorrow? For sure?"

"You bet."

"Because you've had a habit lately of not showing up."

Raven grinned. "Skipp is in a flat calm now. He's had us flying in circles for weeks but today he had the fighters defueled and the ammo removed. They'll sit on the runway pretty much all weekend. I'll be at church tomorrow morning, beauty."

"Then I'll stay until the moon is over the water and blazing like gold." She counted the stars that began to glint against the black. "I used to think you and I alternated between being spiritual and passionate. Now I know our passionate is spiritual and our spiritual is passionate."

He glanced down at the aquamarine gem around her throat and twined the gold chain in his finger. "Forever, Stardust. That's what I'd like for you and me."

She put her hand on his. "That's what I want too, Thunderbird. Even if the world dissolves like snow and the sun refuses to shine."

Twenty-Five

Becky woke at five-thirty and prayed a prayer while she lay in her bed. Dressing quickly and quietly in a clean T-shirt and jeans she left Ruth asleep as she stepped softly down the stairs to the washroom and had a shower. Pulling her clothes on again, she went into the kitchen and glanced at the calendar on the wall, running her finger down the items penciled in for December seven—flying instruction until ten-thirty, a break for church, the next student at twelve-thirty, lessons through to five, a rehearsal for the Christmas dance band at seven. She bit into an apple and wrote in *Thunderbird, The Black Cat, nine-thirty.*

She closed the door slowly behind her because everyone was sleeping in, and she climbed into the jeep. Before she started the engine she threw on her leather jacket and pulled the aquamarine gem from one of its pockets, drawing the gold chain down over her head.

When she pulled up next to Flapjack's hut, he met her and handed her a sheet of paper.

"Meteorologists are giving us a typical morning. As the land warms up the trade winds will be offset. In the afternoon the effect is going to be lessened, but the trades won't be strong enough to make flying the J-3s difficult."

"Okay."

"Nothing special going on with the military, no exercises, but there will be a flight of B-17s coming in. You won't have trouble spotting them or staying out of their way."

"Right. I'm taking Kalino up first thing."

"Manuku's already landed from two lessons and he's taking off again in ten minutes. Sunday's the craziest day of the week and I don't have your mom and dad. I'm giving you church, but you may have to fly until six or seven."

Becky wrinkled her face. "Oh, come on, Flapjack. The band is rehearsing for the Christmas party tonight. I promised Batman and Juggler I'd be there."

"Well, we gotta teach the students and bring in the moola or no paychecks for the Whetstone Flying Circus." He gestured with his chin. "Nice stone. Find it on the beach?"

"Sure, Flapjack. It was a gift from Thunderbird. My birthstone."

"Love the color. Chain's nice too. Guess he finally did fall for the gal with two fangs and horns—you know, the ugly one who ate concrete for breakfast?"

"Ha ha. That's me." She opened the door and looked out across the airfield. "Kalino's already by the plane. See you later."

"You bet."

Becky gripped Kalino's hand when she got to the yellow Piper. "*Aloha.* You're going to get in a lot of solo time this morning. Do you feel good about that?"

"Really good. My goal is to take Lockjaw up for Christmas Day."

"Oh, you'll be in great shape by Christmas. I hope you plan to throw a few barrel rolls into the flight plan."

"I do."

"One thing about some of these combat pilots. They don't like stunts unless they're doing them. Maybe you'll get him to turn green."

Kalino laughed, tossing her gleaming black hair. "Now wouldn't that be a treat?"

Becky's watch was strapped on with the face under her wrist. She flicked her hand over and glanced at it. "Five after seven. We should get going."

"Okay, Stardust."

"Stardust, hm? I see word's getting around. What do you think of it, Kali?"

"It's kind of magical. It works for you."

"Yeah? Let's do our sky prayer."

They held each other's hands and lifted their heads, praying out loud together. "Lord Jesus Christ, touch us so that we mount up with wings like eagles. Keep us strong, keep us safe, keep us wise. Bless us as we find your life in your sky. Amen."

Becky slapped Kalino on the back. "Let's go, Kali." She leaped up into the front cockpit. "You know, you never told me the call sign the guys gave you."

Kalino shrugged and smiled an awkward smile. "*Diamonds.* But they don't mean the jewels. They say I'm like the dance of the sun on the ocean. Especially on the back of a perfect wave."

"That's beautiful. Didn't you tell us Kalino means bright one?"

"Yes."

"So your call sign is perfect." She waved at one of the ground crew. "Sam, can you get the prop?"

"Sure thing, Stardust."

"Oh, Sam, does everybody know that name now?"

"Yessir. And we all love it. It's you, Becky. Ever seen the stardust of the Milky Way? How it shines and covers over the dark? It's you."

"You're going to make me blush. Thanks, Sam. We should touch down again around eight-thirty."

"I'll have my eye out for you."

Once they were up, Becky waggled the stick and jabbed her thumb at Kalino. "Take over, Diamonds."

"Sure thing. Where do you want me to go? Out over the water?"

"No. Go inland. There's mist over the highlands. I want you to practice flying in that." Becky pointed with her whole hand, fingers held together. "Head north for the Ko'olau Mountains."

"Roger."

Kalino banked the J-3 and took it north. High white cumulus clouds kept the distant mountaintops out of sight. Other yellow Pipers popped up all around, as well as a number of blue Culver Cadets from a different flight school. Kalino sailed smoothly between them, waving once at Manuku, who was on their left. He gave her a thumbs-up.

Becky twisted around in her seat to speak to Kalino. "Go for some height as we get closer to the range. Not all at once. Just a few hundred feet at a time."

"All right."

The mountain slopes and white clouds drew nearer. Kalino was slowly ascending as they flew from one end of Oahu to the other. Some Cadets and Pipers were following them, most at a lower elevation—but a few, like Manuku, were farther ahead and higher up.

Fighter planes began to dart out of the silver mist.

Flapjack, you said there wouldn't be any military activity except for the B-17s!

"Kalino! Go higher! Now!"

"Becky—"

"Now! Pull the stick into your stomach!"

The nose of the Piper jerked upward sharply. Olive green aircraft veered to the left and right of them as the Piper lifted. Angry at the recklessness of the pilots, Becky tried frantically to take in their markings so she could report them to Billy Skipp. She read the numbers on the tailfins out loud but realized there were no stars and the paint was not army green.

"Red suns!" Kalino was shouting. "Red suns on the wings and fuselage! These planes are Japanese!"

Becky craned her neck back to see where the formation was going. Two of the planes broke away from the main group. One dove toward a blue Cadet. In moments the smaller plane was throwing off sparks and smoke and falling out of the sky. The fighter roared through the smoke and bore up on the tail of another Cadet. The small blue plane turned toward them and Becky could clearly see the winking lights on the wings and cowling of the fighter as it followed. The tail of the Cadet snapped off and it went into a spin as flames blazed over its fuselage.

"They're shooting!" Becky could hear herself almost screaming. "They're shooting the trainers down!"

Kalino was staring at the mountains and clouds and didn't look to see what was going on behind them. "What?"

"Bank left! Quickly!"

A fighter overshot their craft and turned quickly to come back.

Becky grabbed the stick in her cockpit. "Relinquish the controls to me, Kali!"

Kalino continued to grip her stick tightly, face rigid as the Japanese plane streaked at them. The front edges of its wings flashed. Moments later the canopy broke open and splintered as bullets cracked into the glass and into both cockpits.

"Let go of the stick!" cried Becky.

But her student's hand remained frozen.

Becky jumped out of her seat and turned around. "Kali! You have to let go!"

Cold ripped through her head and body at the sight of her lifeless pilot and friend. She reached for her hand, pried it free, squeezed it, and let it fall. Unable to think, she put the Piper into a dive and turned it over and over as she did so. The dark shape of the Japanese plane swept past overhead.

She dropped hundreds of feet before pulling up. Trails of thick smoke littered the sky where Cadets and Pipers had gone down. The two fighters had both pounced on a yellow J-3 that was zigzagging desperately to throw off their aim. Finally it dove but the fighters hurtled after it. Their cowlings flickered. Becky took in her breath sharply as the Piper exploded in a ball of black and orange fire. At the last instant she saw the number on the fuselage and under the wing.

"Manuku!"

Twenty-Six

"Hey, Wiz. Hey, Batman." Raven cracked the door to their room. "You guys getting up?"

"What time is it?" mumbled Batman.

"Just getting on to oh-eight-hundred."

"Church isn't till eleven."

"Yeah, but you said you were going to go for a five-mile run with me."

Batman lifted his head and stared at Raven. "I lied."

"What about Wizard? Wiz, you want to go for a run and clean out the pipes?"

Wizard had his pillow over his head and didn't respond. Batman grunted and rolled over. "Wiz was at the Wheeler Officers' Club dance last night. Him and Hani. After he took her home there was an all-night poker game he got suckered into. He might rise from the dead at noon."

Raven shook his head and closed their door. He spotted Lockjaw and Juggler heading down the corridor. "Hey. Either of you two want to put in a five-mile run?"

"Run?" Lockjaw glanced back. "We're both looking for coffee. That's the first order of the day."

"Maybe after," said Juggler opening the door of the bachelor officers' quarters and stepping into the sunshine. "First I need some of Ground Chief Archer's brew. He always cooks up a pot in one of the hangars."

Raven joined them. "I can't run with coffee sloshing around in an empty stomach."

267

"He might have water," said Lockjaw.

"He won't have water," responded Raven.

"No, probably not."

"Just one cup." Juggler grinned. "One cup, Thunderbird, and I'll race you to the Ko'olau Mountains."

"That's a deal."

Raven glanced at the P-40s lined up in rows wingtip to wingtip. Suddenly they all rose in the air along with tall columns of dirt and concrete, wings breaking, canopies shattering, huge streaks of red flame rising with them. Raven heard no sound. The planes lifted and turned over, the mud and dirt continued to billow upward, flames and smoke shot into the sky, but still it happened in silence as if it were not real but something he had dreamed up.

Lockjaw saw Raven's stare and looked. "Hey—" he began.

A wave of sound and heat hit them. The three men winced and ducked as their hair blew backward and the roar of multiple explosions slammed into them. At the same instant several aircraft tore through the air right above their heads.

"Look at the paint scheme!" shouted Juggler. "Look at the red suns! They're Japanese!"

"That's a Zeke!" Lockjaw pointed at an olive green fighter banking. "It's coming in for a strafing run!"

He threw his arms around Raven and Juggler and hauled both of them down with him. The front edges of the fighter's wings flashed and concrete flew. They kept their arms over their heads as the Zero snarled past and more P-40s burst into flame. Juggler opened one eye to see a dive bomber pull up as black smoke boiled over the airbase.

"Vals are dropping the bombs!" he yelled. "They're coming in from about five thousand feet! There are at least two dozen of them!"

Lockjaw rammed Juggler's face into the tarmac. "Everything's blowing up, Juggler. Keep your mug down or you'll lose an eye."

Raven felt the ground shudder beneath him as bomb after bomb targeted the P-40s. The reek of the smoke made him cough and he covered his nose and mouth with his hand. A sudden shock wave that rippled over his back made him glance over his shoulder. A building had just erupted, spewing yellow fire. Two hangars were blazing and overheated ammunition began banging away inside one of them.

"They're going after everything." Raven propped himself up on his elbows. "We have to try and save some of our fighters. They could be sending troopships in after this. We need something to fight back with."

"Yeah." Lockjaw scanned the sky. "No more Vals. What do you think?"

"Let's go."

The three men ran across the airstrip toward several P-40s that hadn't caught fire. Kicking the blocks from the tires they began to push them away from the flight line to the edge of the runway one after another. After a few minutes Wizard and Batman ran up in their pajamas to help, followed by Whistler and Shooter, both in their boxer shorts.

"Zeros!" Batman shouted. "Scatter!"

Two fighters bore down on the airbase again, shooting up jeeps and trucks and planes and any man in sight. Raven saw tracers take down several of the ground crew. He flattened himself over a grease patch on the cement. The Zeros left and streaked south.

"Okay, that's it, let's get back at it." Lockjaw jumped to his feet. "How many have we saved so far?"

"Twelve," replied Whistler.

"There's still a bunch that weren't hit. Let's roll them away from the ones that are burning."

Raven hung back. "I'm going up."

Lockjaw stopped running. "In what?"

"They never hit my P-36. I'm getting it gassed up and armed and I'm going after those Zekes. The Japanese aren't going to pull another Nanking here."

"Nanking? Who's talking about Nanking? No way can your P-36 go up against a Zero."

"I'm going up."

"You're my wingman, Thunderbird."

"So crawl into one of your P-40s and let's do our stuff. If they're hitting us they're hitting the other airbases, Lockjaw. For all we know they're bombing Honolulu. They go after civilian targets in China all the time."

Lockjaw's eyes hardened. "Yeah. I'm with you." He called to the others. "Me and Thunderbird are getting refueled and rearmed and going after those bandits! If you can find a working plane jump in and run it over to one of the bunkers for gas and ammo!"

Raven leaped into his undamaged P-36, which was parked well away from the P-40s, and started the engine. He took it slowly across the runway to a refueling station and shouted to a few of the ground crew to give him a hand. Smoke and the stink of burning rubber tumbled over them as they pumped gas into the plane and loaded its machine guns with thirty- and fifty-caliber ammunition. Lockjaw was just preparing to make his run for takeoff when Raven's plane lined up behind his.

"You hear me, Thunderbird?" Raven's radio crackled.

"Roger."

"Let's get airborne."

One of Raven's refuelers waved for him to open his canopy. He hauled it back.

"What is it?" he asked.

"We just received word they're hitting Pearl Harbor. Dive bombers, torpedo bombers, Zeros, the works."

"They're attacking Pearl Harbor," Raven told Lockjaw. "They must be after the fleet."

Lockjaw's voice crackled back. "They've probably taken out the planes at Hickam and Ford too. We better get over there and give our navy boys a hand."

"You get up. I'll be right behind you."

Raven began to pull his canopy shut when the refueler shouted, "Something else, sir!"

"What is it?"

The man hesitated. "It's not confirmed. But I thought you'd better know."

"Spit it out."

"Word is they went after civilian aircraft too, sir. Peterson's Air Service was strafed. Every Piper J-3 he had up in the air this morning has been shot down."

TWENTY-SEVEN

Man battle stations!"

Dave Goff jumped out of his bunk, stripped off his pajamas, and threw on his uniform.

"What's up?" he asked the man next to him who was yanking on his shoes.

The man shook his head. "Another crazy drill. Why Sunday morning?"

They joined scores of other men who were pounding up the metal staircase. Rushing onto the top deck, Goff saw clouds of smoke pouring from Ford Island.

"What's the fire?" a man shouted. "What's the fire?"

"Airplanes and hangars are burning!" an officer yelled back.

"How did it start?"

Five or six aircraft zoomed past the *Arizona* flying low.

The paint is wrong for army planes, thought Goff. *It's like an olive tan. Who uses that?*

"They're dropping torpedoes!" A sailor pointed. "Are they nuts?"

Long black shapes fell into the water. Everyone on deck could see them streak toward the *West Virginia* a few hundred yards away. Water and smoke shot into the sky with a roar and the *West Virginia* rocked at its mooring. Seconds later pillars of flame blasted up from the *Oklahoma* and the huge ship jerked sideways.

"Zekes!"

Several fighters raced through the harbor, machine-gunning the decks of the battleships and the men struggling in the water. A column of spray suddenly erupted off the *Arizona's* port bow and drenched Goff as he ran forward.

"Enemy dive bombers!"

Airplanes with red suns snarled past. Near misses sent seawater soaring into the air. Bombs whistled and groaned. The steel of the *Arizona* shrieked as a bomb exploded at the stern.

"What's been hit? What's been hit?"

Goff continued to make his way forward to gun turret II. Blasts on the port side, one striking the five-inch antiaircraft battery, knocked him off balance. Gunfire from the *Maryland* peppered the olive-green aircraft that swooped down on Pearl Harbor. One disintegrated in front of him, fire peeling open its wings and canopy, the pilot a screaming torch, the fuselage flying into dozens of pieces and scattering over the water.

"The *Nevada* is making steam!"

The AA batteries on the *Nevada* were thumping and smoke streamed from its single funnel as it prepared to cast off. Goff watched its flak pluck a Kate torpedo bomber out of the air and hurl it blazing into the sea.

"Goff! You made it!" An officer slapped him on the back as he entered turret II, just back from the bow and behind turret I. "How is it out there?"

"The sky's thick with enemy planes, sir. They've torpedoed the *West Virginia* and the *Oklahoma*. The *Nevada's* getting ready to make way. She's not anchored next to anyone so she's free to move."

"The *Tennessee*? The *Maryland*?"

"There's so much smoke and confusion, sir. They're afloat and fighting back. That's all I can tell."

"What about ourselves? I heard explosions."

"Dive bombers hit us. At the stern. And on the port side. One of our AA guns is out."

"All right. Our turn to give it back. I need you to bring the ammo up from the forward magazine with the hoist, feed it, and handle the ejected shell casings. I have no idea where our loaders are."

"Aye, aye, sir."

"We've got a few shells ready to go here in the turret. Can't do much against the planes unless they come in at mast level. But for all we know the Japanese are sending ships up the inlet past Hospital Point. If we spot 'em we'll blow 'em out of the water."

The gunner's mate hollered, "Maximum elevation, thirty degrees!"

"Aye!" came the response. "Maximum elevation, thirty degrees!"

The officer hissed, "We'll try to pick off the torpedo bombers coming in low over Ford Island."

"We're loaded up! Commence firing!"

"Open fire!"

Goff clapped his hands to his ears as the three fourteen-inch guns thundered. Brown smoke curled around the turret. He worked the machinery with another sailor, got the casings free, and propelled another set of shells into the triple breeches. Part of his mind worked at loading while another part prayed.

Men are going to die. Men have already died. I might be one of them. Whatever happens, Lord, stick with me. Stick closer than a brother.

The turret lurched and Goff thrust out his hand and braced it against the bulkhead.

"What was that?" someone asked.

"A bomb must have hit just forward of the turret," responded the officer.

"That's not much of a blast."

"It hasn't detonated."

Goff looked at the officer. "We're going to feel it if it goes off below decks."

"Right. Hold on."

Goff held his breath. The turret suddenly vanished in a flash of white. He never heard a sound.

TWENTY-EIGHT

Harrison took a sip from his coffee and headed up the ladder to the radio room of the *Taney*, just behind the bridge. The air was clear but he picked up a scent of something burning. He didn't think twice about it. The navy or the army was likely taking care of garbage somewhere.

He took over from another radioman and slipped on his earphones to monitor radio traffic and signals. On a scratch pad he penciled, *Pick up Dave for band rehearsal tonight at seven.* He adjusted the volume on the radio set and leaned back, coffee in hand. He checked his watch. It was five minutes to eight. He had another sip from the warm mug.

Suddenly the radio sprang to life and a signal came in uncoded and in plain English. "Air raid, Pearl Harbor! This is no drill! Air raid, Pearl Harbor! This is no drill!"

Harrison stared at the set. *This has got to be a mistake.* He yanked off the headphones and ran from the room and looked west toward Pearl Harbor. Plumes of thick smoke were rising into the sky and he spotted several tall splashes of water.

"Hey!" He called down to some of the sailors on deck who had gathered to stare. "What's up?"

"Looks like a training exercise," one of them responded. "The navy planes are doing a mock bombing run and the ships are firing their guns."

"Can't be," said Harrison.

"What else would it be?"

"The smoke going up is black. Stuff is really burning. If the ships were just firing their guns it would be brown."

Several booms overlapped one another and reached them at the same time. They watched flame soar into the sky as a battleship was hit.

"Someone screwed up!" A sailor gripped the rail with both hands. "He'll catch it for dropping a bomb right on one of the ships!"

Harrison felt a wave of ice go through him from head to feet. "Nobody screwed up. They meant to hit that ship. We're under attack. I just got the radio message. This is an air raid. Not a live-fire exercise." Harrison looked at the bridge. "Is the CO back?"

"No. He stayed on shore leave overnight."

Harrison ran onto the bridge and saluted the second in command. "Sir. I just received an urgent message. It was uncoded. The signal was, *Air raid, Pearl Harbor—this is no drill.*"

The second-in-command's face filled with blood. "Are you sure, sailor?"

"Absolutely, sir."

The second-in-command looked at the smoke boiling over Pearl Harbor. "I thought it was a training exercise."

"No, sir. Real bombs are falling and ships are taking damage."

"I…I…uh…I'm not sure what the CO would want me to do—"

"General quarters, sir. Every time I look over that way there are more planes diving and firing. They could hit Honolulu Harbor next."

"I…yes…right—" He turned to a sailor standing behind him. "Sound general quarters. Pearl Harbor is under attack."

"Aye, aye, sir."

The klaxon blared and the sailor spoke loudly into the microphone. "All hands! Man battle stations! All hands! Man battle stations!"

Harrison went quickly down to the deck and helped the gunner's mate clear the area around the three-inch gun for action.

"This won't do much good, Harrison," he said. "We need an AA battery to bring down aircraft."

"It's better than nothing, I guess, Gunny."

"Yeah. Just. I'll crank it to maximum elevation. Help me haul a couple of thirties out, will ya?"

Harrison hauled a thirty-caliber machine gun out of storage, and several other men brought out belts of ammunition. Gunny bolted one in place on the port side and another in place on the starboard side. He assigned two men to each gun, one to aim and fire, the other to feed the belt. Then he ordered several sailors to bring over the shells for the three-inch.

"Enemy Zero!" one man yelled.

A plane shot low over Honolulu Harbor heading west. It was olive green with large red suns.

"That's no Zero." Harrison squinted. "That's a torpedo bomber. A Kate. Probably heading in to make a run at Battleship Row."

One of the thirty-calibers opened up too late. The crashing of the gun jarred everyone on deck. The Kate carried on toward Hickam and Pearl, its torpedo obvious, long and dark and sleek under its belly.

"There must be a hundred planes over Pearl now," a sailor said. "The ships are sitting ducks. Why aren't our fighters engaging?"

Harrison pointed. "Look at the smoke coming from the direction of Hickam. Look at the smoke on Ford Island. They're blowing up our fighter force on the ground."

Two planes Harrison recognized as Val dive bombers tore overhead, and Gunny cut loose with his three-inch gun, firing two shells as quickly as his men could reload. He didn't hit anything but prepared to fire at the next plane that flew near the *Taney* nevertheless.

"It's better to do something," he growled, "than sit on our cans and watch. Hey, Harrison, I want you to spell on the port machine gun in ten."

"Aye, aye, Gunny. I'll have to check on the radio though."

"Get another radioman. Maybe you'll—"

A huge explosion of black and red smoke burst up into the air over Pearl Harbor. Everyone's eyes were riveted even though they could not hear it. The explosion hung like a black wall against the blue sky.

"They got one of the big ships," rumbled Gunny. "Must of hit the ammo or the fuel. That's rough."

"It looks like an evil genie pouring out of a lamp," a sailor said. "Gives me the creeps."

"You can thank the God you worship you're not on the battlewagon and going down. That'd give you more of the creeps than anything you're feeling now."

The blast wave struck—the noise, the heat, the wind. Harrison cringed. It seemed like a blow to the face from someone who knew him and hated him. The pillar of black rose and rose, and fire rocketed over the water. Still the planes came like dark insects. Still the bombs and torpedoes dropped like hard stones.

"Here's another bunch!" spat Gunny. "Open fire!"

Five torpedo bombers slipped across the mouth of Honolulu Harbor heading toward the flames. The three-inch gun barked and both thirty-caliber machine guns hammered, empty casings bouncing and pinging over the deck. The Kates didn't alter course or spurt smoke or oil. It was as if the *Taney* had never fired.

Gunny's face was like rock. "In less than a minute they'll be putting those fish right into the side of another one of our ships. And there's nothing we can do about it."

Harrison ran up to the radio room. The height helped him see Pearl Harbor better. It was an inferno. The fire and darkness reminded him of illustrations in a volume of Dante's *Inferno* he had flipped through. Pictures of hell and suffering and men crying for help as flames surrounded them.

Dear God, be with those men. I don't know what they believe or don't believe but be with their souls. God of all grace, be with their souls.

He rested his hands on the rail. A deep pain gathered in his stomach and pushed its way into his chest and out through his mouth. It was one name repeated again and again.

David. David.

Twenty-Nine

Becky nursed her Piper J-3 south toward the haze of smoke that lay on the horizon. The Japanese fighters had darted away after shooting down Manuku and left her to herself. Wind whistled through the bullet holes in the canopy, and now and then oil spurted from the engine and spattered her goggles. With one hand she used a rag to keep them clear and with the other she gripped the stick and kept the plane level and pointed in the right direction.

Lord, please help me get back to the airfield. Help those who are trying to fend off this vicious attack. Protect Christian when he takes to the air. Have mercy. It's hard enough to lose Manuku and Kalino.

She had looked back at Kalino a second time once the Zeros were gone. Perhaps her first glance had been wrong. Perhaps she'd been confused by blood that covered Kalino's face from a wound in the forehead. But the rigidness of her friend's body told Becky she had not been mistaken. Her throat tight, she returned to flying the plane.

"This isn't right!" she cried out loud. "It makes no sense!"

Japanese fighters breaking out of the clouds. Raging through a small formation of Pipers and Cadets. Blasting unarmed civilian aircraft out of the sky. Was this how Japanese aviators made war? By striking down the helpless and defenseless? How could such killings possibly make any difference to their plans to attack Hawaii from the air or sea?

But what they did in Manchuria ten years ago made no sense, did it? What they did when they invaded China in 1937 made no sense. The murders and barbarities they committed in Nanking in 1938 made no sense.

What's the death of a few flight instructors and their students over Oahu in 1941?

"God. My mother and father will be worried because they know I'm in the air. Christian will be worried because he'll fly in circles and won't find me. Nate will be panicking because the Japanese may put troops ashore this afternoon or tonight and ring Honolulu with bayonets and fire. Ruth will be praying desperately, but she doesn't know she has lost Manuku—how will you comfort her? How is it possible to comfort her?"

The closer she got to Honolulu the more smoke she could see choking the water and ships of Pearl Harbor. There were no Japanese planes in sight but she knew they had caused the destruction. While she was still miles away she had seen them diving and swooping over the battleships. Now they were gone. She glanced at her wristwatch and was surprised to see there was a tear in her flight jacket and a dark clot of blood on the skin that was exposed. The watch face was smashed but the hands were still moving. It was a quarter to eight.

The Wheeler airfield was churning with flame and smoke as Becky flew past. She clenched her fists. P-40s and P-36s were burning. Hangars were burning. She was low enough to see bodies on the tarmac.

Not him. Not Christian. Please, God. I can't go through that again.

Peterson's Air Service was just as much a wreck. She circled the airfield and saw three broken Pipers scattered on the runway. She also saw canvas tarps covering two bodies. The office was untouched. No one waved to her. But she prepared to land.

The Piper shook and swung wildly from side to side as if it were being struck by rock and stones. Becky shot a look over her shoulder. A Zero had latched onto her tail. Tracers zipped past her canopy. She pulled up sharply and rolled to the right. The fighter howled by underneath her. It strafed two untouched Pipers parked at the end of the field near the office. Both exploded.

Becky climbed, stick jammed frantically into her stomach. She saw wave after wave of planes slashing through the smoke south of her and diving on Pearl Harbor. Another attack. It convinced her that Japanese troops were only hours from landing on Hawaiian beaches, with few American warships or fighters to threaten them. The black fear that caught in her throat hardened into stone as she saw a strip of fabric tear free of the Piper's wing and felt the plane shake and begin to fall. It couldn't complete the climb. The bullets had caused too much damage.

Help me!

She fought to bring the plane under control so she could level out and attempt some kind of landing. Three or four Zeros tore past, ignoring her. Oil began to gush from the Piper's engine, and the needles on her gauges either spun wildly or refused to work. The wing dipped left and then sharply right. It was impossible to see out of her goggles and she ripped them from her face. Wrestling with the stick she finally achieved a balance she felt she could hold until she touched down. Suddenly a Zero hurtled at her head on and its wings began to flash. The Piper began to break apart.

This is not how I die. This is not how I die.

The plane went into a spin she couldn't break. The stick was wrenched from her grasp as if by a giant. The force of the spin slammed her back against her seat.

This is how I die.

"I'm sorry, baby." Her eyes were closed and her face spattered with oil and grease. "I wanted to make it home to you. I wanted to hold you in my arms. But I can't do it, my love. I can't get there."

THIRTY

"Thunderbird!"

"Got you!"

"Port wing! Now!"

Raven glanced to his left and down. Four Zeros had opened their throttles and were racing for Pearl Harbor.

Lockjaw's voice was clear. "That's the same group that did a strafing run on Wheeler as we were getting up. I recognize the numbers on two of them. Get one for me, will you?"

"Right after you, Lockjaw."

Raven banked his P-36 and followed Lockjaw into a steep dive. Smoke suddenly streamed from the wings of the P-40 and Raven knew Lockjaw had opened fire with a long sustained burst. The Zeros swiftly split up, but not before one broke into bright blue flames and began to fall. Raven tracked it as the pilot struggled to control his burning plane, dropping down with the stricken fighter. It tumbled from the sky near Peterson's airfield and blew up when it hit the grass.

"You scratched your Zero," Raven announced.

"Good riddance. Heading to Pearl. You with me?"

A yellow Piper trailing smoke and oil careened wildly above the airstrip. Its pilot tried to land but a Zero swooped, spraying the Piper, the building below it, and a pair of jeeps that were driving up. The Piper crashed, skidding over the tarmac spewing sparks. It snapped in half. One part of the wing folded over, exposing the number eleven.

"Yo, Thunderbird. You with me?"

Raven felt completely empty. His mind was white. The Zero was pulling up and heading after him. He did not dodge or bank or roll. Feeling nothing but distance from everything that was taking place he put his nose down and went straight at the Japanese fighter. The machine guns housed in the engine cowling of the P-36 flamed as Raven fired. And fired. And fired. The canopy of the Zero shattered and red flames wrapped the front end of the plane. It exploded and the P-36 flew straight over the debris and began to climb.

"What was all that about?" asked Lockjaw.

"I got my Zero."

"I see that. Do you think you have any ammo left?"

"I'll ram the next one."

"Easy, cowboy. Mind telling me what's up?"

"He shot down Becky. She's dead."

Raven watched as Lockjaw dropped low over Peterson's Air Service. The P-40 circled the runway and climbed, drawing level with Raven.

"Take it easy, Bird. A bunch of people came out of one of the jeeps. They're at the Piper."

"Did you see her?"

"Bird—"

"Did you?"

"No."

"Kalino was in that airplane."

"She wasn't going up for her lesson till oh-nine-hundred," Lockjaw protested.

"They went up at seven, Lockjaw. Becky told me last night."

"No, Bird, her lesson was scheduled for oh-nine-hundred hours."

Raven opened up the throttle, still feeling removed from what was happening. "Let's go to Pearl."

The harbor was engulfed by smoke and flame. Flak ripped open a sky where Zeros circled like sharks. His eyes scanned Battleship Row and he saw that the *Arizona* had sunk and the *Oklahoma* had capsized. All the big ships were burning and Val dive bombers were attacking the *Pennsylvania*. The *Nevada*, streaming fire, was trying to leave the harbor for open sea. It was just about at Hospital Point, where the naval hospital was located, when Vals began to snarl around it like wasps.

"Going after the Vals bombing *Nevada*," said Lockjaw.

"I'll cover," replied Raven. "Watch out for the flak from our boats."

Lockjaw went into a dive. Immediately two Zeros swung down after him. He lit one Val like a match and it staggered out to sea pouring purple smoke. The Zeros got on Lockjaw's tail and peppered him with machine-gun fire. But Raven got on theirs and sent long strings of tracers into both. They scattered, one banking left and climbing swiftly, the other accelerating and racing straight ahead. Raven went after him.

"Zeke on your tail! On your tail, Thunderbird!" It was Batman's voice.

Raven felt his P-36 shake as tracers hit. "I'll run straight."

"He'll catch you."

"I'll climb and do some rolls."

"His plane is better at those tricks than yours."

The P-36 took more hits.

"What do you want me to do, Batman? Just sit still and let him take me apart?"

A low whistling came over the radio. It was a tune Raven did not recognize. He never recognized it.

"Whistler! Where are you?"

"Right behind the Zero that's right behind you. Hold steady now, please. Don't blink or fidget." The whistling began again.

"Whistler—"

"Steady, man, steady. Hold for the picture."

A loud boom was followed by a Zero plummeting into the water of the harbor just off Raven's left wing. He pulled up and could see Whistler behind him and Batman just above Whistler. Both were in their P-40s.

"What is that tune anyway?" Raven asked.

"Never tell. Family secret."

"Thanks for the straight shooting."

"My pleasure. Let's get back to work. Lockjaw is still chasing Vals."

Raven planted himself above and behind Lockjaw as swiftly as he could. *Nevada* had been rocked by explosions but not enough to sink her and block the channel. She took aim for Hospital Point and ran ashore. Vals were still falling on her like hawks. Lockjaw burst into the midst of them, sending another limping away boiling with smoke. A huge explosion shattered a ship close to the *Nevada*. The vivid flash of light made Raven blink.

"What's that? What's that?" Batman's voice.

"The Vals hit a destroyer," Lockjaw said. "The fires must have ignited one of her magazines."

Spider trails of smoke and flame arched over the stricken ship.

Radio crackle, and then, "Who's out there? Batman? Whistler? Lockjaw? Bird? Who's out there? This is Wheeler Air Base."

"Lockjaw's here. All the others are accounted for as well."

"What's your position?"

"We're over Pearl."

"Vals are hitting us from altitude. Can you make it back to Wheeler and help us out?"

"Will do. What about Wiz and Juggler and Shooter?"

"Confirm another P-40 and another P-36 got up. The P-36 was shot down."

"Who's down?" Batman's voice. "Who's down?"

"Taking a lot of bombs. Request you return to base."

"On our way." Lockjaw banked his plane to the north. "You guys with me?"

"We're with you," responded Raven. "Go."

They passed over Peterson's on their way back. At first Raven refused to look. But he couldn't help himself. Becky's Piper was burning and a plume of smoke reached up to his wingtips. The office was burning too. Both jeeps were gone. No one stood on the runway. There was no sign of life.

"You still with me, Thunderbird?" asked Lockjaw.

"Roger. I'm with you."

"Let's get some altitude and go after those Vals."

Raven didn't respond. He still felt locked away in a room watching the day's events unfold through a narrow window. Why was there no rage? Why didn't he cry? Why couldn't he speak her name?

Dear God. What kind of man am I? My world has blown apart and I feel nothing.

"Time check," announced Lockjaw. "I'm at oh-nine-forty-five hours."

"Time is oh-nine-forty-five hours, yes, sir," replied Batman.

"Prepare to attack. Get some more height."

"Gaining more height," Batman said. "Whistler? Bird?"

"Gaining height," responded Whistler.

"Bird?"

Raven checked his watch. "At altitude. Oh-nine-forty-six hours. Val bomber off my starboard wing. Attacking now."

"Bird," Batman cautioned. "Hold up until the rest of us are in position."

Raven threw his fighter into a dive. "Confirm I am in position. Val bomber in my sights. Attacking now."

Thirty-One

"Cease fire! Cease fire!" Gunny waved his arms at both machine gunners. "You're firing at American planes! Can't you see the stars?"

The guns went silent.

He checked his watch. "Ten-ten hours. Maybe there won't be another wave."

"Or they're fueling up and rearming." A sailor squinted at the sky. "Getting ready to provide air cover for their army when it hits Waikiki."

"In that case we'll be in the thick of it here in Honolulu Harbor. So let's preserve ammo."

Harrison stepped out of the radio room behind the bridge.

Gunny looked up at him. "What's up?"

"No more attacks. Not yet. They're asking for help from all ships. Trying to pick up survivors."

"That's Pearl's job."

"Half their ships are burning or sunk, Gunny."

Gunny looked at the smoke roiling up from Pearl Harbor. "Yeah. We could use the launch. But I don't give the orders."

Harrison went to the bridge. "Sir. I'd like permission to take the launch over to Pearl and help out."

The second-in-command stared at him. "Help? Help with what?"

"Survivors, sir. There are still all kinds of men in the water."

"It's not that far to shore in a harbor, Harrison."

"Some of them can't swim, sir. They're injured. They're trapped in wreckage."

"That's the navy's problem, Harrison."

"We're the Coast Guard, sir. We rescue people from the sea. It's our duty."

The second-in-command turned away and waved a hand. "Carry on, Harrison. If you want to get yourself killed, go ahead."

"May I use the launch, sir?"

The officer hesitated. "All right. All right. You'll probably want to take a couple of men."

"Yes, sir."

"Volunteers only. And no more than three."

"Aye, aye, sir." Harrison saluted.

The officer returned the salute. "Good luck, Harrison. I admire your spirit."

"Thank you, sir."

Harrison came down the stairs to the deck. "I'm heading out. Anyone with me?"

Gunny grunted. "It's a mess over there. If the Zeros and dive bombers come back you'll be a sitting duck."

"The navy has been a sitting duck all morning, Gunny."

"So—"

Harrison' temper flared. "So we're the Coast Guard. We go into messes and pull people out of the messes. If they can't swim we do their swimming for them. If they need a rope we make sure they get a rope and then we haul them on board. If they're drowning we keep them from drowning. We save lives, Gunny. We're the Coast Guard. That's one of the ways we protect our country."

Gunny looked at him and blew out a stream of air. "Maybe you should be running for president. Okay, I'm with you. Get the flags out of storage and rig one up. A big one. As big as we've got. I don't want anyone wondering who we are as we come around Hospital Point." He glanced around him. "Who else?"

A tall sailor with massive arms and huge shoulders stood up. "I'll rig the flag, Gunny. And make sure we got all the fuel we need."

"Yeah, I'll join y'all. Gunny, Harrison."

"Me too. I'm in."

"I can only take three," Harrison said. "Orders."

Gunny smiled. "My ears are still ringing from the explosions. Did you say three or four? Four'll do nicely."

In ten minutes the launch was motoring out of Honolulu Harbor and heading west toward the black smoke and fires. They kept close to the coastline at starboard and went past a civilian airfield that had been strafed and bombed. Then they swung north and headed up the inlet into Pearl Harbor, the Stars and Stripes prominent on their stern.

"Now you'll see something you've never seen before," Gunny told them. "The dead and the dying. Men who have been shot and burned and drowned. Bear up. We'll all lend a hand." As they came into Pearl and the extent of the destruction hit them—ships blazing, ships listing crookedly, ships that had capsized, their hulls wet and naked to the sun—Gunny glanced around at the others. "A prayer for us all would be a good thing right now, Mr. Harrison."

THIRTY-TWO

Nate and Jude carried Flapjack into the Petersons' home and placed him on the bed. Shirley arranged his hands so they were folded in his lap, smoothed back his hair, and kissed him on the cheek. Then she sat in a chair beside him, wiping her eyes with a Kleenex, gazing at his face. Lyyndaya knelt by her chair and hugged her.

"We loved him, Shirley."

"I know. Twenty years...You knew him longer than I did."

Ruth and Becky came in with a blanket and draped it over his body, covering the bullet wounds in his chest but leaving his face uncovered.

"Thank you." Shirley looked up at Becky, her eyes coming back to the present. "You've been through a terrible ordeal too. Please feel free to clean yourself up while you're here."

"Maybe later." Becky's flight jacket was still on, the blood was still clotted at the cut on her arm, grease and oil still streaked and spattered her face. "I never saw what happened. One of the ground crew told me—told us—after Dad and Nate hauled me clear of the Piper. Flapjack was out on the runway helping with a plane when the Zeros came in. They sprayed the field with bullets. I was still trying to get back from the Ko'olau Range."

Shirley squeezed her hand. "Ram thought a lot of you. You were like a daughter." She dabbed absently at a patch of grease under Becky's right eye. "How many...how many others were killed?"

"Two or three on the ground. I'm not sure. I...uh..."

"Students and instructors?"

Becky bit her lip. "Quite a few."

Ruth turned and left the room.

Shirley's eyes followed her. "Wasn't your aunt close to one of the instructors?"

"Yes."

"Did he make it?"

Becky shook her head. "She knows. I told her after they pulled me out of the plane."

"How's she doing?"

"I think it's just starting to sink in."

Shirley nodded and blew her nose. "Like it is with me...Go to her. Your family's here with me but she's all alone."

Becky found her aunt outside on the patio, which was ringed by tall palm trees. She had one hand against a trunk and was leaning toward it. Becky wrapped her arms around her from behind.

"This house must be close to the harbor." Ruth gripped one of Becky's hands. "I can smell the smoke."

"He was never in pain."

"You told me that in the jeep."

"He couldn't have been, Ruth. It all happened too fast. In an instant."

Ruth put her head against the palm tree. "I've had so little time to think since you told me. Part of me says I should never have left Pennsylvania. That I should never have followed the four of you to Hawaii."

"Then you never would have met him."

"Wouldn't that have been best?"

"Do you really think so? Knowing none of his words? None of his affection for you? No flying? No dancing? No *love*?"

"Will you say that if they tell you Christian has been shot down?"

Ice seized Becky's spine. "Is that what you've heard?"

Ruth turned around, her eyes dark and swollen. "Of course not. I would never keep something like that from you."

"I know he'll be up and flying. Flying as much as he can. Nate told me he saw two American fighters over the Peterson airfield when they arrived in the jeeps. One of them shot down the Japanese Zero that attacked me."

"The phone lines are jammed," Ruth said. "We have heard nothing from Billy Skipp. Jude has been trying all morning. He tried to get over there before we went looking for you, but the way in was blocked." She dropped her eyes. "There was a lot of smoke. The smell of rubber burning."

"I flew over the field. The Japanese destroyed most of the planes on the ground."

Ruth rubbed a spot of oil off Becky's cheek with her thumb. "If I hiked up there would I find him? By the Ko'olaus?"

"No, you won't find him."

"Or his plane? The one we flew in?"

"No."

"Why not? Your plane made it down."

"But I landed. Even if it was a bad landing. Manuku never had that chance. He was shot down. He was killed in his cockpit."

Ruth wiped away another smudge. "Just shot down?"

"Yes."

"Then there will be wreckage. I will find it."

Becky held Ruth's arms. "You can't go up there. There could be Japanese soldiers on Oahu by nightfall. They'd do to you what they did to the women in China."

"Right now, I wouldn't mind being bayoneted. God forgive me for saying so. It would end my suffering quickly."

"Aunt Ruth—"

She held up her hand. "I won't do anything rash. But you must tell me the truth and not spare me any longer. What really happened up there? What happened to Manuku?"

Becky stalled. "It happened so fast, I told you. I was in one place, he was in another, both of us were trying to shake a Zero loose, I couldn't keep my eyes on him the whole time."

"You saw exactly what occurred. Be honest with me, Rebecca."

Becky closed her eyes. "The plane exploded."

"What?"

"It blew up and it was gone. Manuku and his student were gone… He couldn't have felt a thing…He was there and then he wasn't there." She opened her eyes. "I'm sorry."

Ruth face had lost its color. "I…I think I want to be alone for now."

They hugged each other. Becky walked to the far side of the house. She hadn't gone far before she heard Ruth's sobs. She swiped at her cheeks with the back of her hand. A bench was tucked in among banana plants and she sat down on it, having no desire to take another step.

Could we have outrun them? No. Could we have outmaneuvered them? Outwitted them? Not a Piper Cub against a Zero.

Her mind spun and churned as she relived the morning and Kalino's and Manuku's deaths. Images of green mountains and blue sky clashed with breaking glass and streams of smoke and the hard flash of tracer bullets. She could smell the burning of her plane and taste the blood when she had bitten her tongue, and she could feel the shock when the Piper crash landed on the runway. She let her head sink into her hands.

Oh, Lord, I don't have words. Help Ruth. Bring people who can help her better than I can. Help Kalino's mother and father. And what about Lockjaw? What can I say to him? He acts like he is so strong but this will crush him inside like a fist crumpling paper.

An arm went around her shoulder.

She looked up. "Nate."

"I came looking for you. How are you doing?"

"Not so good…Everything keeps coming back to me."

"I know. Yes, I know. It always comes back and cuts you up. I'm sorry."

"I've been worried about you, Nate. I…uh…I thought you would be in a panic—the Japanese bombings—just like China."

"A lot of things are boiling up in me. But I'm not falling apart."

"They could land troops any time, Nate."

"I'm aware of that. I run it through my mind and the only thing I feel is that I want to do something. Just do something. So if they come, let them come. If we lose on the beaches we'll make them fight us in the jungle and on the mountains."

She couldn't keep the small smile from coming to her lips. "You sound like Winston Churchill when you talk like that. How did you change so much? How did you get rid of all that fear?"

"It's not all gone. There's a good chunk of it still inside me. It's like a cold, black rock. I know what war does, I know how ugly it is. But somehow I've reached a point where I can say to the fear, *You don't rule—you don't decide who I am or what I do with my life.*" He hugged her. "I'm going to enlist. Just so you know. I'll be one of those people Bishop Zook spoke about in his letter. The ones God calls to fight and defend while he calls the Amish to pray and do no harm."

"Enlist? Can you do that? What—"

"I don't know how the day is going to end. But what's happened today isn't something like the sinking of the *Lusitania.* Washington tried to ignore that. This is like a hundred *Lusitanias.* Roosevelt will ask Congress to declare war on Japan. He'll have to."

"And you feel all right with this?"

"Being an army or navy pilot? Yes, I do."

"What about Mom and Dad?"

He lifted one shoulder in a shrug. "I told them when we drove over to Peterson's to find you. They just nodded. I think they realized what I was going to say the moment we watched the smoke rolling up out of the harbor and the planes attacking. I'll talk to Billy Skipp."

"I can't believe you feel up to this."

Nate's face became grim, his mouth tightening. "I was in the shadows long enough. For years I had so little to fight the bullies with. Now God has brought me back into the light. And I can fly, Becky. I can fly."

Her eyes glimmering, she hugged him back.

He patted her on the shoulder. "And speaking of Billy Skipp, Dad got through to the folks at Wheeler. We're heading out there. We'll be cleared through any roadblocks."

"Did Dad talk to him?"

"No. Skipp was up. It was someone else."

Becky rubbed her hand over her eyes. "Did he…did he ask about Christian?"

"It was just a quick call."

"Did he or didn't he? It wouldn't be like Dad not to ask."

Nate let out his breath in a gust. "Okay—yeah, he did. The guy didn't know where he was or wasn't."

"Is that all?"

Nate hesitated. "No, that's not all. They've taken casualties. On the ground and in the air."

"What kind of casualties?"

"Ground crew and pilots were strafed. Just like Flapjack. And they have a plane down."

"What kind?"

"Look, we don't know who was in it—"

"What kind?"

"Thunderbird's kind. A P-36."

"Oh." Becky felt a sharp pain stab her deep in the stomach.

"Becky, any pilot could have been in it—how could this guy know what's what? He's been firefighting and ducking bombs and—"

Becky got to her feet. "We can go there now?"

"Yeah. Mom's going to stay with Shirley and Aunt Ruth."

"I'm not sure what to say to Lockjaw. About Kalino."

"He's an army pilot. Give it to him straight. He'll thank you for that. Don't beat around the bush."

"All right."

Nate stood. "Hey. The fighting's over. There hasn't been an attack on Wheeler for—" he checked his watch "—well over an hour and a half. If Raven's alive he's going to stay that way."

Becky folded her arms over her chest, over the flight jacket whose oil spatters matched her face and hands. Her voice was quiet. "And if he's not, he's going to stay that way too, Nate. Just like Moses."

THIRTY-THREE

Billy Skipp stood with hands on hips and counted the aircraft as they approached from the north. All four of them were there. The P-36 was trailing smoke but Thunderbird was keeping it rock-steady as he came in for a landing. The others followed. He watched them as they climbed out and walked in a group toward him. Whistler and Batman were wearing flight jackets over their pajamas. Smoke from the burning planes and hangars drifted over them.

"Sir." The men saluted as they stopped in front of him.

"Gentlemen." Skipp returned the salute. "You have the honor of giving America its first victories in this war. Antiaircraft on the ships brought down some enemy aircraft and a soldier at Schofield brought down a plane with his Browning automatic, if you can believe that. But you have given us our first victories in the air. Congratulations."

"Thank you, sir."

Skipp looked at Thunderbird's unshaven face. "I was up when you were tangling with that Zero over our airfield."

"Yes, sir. I saw you, sir."

Skipp grinned. "I never saw such combat flying in my life. The Zero is faster and far better at dogfighting than the P-36. But you turned that pilot inside out before you brought him down. Someone taught you stunt flying pretty darn well, Lieutenant."

Raven's eyes went flat. "Yes, sir." He put on his aviator glasses. "We were hoping to see Wiz and the others up there with us. Where'd they go?"

Skipp's smile left his face. "Wizard got up in a P-36. It was all he

299

could get his hands on. He flew it well but three Zeros jumped him. He crashed in the jungle north of here. We've found the wreckage and brought back the body."

Skipp could see the arms and shoulders of all four pilots tighten.

"Where…" Lockjaw stopped and started again. "And Juggler and Shooter?"

"They ran for some undamaged P-40s not long after you left. Juggler had been brushing his teeth and left his toothbrush on the runway. The enemy came in again. Juggler and Shooter were strafed as they tried to climb into their craft. They're both dead."

The pilots stared at Skipp as if they thought he was making things up.

Lockjaw spoke again, very quietly. "Where are they?"

"In the hangar behind me. On the table under a tarp."

The four men walked slowly into the dark of the hangar. The table was off in a corner. They stood beside it but did nothing until Raven finally reached out a hand and drew the canvas away from their faces.

"Wizard," Batman said.

The faces and heads seemed all wrong. Color was gone. Shooter's eyes were partly open. Raven reached out again and closed them gently with his fingers.

Lord. I don't know what to say to you. I don't know what to pray.

After a few minutes Raven was the only one still standing at the table in the hangar. The others had walked back outside. He covered his friends' faces again. No thoughts came to him except that he had lost Becky and now these three men. The lines from the hymn Jude Whetstone loved worked through his mind.

> *Save all who dare the eagle's flight,*
> *And keep them by thy watchful care*
> *From every peril in the air.*

He wandered away from the table and came to an area full of engine parts. He put his hands in his pockets and stared at them. Someone stepped into the entrance to the hangar. But right now he didn't care.

"What is it?" he finally asked.

There was no response. He looked up, annoyed, and squinted at the rectangle of light. A slender dark figure was there and wasn't there. He shielded his eyes.

Becky.

He didn't move. She came inside in her flight jacket and jeans and white tee. Her face was spattered with grease and oil and long black streaks from tears. She stood in front of him.

"Dead." He spoke the word. "I know you're dead."

Her face was white as bone. "I guess you're right. Whatever I was before is gone. I don't know what God will make of me now."

She put her hand to his cheek.

"I feel a million things," he said.

His kiss was sudden and full. She gripped his back as if she were clinging to something that could keep her above water and give her air.

He pulled back from her for a moment. "God knows I'd lost you. In my head I'd lost you."

"I'm here. It's okay. I'm here."

"I saw your plane…"

"Marry me, Thunderbird. Just take me and marry me and carry me to your room and be my husband."

"Beck—"

"I mean it."

"Not today, we can't marry today."

"Why not?" She gripped his face in her hands. "It's a day full of death and hate. Why should that be the final word? Why can't we put life into it? And love?"

He stared at her. "Are you serious?"

"Yes, I'm serious. Kalino is dead. And Manuku."

"What? Did you tell Lockjaw?"

"I told him. It's not just Kalino and Manuku. Flapjack is dead. Shooter. Juggler. Wizard. My dad was told the *Arizona* went down with practically everybody on board."

"David—"

"Yes, David too. So much death. So much pain. Why shouldn't we fight back by loving each other? Why shouldn't we give our family and friends something when all around them is hell? Why not?"

Raven shook his head. "But how could that work?" He looked in her eyes, then hugged her to himself. "Well, okay, then. Marry me, crazy girl."

She clutched him. "Today. I want to look back on December seventh and remember it as the day we became one. I want it to be a day of happiness. I want to love the ones we lost by becoming man and wife and honoring each of them with all the life we can muster."

"We can't just walk into a church—"

"Why can't we? Isn't the chaplain around here somewhere? Helping the wounded? Didn't you talk to him about me months ago? Let's find him."

"I don't know where he is, Beck—it's nuts out there."

Grabbing his hand she pulled him through a door at the back of the hangar. Two ground crew were running past.

"Soldier!" she barked. "Where's the army chaplain?"

They both came to a stop.

"I'm not sure, ma'am," one of them replied.

"Do you know where they've collected the wounded?"

He pointed. "Way back behind the hangars. In case the Japs hit us again. They're setting up a tent. You can see it. That's one place anyway."

"Thanks." She still had Raven's hand and she began to drag him. "What's wrong with my face?"

"Nothing."

"They both stared as if I had two heads."

"I guess it's because we've smeared the grease and oil all over ourselves. Your whole face is covered."

"But you'll still marry me, right?"

"Sure, I'll marry you. Love is blind."

"Come on. Quick. They'll be sending people after you to fly the next sortie."

The tent was full of wounded, many with burns, and the groans of pain immediately took the good feeling out of Becky's spirit. Her face went rigid as she scanned the tent, but she didn't let go of Raven's hand.

"What does he look like?" she asked.

"He's not here."

"Where would he go?"

"Maybe he's with Skipp for some reason."

"No, not likely. Skipp was going up again in an hour. They're heading out to look for troopships and the Japanese task force." She wiped oil off his eyebrows and rubbed it between her fingers. "Which means you."

"The wedding can wait."

"No, it can't wait."

A tall man holding a Bible bent as he entered the tent.

Raven came to attention. "Reverend Captain."

The chaplain returned the salute. "*Captain* will do." He hesitated. "You're Thunderbird, aren't you?"

"Yes, sir."

"Are you hurt?"

"No, sir."

"Then maybe you can help me since you're here. I want to pray with the wounded men and encourage them." He nodded his head at Becky. "Miss Whetstone, isn't it? I know your parents." He narrowed his eyes. "You don't seem too well off yourself. Perhaps you'd better see a nurse or doctor."

"Captain. Marry us."

"Excuse me?"

"As soon as you've seen to the wounded. Or right now."

The chaplain took their arms and pulled them out of the tent with him.

"What on earth are you jabbering about, Miss Whetstone?" he demanded. "You know what kind of day this is?"

"Yes, sir, that's why I want to do it. This day shouldn't be all about death and destruction. There should be love and hope in it. I want to tell Hawaii and America I married the man I love the day our enemy tried to defeat us."

"Every day has its share of love and hope, Miss Whetstone."

"Yes, sir. But some days need a lot more. Some need all they can get."

The chaplain scowled at Raven. "Are you serious, Lieutenant?"

"Well, I—"

"You want to marry her today? Just like that? With Pearl Harbor and Wheeler burning?"

"Angel's wings." Becky smiled through the oil and grease on her face. "Angel's wings beating where you least expect it."

"Miss Whetstone—"

"I know it's crazy, sir." Raven spoke up. "But it's a crazy day. Some of our best friends are dead. There could be Japanese troops all over Oahu by sunset. This whole island may be overrun. So maybe Becky just wants one moment of beauty in a day that doesn't have many of them."

The chaplain looked from one to the other. "As God is my witness you both mean it." He poked his head into the tent. "Corporal. I need you to run an errand for me."

A tall man with a boy's face covered in freckles stepped outside. "Yes, sir."

The chaplain held a piece of paper to his Bible and was scribbling with a pen. "Go to the runway. Find Colonel Skipp. Do you know him by sight?"

"No, sir, I'm afraid I don't."

"Ask." He folded the paper twice and handed it to the corporal. "As soon as you've delivered it you can report back here."

"Yes, sir."

A cluster of P-40s suddenly screamed overhead. The chaplain and the corporal ducked. Becky smiled once the two men straightened.

"No red suns," she said.

The chaplain didn't smile back. "I hope you'll both help me. After that we can talk about your wedding."

"Of course we'll help."

"Prayer. Some food. Kindness. All this helps as much as the morphine." He put a hand on Becky's shoulder. "They will be glad to see you. But there are about fifty casualties. We can cover more ground if we all take a different patient. Are you comfortable praying with the soldiers on your own?"

"Yes, sir. I can do that."

The first man Becky came to had a bandage over his eyes. Blood was seeping through gauze on his chest. Instinctively she took his hand. He almost pulled it away.

"Who's that?" he demanded.

"Becky Whetstone. I'm working with the chaplain. Is that okay?"

The man relaxed. "Yeah. Sure."

"Where are you from, soldier? What's your name?"

"Max. From Michigan. Detroit. I'm a mechanic. Work on the trucks and jeeps here."

"No airplanes?"

"Haven't got my ticket yet. But I'm learning."

"That's good. Because my boyfriend flies. He stakes his life on what you guys do."

The man lifted his head off the pillow. "What's his call sign?"

"Thunderbird."

"The Bird? Sure, I know him. He's all right."

"Do you need anything? Some water? Anything to eat?"

"I want to know what's happening with the bombs. Is it...over?"

"We hope it's over. No more planes. No more bombing runs."

"They're getting ready to land troops."

"We have fighters up. So far nothing is near the coast."

"They could still be coming," Max said.

"I know."

"They sunk all our ships."

"They didn't get the carriers, Max. The *Lex* and *Enterprise* are still out there with their planes."

Max put both hands on hers. "That's right. Good. Hey. I'm a lapsed Catholic, as the priest always tells me." He barked a laugh. "Have you got a prayer for a lapsed Catholic, sister? I want to see again."

"Sure, Max. I have all kinds of prayers." She lowered her voice and prayed quietly over him. "Give him his sight back, Lord. Give him hope. Raise him off his sickbed. In Christ's name."

Max crunched her hand. "Hey. That means a lot. Thank you. Will you come by again?"

"I will. Today or tomorrow. God bless you, Max."

"Yeah, sister. You too."

Becky made her way slowly from bed to bed, sometimes talking and praying with those Raven or the chaplain had already seen. A few she kissed on the forehead. One reminded her of Wizard, and she combed his hair for him when he asked. Another had pictures in his wallet he tried to show her but they were glued together with his blood. Forty-five minutes had passed before she joined Raven and the chaplain at the front of the tent, and she kept rubbing her eyes to keep the tears back.

The chaplain's voice was gentle. "You're a flight instructor at Peterson's, aren't you? I sure could use you at my side over the next few days."

Becky wiped her fingers against her jeans and blinked. "I'd be happy to help. There won't be any flying at Peterson's for a long time."

Raven took her hand. "You okay?"

"No, I'm not okay."

"How'd you get the oil and grease off your face?"

"One of the guys did that."

"Look, we don't have to go ahead with the marriage stuff. Maybe—"

She flared up. "Of course we have to go ahead with the marriage stuff. What other bright spot can I give the guys but that?" She swung her blazing green eyes on the chaplain. "I want to do it here. In this tent. They can all be my witnesses. And the nurse here, Cathy, she can be my maid of honor."

He smiled. "All right."

She had expected an argument. "All right?"

"I thought it might come to that."

Tires screeched outside the tent opening.

"What's that?" she asked, drawing back the flap.

"My marriage preparations," the chaplain replied.

The three of them stepped outside. Two jeeps full of men had pulled up in front. Billy Skipp jumped out.

"Are you kidding me, Thunderbird?" he shouted. "The sky's falling, we're at war with Japan, I need planes up to look for the Japanese carriers and troopships, and you want to get married?"

"Well, sir—"

"Yes, we do!" snapped Becky.

Skipp looked from her father, who was driving one of the jeeps, to her. "Are you behind this, Becky?"

"Yes, I am, Billy." It was the first time she had ever used his Christian name. "All I can tell the guys to buck them up—" she jerked her thumb at the tent "—is remind them the carriers weren't in port when the bombs started dropping this morning. Well, I'm going to give them another shot in the arm. I'm getting married—here, now—to an army pilot before he goes on his next sortie. Two Americans are getting married and they'll be back to celebrate their anniversary five years from now, ten years from now, in Hawaii, in America—because Hawaii is still going to be here and it is still going to be American." She turned her eyes on her father. "Dad, you can give me away. And Nate can help."

"Honey," Jude responded, "your mother's not here."

"I know that. And neither is Aunt Ruth. But we don't have time to give them a call and wait for them to show up. I'd love to have them here but we have to move ahead." She looked over the men in both jeeps. "Since the chaplain decided to tell the world, the world can help too. Batman, Lockjaw, Whistler, you stand with Thunderbird. I'm asking a nurse to stand with me. That's all we need." She paused as her eyes met Lockjaw's. "You can pass on this, Lockjaw. I'm sorry."

"No." He adjusted his aviator glasses. "Kali knows where I need to be."

"Lockjaw—"

"I need to be here, Becky."

"Thank you," she said quietly.

Skipp put up both hands. "Now hold your horses, Little Missy. If it's all about putting on a show for the boys—"

Becky took her eyes off Lockjaw and they immediately flamed again. "Hold your own horses. It's not just about putting on a show for the boys. I love Christian. I want him in my arms tonight when it gets dark. I want him there all night, Colonel."

"Becky, I need him in the air."

"I'll bet you have other pilots up. You don't need Thunderbird and the others right away."

"We are under attack—"

"No, you're not—sir. There hasn't been a Japanese plane in the sky for hours."

"Becky, they could send in another wave at any time."

"Which is why we'd better hurry this along. It won't take five minutes." She walked back into the tent. "Guys. Hey. Can you all help me out with something?"

Heads lifted.

"What's up?" asked half a dozen men.

"Do you mind being part of a wedding ceremony in this tent? I want to tie the knot with my boyfriend the army pilot before he goes on another sortie. I need you guys as witnesses. I don't care if you're all witnesses but I need at least one or two."

Billy Skipp and Jude Whetstone entered as men were falling out of their beds and shouting and raising their hands to get Becky's attention. When the chaplain stepped inside she turned to him.

"Captain. Can we use them all?"

"I don't need fifty names. But I'll attach an extra sheet. Just so they can all say they were here when Becky Whetstone married a fighter pilot the day Japan bombed Pearl Harbor."

"And do you have the book you do weddings and funerals with?"

"Yes. It's in my bag."

Becky called to the nurse at the far end of the tent. "Cathy. Will you be my maid of honor?"

Cathy smiled, hung her stethoscope around her neck, and wrote on her clipboard. "I thought you'd never ask."

Becky put her hands on her hips. "Colonel, do you want to say something to the boys?"

Skipp stared at her and at the men sitting up in their beds. Many of them were covered in bandages and blood. "God bless you, boys. I'm honored to be here."

She suddenly flashed a grin. "Why, you *are* my guest of honor, sir."

Lockjaw, Batman, and Whistler stood with Raven by the tent flap. Jude and Nate walked Becky up the aisle between the beds right behind Cathy Brown, the nurse. The chaplain led Becky and Raven through their vows. When he told Raven he could kiss the bride the tent was in an uproar, all the men cheering and whistling and shouting.

Raven curled his finger around her gold chain and gemstone. "I never noticed. You still have this."

"Yeah. I still have it. It's my ring."

"I'll get you a proper ring, Beck."

"I don't care. I really don't. This is good enough." She kissed him again.

The chaplain made the sign of the cross over them. "Highly irregular but that's it." The chaplain shook Raven's hand. "Congratulations, Lieutenant. You've got a real firecracker on your hands. May God be with you."

"Thank you, sir."

Cathy got signatures from Lockjaw, Whistler, and Batman, attached a clean sheet to her clipboard, and began to move among the beds, helping the wounded scribble their names.

"Rebecca." Skipp kissed Becky on the cheek. "You look radiant in your flight jacket and white T-shirt and grease. I just wish I could drop you into a P-40. Your husband will have to do instead."

She kissed him back. "Thanks for putting up with me, Billy Skipp."

"I have to get your guy…your husband in the air."

"I know."

Raven leaned over and kissed her quickly on the lips. "I'm the happiest man on earth. But I gotta go. Even though you're the most beautiful thing alive."

Becky hugged him. "Oh, sure—love me and leave me."

"Jump in the jeep with us. Come on."

"Is there room?"

"We'll make room." He turned to Batman, Lockjaw, and Whistler. "Let's go, guys."

The jeeps raced back to the runway, Skinny at the wheel of one and Jude steering the other. As they neared the smoke and firefighting and airplanes Skinny suddenly started leaning on the horn. Skipp looked at his driver in surprise but did nothing to stop him. Heads turned. Skinny jumped up from his seat as he jammed on the brakes.

"Married!" he shouted. "Becky and Bird got married!"

Becky reddened and put her hand to her mouth. "Becky and Bird. That sounds awful."

Skinny continued to honk the horn. "The chaplain married them ten minutes ago! Tell that to the Japanese!"

Laughter erupted from the throats of smoke-blackened ground crew and pilots still in their pajamas and soldiers rushing past with helmets on. Hands came together and clapped as Skinny continued to press his hand against the horn. Finally Jude shrugged and did it too.

Skipp shook his head. "Holy smoke, Becky, you are something else for morale."

"They just needed something to cheer about, sir."

"A wedding in a war zone looks to be it." He nodded at Raven. "Your fighter is patched up and rearmed and ready to go. Head west toward Japan. See what you can see. Maintain radio contact. Stick together."

"Yes, sir."

Raven kissed Becky a final time and began to run toward his P-36. His fellow pilots were already climbing into their P-40s. The honking stopped and smoke drifted over the jeeps. Becky stood up as Raven headed down the runway and lifted into the air. She waved. Then collapsed into her seat.

Her father's arm went around her shoulders. "Hey, my little girl. Chin up. You'll have the rest of your lives together to look forward to."

Becky was biting her knuckle. "Sure. If he comes back. What a wild and crazy thing for me to do. Typical."

"He'll come back."

"How do you know, Dad? Anything could happen up there. The Japanese could launch another bombing run."

He hugged her and kissed the top of her head. "He'll come back. God knows he has to come back."

THIRTY-FOUR

We're coming up on the *Arizona* now." Gunny began to tie a water-soaked cloth over his nose and mouth. "Most of it's underwater. But what's on top is sure burning. And it's spread to the *West Virginia.*" He handed Harrison a handful of cloths like the one he had put on. "Better pass these around."

Harrison stared at the sunken ship as the launch slowed. "Where are the men?"

"Already picked up. Or still inside."

Harrison narrowed his eyes. "God have mercy."

Gunny nodded. "Aye. Mercy."

Harrison began to cough as the black smoke smothered their boat. He tied the cloth over his face but still had trouble breathing. One body bobbed near the wreck, covered in oil, on fire. Glancing behind him he shook his head grimly. The last two men they had recovered lay dead in water and blood, rocking with the motion of the launch.

All the living they had plucked from the sea had been taken to the naval hospital at Hospital Point, near the beached battleship *Nevada* and the heavily bombed destroyer *USS Shaw.* They had made the trip seven times as they inched their way along Battleship Row, searching the debris for signs of life, passing the *Pennsylvania, California, Maryland,* and the other great ships. Everywhere there had been smoke and flame and drowned sailors. The *California* and *West Virginia* had sunk, the *Oklahoma* had capsized. The *Arizona* was the last in the row, moored at the north end of Ford Island. Its oily smoke clung to them like a fog bank.

"D'you see anything?' asked Gunny, squinting through the haze. "The navy's been looking for hours but you never know when someone might pop up."

"Gunny! A swimmer!"

A man was stroking furiously to get away from the *Arizona*'s wreckage and the burning oil. "Help!" he screamed. "Please help!"

"Bring the boat in!" hollered Gunny. "Bring it in!"

"We're too close to the fire," argued the helmsman.

"I said, *Bring it in!* Do you hear me?"

"Gunny—"

Gunny threw the man off the rudder and took the helm himself. "Harrison! You others! Haul him in! Haul him in and be quick about it!"

The launch went right up to the *Arizona*. Flames leaped up blue and white and yellow on all sides of them. Harrison reached over and grabbed one of the man's arms. The heat cut into his face. A sailor grabbed the other arm. But they could not get him over the side. The oil made him slide right through their fingers. He began to sink, his features rigid with fear.

"Oh, no, please, God, please, Jesus, help me!" the man cried.

Harrison dove straight into the flames.

THIRTY-FIVE

"Becky."

She turned to peer through the smoke. Her mother was standing on the runway. Behind her was Ruth.

"Mom!" They hugged. Then Becky extended her arm to bring her aunt into the embrace. "I'm sorry. I just had this feeling come over me. That I needed to marry Christian right now, today, that there wasn't a moment to lose. Forgive me."

Her mother patted her back. "Shh. Shh. Billy explained all this to us. We're not angry. From the moment we heard, we've been praying for you."

"Colonel Skipp phoned you?"

"Yes, dear. He thought we should know. Then he put your father on the phone, and he gave me more details." She smiled a full smile. "It sounded very much like a straightforward, no-nonsense thing that Becky Whetstone might do. Astonishingly, it was even done officially, with all the correct paperwork. So now you really are Mrs. Rebecca Raven." She kissed her daughter on the cheek.

Ruth added another kiss. "The Lord be with you forever and ever, amen. How delighted Bishop Zook would be to see you married to a Christian man. Even though it took place on a day of war, it remains God's peace in the midst of storm and conflict. How happy I am for you."

Becky put her head on her aunt's chest. "How can you be happy for me when you have lost so much? How can Lockjaw stand with me and Raven when he has lost so much?"

"Lockjaw and I have lost a great deal, it's true. But we haven't lost our capacity to love. And we both love you and Christian."

The three women continued to hug each other.

"Who will talk to Hani?" asked Becky.

"Your father told us who had been killed." Lyyndaya smoothed her daughter's unbrushed hair. "Ruth and I will go to her and tell her about Wizard. The colonel will stop by later. But he agreed it would be best if we could go first."

"Perhaps you should leave now."

"No, my dear. We will see your husband safely down first. Then we'll go to Hani."

Ruth smiled. "And there's something we must show you."

Becky had been standing by herself at the edge of the runway. They led her to a small Quonset hut behind one of the larger hangars. A sign posted outside informed Army Air Forces personnel that the hut was for the storage of rope and hoses. But a sheet of paper tacked to the door said in bright orange crayon, *Honeymoon hut of Mr. and Mrs. Raven, December 7, 1941.*

"What?" Becky touched the orange-crayon writing. "Who did this?"

"Billy Skipp ordered it," her mother replied. "He asked us to help make a home out of the hut after we drove up to Wheeler. So a bunch of soldiers and airmen moved the rope and hoses and other gear and brought in what they thought would make it charming. Ruth and I did the rest."

Becky wrapped her fingers around the door handle, looked at her mother and aunt, and bit her lip. "Should I?"

"Of course. There may be other things you wish to fix up before Christian lands."

Becky opened the door. There was a groan of metal on metal. Sunshine tumbled through the doorway. Inside were two chairs around a small round table. On the table was a vase of roses. To Becky's left was a bed with two pillows, covered with the Amish quilt Ruth had stitched for Manuku. Right next to the bed was a table with a candle.

"My goodness." Becky's mouth was open in surprise. "The boys did this for me?"

Ruth nodded. "They were glad to do it, believe me. The one bright spot in their day. Now they're back at their fires and trying to salvage as many planes as they can. Or on the beaches preparing for an attack."

"They've been so kind." Becky pulled back the quilt to look at the sheets. They were white and soft. She looked up. "And you, both of you, look at what you've done for me. Yet you didn't even get an invitation to the wedding."

"Well." Her mother had her small smile. "We were hoping we would get one to the reception."

"A reception. When will I be able to do that?"

"Not this week. But someday soon, I pray, you will remember your mother and your aunt when it comes time to open your home to visitors."

She hugged her mother and Ruth again with a sudden burst of happiness and strength. "Of course I will. Thank you for everything."

There was a sudden banging on the door that made them jump and turn around.

Forgetting herself, Ruth blurted, "*Was ist das?*"

A young man's voice responded, "I'm sorry to disturb you, but is Becky Whetstone in there? Or her mother or aunt?"

"*Wir sind alle hier.*"

"Pardon me?"

Lyyndaya put a hand on her sister's arm. "The three of us are in here."

Skinny stepped into view. "I didn't want to barge in on something personal."

"You didn't. What is it you want?"

"The colonel wanted me to relay this message to you right away. If you wish to join him at his office my jeep is at your disposal."

"What is the message?"

Skinny handed Lyyndaya a sheet of paper folded in half. "Ma'am."

Becky, Lyyndaya, Ruth—

Our own antiaircraft guns have been firing at American planes because they think they are Japanese. We have lost two fighters and their pilots. Please join me immediately.

Billy Skipp

THIRTY-SIX

"**B**reak left and right! Break left and right! They've got our altitude!"

"Wheeler, we're being fired on by our own AA."

"Roger. Get clear of Pearl Harbor. Get clear. They can't recognize your insignia."

"Breaking left!"

"Thunderbird! Thunderbird! Does anyone have a visual of Bird?"

"Negative. He's not off either wing here."

"Did his plane go down? Did anyone see the P-36 go down? Can you confirm?"

"More AA. Head inland. Head for base."

"Boxcars. Who can give me a report on Boxcars?"

"He's down. Never saw smoke but he's down."

"Did you see him crash? Can you verify a crash?"

"Low on fuel. Heading back."

"This is Wheeler. Did you spot enemy troopships? Did you spot a task force?"

"No troopships close to Oahu. Repeat. No troopships. No carriers. No task force."

"Our formation is clear of Pearl, Wheeler."

"If any of you eyeball Bird shout it out."

"Roger, Lockjaw."

Raven tried again and again to make radio contact but a flak burst had knocked out his microphone—he could hear his squadron but they couldn't hear him. He had taken a long loop out to sea to avoid antiaircraft fire and was now trying to get to Wheeler from the east coast, his needle trembling just above empty, his engine stuttering, fabric torn by AA flapping wildly on his port wing. The sun was low on the horizon and the sea was full of shadows.

Just a few nights ago it was the full moon. What will it be tonight? Half of that? Lord, I have to get home, sun or no sun, moon or no moon. I'm a married man now. Have to make it. My guys think I'm gone.

He made his way past the beaches and over the palms. To his left he could just catch a glimpse of antiaircraft going up and bursting in the late afternoon sky. He glanced at his watch. The crystal was smashed and the hands had stopped at 0437 hours. He had no idea what the time was. Scanning the instrument panel he could see the oil pressure dropping and the gas gauge about to indicate an empty tank. He rubbed a hand over his face and his day's growth of beard.

There's nothing I can do but nurse it along—reduce my airspeed, take more time, and hope I don't crash into a hillside in the dark. Or I could speed up and get to Wheeler faster and risk having the engine cut out—and I would drop like a stone right in front of Becky's eyes.

"Asking again—any sign of Boxcars? Any sign of Bird?"

"Negative."

"No one up here but us, boss."

Miles ahead, still specks to him, Raven watched his squadron descend and land where a tall plume of black smoke hung in the golden sky. He was already flying as low as he dared in order to conserve fuel, confident there were no AA batteries on his route and, if there were, the gunners would see the stars on his plane. Now and then a white or bronzed face gaped up at him, and some people ran.

I don't blame you. I guess I would run too after what's happened today.

Jungle and fields swept past under his wings. The light took on a copper color as the sun sank. His engine coughed and rumbled and then coughed again. The plume of smoke was close but not close enough. He was too low to parachute and didn't like using a chute anyway.

If I could just reach an open field near the runway. Just a long-enough stretch to handle my slide. Flat would be great too.

He smiled. "What would you say about a prayer like that, Beck?"

he asked out loud. "Nothing much to it, is there? But I sure mean it. Every part of me means it."

The engine cut out.

"We have an unidentified aircraft approaching from the east. He is coming in low and looks to be preparing to strafe the airfield. Who's still up?"

"Batman's up."

"Whistler's up."

"Engage fighter. Repeat. Engage fighter. He is descending rapidly to treetop level."

"Got him."

"On him with Batman."

"Hey. That's one of ours. Say again, that's one of ours. It's a P-36."

"Thunderbird. A definite. It's the Bird. Can you read us? Bird, can you read us?"

"Wheeler. We have Thunderbird. He doesn't appear to be under power. We identify him as the plane approaching from the east. Do not fire on him. Repeat. Do not open fire. It is Thunderbird."

"Mayday! Mayday! Mayday! Thunderbird is hitting trees and losing control. He may have enough to get to the edge of the airstrip. Clear personnel from the runway immediately."

Raven fought the stick, forcing the nose up. The P-36 struck the grass with a loud bang and the canopy split. He kept thinking, *Too much speed, too much speed,* but his brakes did nothing. The metal screeched and the wings bounced against the ground. One snapped off and flipped back over the top of the plane, just missing him. Mud and stones spattered the glass. The only words that sped through Raven's mind were from an old hymn his mother always sang.

> *Abide with me; fast falls the eventide;*
> *The darkness deepens; Lord with me abide.*
> *When other helpers fail and comforts flee,*
> *Help of the helpless, O abide with me.*

Then even that was taken away as his P-36 skidded onto the concrete of the runway. Sparks and flame showered its wings, and it hurtled toward the still burning wreckage of the morning's attack.

Thirty-Seven

"We got the guy up to the hospital okay," Gunny said to his men. "They say it looks good but we can check back on him tomorrow or Tuesday if we're not fighting off an invasion."

"All right."

"They bandaged Harrison's hands from the oil burns. He wouldn't stay up there. Said there were too many people worse off than him and he'd be taking space from someone who needed it."

The sailor glanced over at Harrison who was leaning against the gunwale and saying nothing, his uniform oil and blood, his hands white with the bandages.

Gunny gauged the location of the sun. "We got just enough time to drop you back at the *Taney*. But we may spot someone else. In which case we'll do whatever we can to pick him up. Understood?"

"Understood."

"Take the helm back. Get us home. Maybe we have enough fuel, maybe we don't. Do your best. You're a good sailor. Just remember. We're the Coast Guard. And we're at war. Every life we save is a victory. Everybody we recover is a victory."

"Got it."

Gunny slapped him on the back. "Take the helm. Get us to our berth."

The sailor gunned the engine and began to steer the launch around Hospital Point. In a few minutes they were cruising through the inlet that led to the open sea. Flak burst overhead as AA guns continued to hammer the sky. Gunny went over to Harrison.

"How do your hands feel?"

"They feel good."

"Good? You're a crazy fool, Harrison. You could have been burned alive in that mess you jumped into."

"Better me than you."

"What?"

"You would have done it. I saw you taking your shoes off. I beat you to it because I went in with them on."

Gunny gave a lopsided grin. "You ruined those black leather shoes of yours, sailor."

"I'll buy another pair. No one cries out like that man did without getting a response from me. I don't care what I have to jump into."

"Gunny!" A sailor called to him from the bow. "We've got company."

Gunny and Harrison hadn't paid any notice to a destroyer moving along the far shore of the inlet. It had swerved and was now headed straight across their bow. The helmsman slowed down their launch. In a few moments they were being hailed.

"Where from? Where to?"

Gunny gazed up at the officers and men at the rail. "We're from the *Taney.* A Coast Guard cutter moored in Honolulu Harbor."

"What brought you into Pearl on a day like this?"

"To do what we can. To help out."

The captain smiled. "I saw that. Back and forth all afternoon. How many trips did you make to the hospital?"

"I can't say. Seven, maybe?"

"Closer to ten. My math skills are pretty good. How many were alive?"

Gunny laughed. "My math skills aren't that good, skipper. A dozen? Sixteen, seventeen, eighteen?"

"What if the enemy had come back for another run? You were sitting ducks."

"They wouldn't have wasted a bomb on us, sir."

"A few machine-gun bullets would have been all it took."

"Seemed worth the risk."

The captain nodded. "You must be low on fuel."

"We'll make it, sir."

"Let's be sure of that." The captain turned to a man beside him. "I think we can spare a drum, Mr. Gibbs?"

"I believe we can, Captain."

A fuel drum was lowered in a net. The Coast Guard men secured it near the engine in the stern. Harrison waved up at the destroyer.

"Thanks, Navy!" he called.

"It's the navy who thanks you, sailor." The captain looked them over once again. "You're all enlisted men."

"Yes, sir."

"You came out here on your own?"

"We were granted leave to do so—yes, sir."

Suddenly the captain stood up straight and bellowed in a voice that seemed to carry right across Pearl Harbor. "Officer on deck!"

The other officers and sailors at the rail snapped to attention and saluted the men in the launch. The captain held the salute for several long seconds. The surprised Coast Guard men—Gunny, Harrison, and all—finally came to attention in their bloody and blackened clothing and returned the honor. Smoke drifted over them from the burning battleships as the AA guns still banged and thumped.

Finally the captain dropped his arm. "Godspeed. And if the enemy should come again, night or morning, make sure the Coast Guard lays into them with everything they've got."

Gunny grinned and snapped off a final salute. "Aye, aye, Skipper."

The launch moved around the destroyer's bow and headed for the ocean. Off to starboard the sun hovered just above the horizon. Harrison watched as the smoke from the attack turned it the color of blood. Then he stared straight ahead where sea and sky met in a long line of gold.

"There's something you don't see every day, Harrison." Gunny was at his elbow.

"What's that?"

"The navy paying tribute to the Coast Guard. Shall we let the CO or second-in-command know?"

Harrison leaned on the gunwale as fine spray blew back over their faces. "Why spoil it, Gunny? It was for the men in the launch. The volunteers. And it can stay with them to the grave."

"I was thinking the same thing. It was a hard day. And they did a marvelous thing on a hard day."

"Tell the men that, Gunny. Tell them you're proud of them."

Gunny laughed. "Why spoil it, Harrison? They've been told that in a way far better than I could ever tell them. Any words of mine would just take the bloom off the rose. Or the shine off the sea to put it in nautical terms."

Harrison nodded and folded his bandaged hands one over the other. "Aye, aye, Gunny. Let's keep the day under our caps. All of it." He fell silent, recalling the conversation he'd had at the hospital with the survivor from the *Arizona*:

I heard a lot of boats go by. I knew they were looking for survivors. But I was trapped under a piece of wreckage and it was all I could do to hang on and keep breathing. Finally I yanked my foot loose. It broke my ankle but I got to you guys.

Better a busted ankle than a drowning.

It would have been a drowning if you hadn't jumped in after me. Thanks again, Harrison.

You mend up. That'll be thanks enough. I'll try and drop by Tuesday or Wednesday if there isn't an invasion first.

That'd be swell.

Listen. I know you had a big crew. But a buddy of mine was on your boat. Maybe there's a chance you knew him?

Slim chance. But you never know. What was his name?

Goff. David Goff.

What? Goff? The singer? Sure, I knew him. We messed together a lot. He mentioned he had friends in the Coast Guard and the air forces. Isn't that something?...I wish I had better news to give you about him. I saw Dave in the water.

In the water? Maybe another boat picked him up. Maybe he got to shore.

He was floating facedown. The waves turned him over and I saw his eyes. I'm sorry.

Thirty-Eight

No! *No!*" Becky began running across the runway toward the flames.

Nate grabbed her from behind and wrestled her down onto the concrete. She thrashed and yelled and bit and pulled his hair with a ferocity that made him cry out. But he wouldn't let her go.

"Stop it, Becky! There's nothing you can do! Either he walks out of it or he doesn't! No one can pull him clear of that!"

"I can! I can! If you men are so afraid then let a woman show you how!" She almost broke free but Nate pinned her again. "I'll hate you forever if you don't let me go to him!"

"And burn up? Hate away."

Tears began to streak down Becky's face as she lay with her back against the concrete. "I can't believe God is going to do this again. First Moses and now Christian. Why does he hate me? Isn't that what the Amish would say? That he hates me because I love men like Moses and Christian with too much of my heart?"

"Beck—"

"He's my husband." She struggled with his grip. "Nate! Let me go to him!"

A jeep roared past with Billy Skipp shouting to Skinny. "Go right in there! I don't care if we eat fire!"

"Yes, sir!"

Nate looked up. "It's Raven."

Becky pushed him away and sprang to her feet. The jeep was racing toward the fire engulfing the P-36. Smoke from the still-smoldering P-40s rolled over it. A man was crawling across the runway.

"Christian!"

She began to run again. The jeep reached Raven. Billy Skipp leaped out to grab him under the arms. The P-36 exploded. Becky saw the fireball, saw Billy Skipp and Skinny get blown backward, heard the sound, and felt the heat like a slap to her face seconds after the blast.

Another jeep screeched to a stop in front of her. Her father and Nate were in it.

"Let's go!" Jude barked.

She leaped inside and they sped to Skipp's jeep. Skinny was up, trying to get Skipp to his feet. Jude and Nate rushed over to help, but Becky knelt by Raven and took him in her arms.

"Help me!" she shouted. "I have to get him to a medic! One of you help me!"

It was Billy Skipp and Jude who each took one of Raven's arms over their shoulders and placed him in the jeep. Skinny was already behind the wheel. Becky jumped in and cradled Raven while they tore across the runway for the medical tents. The other jeep followed, Jude ripping through the gears.

The army surgeons wouldn't let Becky stay in the surgical tent. She made her way back to the runway. Raven's plane burned orange while wreckage from the P-40s glowed yellow in the darkness. She squatted down with her back to the wall of one of the hangars. The moon came up, about half-full. For a long time it was red in the smoke that drifted through the air. Then it rose higher and turned amber.

Mein Herr, mein Gott, in der Stunde meiner Brauche komme ich zu dir. My Lord, my God, in my hour of need I come to thee.

Unable to relax she got up and walked as close to the P-36 as she could, the heat penetrating like a knifepoint. Hands in her pockets, she turned and made her way into the black night that covered the island.

Too much death today. Too much death for a Sunday. Too much for a day on which you rose from the dead.

She did not think. She scarcely felt. Her feet took her to the Quonset hut—when her awareness returned she was surprised to see it only a few yards away. The sheet of paper with the crayoned writing was still on the door. She went inside, felt her way along the bed frame to the small table, fumbled with the box of matches sitting there, and lit the candle.

She lay on the bed for what seemed like only minutes…and then she awoke to a familiar voice.

"Hey."

She sat up in surprise. The voice asked, "Remember me? The guy who married you?"

She stood to her feet. "You're not supposed to be here. I left you in surgery."

"Almost three hours ago. Did you think they needed to sew my head back on?"

A white bandage circled his forehead. He touched it. "Makes me look like that guy in the Spirit of '76 painting." He held up his left hand. Two of his fingers were taped together with a splint. "Broken." He lifted a bare foot that was wrapped tightly in gauze and tape. "Sprained."

"That's all? A cut to the head? Broken fingers? A sprain? But you looked half dead!"

"You should have seen the other guy."

"What other guy?"

"Boxcars. He got pulled out of his plane by a couple of hula dancers after he crashed on Maui. I'm not kidding. Two broken arms, two broken legs. One of the dancers refused to leave him when they brought him over here by destroyer."

"Two broken arms and two broken legs! He probably needed her to hold him tight so he wouldn't fall apart. You don't appear to be in quite the dire condition he is."

"Well. I'm lonely."

She had her fingers to her eyes. She laughed. "You're absolutely nuts. Does the doctor know you're here?"

"Nobody knows I'm here. I told them I'd walk myself to the recovery tent, the same one we got married in. I did that and said hi to the guys. We all agreed it was not the place for me. Not on my wedding night. They suggested I take you to the beach. But as I went looking for you I realized all the beaches would be strung with barbed wire and dug up with gun emplacements. They'd be crawling with soldiers. So I thought you might wind up here in the Quonset. I prayed you would, actually. In Cherokee though. Not in German."

"You prayed in Cherokee."

"Yes, ma'am."

Becky knelt on the bed beside him and took his wounded hand in hers. "This has been a black day. Only the marriage was something good. And I thought I was going to lose that too."

"Yeah. I'm sorry. I don't know if using a chute would have been any safer than a crash landing."

She saw burn marks all over his flight gear. There were large holes right through to the skin in some places. One cheek had been scraped raw. The knuckles of the hand she held were cut and nicked.

"I can't believe you're in one piece," she said.

"I could say the same about you."

Slowly she lay down beside him, still holding his hand. He kissed her hair and laughed.

"What's funny?" she asked. "I just want a peaceful time now."

"I've never seen your hair so greasy. It's always clean and fresh even after you've been flying all day."

"Pardon me. It's been a difficult twenty-four hours even for a perfectionist like me."

"As if I care whether you come with grease spots or not."

"There is a shower set aside just for my use. And a latrine. Shall I go freshen up, Lieutenant?"

"No, you shall not." He kissed her hair again.

She put a hand to his beard. "This is a bit heavier than the five o'clock shadow I prefer."

"Shaving kit's in the BOQ." He swung a leg over the side of the bed. "I'll only be a minute."

She pushed him down. "It would be just like you to go and do it simply to annoy me. Stay here. I want a moment's peace and quiet with my husband. I want to tell him something."

"Tell him what?"

Becky laid her head on his chest. "Do you remember the first time we met?"

"When you wouldn't shake my hand?"

"A few minutes before that. When you said seeing me was like a lightning strike."

"I never said that."

"You did too. Don't tease. I want to be peaceful and serious."

"Okay. I was hit by lightning."

"At the same time it happened to you it happened to me."

He lifted his head to look at her, but groaned and put it back on the pillow. "It feels like Zero bullets are bouncing off the inside of my skull."

"I'm sorry, love, but my story will help. I was crouched down checking over my Piper. I straightened up and looked around. You were standing by Peterson's hut. I know you were far away but I could see how blond your hair was and that your eyes were blue—I swear it. You were so handsome I felt like I'd been punched. I turned away as quick as I could because the last thing I wanted was to be attracted to you. Of course from that moment on I was. So I spent the rest of my time fighting it."

He played with her hair while he stared up at the candle shadows on the ceiling. "We both got hit at the same time then. What does it mean?"

"God's in his heaven and we're meant for each other. Even on a day as bad as this."

"A day as good as this. I got married today to a whole lot of beauty, you know. It's still hard to believe. But here you are in my arms and God's giving me the thumbs-up. I'm cleared for takeoff."

"Oh, you're cleared for takeoff, are you?" She propped herself up on her elbow. "What's our destination?"

"Why, heaven. But this is heaven so I guess we'll stay put and make the best of it."

"This is heaven?"

"Remember that tune?" He began to sing softly. "*It's heaven in Hawaii…*"

She put a small kiss on his lips. "Does that hurt?"

In answer, he brought her head down with his wounded hand and kissed her with all the day's pain and fear and hope. He had no interest in stopping. When she tried to pull away to catch her breath he drew her back. Finally she put her hands on his chest and pushed, breaking the kiss.

"You're crazy!" she gasped. "You're supposed to be in sick bay and I can't handle you. What's going to happen when the doc gives you a clean bill of health?"

He pulled her back. "Could be a long marriage, baby."

The candle burned down into a pool of wax, and the flame there lasted for hours before finally vanishing. The hut was completely dark.

A half hour before dawn Becky got up, dressed, kissed her husband on his bandaged forehead, and pried open the door as slowly and quietly as she could. There was still the smell of burning oil and rubber and metal in the air but she could also pick up the scent of the sea and the green jungle and the tropical flowers. She sat down with her back to the hut and thanked God she was alive and that the man she loved with all her heart was alive too. A line of scarlet traced the eastern horizon.

"Red sky at morning," she said.

Thirty-Nine

"H ey. Hotshot. Want some coffee?"

"Mm." Raven opened one eye. "What time is it? And who are you?"

"It's oh-six-oh-five hours. And I'm your wife for the next fifty or sixty years."

"Wow. Must have been some poker game."

"Yup. And you won the jackpot." She put the coffee mug in his hand as he sat up. "I have a plate of bacon and eggs from the mess too. I hope you like yours over easy."

"That would be a good call sign—*Overeasy.*" He dug into the food. "This is great. You're a terrific cook."

"Thanks. I got up before dawn like the woman in the Bible—Ruby."

"Ruby?"

"Yeah. The one whose worth is far above rubies. That's what I call her."

Raven's blue eyes lingered on her as he drank his coffee. "You're pretty crazy beautiful, Stardust."

"Oh, sure I am. I'm a ball of grease is what I am."

"Who notices? But have a shower if you like."

"I will. After you have yours and you're up in the air."

He put an egg on a piece of toast. "Don't rush me."

"Rush you? You'd better wolf that breakfast down before Billy Skipp shows up. You've only got about fifteen minutes."

He put the plate aside and reached for her. "I don't need fifteen minutes." Hugging her, he whispered in her ear, "We could hide out here all morning."

She kissed his cheek and hugged him back. "They know we're in this hut. It's not a very good hiding place."

"Nanakuli Beach then."

"It's strung with barbed wire and thick with soldiers."

"I've got a new P-36. Squeeze in with me. Fly with me. We're on our honeymoon for pity's sake."

She rubbed her nose against his. "I know we're on a honeymoon. I'd love to be squirreled away with you all day. But when you open that door you'll remember yesterday."

"There's lots I'd like to forget. But not you. Never you."

"I get that impression."

After Raven had shaved and showered—awkwardly to keep his bandages intact—they walked together to the plane. A haze was all around them. The sun rose red in the smoke. He moved with a limp and Becky had tied a new strip of gauze over the wound on his forehead. Skinny drove up with Billy Skipp just as Raven was giving Becky a goodbye kiss.

"How was the wedding night, lovebirds?" asked Skipp coming over to them. "I hope the hut was comfortable."

Becky hugged Raven's arm. "It was a palace, Colonel. I hope we can use it again tonight."

"Three or four nights if that's okay with you. Then I'll have a house for you in the Married Officers' Residences." The smile was suddenly gone. "You had a pretty big knock yesterday, Bird. How are you feeling?"

"Top-notch."

"We don't know where our carriers are or where the enemy's are. Hunt north and west, Thunderbird. If anything happens to Lockjaw you're squadron leader."

"What about Batman?"

"Batman takes over if you can't perform your duties. He knows that. Now get up. For all we know enemy ships are not far over the horizon."

"Yes, sir."

Raven climbed into his cockpit, gave Becky thumbs-up, and pulled the canopy home. The engine roared and exhaust spilled over her and Skipp. Lockjaw walked up as Raven rolled out onto the runway.

"Hey, Stardust." He offered Becky a Chiclet. "We'll be keeping an eye on your husband today. Lots of eyes."

Becky took the Chiclet. "Thanks, Lockjaw."

"Good morning, sir."

"Lockjaw. North by west. Find the enemy task force. Find the carriers."

"Understood." Lockjaw put on his aviator glasses. "I saw Hani last night, Becky."

"How was she?"

"Not so great." He turned to Skipp. "She was grateful for your visit yesterday, sir. And the time Mrs. Whetstone and Miss Kurtz spent with her. But the night was hard."

"All day—all week—in the United States chaplains and naval and army officers will be knocking on doors. *Your son went down with the* Oklahoma. *Your son went down with the* Utah. *Your son died at Wheeler Army Air Forces Base. We regret to inform you. Our condolences.* Thousands of doors, Lockjaw. My heart breaks for Hani. But she is just one of those thousands of doors."

"Yes, sir."

"I'll visit her again today. How are Kalino's parents? I assume you saw them."

Lockjaw stopped chewing. "I did. They're holding up."

"And you?"

"Right as rain, sir."

"Visit them again tonight."

"Not a problem, sir. That was my intention."

"All right. Now get up." He saluted Lockjaw. "We're at war since five to eight Sunday morning."

Lockjaw returned the salute. "Sir." He began to stride toward his P-40, turning to look back at Becky. "All eyes, girl."

"Bless you, Lockjaw."

Skipp left in the jeep but Becky remained where she was until the whole squadron had taken off, all of them in P-40s but Raven.

A man ran up with a note in his hand, his eyes watching the last of planes leave the runway. "Shoot. I missed them. I have a radio message for Lockjaw or Batman or Thunderbird. From the *Taney.*"

"The *Taney?*" A coldness struck Becky's spine. "From who?"

"Ma'am, I'm sorry, but—"

"For heaven's sake, soldier, Thunderbird is my husband. You know what kind of day it was yesterday. A friend of ours is on the *Taney.* Can't I at least find out if he's alive?"

"Yes, ma'am. Please give this to your husband when he returns."

She took the message from him.

> *I wanted you to know I'm okay. The enemy did not attack Honolulu Harbor. Please let me know if the boys are all right.*
>
> *David went down with the Arizona.*
>
> *Harrison, RM1, USCGC Taney*

Becky choked back a sob. She felt that if she started crying she would never stop. Closing her eyes, she remembered David singing on the beach Saturday night. It felt as if her chest was suddenly full of blackness, heavy as stone.

Gott erbarme, Christus erbarme dich.

God have mercy. Christ have mercy.

She wiped her eyes with her fingertips and put the note in her pocket.

Drifting off the runway, Becky found herself heading toward the medical tents. The chaplain called out when he saw her standing by the opening of one he had just entered.

"If you've got time on your hands, I could use your help, Mrs. Raven."

She came into the tent. "There are no planes at Peterson's to fly,

Chaplain. And even if there were I doubt the navy or army air forces would allow us to put them up. Let me help."

"Talk to Cathy. Some of the men can't feed themselves, and some would feel better if their faces were washed and shaved, but she can't get to it."

"I'll do that. Have you seen one of our army pilots? Boxcars?"

"Boxcars? Was he the one that crashed on the Big Island?"

"Maui."

"Right. His injuries were too severe for us, Becky. He was taken to Tripler Army Hospital as soon as they got him here. Tripler's overflowing but they found him a bed. He'll be fine. I was talking with Pastor Thor. He's been helping me out. You know him, don't you?"

"Yes. Yes, I do."

She began to go up and down the rows of beds. After a few minutes she went to get a basin of hot water and some razors and a cake of shaving soap. Man after man received her attention for whatever needs they had. Even if it was just to talk.

Then at lunch, Becky's mother and father showed up and told her Aunt Ruth was having a difficult day. The three of them got away behind the tent and prayed together.

At four, Raven came by and announced that he was beat and was going to take a nap before going up again.

"There's nothing out there, Beck," he told her. "We've gone in every direction. The sea is empty."

"They could come tomorrow. Or Wednesday."

He shook his head. "Not troops. And I don't believe dive bombers or torpedo bombers are in the region anymore. I guess no one's given you the news. The Japanese have invaded Malaya and Thailand. That's where their soldiers are. And they're bombing Hong Kong and Singapore and the Philippines—that's where their soldiers are going to be. Canada had already declared war on Japan yesterday—they have regiments in Hong Kong. Roosevelt did it today. So did the Brits and the Dutch and New Zealand. It's another world war, Beck. But it's not happening here. It's happening south and west of us."

"What does Pearl Harbor look like today?"

"Like a bunch of tall buildings have collapsed. And nothing's left but the skeletons—twisted girders and smoke."

She did not see him again. She thought her brother or some of the army pilots might stop by but the day ended without any more visitors. The chaplain ordered her out at sunset.

"Go find your husband and work on your marriage," he said. "But I'd love to have you back here in the morning."

"I'll see you at dawn, sir."

"Thank you, Becky."

The Quonset hut was empty, red sunlight illuminating the bed, the table, and a dresser with a mirror someone had brought in. She opened a few drawers and found most of them contained her own clothing as well as towels and facecloths. Glancing in the mirror she stuck out her tongue and made a face.

"You've never looked as bad as this," she said to her reflection. "Your husband may not come back." Immediately she wished she had not spoken those words. "Shut up, Becky," she muttered to herself.

Taking a towel, soap, and clean clothes she made her way to the shower. As the cold water ran over her in a trickle she thought, *I am cleaning the death off me. All the blood. All the smoke of dying ships.*

Back at the mirror her shirt looked too white, her hair too blond, and her eyes too green. She began to cry and didn't understand why. She put one hand on the dresser to brace herself and put the other to her face.

"Hey." Strong hands gently caressed her shoulders. "What's wrong?"

She gasped and spun and buried her face in his chest. "Oh, thank God, you're back. You made it down safe." She clutched his flight jacket, crying. "I'm sorry. I should be dancing. I don't know what's wrong."

He put his arms around her. "Beck. It's everything. Yesterday and today and tomorrow. You feel it all. It's okay."

"I have no idea what to do. Everything's falling apart. How long does a war last?"

"A war like this lasts a long time." He led her to the bed, took off her boots, and drew the Amish quilt up to her chin. "I talk a lot about how beautiful you look. I don't spend near enough time telling you how beautiful you are inside." He closed her eyelids and kissed them. "You're very special, Becky Raven."

Her tears had not stopped. "You make it worse when you talk like that. You make me cry more." She reached out a hand from under the covers and he took it. "Are we going to make it, Christian? Are we going to make it through?"

"You bet."

"No getting shot down? No missing in action?"

"I promise."

"Liar." Becky laughed and cried. "You'd promise me the world if you could get away with it."

"I do promise you the world."

"Even if you could do it, it won't be the same world. Not after years of war." She caught sight of her jeans crumpled up on the floor where she'd dropped them. The note with the radio message was halfway out of one of the pockets. "There's something I didn't tell you."

His face took on a somber look. "What happened?"

"A radio message came in this morning. It was from Harrison. He's all right."

"That's good news."

"He said that Dave Goff went down with the *Arizona*."

Raven hesitated. He gripped her hand more tightly. "You and I have dealt with a lot of healing. God will have to heal us of this too. All of this. But we'll make it through, Becky. I swear it."

FORTY

*L*obet den Herrn!"

Ruth let the gentle waves wet the bottom of her long Amish dress. After a moment she waded out farther, and a whitecap broke over her stomach and chest. She laughed.

"The Amish would tell me to repent, but I can't repent from falling in love with Manuku. Or dancing with him. Or kissing him. Or singing 'Somewhere Over the Rainbow.' Do you understand that? It's important to me you understand that."

Becky stood on the shore in her jacket, white T-shirt, and jeans. "What will you repent of then?"

"Leaving them. Leaving them and following you to Hawaii. Of course part of me is sorry I ever left, but another part is grateful to God I did."

"If you feel that way, why are you going back?"

"Oh, life between me and God and the Amish is very complicated. The whole world is on fire and I just want to be someplace that feels safe and where I understand what is going on. The Amish are my shelter in the storm. The Amish and God." She smiled. "I will not love again. So now it is good to be with Mother and Father and my people."

"How can you say you won't love again?"

Ruth shook her head as waves broke against her. Her hair began to unravel from its bun. "When I prayed my prayer for Manuku's soul, and asked for God's mercy in Christ, and threw that lei onto the sea at the church service, I knew such a life was not meant to be mine—a life such as yours, with a husband and children."

"Children? Aunt Ruth, I've only been married for ten days."

"Yes, of course, but in time it will fall to you and Christian to raise sons and daughters. As it's fallen to me to bless Mother and Father and other people's children instead. I don't mind that. Now that Manuku is gone I wish to be back in Pennsylvania more than anything in the world."

"And us? What about us? Nate and I. Your sister, Lyyndaya. Jude."

"You have one another."

Becky folded her arms over her chest. A formation of eight P-40s and two P-36s whistled over Waikiki and she watched them disappear across the ocean, wondering if Raven was one of them.

"Not for long," she said. "Nate will be going to the States for pilot training and then he's requested a transfer to Europe. With Christian resigning his commission in the army and going to the naval air station at Pensacola for carrier training—and whatever else they think an army pilot has to learn all over again—well…he'll be gone for months."

Ruth stopped stirring the waves with her foot and waded through the surf to Becky, taking her niece in her arms and hugging her. Despite the cold wetness of the dress Becky tightened her arms around her aunt's back.

"War." Ruth sighed. "I am sorry for war. The Amish are right to oppose it. That's another reason I'm returning to Lancaster County."

"You remember Bishop Zook's letter. He said some Christians were called to defend."

"*Ja.* Well, it is not my calling, my dear Rebecca. But I will always be praying for you and Christian and Nate. It doesn't matter where you are or what you're doing. My prayers will be constant. I'm just sorry you'll be without your brother or your husband."

She linked her arm through her niece's and they began to walk along the beach. "I'm so naïve, Becky. For the first week everyone worried about an invasion. So when it didn't come I thought, *There will be peace quickly.* But then the Japanese attacked so many places and I realized there would be no peace, only more killing."

"I didn't think there could be peace, Aunt Ruth, not after the attack. I just had a hard time believing the whole thing had really happened. That so many of our friends were gone. Even that I was married to Christian. So I would drive down to the harbor and stare at the wrecks of the fleet. Or stand on the runway at Wheeler and look at the burnt-out fighters. Go to the army cemetery and look at the graves of Wizard and Shooter and Juggler. I would stand and wait for Christian at the road to the Married Officers' Quarters, sure he wouldn't come, sure I had dreamed it all up."

Ruth nodded. "I go over and over the day in my mind, wanting to change how it ended, wanting my mind to give me different images than the ones I've held for almost two weeks. I wish so badly to see Manuku smiling at me with red carnations in his hand. But it's no use. I can only give the day to God and try to forgive."

"People in America don't talk about forgiveness, Aunt Ruth."

"The Amish do. I can hear them as if they were walking beside us right now—quoting Scripture, telling us to bless our enemy, to do good to him, to turn the other cheek."

"I can hear them too."

"So I need to put my voice with theirs. It's not for everybody to do this, perhaps. But it is for me to do this. To do this and never leave Paradise again. One day the Japanese will be our friends again, I hope. And the Germans and Italians. I want to be part of that spirit, Becky. Not the other."

Becky stopped walking. "But the Japanese are attacking people. And killing them. All over the world. Just like they've done in Manchuria and China. So are the Italians and the Germans. You make it sound so easy. As if it is just a spat at the dinner table. People are being murdered, Aunt Ruth. Children are being murdered. The Japanese and Germans are not full of remorse. They're not sorry for Nanking or Leningrad or Pearl Harbor."

"It doesn't matter what they do or don't do. It only matters what we do, what I do, how I pray, how I bless."

"Of course it matters what they do. Do you think if I'd shouted out of my cockpit, 'I forgive you!' the Japanese pilot would have stopped from killing Kalino? That if Dave Goff had stood on the deck of the *Arizona* and cried, 'I bless you!' the dive bombers would have gone back to their carriers and never blown up the ship and murdered a thousand men? If it matters what we do, it matters what they do too."

"Your husband is an army pilot—"

Becky's face darkened with blood. "I don't care if he's a used-car salesman. Nate was in China long before I met Christian Scott Raven. He prayed, he begged, he turned the other cheek. And they bayoneted and decapitated women and children anyway. Someone has to defend. Someone has to be there between the prayer for peace and when peace finally shows up. I'm not saying that because Christian's a fighter pilot. I'm saying it because I don't want to see a million people slaughtered while everyone else is standing by waiting for peace to come."

"A million will be slaughtered anyway, my dear. War always takes life. It's always greedy for more souls. War doesn't stop the killing."

Becky's voice dropped. "I know that. There will be a lot more killed before peace comes. I could lose my own husband. But one thing won't happen, Aunt Ruth. The murderers won't get away with it. The warlords aren't going to kill the innocent anymore without answering for what they do. It's judgment day."

Becky's eyes had gone a cold green. Ruth stared at her, her mouth partly open.

"Rebecca. It is not for us to judge."

"God is the judge, yes. But the instruments of his judgment will not be surrender and massacre. They'll be resistance."

"My dear. My dear." Ruth stretched out her arms. "Resistance will bring its own evils and fill its own graves."

Becky was stiff. "I know that too. Terrible things happen all around. But the child will know it's remembered. It will know that while you wait safe and warm in Pennsylvania for peace to come, others will defend its life. My husband and others will bless the child. They'll bless the child, Aunt Ruth, by fighting to keep it alive." She suddenly winced and covered her face with her hands. "I didn't want to quarrel. I didn't want to be harsh. You are going away forever and I'm saying such cruel things—"

"Hush, hush, you are as much a bundle of emotions as I am." Ruth gathered her into her arms again. "I feel anger too. And if I let myself go there would be hatred. But I've been Amish all my life. The Spirit of God will not permit it. All the teaching and the prayers have become a forest of oaks inside me and the forest cannot be uprooted."

"I don't want to hate…but I see Manuku and Kalino and Wizard—sharp ends cut into me—black edges—it's as if I had swallowed bits of broken glass—"

"So it may feel that way for some time. But pray for the peace to come. Not just all around you. Pray for what's inside. Just as you prayed for it when you grieved over Moses. Seek it again."

"I want you to stay. Until the war is done and Christian is safe. Until all that can be saved are safe."

"I have to go for the sake of my own soul, Becky. If I remained with you I would eventually become a shell as the war dragged on—all wars last too long. But if I go to my people in Pennsylvania I will have something to give you. I will have heart if I live among them and their worship of God. My words will have strength. So I can bless you."

They stayed on the beach long after the sun was gone. The stars burned in the sea and over their heads. There was no moon. Ruth's dress dried, and they sat together on the sand, side by side, talking very little.

The next morning the family went down to the dock in Honolulu Harbor and Ruth boarded the liner for San Francisco. Nate lugged her suitcases up the gangway after her. She stood at the railing in her dark dress and prayer *kapp*. Along with hundreds of others she looked down at the upturned faces.

"God be with you!" called Lyyndaya.

"And also with you, sister!" Ruth responded.

"There will be a time we all meet again in Pennsylvania. There will be."

Ruth smiled. "The sooner the better."

The gangway was hauled up and secured. The mooring lines were cast off. The ship's whistle blew, cutting its way through the warm

Hawaiian air. The tall vessel moved away from the dock toward the open sea.

Ruth lifted her hand. "Lyyndaya, Jude, Nate, Rebecca—*The Lord bless thee, and keep thee: The Lord make his face shine upon thee, and be gracious unto thee: The Lord lift up his countenance upon thee, and give thee peace.*"

FORTY-ONE

"Captain Whetstone?"

"Mm?"

"It's quarter to twelve, sir," said Skinny.

"All right. Thank you."

Jude straightened his tie in the mirror a final time and walked into the dining room of his home in full dress uniform. The others quietly watched him come. He went to the head of the table, where there was an empty chair. To his left sat Lyyndaya, Billy Skipp and his wife, Nancy, Whistler, Skinny, and Harrison. To his right were his son, Nate, his daughter, Becky, and her husband, Christian, as well as Lockjaw and Batman. All the men, including Nate, were in Army Air Forces uniform. The exception was Harrison, who wore Coast Guard whites. Every uniform was immaculate.

"We gathered tonight to remember," Jude said. "I know that for some it's a time to let off steam. To celebrate being alive and being with friends and family. Believe me, I understand that. It's been a black month for America and the world. Everything is falling to pieces in front of our eyes. The Nazis and the Japanese are conquering and destroying whatever they want and no one can stop them. For a lot of servicemen this will be their last New Year's with their families for years."

He didn't speak the words *or forever*, but he felt them, and he knew everyone in the room felt them too. Lyyndaya dropped her head. Jude paused to place a hand gently on her shoulder.

"In the first war I put on this uniform because I was forced to. Now I put it on because I choose to. You all know my background and that of my wife. What you don't know is that when we came to Hawaii to help Flapjack and Colonel Skipp we closed the door to our Amish community in Pennsylvania. To them we had joined ranks with the military and were continuing to fly aircraft in defiance of Amish beliefs and customs. We cannot return. Weeks ago my wife and I made up our minds that we would not even if we could. Our place is to train and to bless the young men who serve and their families. We feel that is our calling from God.

"And now, all of us here have agreed to come together tonight, at the end of 1941 and the beginning of 1942, to remember those we have lost as well as brace ourselves for what lies ahead. Wars may be won without hate, but not without sacrifice." He paused. "We have empty chairs among us."

"Manuku," said Becky. One of the empty chairs was beside her and Christian.

"Dave." Harrison kept his eyes straight ahead.

"Juggler," said Batman.

Whistler put a hand on the back of a chair on his right. "Shooter."

Lockjaw's voice was quieter than it had ever been. There was an empty chair on either side of him. "Wizard. Kalino."

Billy Skipp stood up. "Flapjack Peterson. A good friend and fellow pilot who flew with Jude and me in the first war. I'm not an expert at offering prayers to the Almighty, but I would like to do that now regardless."

Everyone pushed back their chairs and got to their feet to join Skipp and Jude.

"Eternal Father, strong to save," Skipp began. "Have mercy on those we've lost as only you can have mercy. Give strength to those of us who remain as only you can give strength. Bind our hearts to your purpose—when it's a time for war, help us to wage it swiftly and justly—when it's a time for peace, help us to seek that peace and embrace it with all our might. In the air, on land, at sea, when in harm's way, be with us, Lord, and do not forsake us. In Christ's name. Amen."

"Amen," said Jude. "Your prayers sound okay to me, Billy." He checked his watch. "We have only a couple of minutes. Let's stay on our feet." He smiled. "Most of you have never seen me in a uniform before. When I enlisted they gave me my rank of captain back. I hope to be qualified on the P-40 in January. I won't be a frontline pilot. But I hope to help the young men who are sent our way become ones."

He put his hands in his pockets. "My Amish friends would turn their backs on me if they saw me dressed like this. I could argue I was in a position to make a difference, to train young men in such a way that most of them could be assured of returning home. But the Amish know that our planes shoot down other planes. *Thou shalt not kill.* I am breaking the commandment." Jude shook his head. "What I do is not an easy thing to do. What Lyyndaya does at my side is not an easy thing either. What all of you will be asked to do over the next few years will never be easy. But at least one of our Amish friends understands this. Some are called to lay down their arms, he says. Some are called to pick them up. You have to decide what your calling is. At this table we have made up our minds. We defend until peace comes."

He looked at his wife. "The trick is to do it without hate. Our friends have been killed. Somehow I must defend others against the Japanese and still be prepared to embrace the Japanese when the end has come. How is that done? Lyyndaya helped me do it twenty years ago with the Germans. Now she'll have to help me do it all over again." He glanced at his watch a second time. "It's midnight. God bless Manuku, Kalino, Shooter, and Wizard. God bless Flapjack, Juggler, and Dave. God bless you all."

Jude kissed his wife and then turned and shook his son's hand and gave him a hug. People laughed and began hugging and kissing right around the table. Becky, Nancy, and Lyyndaya went to the kitchen and came back with platters of food and pitchers of fruit punch and a pot of coffee. Christian grabbed a handful of grapes before Becky took his arm and drew him outside.

He smiled. "Wow." The darkness gleamed with silver as a moon that was almost full moved over the ocean and the jungle. "The whole island's under a blackout, your mom has the blackout curtains drawn, you can't see a thing at Pearl, yet Hawaii is lit up like it's Christmas."

Becky smiled at the shining night. "It's like the full moon at the beach. Before everything changed."

"Some things for the worse, Beck." He tilted up her chin with his hand. "But some things for the better."

She tugged on his dog-tag chain as she looked up at him. "Your wife hasn't had her first kiss of 1942 yet."

"I can't yet."

"What do you mean you can't yet?"

"Looking at you in this light is just amazing. I don't want to close my eyes. Not even for a Becky Raven kiss."

She laced her arms around his neck. "Perhaps I can encourage you to change your mind."

"Your eyes are incredible. And your hair is like some kind of white gold. And your skin—"

"Shh. Enough."

"—is like stardust."

"Stardust."

"And it's all over you."

She smiled and smoothed back his hair. "*Ye shall go out with joy, and be led forth with peace: the mountains and the hills shall break forth before you into singing, and all the trees of the field shall clap their hands.* Do you remember that?"

"Sure. It was in that letter you read me from your bishop in Pennsylvania. The one he wrote to Nate just before the attack."

"So do you remember the rest of it?"

"I remember that it's from Isaiah."

"*Instead of the thorn shall come up the fir tree, and instead of the brier shall come up the myrtle tree: and it shall be to the Lord for a name, for an everlasting sign that shall not be cut off.* Nate thinks it's about America now. America and the world coming back to life after years of blight and destruction and war. But I think it's about us—you and me."

He kissed each of her eyes. "How do you figure that?"

"We both lost people we cared for. When we met we started rough. It took a lot for us to admit we loved each other. It took a war to make me want marriage. It may be hell on earth tonight. But for us the love is unstoppable no matter what gets thrown at us. We've come too far and we've fought through too much to toss away what we feel for each other and say it's too hard. The Japanese won't make me do it. Or the Germans. Fear won't. Not even death. It's this *everlasting* thing—you know?"

"Yeah. You make it all pretty clear."

"You're shipping out in the morning. But it's not over between us. It never will be. Do you believe that, Christian?"

He put his lips gently to hers, the moon turning both of them into fire. "Yeah, Becky. I do."

About Murray Pura...

Murray Pura earned his Master of Divinity degree from Acadia University in Wolfville, Nova Scotia, and his ThM degree in theology and interdisciplinary studies from Regent College in Vancouver, British Columbia. For more than 25 years, in addition to his writing, he has pastored churches in Nova Scotia, British Columbia, and Alberta. Murray's writings have been shortlisted for the Dartmouth Book Award, the John Spencer Hill Literary Award, the Paraclete Fiction Award, and Toronto's Kobzar Literary Award. Murray pastors and writes in southern Alberta near the Rocky Mountains. He and his wife, Linda, have a son and a daughter.

Visit Murray's website at www.MurrayPura.com.

Also, for more information about Harvest House books, please visit our website at www.HarvestHousePublishers.com and our Amish reader page at www.AmishReader.com.

If you loved WHISPERS OF A NEW DAWN, you'll want to read about Jude and Lyyndy's earlier adventure in Murray Pura's THE WINGS OF MORNING...

Jude Whetstone and Lyyndaya Kurtz, whose families are converts to the Amish faith, are slowly falling in love. Jude has also fallen in love with flying that newfangled invention, the aeroplane.

The Amish communities have rejected the telephone and have forbidden motorcar ownership but not yet electricity or aeroplanes.

Though exempt from military service on religious grounds, Jude is manipulated by unscrupulous army officers into enlisting in order to protect several other young Amish men. No one in the community understands his sudden enlistment and so he is shunned. Lyyndaya's despair deepens at the reports that Jude has been shot down in France. In her grief, she turns to nursing Spanish flu victims in Philadelphia.

After many months of caring for stricken soldiers, Lyyndaya is stunned when an emaciated Jude turns up in her ward. Her joy at receiving Jude back from the dead is quickly diminished when the Amish leadership insists the shunning remain in force. How then can they marry without the blessing of their families? Will happiness elude them forever?

Book two in the Snapshots in History series...
THE FACE OF HEAVEN

In April 1861, Lyndel Keim discovers two runaway slaves in her family's barn. When the men are captured and returned to their plantation, Lyndel and her young Amish beau, Nathaniel King, find themselves at odds with their pacifist Amish colony.

Nathaniel enlists in what will become the famous Iron Brigade of the Union Army. Lyndel enters the fray as a Brigade nurse on the battlefield, sticking close to Nathaniel as they both witness the horrors of war—including the battles at Chancellorsville, Fredericksburg, and Antietam. Despite the pair's heroic sacrifices, the Amish only see that Lyndel and Nathaniel have become part of the war effort, and both are banished.

And a severe battle wound at Gettysburg threatens Nathaniel's life. Lyndel must call upon her faith in God to endure the savage conflict and to face its painful aftermath, not knowing if Nathaniel is alive or dead. Will the momentous battle change her life forever, just as it will change the course of the war and the history of her country?

- Exclusive Book Previews
- Authentic Amish Recipes
- Q & A with Your Favorite Authors
- Free Downloads
- Author Interviews & Extras

AMISHREADER.COM

FOLLOW US:

facebook twitter

Visit **AmishReader.com** today
and download your free copy of

LEFT HOMELESS

a short story by Jerry Eicher